CHAOS
IN THE
DARK DAYS

LET HIM BEWARE WHO READS,

THE LURE FOR CONQUEST, IS INEVITABLY ALLOYED WITH PHYRRIC GALL.

—*KEN. C. OKONKWO*

THE DARK DAYS' SERIES

CHAOS
IN THE
DARK
DAYS

KEN OKONKWO

Chaos in the Dark Days
Copyright © 2019 by Ken Okonkwo. All rights reserved.

No part of this publication may be reproduced, stored in a retrieval system or transmitted in any way by any means, electronic, mechanical, photocopy, recording or otherwise without the prior permission of the author except as provided by USA copyright law.

This novel is a work of fiction. Names, descriptions, entities, and incidents included in the story are products of the author's imagination. Any resemblance to actual persons, events, and entities is entirely coincidental.

The opinions expressed by the author are not necessarily those of URLink Print and Media.

1603 Capitol Ave., Suite 310 Cheyenne, Wyoming USA 82001
1-888-980-6523 | admin@urlinkpublishing.com

URLink Print and Media is committed to excellence in the publishing industry.

Book design copyright © 2019 by URLink Print and Media. All rights reserved.

Published in the United States of America
ISBN 978-1-64367-422-3 (Paperback)
ISBN 978-1-64367-421-6 (Digital)
10.05.19

DEDICATION

THE BOOK 'CHAOS IN THE DARK DAYS' IS DEDICATD TO THE BLIND, MANY OF WHOM REQUIRE SIMPLE SURGERY OR MEDICATIONTHAT ARE TANTALIZINGLY CLOSE BUT UNAVAILABLE DUE TO POVERTY. PART OF THE REVENUE ACCRUING FROM THIS BOOK GOES TO ASSISTING THE BLIND THROUGH THE 'KINDNESS UNHINDERED ORGANIZATION.'

KEN OKONKWO

Contents

Chapter 1: ABAGANA—OKOKO NDEM viii
Chapter 2: 54TH BRIGADE 3
Chapter 3: SHINE MESS..10
Chapter 4: COLONEL ADAKA EKWO 16
Chapter 5: HONING..25
Chapter 6: IDIGO..29
Chapter 7: LIGHTNING STRIKE FORCE 39
Chapter 8: QUESTIONS..48
Chapter 9: TRAINING SESSION 58
Chapter 10: PATROLS..74
Chapter 11: NIGERIAN PATROL 101
Chapter 12: RUMINATIONS 108
Chapter 13: MILITARY POLICE POSER 127
Chapter 14: FIDELIS UDE..160
Chapter 15: DIOKPA OLISA 181
Chapter 16: 10TH DECEMBER. OKOKO NDEM 200
Chapter 17: THE NEBUCHADNEZZAR 234
Chapter 18: IDES OF MARCH..250

AUTHOR'S NOTE TO THE READER

Science defines chaos as a state of disorder and irregularity that is an intermediate stage between highly ordered motion and entirely random motion.

In all situations and circumstances, disorder and irregularity results in mindless clashes. 1969 through 1970 when the war ended fully represent the foregoing. Activities were painfully chaotic.

May our dear country never experience chaos again.

I highly regret any resemblance or similarity to names of anything, place, event, group, entity, person or persons existing, past, living or dead.

Although woven around hazy historical facts, this is a work of fiction. I wish you bon-apetit as you read to enjoy the story.

KEN CHUKA OKONKWO

CHAPTER ONE

ABAGANA—OKOKO NDEM

Brave and courageous Biafrans, today marks a turning point in this genocidal war being prosecuted by the sick Nigerian government, nose-led by the Hausa-Fulani oligarchy, backed by the senile British government in an unholy alliance with the godless, emotionless, and saturnine communist Russian government.

Yesterday, two infantry divisions and an armoured brigade of the rag-tag Nigerian Army, plentifully supplied with British and Soviet arms, munitions and armour, guarded by heavy Russian tanks, fast British light tanks, armoured cars and armoured personnel-carriers set out on the Herculean task of linking the Enugu-Onitsha road to secure the Niger bridge head. Under the pugnacious cockerel General Muritala Muhammad their easy passage through the deceptive resistance along Oji-River, Ugwuoba, Amansea and Agu-Awka, the light-hearted skirmishes along Ntoko, Ndikpa, Ndiora and Ndiowuu fueled their confidence. Lulled into complacency the untrained Army peopled mainly by Niger and Chadian mercenaries stumbled into the well-set ambush of the gallant Biafran Army at Abagana.

The resulting carnage that left over two hundred vehicles inclusive of haulage trailers, lorries, tanks, armoured cars, staff cars, mounted jeeps, mobile artillery guns, personnel-carriers, and three helicopters blazing like the entrance to the biblical hell, heralded miles of shell, bomb and mortar pock-marked roads up to Afor-Igwe

Umudioka. These were littered with the dead and burnt bodies of thousands of Nigerian soldiers killed in their aborted bid to escape. One man however escaped with a seriously deflated ego—the Hawk, General Muritala Muhammad. The only surviving helicopter picked him up and whisked him away.

About four hundred soldiers were captured alongside a good supply of assault riffles, machine guns, grenades, rocket launchers and ammunition. We thank Nigeria for her benevolence. May they make more of such moves and arm us better. We hereby invite journalists from all over the world to come over and see this unprecedented massacre in what General Gowan described as a Police action. The Biafran Army is ready to stage a repeat performance if and when the Nigerian Army rouses from her doze not minding their emasculating blockade, to attempt another determined putsch.

Fellow Biafrans one thing is certain, as the rag-tag army keeps busy bombing churches, civilians, farms and homesteads, we will seek out and encounter their ground forces over whom we have the advantage of discipline, training and purpose, until they are decimated. We will then turn our attention to their British and Russian assisted blockade before the year runs out. The results of discipline will show now as our troops move into the Republic of Benin to flush out the remnants of the rag-tag army.

This news commentary read by Okoko Ndem is reaching you from Radio Biafra.

CHAPTER TWO

54TH BRIGADE

54TH Brigade Shine Mess was a large twelve room house with a living room the size of a football pitch. It belonged to a former member of the House of Parliament, who was rich enough to purchase the flat, tree-shaded grounds behind St. Barnabas' Church Ojoto. It was bordered by St, Andrews' School Oba. The brigade was located in Oba before the mess and the brigade commander had respect for personalities. The brigade caterer used her charms to both cajole and entice the balding, ageing parliamentarian to relocate. The added bonus was that he received a personal letter from the Biafran Head of State thanking him for his recognized contributions to the war effort. He would at a latter date be invited to the State House for a ceremonial honour. He therefore moved out that day, brandishing the letter and bragging of his future political career that would blossom after the war.

    His children were all grown up and were rushed out of the country as the war threatened under their austere mother's auspices. The randy parliamentarian dreamt of marrying the catering officer Lieutenant Dinah. Desmond Oji, after a heart thumping session with Lieutenant Dinah in his newly rented flat located in Oba, explained between gasps and pants that he was not really randy. He claimed that all he was doing was for the war effort. He fed his weak eyes on Dinah's graceful figure as she stepped out of the shower into the room dripping wet. He said:

"Lieutenant, let me tell you some truths."

Dinah smiled and wiped her pointed breasts with the large, white towel, fondled them and demurely cooed: "Yes honourable, you have told me truths many times before, that you are not like Zik who is quarreling with our God-sent Head of State. You hate your wicked wife and you wish to marry me. I am the most beautiful girl you have ever met. You are not sure that you are as old as the sixty three years your birth certificate suggests and a host of other irrelevancies. The main truth remains that you are a randy old goat with all three daughters of yours older than me. You already owe me a lot of money. Each time you demonstrate your randy nature with me you owe me three pounds. You agreed to sell your house at Bishop Aniogu Street Enugu to me for two hundred and fifty pounds."

Desmond cut in: "I have told you that I do not like your putting a price tag to it as if you are a free girl. I will sign the agreement of the sale today if only you present the papers but do not keep behaving as if I am paying for the favour. It is all for love and marriage being seriously contemplated."

"Stop wasting your scarce breath. I am beautiful and I am a prostitute. I am taking advantage of you and I am wiser than you. You cannot help yourself because I am strong and in control. Now, to make you happy again I command you to flatter me. If you do not do it well I will leave now. If you do it well I will spend the night here."

The brooding eyes and sour countenance of Desmond lightened, and sparkled as he embarked on a poetry-like praise recital. His sing-song voice flowed smoothly from practice as each encounter elicited the same amount of money and flattery except when he got more horny than usual. Like in most things, practice kept improving his performance. Lieutenant Dinah Igbeli left the abode just before 5.00am for her quarters at the brigade headquarters. The brigade commander, whom she suspected was homosexual, had no interest in her charms. He was uncompromising when it came to discipline. Missing out during tattoo roll calls or muster parades resulted in spells at the guard room followed by quarter-guard duty. She had learned first hand of the commander's evil nature. She had entertained two Majors, old acquaintances from Div. Hq. and three Captains from

Afikpo sector, Ukwa sector and Awgu sector respectively. She was assisted by only one entertainment corporal named Ogugua. It all happened during the mobilization for the formation and retraining of the brigade to execute the recapture of Onitsha. This operation was code named 'Hiroshima'. She overslept and did not respond with the required alacrity to the emergency burgle call at 0400hrs, because she went to sleep just an hour earlier, after turning down the insatiable Captains from the war fronts. She had thought herself insatiable, but the exertions of that night surpassed every other escapade of hers with all of her muscles aching. During the ensuing trial, she painstakingly explained that as an army entertainment officer, she had been on active duty until an hour before the burgle call.

"Doing what?" asked the commander. "Do I give the details sir?" asked Dinah.

"Yes Lieutenant" replied the commander.

Dinah then went into a detailed description of the lewd duties she performed, to the discomfort of the military and regimental policemen attending the trial. The brigade Major excused himself to answer the call of nature and burst into a roarous laughter as he stepped outside the door. Dinah, believing that she had got everyone captivated, continued unabated, choosing rawer and dirtier language for her story. She failed to notice the dead fish eyes of Colonel Awoni Mbebo, whose waves to silence her were misinterpreted by her to mean 'carry on'. When she came up for breath and looked around closely to assess her performance, her already formed belief that she had captured the commander evaporated. He was so angry that he could not speak. He kept toying with his service pistol. The brigade Major who had served under Colonel Awoni sensed the tension and hurried in to stand between the Colonel and Lieutenant Dinah. He looked into the dead fish eyes and stretched out his hand to retrieve the pistol from his commander. Dinah then saw how close she had come to death and lost her nerves and composure. Major Ozoadibe turned to the regimental Provost and said:

"Take her to the guardroom."

"Not yet" said Colonel Awoni. "Are you wearing any underwear?"

"Yes sir" whined Lieutenant Dinah.

"Remove your trousers" ordered Awoni. She complied fearfully.

"Somebody get three good canes for me from the guava tree in front of this office." Ordered Colonel Awoni and adjourned the trial, dismissing everyone except the Major and two Provosts. He took the canes and started wielding them until two had broken to pieces before Major Ozo cut in saying:

"Remember, please remember and don't forget."

"Okay" intoned the commander. "Transfer her back to Div. Headquarters after one week in the guardroom."

If not for her stripped buttocks and thighs, Dinah was no worse for wear and tear. She looked forward to her return to the Div. Headquarters which had better facilities and clientele, although she was only an assistant to the entertainment Captain in charge of the Div. Mess.

By the tenth day in the guardroom, she summoned Major Ozo to know the reason for her extended stay in the guardroom and the delay in transfer to Div. Hq.

"See darling" Ozo began but she cut him short saying: "God will punish your mother. I have told you that I am a prostitute and cannot love or be loved. Don't call me darling, honey, sweet, mine or any of those stupid pet names for stupid people. I will pay for what you have been doing for me since I met the devil your boss when I come out but it ends there. Now I want answers to my questions Major."

"Yes sir, madam. Lieutenant Dinah. I love you but you can't see"

"Shut up and give me the answers." Dinah insisted.

Major Ozo shook his head and explained that Dinah was supposed to be transported physically to the Division Headquarters after seven days in the guardroom but that the Div. Hq. had replied to the transfer signal over-ruling the commanding officer. They had also hinted at a possible promotion of Lieutenant Dinah to the rank of Captain to enable her cope with the mustering of men for two big operations to be launched from 54th brigade front lines. Information from Army Headquarters had it that in the Part One Orders her name was on the list of newly promoted Captains. This was to be confirmed by the Part Two Orders. Major Ozo was smiling as he concluded.

"Why then am I still in the guardroom?" asked Dinah.

"I was directed to look for accommodation for you under a different roof from that of the commander. You have to move from your present quarters." Ozo explained.

"So he hates women this much? I have heard of and met with homosexuals who like women and occasionally relate with women sexually" Dinah mused "this total abhorrence of women is strange."

"I have told you that I am not convinced that he is homosexual. In the University, we were in the same hostel and I remember that he had female friends, especially of the severely attired Scripture Union variety. I will rather say that he is a religious bigot, but one thing is certain and that is that he is mad. Avoid him and I will help shield you while you remain in this regiment."

Ozo offered her some Caritas supplied chocolates, cigarettes and a fresh army underwear and vest.

"Thank you but what is keeping you from securing the quarters for me? Hurry up and get something near the muster parade grounds. Then you must get these animals from the guardroom to dig a bunker near it. I have not had a man in the past ten days. Hurry up so that I can start repaying my debts to you." Dinah wriggled her waist as she spoke.

"Listen Dinah, you are not as bad as you make out. You are a good girl pretending to be bad because of this mad war. You are only nineteen years old and pretending to be heartless, I will marry you."

"Get out of here and do as I say." Dinah smiled bewitchingly while Ozo left. The following day, he cleaned out the Headquarters' bungalow at St. Andrews school on the east side of the muster parade ground, built a strong bunker behind it, furnished the place and moved Dinah's property inside it. The next day, the commanding officer, with a grimace, permitted him to release the 'nymphomaniac'. The release was effected and Ozo personally escorted her to the apartment. When he had shown her through the house he turned to leave but she stopped him saying:

"Do not go for I would like to use you now to launch the apartment, start paying the debts I owe and relax this old body of mine. Make yourself ready on the mattress on the floor because the bed looks shaky to me. I will take thirty minutes to wash out the guardroom smell and generally attend to my beautiful body, then like a tornado I will be all over you."

Dinah went into the bath room. Major Ozo left four hours later wondering what hit him. As he shuffled back to his apartment, unknown to him, the commanding officer's eyes followed him disdainfully. The commander's numerous analysis within the next four days arrived at the same conclusion: the girl is strong, energetic, very beautiful, over sexed, bad but not as bad as she makes out.

At this juncture he would start hearing the marriage ban calls and the wedding bells ringing. It would be like in the movie 'Sound of Music' which he watched in his first year at the University. 'I will marry her.' He always concluded. The unsolicited swelling in his crotch whenever he thought of Dinah gave him the impression that he had been bewitched by her. He liked the idea, laughing gleefully and thinking up love potions that would bind both of them inseparably.

CHAPTER THREE

SHINE MESS

Shine Mess was the name given to the Officer's mess of the 54th brigade at Ojoto. It was so named because, the large rambling house and the sprawling grounds that were heavily shaded by large trees, were very well kept by Lieutenant Dinah Igbeli of the army entertainment unit. Chocolate-complexioned, aquiline-nosed, average height, slim, hard-muscled from BOFF training, army training, commando training, secret service training and mellowed by entertainment training which honed her sexual instincts and appetite, she was a stickler for cleanliness. Her girls and male musicians, whom she hated for their weakness and feminine nature, were not exempted from normal military duties. She ensured that after routine duties, the entertainment was plentiful and not restricted to any, from the lowest to the highest ranks. Only dirty and unkempt persons were not allowed into the mess. There was always water, thanks to the ever increasing population of the guardroom. Soap was available too, even though it was mainly of the black variety that was manufactured locally. With the little vote from the Division, she turned the rambling living room into a well furnished modern bar. All kinds of cigarettes including recreational weed were available. However, it was not allowed to smoke weed in the bar. The ever present Provosts and Military Police ensured order and obedience to the rules and regulations. Drunkenness was allowed if it led to stupor but forcefully dissuaded if it led to violence. A horny disposition provoked tolerant smiles and provided work for the entertainment girls. The Shine Mess thus became an oasis to which officers and men from other brigades in the Division came. They converged like bees to honey combs. Any pass that did not result in the sampling of all the forms of entertainment provided by the mess, was considered wasted. Half the total sum of the Division payroll ended up in the Shine Mess treasury. Lieutenant Dinah scoured every nook and cranny of blockaded Biafra to enrich the menu of delicacies at the Shine Mess. From senior officers and mercenaries, she purchased, by cash or kind, all brands of cigarettes, alcoholic beverages, tinned fish and meat, including the mushroom which nobody seemed to like. Only the senior officers with fat pay packets ate the mushrooms as a status symbol. They never failed to mask the rustic metallic taste with equally expensive hot drinks. Only Lieutenant Dinah mixed the drinks so the ingredients remained a mystery. She did not fail to transfer half of her takings to her Amumma town.

She reconstructed her father's pit latrine to be double barreled. One chamber took in the feces while another chamber that slanted from an angle, took in valuables. This was only known to her father who did the construction himself.

The mess was never in short supply of locally available food and drinks. To ensure the health of her workers she purchased penicillin derivatives even by barter and corporal Osita always accompanied her on her trips. Changes were rampant in the mess hence any visit gave the impression of novelty. Dinah's expertise at negotiation and bargaining added another dimension to Shine Mess activities. The stream of clean and rich servicemen into the mess made the trade to blossom. Because of the scarcity of food, drinks and other luxury items, barter was preferred. The mess thus became a clearing house for scarce commodities. From experience, Dinah learnt that chairs and tables were easily wieldable items, just like glasses, plates, spoons, forks and knives in a fight. She therefore built big and heavy chairs as well as tables. They could not be easily moved.

The Division Commander's visit to the Shine Mess was once a month. It always coincided with Lieutenant Dinah's return from her commodity sourcing travels. Nobody questioned her absence from the Shine Mess and how it coincided with that of the Division Commander, or their never varying reappearance at the Shine Mess. When they drank far into the night, everybody expected to see the Div. Commander go to her apartment to spend what was left of the night, but it never happened. No expletives or gestures of endearment ever passed between them. They just drank together and parted solemnly in the early hours of the morning.

Lieutenant Muturu of the Intelligence Unit was pretending to investigate what he deemed suspicious actions that might be classified as treason. He sneaked into Dinah's apartment hoping to end up in her bed. He however ended up in the Casualty Collection Post. He had a broken nose, squashed and swollen scrotum, dislocated hands, a broken jaw, a displaced kneecap and four broken fingers. When he became able to talk a month later, he promptly paid off the five pounds bet he lost to Major Ozo. The wager was that he would bed Dinah and give her more satisfaction than Ozo. He not only lost the money but also would not be able to bed anyone for some time to come. When Major Ozo had counted and pocketed the money, Muturu cleared his throat and re-arranging his squeaky jaws, mumbled as if he had water in his mouth about the invasion of Biafra by ghosts. "This is not surprising considering the number of people killed every day in this mad war. Youths cropped before their prime whose spirits cannot rest."

For up to half an hour, Lieutenant Muturu did his best to convince his friend and former battalion commander Ozo to steer clear of the 'ghost' Dinah. He had been under Ozo for his battle inoculation at Abakaliki and also saw action at Afikpo, Uzuakoli and Okigwe sectors. His eyes were flaming red; the brows creased as much in puzzlement as in fury:

"She was dumb and could not talk for you know that dead people do not talk. Her body was cold and clammy and there was no breath in her. No hissing, wheezing exertion, grunting, whining or sighing. She did not ball her fingers into fists but the blows were hammer blows. They Felt like those of the pugilist Sonny Liston. She seemed not to be sad, angry, anxious, happy, excited or contemplative. She showed no emotion and did not express any sentiments. She oozed of the 'six flowers' perfume used to prepare corpses for burial. She must be a dead person otherwise how could I have got to the Casualty Collection Post without being carried?"

Major Ozo shook his head for he could not understand how a little girl weighing less than Muturu could have bested him in a fight. Muturu was a known brawler and feared all around the night clubs that he favoured. He was also respected all around the amateur boxing rings. He represented his University creditably in boxing tournaments before the outbreak of the war. Ozo wondered how such a beautiful, expressive, warm, succulent, and loving girl could deliver such brutal beating to a known fighter. He had lost his limbs and this talk about ghosts indicated that he had also lost his mind mused Ozo as he calmed Muturu and placing his hands patronizingly on Muturu's shoulder asked:

"How many of them did you meet in her bedroom? Was the Div. Commander there? How many of them beat you?" Ozo took out his pen and notebook to record. Muturu forced himself up and cringing into the bed screamed and fainted. Lieutenant Dinah walked into the room saying: "What has kept you away from me all through last week? Have you married me enough?"

Turning different shades in confusion Ozo replied: "No I mean Yes, I am still marrying, I will marry you."

"Even after you have discovered that I am a ghost? No matter what happens come in this night because I need to relax. Hon. Desmond Oji has been on duty for two stormy weeks and is suffering from exhaustion and is therefore ineffective."

Ozo's eyes gleamed with joy.

"Don't gloat" hissed Dinah "Even at his age, he is more man than you. I take him for two weeks and he is exhausted, if I take you for two days you will be comatose and treated for malaria. You are manageable but don't gloat."

The ghost story spread like wild bush fire and the Shine Mess pedigree had fairy princess added to it. Serving as the Commander-in-Chief's courier, especially for missives that required no response, did not add to Dinah's popularity. She was just seen as the mysterious entertainment officer who was so good at her job that even the Head of State required her lewd services every fortnight. Her frequent travels were evidence of State House relationship. Nobody doubted the authenticity of the not-so-few Commander-in-Chief letters hand delivered by her, not even the Division Commander. Only the entertainment corporal Ogugua knew of the existence of the miniature Imperial90 typewriter, the black, red and green fountain pens with their quink inks and the State House stamps, seals and letter headed sheets. Her loyalty to Dinah being as adhesive as the loyalty of angels to God, there was no fear of anybody ever suspecting the source of the priced State House communications or the fighting ability Of Dinah or the lethal and soulless nature of Ogugua or that both were morse code specialists.

CHAPTER FOUR

COLONEL ADAKA EKWO

The 12th Division of the Biafran army had a nine month lull of sleepy inactivity. This was characterized by half-hearted skirmishes with hit and run patrols to indicate presence. The occasional burst of small arms and rare sound of machine guns were supposed to deter soldiers who may wander into no-man's-land of the forward locations. The ominous crack of the sniper's mate called Mark IV was heard only when the opponents got more brazen. Little streams and bushy shores along the front marked unspoken but acccpted borders, beyond which opposing troops should not wander. There were free zones where soldiers of both sides met and interacted. Weapons were left at some distance behind for no swimmers forded their opponents' shore. Gifts however used to exchange hands despite the risk of court martial for sabotage. The Biafrans would give fish or other local foods in exchange for brands of cigarettes, beer, salt and tinned foods. Gifts of cash were not easily accepted because of the obvious implications.

    The lull in the fighting was seen as a trick of the enemy to allay suspicion, mobilize effectively and lure the Biafrans into offensive. The Nigerians had lost a large number of troops in the capture of Port Harcourt and up to the outskirts of Aba. They wanted Biafra to attack and they would inflict casualties. The unaccustomed terrain and weird topography put the advancing Nigerian troops at a disadvantage. The angry and uncompromising defense of Biafra, cemented by hunger exacted a great toll. Another school of thought had it that the federals were reinforcing and re-supplying to execute a final putsch. Passage of time and the interaction of the opposing troops belied the surmises.

The Biafran High Command, expecting a more determined offensive scoured the sectors for tough, foxy and knowledgeable commanders with which they beefed up 12th Division. Huge, gorilla-stature machine gun sergeants with their crew were moved in. With the top commanders came proven battalion commanders known for their doggedness and enterprise. A sure way of halting the Nigerian advance was the devastating ambush and cut off maneuvers to which they are susceptible.

Colonel Adaka Ekwo, nicknamed 'the bee' was hustled out of the Afikpo sector where he initiated the 'bee' sting. This strategy never gave respite to the invaders. The 39th battalion, 14 Division Afikpo sector utilized most of the Division's munitions but paid back with new FN riffles, K3 and Browning automatic guns. Their constant fighting patrols, sneak incursions, deep penetrations for prime target destructions and lightning strikes and withdrawals provided ample supply of guns, grenades and ammunition as booty from the over supplied federal troops. Colonel Adaka Ekwo, commanding 39th brigade nibbled lethally at the forward lines of the Nigerian troops, harassing and embarrassing them with his success. They were given no rest but 27th and 21st brigades were resting. They had to sit back in defense while Adaka's 39th burrowed through their front lines also. At the Port Harcourt sector, brigadier Bejamin Adikunle was advancing in leaps and bounds after trudging through the marshes with painful turtle gait and much casualties. The casualties increased on dry land but more territories were gained steadily. This continued until Brigadier Eze in command of 12th Division blew up three bridges to slow down the advancing troops and also blew up six bridges behind his retreating troops and mined the rear behind his command, the Divisional Headquarters inclusive. The annual six days non-stop July rains forced a lull in the fighting for the roads pock-marked from the effects of the shell mortar and rocket were marshy, bogging down supply trucks, personnel carriers, light tanks and heavy assault tanks. The blown bridges conclusively halted the

Nigerian advance. Four days of hard manual labour that only left two men at each trench provided the labour force, no distinctions wrought between officers and other ranks, to create three defensive lines. The bunkers were solid shelters against freezing cold, rainfall and the shell, bomb, mortar, canon and machine gun bullet rain which followed the frustrating halt of the enemy advance. When it became obvious that they would be bogged down by these obstacles, the rain of lethal material diminished to a trickle and ceased. Peace entered and Brigadier Eze made a speech.

All the officers and senior non-com's hastily summoned arrived the tactical quarters and made themselves as comfortable as they could under the rain. Bare-headed with his steel helmet slung behind his apron. Looking dirty, tired, and disheveled without the insignia of rank, the commander stood at the centre of the clearing like an advance guard waiting for the arrival of the commander. No soldier looked in his direction. A king-kong like sergeant in charge of a mortar section sheltering under a tree cleared his throat and getting Brigadier Eze's attention addressed him:

"Boy, you are in the army. You are no longer an idle civilian. You don't have to be shy, stupid or afraid. Look for a shelter and rest until the big man comes . . ."

The Brigadier did not react so the sergeant believing that his timidity was born out of fear offered him a space under his own shelter. The Brigadier smiled and told him in his low, slow and quiet voice that he was about to start and added:

"Thank you anyway; I can see that you are a thoughtful person. However meet me immediately I am through here."

The authority in his quiet voice belied the voice, his demeanor, the below average height, and the slim build. He cleared his throat to draw attention and the Sergeant wonderingly stood up. As the Senior Officers hastened up to attention position, Sergeant King Kong belatedly came to attention and saluted.

"I am sorry sir!" he thundered

"I did not know you" he finished.

A fat-headed Colonel warned him to silence and the Brigadier began: "Stand-at-aise everybody. Make yourself as comfortable as you can sitting, standing, kneeling, or lying down. Just listen attentively and no matter your rank, ask whatever questions that comes into your mind after you have heard me. I was with the 1st Battalion at Gakem when Gowan unleashed a Division of his well trained, armed, well supplied army in what he dubbed 'Police Action' against the then fledgling Biafra. It was supposed to last for seven days, within which period they would have overrun us. In the two month period of heavy fighting that never let up, day or night, we held them at the border towns not loosing an inch of our land. By the third month it became a see-saw kind of motion. They deployed more troops, armoured cars, tanks and aircrafts. Our predominantly double barreled guns, mark 2 and mark 4 riffles, Dane guns and machetes wilted before them in a proud, orderly and systematic slow withdrawal to Opi town. Licking their wounds they approached the Opi offensive with trepidation and caution. With comrades like Major Chukwuma Nzogwu, Captain Ude and Captain Oboyo, we were able to contain them for a further six weeks within which period their armouries fell to us supplying us better. The weapons captured at Okpatu, Gakem, Ukehe, and their other routes helped fortify Opi. The men and material they lost was compensated for by the loss of my Commander Major Nzogwu. With less than a brigade, we contained their many Divisions in addition to British and Soviet military advisers and Chadian mercenaries. We held on for close to six months before they penetrated and widened the fronts. Then officers and men of the Biafran Army were fighting men. Casualties were few on our side and more on the Nigerian side. We were soldiers then determined in the fight to save our land. Then the spirit of flight arrived and in less than six months we lost almost half the land mass of Biafra. Withdrawals became the norm in every sector and we could no longer avail ourselves of their supply stores and arms. There were no more counter attacks, pre-emptive attacks, and sneak penetrations with devastating effects. We got impotent and learnt to turn our backs, and run from the enemy. Those of us concerned, with the assistance of military intelligence found out the source of the spirit of flight. A few saboteurs were arrested, given a fair trial and executed. The spirit fled. We were able to contain them again. We pinned them down in impossible locations, and recovered some of our lost lands. The fighting evened out and we moved again into the Republic of Benin. This is my fourth command and the first Division I have commanded. I do not intend to fail. I have noticed that the spirit of flight has returned to the fields. The war has broadened into many sectors, and we are getting more desperate. The infernal blockade is inflicting more pain than the actual fighting. There is no time for the cloak and dagger work that exposed the saboteurs now so I have decided and tried us all and not finding the saboteurs, I have condemned us all."

He paused, wiped his sagging wet head and face and then donned his steel helmet. He surveyed the now tense and expectant soldiers. He continued: "I am a very fair man. I will give a chance to those of you whose hearts cannot take the fighting. Any of you here who has not got the heart, health, conscience or will to continue this fight for survival should indicate by stepping out before me. I will count up to ten. One . . . . two   "

Sergeant King-Kong, whose real name was Kingsley stepped out and marched briskly to the Brigadier, Eze's huge Beretta pistol was pointing rock steady at the Sergeant's navel. He ignored it and stopped at a respectable distance from Brigadier Eze. He saluted briskly and waited. No one else came out. The pistol disappeared as briskly as it appeared.

"Which is your reason for wanting out?" enquired the Brigadier. "None of the reasons you mentioned Sir. I know that I am not very sensible. I talk out of turn. I do not think that I am good enough for the unit you intend to build from what you presently have. I however plead to be retained in this Division to hew wood, fetch water and do manual labour until I either learn or die in the bid to learn"

"Why do you judge yourself so severely?" Eze asked.

"I lost every member of my family, father, mother, brothers and sisters, an uncle and my cousins to the pogrom in the north, yet I cannot feel very bitter towards our enemies. I have even on the occasions, catching some of them helpless in my sections cross-fire let them slip away by easing up the sight of my gun, or ordering a cut when we should be raking and combing the area."

"Stop!" ordered the Brigadier.

"Talk to no man and see me immediately as I said before."

He saluted, spun around and marched back to his former position. "All of you want to fight as I can see" continued Brigadier Eze:

"If you know any unsuitable soldiers in your sections then please send their names, rank, unit and observed flaws to my ADC by 1400 hrs tomorrow. They will be excused. Now as I said, I have tried us all and found us all guilty of unsoldierly acts and condemned us to ether stand and fight to push back these our enemies, or turn tail as usual and die here when they attack. You will like to know how I did it. It is simply that I blew up six of the bridges behind us. That means that I cut off our supply and reinforcement routes and mined our rear area. The engineers will also tell you that I seized the map of the minefields so there will be no charting a safe route through them. Any attempt at withdrawal means death. We have enough supplies to last until they attack and after that our supply will come from their bases and depots. We will again fight like Biafran Soldiers. Nzogwu, Ude, Okafor, Ilo, Uzo and others will smile again when they see us fight as we should, and are used to. They have for months covered their faces with their palms for shame in their graves. Now make them glad again. Show them that they did not die in vain. Fight for your lives and for our nation. You stand more chances of living if you stand and fight than if you chicken out and run. You cannot shoot at your enemy with your back turned to him. By 1800 hours tomorrow anybody here is a soldier, and the trial and punishment for cowardice is summary and punishable by death. We have enlarged and upgraded our Casualty Collecting Post and the Divisional (MRS) Medical unit to hospital status. We have two Doctors, five interns and six nurses. If the need for more nurses arises the wounded will assist and deputize. From this moment on every member of this Division has been de-specialized. This is an infantry division therefore engineers, provosts, snipers, Reece men, armourers, cooks, clerks etcetera are all gunners of this infantry division. When we get locked in battle as the fields mature to confusion, switch to discretion and fight to possess the enemy trenches. Gaining the trenches mean a cut off has been established and the enemy caught in a cross fire. Activate the second defensive line by firing blue airbursts. Dig in and stay put. Armour bearers will locate you as you indicate need by firing green airbursts. Training and refresher battle drills will commence day after tomorrow. It is my pleasure to introduce to you, now, and hand you over to the training officer from the 14th Division Afikpo sector. He was until yesterday the commander of 39th Brigade of the 14th Division."

A weary groan swelled and burst into a wail that appeared to signify consternation.

"He is Colonel Adaka Ekwo!"

Many of the listeners stared in confusion at the short, fat headed Colonel as he marched out and halted before the Brigadier. He saluted staring expectantly.

"Your men" said Brigadier Eze waving over to the soldiers

"Turn them into soldiers. You have just about two months to effect this miracle. If you fail there will be plenty of human bones bleaching in the sun around this location, including yours and mine. Tales, and speeches, have ended. Orders have arrived. Division At-ten-tion."

He hollered, in his loudest voice. Everyone complied.

"As soon as the enemy attacks you will never be at ease until, you wipe them off our lands. Any questions?"

Silence reigned. Brigadier Eze turned and walked away from the Tac HQ, to his office.

"Stand-at-aise!"

Bellowed the fat headed Colonel whose reputation preceded him. The drizzle had intensified to a moderately heavy rain. Colonel Adaka sidled to some plantain trees, cupped his palm and catching the water sleuthing down the leaves drank thirstily. He smacked his thick lips and donned his helmet and without ceremony he started:

"I am Colonel Adakamma Ekwosimba. I have been posted to the 12th Division Biafran Army seemingly to command a Brigade of the Division, but in truth I am here to re-train soldiers of the division. Irrespective of rank, size, language, or creed, we are one and as soldiers are manufactured to be dangerous. We are like knives manufactured for cutting but will never be effective for that purpose until our cutting edges are honed. We can also be put to other related uses. We must learn to kill. In a month we will become good soldiers that can be truthfully described as dangerous. In two months, practice would have perfected us in this work of killing. By the sixth week, less than one percent of trainees would discover that killing is a way of life with them, and will be seen to be lethal. This will increase the effectiveness and efficiency of the Division. The training procedures will be ninety percent practical. We value words but they will represent only about two percent of the procedure. We will rely a lot on the correct type of mindset. This is variously described as brainwork, number six, intuition, psychological work, thinking, spiritual work etc. This is the heart or engine of all our doings. In this training period there will be lots of casualties because mistakes will be paid for with the life of the person who made it. Do not let that bother you. You will not know that you are dead. Believe me, the dead do not know or feel anything. The training has commenced—now!"

The somewhat heavy rainfall had increased in strength.

"All who wish to die for Biafra signify by raising your right hand!" all hands shot up.

"All with raised hands step out of your shelters"

Everybody complied, the Senior Officers less readily. Before Colonel Adaka could continue some of the Senior Officers including all three Brigade commanders withdrew to their shelters.

"You are not permitted to withdraw. Step out and do not repeat this error"

They stepped out again, donning their helmets.

"Kneel down where you now stand and instruct yourself to feel relaxed and comfortable in that position for the two training courses"

Groans of concern swelled filling the air and murmurs peremptorily began and stopped as Adaka stared at them without blinking.

"You will learn to close your minds to hunger, pain, discomfort, shame, sentiments, emotion, and fear. You will learn patience. You will shun remorse and regret."

CHAPTER FIVE

HONING

Colonel Adaka continued with his eyes shielded from the rain by his helmet: "You will learn to keep alive with the odds heavily against you for as sure as you have a name there is someone out there who is better than you. To keep alive you will learn to kill. You will learn courage. You will learn to think like the enemy. You will learn to posses the mind of others. You will learn to be frugal with words. You will learn to economize action and to maximize results. Most importantly you will learn to keep alive. You are all serving this punishment because you failed the first test. You all indicated willingness to die for Biafra. You will live and not die. How will it help Biafra if all her soldiers die? It will not help for then Biafra will no longer exist. Do not die for anyone or anything. Nothing and nobody is worth dying for."

"But someone died for us. Jesus Christ gave his life for us. Why can we not follow his example?"

Lieutenant Ahukanna, the Signals Commander who was totally fanatical about his Christian faith had cut in.

"Good" replied Adaka "That was an insured risk. He gave his life knowing that he would take it up again. You will not live again if you die, so try not to die for anything or anybody. Jesus has done it for us and that is sufficient. If that satisfies you I would like to continue."

He looked at Ahukanna inquiringly, who with a moronic grin on his face nodded his head in the affirmative saying sotto-voce:

"A good answer, I never heard it told that way before. It suits."

Adaka continued: "Majority of you, with the honing you will receive, will become dangerous to foes but less than one percent like I said before will be lethal. These ones are born killers. The instinct is there but unhoned. With honing they will emerge from their shells of inhibition, and stand apart from other soldiers. They will be proficient in destruction and they will be well sought after. The army will not retain them for they cannot be controlled when the fighting is over. The secret service, the intelligence services and the crime services will require their services. They can only hibernate in the hope of future activity. They are feared, dreaded and hated. They appear indestructible but they normally die young. One may be tempted to ask why this is so. It is because their restive natures, urge for dangerous activities, and desire for lethal excitement cannot be restrained, and finally, taking on more than they can chew, they self-destruct. They know this and expect it."

He paused reflectively.

"There is one ingredient of honing that we do not have enough of and that is time. We cannot have more so we stretch what we have to its limit. From this moment on we cancel the time for sleep. Steal it when you can but do not be caught sleeping on duty. The punishment is very severe. All twenty-four hours of the day will be used up for this training and the practical that will perfect our deadly application of the lethal science of destruction. A well-trained platoon of soldiers can destabilize, rout, decimate and destroy a full-fledged brigade beyond the ability to regroup. This will for now look like a pipe dream to you, but you will in six weeks time know that I speak only truths, verifiable truths. A platoon of lethal troops can do the same to a Division more effectively and with more devastating results. This however is hypothetical for it is very unlikely to put together a platoon of lethal fighters. They come in singles and are very difficult to hold together. When we are through with defying this rain, the Battalion Commanders, Specialized Unit Commanders, Signals, Reece, Engineers, Intelligence and others with their second-in-command, Adjutants and Administrative Officers will meet with the Brigade Commanders and their support officers to plan the twenty four hour training programme chart. This is to ensure that all hands are on deck to ensure full willing and complete participation. There will never be an official dull moment as the training commences at 1800 hours today. The only dull moment will be when you steal sleep. Do not be caught. I have thirty questions to ask and I expect answers to all of them, from all of you separately seven days after I have asked these questions. I will ask the questions after you have asked me yours. You have listened to my windy parroting for exactly fifty-six minutes now and as intelligent persons I expect you to have some issues agitating your minds within or without what I have said. I therefore expect questions from you to clarify whatever confusion or disagreements exist. The Brigade commanders will please walk up to me now and assist in this question and answer session. It will last for at least one hour. The second question time will be of about thirty minutes duration."

CHAPTER SIX

IDIGO

The relieved Colonels slowly rose to their feet and walked to Colonel Adaka. Colonel ldigo of the 17th Brigade was elected Director of the session. Colonel Oboyo was elected Provost, while Colonel Dennis was elected Secretary. This took less than three minutes. These three took over from the former Commanders.

Standing six feet five inches, Colonel ldigo, was a constant reminder of a ladder, a scarecrow and a tottering reed. His height made it seem as if he had no bulk. To make matters worse, his voice was at the same time childish, feminine, whining, rushed and breathless. These resulted in a blurred diction. A final year student of Engineering with a G.P depicting undoubtedly a first class honours, he was endowed with a razor sharp brain and phenomenal memory. Like most of his ilk, the rage generated by the animalistic pogrom in the northern part of Nigeria directed his footsteps from the academia into the army. In the army while still at the school of infantry, despite his gaunt frame, he excelled in every thing; beating renowned athletes and making Instructors look like recruits. Naturally he stuck out like a sore finger, and was commissioned Lieutenant, three months before his course mates. He was then posted to D.M.I [Directorate of Military Intelligence] where he not only solved all the code breaking problems, but also produced the foolproof 'Diarrhea' code. The simplicity of this code belied its resilience. All the code experts even with ninety percent tips of make up, could not crack the code.

Questioning of prisoners of war, one of his numerous duties at DMI, furnished him with facts to make uncannily accurate predictions of enemy movements and actions. Sieving out the truth from glucky rubbish spewed by prisoners of war was as nothing to him. He usually dropped the report, which invariably proved revealing and helpful to the Biafra Army strategists, with his Commanding Officer as he stepped out of the interrogation cell.

Other officers normally needed to muse on their fat facts files for some days before producing a report that rarely proffers relevant or valuable facts. While others would need a week of long hours of daily windy jawing to be seen to have thoroughly interviewed a prisoner, Idigo would spend less than an hour and come out with very revealing facts and tid bits to confirm other INTEL gathered else where. The fond nickname 'ORACLE' stuck to him like an adhesive while his detractors would in their derogatory remarks allude to a 'long juju' presumably of Arochukwu origin. These were the officers jealous of his prowess. When his rare talent was also put to debriefing intelligence officers back from reconnaissance trips, the Reece regiment was transferred to DMI garrison so as to be near the oracle for maximal utilization. The oracle kept churning out back breaking facts, and the outmatched Biafran Army began to slow down the pace of enemy advance, and counter attacks more often than not. Soon they started attacking to regain lost ground. Part One Orders graced DHQ notice board and a strange Fabian Idigo was promoted to Major. It was strange because no one knew of a Captain Fabian Idigo. It took the publication of the confirmatory Part Two Orders to establish that the "Oracle", Lieutenant Idigo, who did not wear the single star pip of a second Lieutenant, had again skipped the three star Captain pip and vaulted to the difficult-to-attain rank of Major. This time even his friends took offense. His admirers who surreptitiously added 'Brain Box' to his many nicknames stopped using it, and loudly stressed the derogatory 'long juju' title. The successes recorded in all sectors of the war coincided with his appointment as Head of Intel Analysis Bureau of the DMI, and his induction into the War Cabinet. It will be noted that the lowest ranking officer in the war cabinet was a full-blooded Colonel.

Thus with his lowly rank of Major he was not allowed to speak at the meetings. Issues of import were normally introduced and thoroughly discussed and canvassed, after which the Idigo who had been listening and whom the chairman had co-opted as assistant secretary to war cabinet, would produce the minutes. Momentous decisions and strategies are born to the detriment and pain of the Nigerian soldiers, albeit to the joy of the Biafran troops. Members of the war cabinet fail to recognize their contributions but quickly acknowledge the thoughts as lurking in their minds. In other words Idigo became the War Cabinet, churning out successful strategies and devious plans for the successful military activities that resulted. Such strategies gave birth to the five twin-engine gunboats and thirty single-engine canoes whose success in the riverside areas gave to Biafra a credible Navy. Even the Air force that was moribund came alive, as crafts made up of patched up dilapidated high fixed-wing aircraft, mostly Cessna and Navajo Chieftains, started making sorties. The Air force had arrived. Deep penetration bombing raids were soon carried out. The most potent addition ldigo spearheaded to the Biafran arsenal, was the Helicopter-gun-Ships. This gave a new leverage and bite to infantry activities. The Biafra military capability, through unerring interpretation of collated intelligence and the development of successful strategies in-line with the Biafra military capability, gave Brigadier Madiebo, the Chief of Army staff, an inspiration of how to do less work and get better results The Brigadier received recommendations from the different Commanders under whom Idigo had served and these were many, including Weapons, Research and Production, Signals, Intelligence-Analysis, Investigations and War Cabinet among others. These were for his promotion to the rank of Colonel. Madiebo considered this a tall hope but neither unreasonable nor unrealistic. He knew that the Commander-in-Chief would do a double take on the recommendations. He therefore laid the solid foundation to necessitate a promotion. He discussed with ldigo and his helicopter pilots that formed the strongest arm of the Biafran Air force and in addition to their devastating front-line activities; they began and sustained behind-the-line strikes. The objective was the demolition of enemy armouries and their munitions, transport and supply bases. They succeeded so well that not only the Biafra propaganda machinery, but also the Nigerian radio stations broadcast their destructive potency. The publication of the quarterly Part One Orders carried Idigo's promotion to the rank of Colonel, and the Chief of General Staff, Major General Effong protested vehemently:

"What are we running here?" he queried "A boy's scout organization of tantalizing nomenclature. This boy has never fired a shot in anger. He has not gone through battle inoculation. If he has so much brains what about brawn? Under pressure how will he react? What is his physical condition? What is his courage assessment? Can he effectively lead men in a desperate battle? I concede he is brilliant, ingenious, has nerves but what about good old bravery, hardiness and native cunning which have always served as a foundation for a good army career? Give me answers Brigadier. Must we abuse rank because of this chaotic war situation?"

"Well sir" replied Brigadier Madiebo "I do not know exactly where and how to start but l crave your indulgence to tell you a story."

"Stand-at-aise" drawled Effong askance turning up his nose in disapproval.

"Tell the story."

Brigadier Madiebo relaxed and with a smile on his face began:

"In December 1967, the 'Red findings' of the military intelligence was that our forward lines were being breached without enemy efforts. Battles were not fought, skirmishes were light, artillery and mortar fire were not in barrages but in scanty and solitary droppings. Yet our forces were loosing ground, our men were turning tail without enemy persuasion. The war cabinet was perplexed. When the situation could not be stemmed, Lt. Idigo who was newly posted to DMI, from the school of infantry, approached his unit commander Major Egbue and inquired as to the cause of the restiveness. He had inferred from the ceaseless chattering of the signals and the milling around of staff officers. Egbue, neck deep in confusion told him of the DMI's findings. Idigo then requested for the Intel file, and when they were provided, he sat in Egbue's office to study them. An hour later he came out with the report that the sequence of withdrawals and AWOLs spoke of a well-coordinated sabotage with well defined goals that were being achieved without much loss of men and materials on the Federal side, and loss of much materials but fewer loss of life on the Biafran side. The greater loss of personnel could be traced to desertions, AWOLs, and self-inflicted hand and leg injuries by unwilling Biafran soldiers. Idigo made a detailed report that caught the C-In-C's interest. Within the week three reconnaissance sorties into enemy territory by our Intel boys failed, and more of our Intel staff were in enemy hands. Idigo volunteered, and was dropped behind enemy lines in naval motor boats. Swimming into Umuoba Anam from the canoe parked out of sight of the lonely shores he acquired a nest in a long abandoned, half sunk, rotting vessel just a few steps from the shore. From there he rowed to Ozugono disguised as a fisherman. There he killed a tall army Lieutenant and using the uniform of the man he impersonated as a Nigerian Army Lieutenant. In two days he abducted and ferried across to his nest, a Corporal, a Warrant Officer and a Lieutenant. He fed them well and interrogated them promising them a good drink after the interrogation. Except for lashing them securely on the rotting deck, any violent forceful action of theirs being capable of disintegrating the deck and hence dropping them into the water logged hold of the ship, he explained the circumstances neither threatening nor maltreating them. Although he himself does not drink he freely fed them raffia palm gin and rice for the two days it took to successfully interrogate them. Because their hands and legs were tied together, turkey style with the fisherman's knot, he had to spoon feed and cup feed them. He however deprived them of cigarettes. They talked loosely and carelessly to him, believing they were giving him sludge of rubbish. When he was through he thanked them profusely repeating his promise of a good drink. He left them and slid into dark waters. Thirty minutes later after mining the vessel he swam out to his canoe. He rowed into the night but not before he heard the explosion that sent the vessel to the bottom of the water creating a lot of flotsam. He had made good his promise of a good drink. His next port of call was Abudu where he successfully reconnoitered, killing a Captain and a Regimental Sergeant Major. Thence he returned through Agbor, where he slit the throats of two cell guards before releasing two of the missing Biafran Intelligence Officers. He debriefed them that same night before they made their tortuous way back to Abala Oshimili. They returned to Biafra with ldigos intelligence reports, and his interpretation of them. He surfaced at Omoh in a Nigerian Army Signals Land rover and left that same night leaving three dead bodies. He rode into Enugu on a motorcycle, breached the prison fence and rescued four more of the missing intelligence officers. A week and over twenty dead bodies later he rescued a dozen prisoners of war including five intelligence Officers, his colleagues at DMI, from Uzuakoli prison. In his escape bid, he stopped a bullet in his thigh and was captured while trying at snail speed to swim across the rushing Ogwe River. The rescued prisoners of war reported and there was a great hue and cry of despondency at Army Headquarters. Before the Army Headquarters could react, Captain Adaka had sent an action signal to his Division Commander and vanished into enemy territory. Two weeks later, while sneaking around 82nd Division Garrison, at Eha-Amufu, explosions started rocking the whole Barracks. The volcano like eruption of the armory heralded intermittent loud and angry explosions as important facilities in the garrison vapourised. Idigo pulled his game leg over the high wall fence to the leeward side of the garrison. Adaka like a big cat on all fours padded, blade between his teeth under where Idigo was poised to jump from. In time he recognized the wonder boy of military intelligence, severally known as Occult or Oracle and sheathed his blade. Idigo jumped unsuspectingly into Adaka hands, and was forced to stand still as an expertly applied neck lock told him that he would be dead if he showed any resistance. He relaxed as Adaka mulled: "Welcome long juju" into his ears.

The increasing thunderous explosions and accompanying bonfires hurried them on their way. Both rescuer and the rescued left a bloody trail of dead bodies with slit throats on their way back out of the enemy territory. What I have narrated to you sir is only one of his many mental and physical escapades. I would like you to ask him all those questions you asked me so that you can personally assess and evaluate him."

Looking somewhat puzzled and contemplative but definitely more mellowed from his earlier rage, Major General Effong in a weak voice requested for the interview to be held immediately.

Ten minutes later Idigo was marched in and saluting he stood stiff still.

Effong ignored him and he continued his stiff salute poise and rigid attention for almost ten minutes. Effong looked at him dourly, minutely inspecting every part of him. He directed his gaze to Madiebo and asked in a sour voice:

'What have we got here? He is gangly and awkward and foolishly tall. He is as thin as a rake and like a reed will break if visited by strong wind." He got up and walked around him in inspection and made riling comments: 'This long, weak-kneed, ridiculous walking stick in uniform is an embarrassment to the Army. Madiebo what do you think?"

Another ten minutes had elapsed. "I think sir that he should speak for himself. Major Idigo give answers to the CGS's questions and meanwhile stand at ease."

Idigo relaxed as Madiebo returned the salute on behalf of the CGS. "Which of the questions sir?" Idigo inquired.

"I have only asked a question. It will do you a world of good not to play that stupid brains game with me. What questions did you say I asked?"

"Sir you wish to known if I am an impostor. If what you have heard about me is true. If I am a normal person, if I am a freak, what my weaknesses are. Whether I am related to Giant Alakuku? Most importantly you wish to discover my Achilles heels. You are very impressed with the resume you have gathered, but you are displaying a dour countenance to dissuade my acting swollen headed. You wish to evaluate my temperament . . ."

"Stop" ordered Effong raising his hands palm open to buttress the verbal order and reclining in his high backed chair against the wall. He dismissed him with a wave of the hand. Uncorrupted by familiarity, Idigo awkwardly came to attention saluted, wheeled about and marched out of the office. As the door closed behind him Effong's lopsided grin widened into a broad smile.

"I saw something like this during my peace keeping tour of the Congo from a Ghanaian egg-head lieutenant, who had reconnoitered almost half of the Congo, within the eighteen-month period of his tour. When he read my mind everything he said up to the Alakuku reference was true. When he left we discovered that he represented ninety percent of our intelligence activities. He learnt and spoke fluently four Congolese dialects during his tour. This was in addition to his flawless English, French, Italian, Spanish and German Languages. He was working on Russian, Chinese and Arabic when he left. He never drank, smoked or womanized. He was not homosexual either. He ate only one meal a day but quadruple ration. He would spend all his leisure time at the shooting range practicing with all manners of guns and knives. I was then a good knife thrower but Lieutenant Kwaku Arya made me look ordinary. When he left, we though without proof connected most of the mystery killings in our area of operation to his frequent unauthorized absences from camp. On my return l made enquiries about him and his whereabouts all to no avail. Even my close friend, Kotoka, blanked out on me when l mentioned Kwaku. This Idigo is like him except in physical features. Kwaku was average in size and handsome beyond imagination. Everything about him was perfect but he was mulatto."

He mused for over ten minutes especially with fleeting changes in facial expressions until he realized once more that Brigadier Madiebo was still in attendance to him. He turned to him with a smile and said: "Yes Alex l have got it. I will add my own recommendation but will insist on his having a full scale battle inoculation. He will join battalion grade strike force attacks. He will assist in the command of a brigade grade attack and then he will command a brigade in dire combat. If he survives we will start adding brief special duty commands to his other functions so that in this way he will justify his rare brain, brawn and lightning fast promotions."

Effiong opened his leather-bound minute pad and started writing furiously.

"Would this not amount to riding a willing horse to death?" Madiebo asked quietly.

Effiong did not look up. He continued writing and requested for an envelope and a glass of gin-with-milk. As he sipped the drink he looked at Madiebo saying: "No Alex. This willing horse cannot be ridden to death. He will get better as his work load increases. Inactivity will lead to boredom, which is the only thing that will destroy him. I have met this type before. I am sure you have heard of the American special assignment group called Navy Seals. I have not only seen one but joined in debriefing him after a deep penetration strike. During the debriefing I thought he was hallucinating but when proofs of his mind-boggling exploits were presented I feared for the safety of the world. I was a second lieutenant then. Now I know better. If we can put together a squad of such lethal fighters, it will effectively counter-balance Nigeria's superiority in arms and personnel. I know of two such people. They are Adaka, running raids along Ehamufu, Afikpo, Uzuakoli and Okigwe sectors, and the chameleon Oboyo, commanding the Special Task Force that has helped curb enemy incursion in almost all sectors of this war. Six more of these types and we will be able to build a very mobile and highly effective force to plague our enemies. I am sure that if we search especially among the other ranks we will locate more of these fellows. I have a feeling in my bones that Lightning Strike Force is born."

CHAPTER SEVEN

LIGHTNING STRIKE FORCE

INTRA DEPT MEMO
Date:—28-02-69
Source:—C.G.S
Destination:—C-in-C. BA.
Courier:—

SUBJECT: MAJOR IDIGO / PROMOTION TO COLONEL
Recommendation

1. Personal worth Assessment and Evaluation. Agree with C.O.A.S' recommendation. Pedigree indicates effective, efficient and reliable under pressure. Self confident and very courageous. Ingenious and emotionally stable. Highly analytical and intuitive. Quick of mind. Independent non-regular service type. Photographic memory. Highly productive under pressure. Inspires confidence in persons around him. Gets the best out of subordinates. Core nature not definable. No known weaknesses. Homicidal mania suspected. Natural leader. Natural killer *Lethal*. Handle with care. No fear. No sentiments. No remorse.

EYES ONLY C-in-C
RECOMMENDATION: PROMOTE COLONEL. PUT ASSIDUOUS THROUGH INOCULATION RE-HIGH

DANGER / RISK ASSIGNMENTS. UTILIZE MAXIMALLY DURING THE WAR SITUATION. CANNOT FUNCTION IN SERENITY. WILL SELF-DESTRUCT IN PEACETIME. CONFIRM PART ONE AWAIT FURTHER ORDERS.

SUGGEST:

(a) PRO PSYCHOANALYSIS EVALUATION ASSESSMENT REPORT PREREQUISITE FOR EFFECTIVE CONTROL OF SUBJECT
(b) SIFT THROUGH FORMATIONS FOR COMBATANT INDIVIDUALS OF THIS LETHAL ILK TO FORM THE CORE OF THE EARLIER PROPOSED HIGHLY MOBILE STRIKE FORCE
(c) COLONELS OBOYO AND ADAKA OF THE SAME MAKE. AWAIT ORDERS.

The two combat Land Rovers slugged their slippery way through the mud, splashing everything within their sphere dirty brown. They skidded to a halt before the D.H.Q's main office and the inmates briskly disembarked. Brigadier Eze stepped into his office and halted as if he jammed a brickwall. He donned his helmet and saluted. General Madiebo the C.O.A.S waved him into a seat and pushed a glass of amber liquid in a large drinking glass towards him. They both drank meditatively until the C.O.A.S spoke:

"What is the problem? We got your signal asking to be relieved. Why?

Are you battle weary?"

"No sir" replied Brigadier Eze.

"I am in the dark. I may have wasted time halting the Nigerian advance but there was no other way. The battle had to be frontal because of the flat terrain. Yet I got more than I lost in men and materials. I asked myself if I was being suspected of being a saboteur. I wonder. I have got the Bee, the Chameleon and the Oracle from different regiments and no further information except that Adaka will train the Division. I have got definite instruction not to go on the offensive. I have been warned not to expect reinforcement in men or ammunitions. I am at a loss as to what is going on. Situation report shows enemy docility. They don't initiate skirmishes, patrols or target strikes. They are not reinforcing in men or supplies. They are not clearing the littered roads or filling up obstacles. Their small guns rarely speak. Their 105mm and 106mm guns fire scantily but purposely beyond our locations into the Ojuru and Uyo Rivers at Ngor Okpalla. Reece patrols show that having rested and re-armed, we can without much difficulty beat them back to Obigbo and if well supplied recapture Port Harcourt. But the AHQ says 'stay put'. I talk to the COAS and he threatens to relieve me if I should talk again of offensive action. He even threatens to court martial me if any unit of my division should as much as engage in any skirmish no matter how light. I have a very fit Division, well armed, motivated and raring to go yet I am hamstrung by the very people who armed me. How can you stripple a rifle, clean and assemble it, oil it well and load it, cock it and despite the prevailing prospect of action lock it away from use. I don't understand this. My course mate Oboyo whose mind is a closed book has been posted here to serve under me. He was my junior by dint of the alphabet of my name coming before his. A very well trained devil and a soldier to the core but where is his loyalty? At the school of infantry during strategy sessions he excelled besting everyone including the instructors because he never did anything according to the rules. This earned him the nick name Chameleon. He has proved himself commanding sturdy platoons, effective companies after which he put together the crack 18th battalion. He deployed these against orders to withdraw from the Republic of Benin when it fell to the federal troops. Truly he discomfited the enemy, decimating their isolated formations in guerilla warfare actions that did not allow the federal troops affect a concerted effort at capturing Onitsha through the Niger bridge head. He disobeyed the COAS' order to withdraw to Onitsha before the bridge was blown and thumbed his nose at the C-in-C's order halting all supplies and reinforcement to 18th and 21st battalions cut off in the Republic of Benin. Oboyo in a lightning fast move cut out the surrounded 21st battalion, destroying after looting, the supply bases of the federal troops from Agbor to

Asaba. He merged the two troops and formed the Biafran Vandals who were subject only to himself and his subordinates. He posted his men to towns adjoining Nigerian Army formations. Each unit was responsible for its arms, ammunition and essential supplies which it got albeit from the Nigerian army supply bases nearest to it. Their food supplies came from the natives who became cooperative after they felt the wrath of the vandals. It took me, Nwobosi and Nebo to negotiate Abala-Oshimili, Abala-Agada, Ukwuo, and Olona to his headquarters and talk him out of there and into coming back to Biafra. He refused withdrawing his men but reported a week later at AHQ. The following day he was driven to the State House at Umuahia and marched into the presence of the C-in-C. The military policemen who marched in with him had earlier disarmed him. They stood around expectant and tense. The C-in-C fingered his bushy beard contemplatively saying:

"You served under me at Logistics Kaduna as a Lieutenant. Am I right?"

"Yes sir" replied Oboyo.

"I promoted you to the rank of Captain at 82nd division N.A Enugu.

Is that right?" "Yes sir"

"You are now a Major. Am I right?" "Yes sir."

"You disobeyed my command to withdraw to the Niger Bridge Head Onitsha and thereby jeopardized the safety of your command and that of Major Azunna in command of 21st battalion?" the C-in-C's eyes were blazing now and all was still.

"Yes sir but only to the extent that I disobeyed the order to withdraw. When Major Azunna saw his command cut off he set up a defensive square and was ready to according to him commit suicide rather than fall into the hands of the enemy. I salvaged his command in full, loosing only twelve men." Replied Oboyo

"Why did you come into Biafra?" "Because you sent for me." "What do you expect now?"

"To hear the problem and contribute my own quota." "Don't you expect to be court marshaled?"

"No sir."

"Why?"

"You have integrity. As a gentleman you cannot send worthy officers with your word and go back on it."

"What if it is a trick?"

"This level of trickery is below you."

"You are the chameleon so you should understand trickery." "I made a study of it and i use it effectively", Oboyo answered.

"Why did you disobey the order to fall back to the Onitsha end of the Niger Bridge?"

"To save Onitsha and allow 11th Division stabilize and dig in defensively. That has been achieved and to ensure that no concerted effort is made and sustained to take Onitsha from the Republic of Benin. We are a large poisonous thorn in their flesh. Also to assist in arming Biafra from their stock and we have sent over ten thousand riffles and twenty thousand boxes of different calibers of ammunition to Biafra through Ndoni, Osamara, Ogbaru, Atani and Akiri Ogidi. My men monitored them until they were delivered to Supply and Transport logistics unit at 11th Division. Otherwise Onitsha would have fallen and Biafra ceased to exist.

"Thank you" said Colonel Ojukwu. "I swore to defend the Biafran State", replied Oboyo.

"Thank you anyway" continued Ojuku. He moved across and embraced Oboyo. He then went behind his table and pulled out a drawer from where he withdrew a black box. He opened it and extracted two stars and pinned them to Oboyo's shoulders after the eagle.

"You are promoted to the rank of Lieutenant Colonel. Report to planning and Strategies Office AHQ and await further orders. You are free to discuss with the Chief of Army Staff. You have my ear through him."

The bodyguards and Military Policemen had quietly melted away. The ADC who was now translating the discussion into long hand pretended that he was not there as glasses clicked and two hefty slugs of Gordon's Dry Gin burned their way down the throats of the newly promoted Colonel and the Static Colonel whose subordinates were General Officers. I was there so I saw and heard it all because during my convalescence period I acted ADC to the C-in-C. I went into the ROB with two 9mm bullets embedded in my foot and thigh and brought Oboyo back from an obvious rebellion. The injuries I sustained while slugging it out with Brigadier Benjamin Adikunle in and around Port Harcourt had not healed when I requested to return to unit. The C-in-C granted my request and I came to realize that we had been beaten back to beyond Ukwa. While I was lazing around with little scratches of injury as excuse, my Division lost thirty-six kilometers of Biafra land to Adikunle who was now ensconced at Obinze breathing down Owerri town. I stopped their advance and pushed them back to Ukwa. I then stabilized the defensive line, rested my troops and called for reinforcement and re-supply. The first blow I received was:

'Dig in. No logistic support.'

I did not bother much because strange but ultimately realistic and sensible orders fly around in dire situations. I reconnoitered the enemy locations and found that they were not poised to begin the offensive. I noted that they could be easily dislodged. Their fear of thick forests, uncharted rivers, many twisting and turning deep streams, that rush angrily to what appear to them like unknown destinations, cowed them into procrastination. I requested permission to launch an offensive that would rout them. I planned to push them back to Port Harcourt where we will stand at advantage in street to street fighting. Their big guns and armoured vehicles will not serve much purpose against our close combat Rangers battalion. The response signal read thus:

"No action. Maintain present defensive line. Out."

There was no more use of Diarrhea code. The SITREPS were in pidgin and delivered by hand carry COAS, so I knew that something was wrong. The smell of sabotage pervaded the air and I felt that either I was suspected of sabotage or the saboteurs were blanking me out. They are also keeping a meaningful percentage of Biafra's military might in the dark. Though we are well armed we are being immobilized. When I saw the tracks of your amphibious vehicles, I came in expecting to be arrested but you are alone. You are without your bodyguards and without Military Policemen. What is happening?"

He downed the drink and pushed the glass aside. Madiebo refilled both glasses and pushed his towards him.

"Why are the Bee, the Chameleon and the Oracle here? Why this retraining order? Why am I now excluded from the Diarrhea code and the War Cabinet meetings? I have not received my code digits for two weeks now. Please enlighten me before you take any other action."

Madiebo corked his flask from where he had poured out the drinks. He drained his glass, leaned back and said:

"The C-in-C sent me to brief you because he is aware of the turmoil in your mind. The SITREP you sent was coded over you by the Oracle explaining your confusion. Your bridge busting mood told the Oracle that you were only sure of yourself and your Division. Others, including myself are suspect. You believe that the Office of Planning and Strategies, DMI, AHQ and even Signals are compromised. You think that Biafra will capitulate within the month and so as a true soldier and a loyal Biafran will rather die than go along with any plan to surrender or sell Biafra. You prepared for the worthy exit. That is why I have been sent to brief you. All is well and the plan is to throw a deadly weapon into the foray against Nigeria. It is neither a nuclear nor atomic weapon but a weapon made up of flesh and blood. Not ordinary flesh and ordinary blood but rare flesh and rare blood. Science has given us dangerous weapons but we are putting together a hydra-headed lethal weapon to end this war. I saw a squad of lethal persons acting separately to outdo the American Army in Vietnam. They are called the Navy Seals. Now we are about to put these lethal persons together to act in concert for maximum effect called synergy. The grouse of Adikunle's Army is the environment we require for the said mobilization and interaction. The Lightning Strike Force is born and as I am in command of the project, I think that you are the right person to hold together the bunch of lethal persons we are bringing together. You are the trigger to this gun. During training, they will operate from here but not in this sector. Oboyo is the infiltration expert and his Reece reports are usually ninety percent accurate. Adaka's non-stop aggression and persistence will wear down any regiment no matter how resilient. Idigo the catalyst will provide all the necessary intelligence reports. Oboyo and Idigo are better at killing with the knife than with any other weapon. Adaka requires only a squad to disintegrate a well knit regiment of conventional fighters. Colonel Dennis may not possess all these qualities but he is the best Ordnance Officer in the Biafran army. He ran Supply and Transport Headquarters like clockwork and is expert at rapid deployment, personnel management and control, management analysis, general logistics and is a military historian. Although a well trained soldier he hasn't the maniacal courage of Adaka, Idigo and Oboyo. He will within this training period sniff out the kind of lethal persons required for this force. You are now in the know. The weapon will become fully operational forty days from today when the Office of Planning and Strategies would have submitted the programme of activities to the War Cabinet. Your hands will be too full to continue in the War Cabinet but your diarrhea status will be restored. Carry on from here and do a good job. The three best marksmen in the Biafran army are on their way to this Division. Unarmed combat specialists are already here for the training programme. Physical health instructors are jogging into your command post this moment if you will look through the window behind you, you will see them. Experienced armourers with didactic qualities will report tomorrow for your weapons management training. Keep communications with the AHQ at the barest minimum. Hand carry via officer couriers are preferable. Thirty days from now targets will be communicated to you for Reece purposes. Your opinion will reach us before you start striking as we need to compare notes. You can now see why your relieved Brigade commanders were ordered to remain with you. When the training programme is completed, the Lightning Strike Force will become mobile under your new command with another General Officer taking over your 12th Division and reinstating the now relieved but then better trained brigade and battalion commanders. Your present command has an estimated life span of forty days from today."

The COAS left the way he arrived, unannounced as a whirlwind.

CHAPTER EIGHT

QUESTIONS

Brigadier Eze at 1620hrs, over two hours after the departure of the COAS was still prancing about his office with a fixed wide grin on his face, studying maps on the walls of his office and nodding meditatively. The mug of gin he poured with which to celebrate remained forgotten on the table alongside the pad and pen for making notes. Pleasant thoughts of devastating blows struck at the brutes who wiped out his wife and children chased themselves around his mind. He could not control them and was in the middle of a wild laugh appreciating another deadly use to which he would put his lethal force when he heard the knock. He stopped and looking up saw Sergeant Mbagwu put his head to announce:

"Sergeant Kingsley to see the Div. Commander sir."

Kingsley entered and stood at attention for many minutes before Eze remembered him and returned the salute with a touch to his forehead.

"What do you do best in the Army?"

"I command a heavy weapons squadron sir. I am said to be good at the use of machine guns for I understand them."

"Give my clerk your particulars and try to keep alive until I contact you. Fall out."

Kingsley left wondering what was happening. As Kingsley stepped out of the command post he saw many bicycles standing besides the building. He stepped back into Sergeant Mbagwu's office asking to borrow one. Before Mbagwu could reply he vaulted across the verandah railing onto a Hercules bicycle pedaling furiously downhill towards the forward locations. The cassava and yam mounds just before the tactical post grounds did not allow for a smooth ride. He got down and ran the last lap with the bicycle lifted over his head with one hand. He bounded into the clearing while the questions were being asked and Colonel Adaka was giving answers to them as follows:

"I am Corporal Nwafor, C Company, 30th battalion, 17th brigade, 12th Division. Is your name Adaka or Adakamma?"

"My name is Adakamma. Adaka is short for Adakamma so you are right to call me either if you care to. I am not kin to the gorilla."

"What do you mean by crime services?" "Talking about crime, what is your name?"

"I am sorry sir. I am Warrant Officer Grade II, John Egbue of the 12th Division signals."

"Lieutenant Fidelis Onyia. Reece regiment, 12th Div. When did you join Biafran army?"

"I transferred from the Nigeria army at secession."

"Lieutenant Ephraim Taribo, 30th battalion, 17th brigade, 12th Division. Can we bounce the enemies back and out of Port Harcourt? If so how soon?"

"It is possible immediately we are through with this training. We will commence offensive action aimed at recovering all our lost lands."

"Are you not afraid of death?"

"I am but what bothers me more is dying."

"When we are through with training will you remain and lead us in combat? Colonel Mewu M.O, relieved commander 19th brigade, 12th Division."

"Training is on the job, which means practicals not theory. Combat starts today, this very night."

"2nd Lieutenant Maliki Odakosa, B Company, 7th of 28th, 12 Div. What are our targets, objectives and goals?"

"Efficiency, proficiency and defeat of the enemy which is deadly enough to achieve as set goals."

"My question is not answered sir, I mean operational targets." "Unknown to me if already formulated."

"Private Justus Okwara, 27th battalion 29th brigade. How sir can I become lethal?"

"Excel in this programme and you are lethal."

"Obidi Amaka, Major 7th battalion, 29th brigade. How can you describe a lethal person?"

"A person, who disregards personal safety, manifests extraordinary courage and rare bravery in the face of grave danger and overwhelming enemy activities. Stands two shades deeper than being ordinarily dangerous and cannot be termed kind or wicked so is not known to possess emotions or sentiments. Reads situations and circumstances accurately and anticipates orders that shortly arrive even after they have been executed. Can read others like a book. It is not common but happens as a result of honing. Well I can see that you have exhausted your questions so we cannot afford to waste time on irrelevancies.

"Sorry sir" droned Sergeant Kingsley

"I just rode in from the Div. Command Post. I have a question." "Yes ask" replied Adaka.

"I am Sergeant Kingsley Okoh of 12th Div. Heavy Weapons and Backup Guns. The last fourteen days have shown an unusual flurry of activities and it is obvious that something is brewing. What is it?"

"It is an attempt to make soldiers out of the untrained personnel of a rag-tag quasi armed army."

"How can I help?"

"By submitting yourself for training, and being committed."

"Thank you sir. In case heavy weapons training is required, I am the expert. Nobody and by that I mean nobody, knows it like me. I even understand light machine guns also. I am available."

Adaka waited until he finished then said:

"They call you King Kong. Now I know why for your stature is not overly baboonish. Raise your left thumb and forefinger."

Kingsley complied. "Show your tongue."

When the tongue came out of the perplexed face Adaka ordered: "Hold your tongue with your thumb and forefinger until I finish here.

You talk too much."

Kingsley obeyed standing stock still. Adaka resumed:

"Dig for paper and pen or pencil out of your kit and take down the questions. Think on them and give your answers within seven days. Submit your answers as soon as you finish to my aide."

He cleared his throat, spat out and began:

1. What do you do in a jungle situation?
2. When action matures to a maelstrom what do you do?
3. What do you do when you come under effective enemy fire?
4. What do you do under ineffective enemy fire?
5. What do you do when outmatched by the enemy fire power?
6. What do you do when fatally wounded in action?
7. What do you do when located by the enemy?
8. What do you do when in doubt?
9. What do you do when outmatched?
10. What do you do when you are finished?
11. What do you do when confused?
12. What do you do when cut off?
13. What do you do when caught in an ambush?
14. What do you do when you run out of ammunition?
15. What do you do when caught in a cross fire?
16. What do you do when you can't locate the enemy?
17. What do you do when faced with female soldiers?
18. What do you do when lost?
19. What do you do when captured?
20. What do you do when you are out of your depth?
21. What do you do when wounded in action?
22. What is the difference between a withdrawal and a retreat?
23. What do you do when a situation is too good?
24. How do you become combat effective?
25. What is mature jungle language?
26. How do you retain relevance in your environment?
27. What is jungle motion?

28. How do you react to things you can do nothing about?
29. What do you do when in enemy territory?
30. What do you do in a no win situation?

That is all for now. Make your answers simple, straight forward to the point and without semantics. Please no proverbs or idioms. There is not enough time to accommodate academic gallivanting. You should report in your tugs and vests at St. Dominic's school field behind the Div. Command Post at 1800hrs. Dismiss."

Everybody slunk away soaked to the skin. Dennis, Oboyo and Adaka uncorked their flasks and sipped the inevitable fiery illicit gin as they walked to the Tac bunker. Their aides did the same to defy the cold but kept a respectable distance though within earshot. They settled under the leafy shrubs camouflaging the bunker. The Colonels sat at the large table and Idigo shared out plain sheets and pencils saying:

"It is obvious that the principle of division of labour is appropriate for achieving our purpose in this training programme. One will act as supervisor and the other act as instructor in our specialized fields. Dennis will continue as secretary, recorder, administrator and liaison officer to the Div. commander. He will instruct on administration, ordnance, observation post and sentry duties. He will handle liaison, logistics and act as executive officer to our Training Commandant Colonel Adaka. He can adjust as he sees fit with the approval of the commandant. Colonel Oboyo will handle guerilla warfare, penetration, infiltration, terrorism, survival, camouflaging, obstacle strategies and tactics. He will also adjust as he sees fit with the approval of the commandant. Colonel Adaka will handle skirmishes, patrols, demolition attacks which will include offensive and defensive actions. He will also adjust as he sees fit. Combat maneuvers are his exclusive preserve. I will handle and supervise intelligence planning and disguise. I will personally lead or assist the leaders in practical sessions. All these will of course be under Adaka's overall supervision and approval. I believe that specialists should be invited to handle marksmanship, unarmed combat, physical health, mental health, and group weapons such as machine guns, rockets, mobile grenades and mines. I reiterate that these are all subject to the approval of the commandant."

Idigo leaned back pushing across to Adaka the paper on which he was writing out all that he said. Adaka picked it up and studied it closely while referring to what he himself wrote as Idigo was talking and said:

"I have heard of your phenomenal ability of invading people's minds and culling their thoughts. Today I have seen it. You x-rayed my mind fully and I am amazed. Your renowned phenomenon of talking while thinking and writing has also been demonstrated. I watched you do it and tried to write along with you yet I could not keep up with you. You are really strange. I accept this input without reservations. Are there any further inputs?" he asked looking at Oboyo and Dennis. They shook their heads and drank deeply from their flasks.

"Then let us see the Div. Commander."

Adaka got up and led the way out of the Tac bunker. He adjusted his pouch and bounded into a slow jog while the others followed. He reached the Div. command post just ahead of Oboyo but far ahead of Dennis and far behind Idigo. As they waited to catch their breath, panting, puffing, wheezing and sneezing, Idigo showed no sign of the exertion as he bent over the verandah wall writing with full concentration. Adaka put on his beret and the others followed suit including Idigo who was till busy writing but stopped abruptly as Adaka took out his beret.

"You even read minds without looking at your prey."

They all entered the commander's office and came to attention.

"Relax!" ordered Eze. "Sit down." As they sat down he ordered: "Brief me."

Adaka turned to Idigo and said:

"Do the briefing and say everything you deem necessary. Oboyo, Dennis and I will take notes."

Eze drew his pad to himself, took out a ball point pen and started writing as Idigo reeled out much more than he wrote before. The monologue of a meeting rose at 1845hrs after Adaka had left for the 1800hrs rendezvous behind the command post.

Brigadier Eze led the Colonels onto the field where they joined the jog around the field. After that they participated fully in the physical exercises and sat meekly on the grass listening to the leader of the Physical health Team as he was saying:

"You cannot be good at anything if you are not physically fit. Weaklings do not survive wars. You need to learn how to run, jump, dive, crawl, climb, swim, endure, fight, kick, slap, punch, hook, jab and slither in order to be able to survive in this war of bullets, shrapnel and explosives. You feed well so all you need is to excite your muscles and brain cells. We have planned an all round regime to put you into shape. I do not intend to fail and as many as pass through me for the planned thirty days training period will emerge physically and mentally fit. Your psychological state is outside my scope. You will be split into groups of fifty for ease of control. I don't want any segregation. By this I mean that groups will have a good mix of officers as well as rank and file. Rank will mean nothing once you are on this field. Endurance training periods will last for two hours. A one hour rest period will be observed which will be utilized for unarmed combat training and practice. You will be introduced to judo, wrestling, boxing, karate and savate but will only be told of kung fu and taekwando for which we have no instructors. Knife skills which include stabbing, cutting and throwing are a must for everyone. Three hour periods for each group means that four groups will train daily. While training, huffing, puffing, wheezing, sneezing, coughing, noisy inhalation and exhalation must be kept at the barest minimum. The idea of this training is to make you combat effective and noise reduces your effectiveness by about eighty percent. You should strive to be strong, diligent, persistent, ferocious, courageous but above all silent. Four hours sleep daily is enough for a healthy man. Go to bed by 2300hrs or earlier if you can and wake up by 0300hrs. I have the exercise regime typed out for you to hold and refer to. Half of your aerobic needs will be done by you without supervision until the ninety minutes before you join others for jogging. Be diligently religious about this for your life depends primarily on it."

Pausing he signaled his batman to share out the sheets of paper containing the regime. The time table and activities will be pasted by tomorrow on the Div. notice board.

EXERCISE REGIME.

1. Wake up with breathing exercises. While praying, thinking or meditating do 100 deep inhalations and exhalations alternatively.
2. Roll your eyes vertically and horizontally twenty times without moving your head.
3. Rise with 100 press-ups, fifty fast and fifty slow.
4. Follow up with 100 sit ups
5. Relax with 50 fast 'touch your toes'.
6. Relax further with 50 slow 'touch your toes'.
7. Execute 10 forward low kicks and 10 backward low kicks.
8. Execute 10 high kicks with each foot.
9. Execute 10 mule kicks with each heel.
10. Execute 50 deep knee bends.
11. Run 300 steps on the spot.
12. Relax with 500 marking time.
13. Execute five throw backs.
14. Throw 50 punches, 50 hooks, 50 jabs and 50 elbow hits with each hand.
15. Skip an imaginary rope 300 times and double skip if you know how.
16. Execute grabbing. Ball your fists and open them forcefully 200 times.
17. Rotate your neck 50 times in each direction with your eyes open.
18. Revolve your wrists 100 times in each direction.
19. Revolve your waist 50 times in each direction.
20. Push your waist forward forcefully 10 times and backwards ten times.
21. Forcefully knee high 20 times alternating with each knee.
22. Twist your body parts.
23. Train on weights using your munition pouches.
24. Frog jump with your riffle above your head briskly and in all directions.
25. Bare your mind of all thoughts.
26. Learn concentration on specific targets or thoughts.

These and any other physicals that come to your mind should not take over ninety minutes of your time utilize the remaining thirty minutes of your personal time to practice deep thinking on specific issues. Fleeting thoughts should not be encouraged within this most important time of your day. Report for Physical Training."

CHAPTER NINE

TRAINING SESSION

The effect of the wooly dew was short-lived for the gazelle-like pace of the Physical Training instructors and the sharp prods of their staff between shoulder blades increased the pace of the slower trainees. The mist hid the identities of the joggers so the instructors' staff lashed and prodded indiscriminately. In the initial melee, rank had no effect because of the thick mist but the mischievous instructors were able to pick out some ranking officers by their girth. This was easily established by too much eating and drinking. They vindictively encouraged them to keep up with not-so-gentle wields and prods of their staff.

One scarecrow-like urchin picked on Adaka and kept ministering to him no matter how fast Adaka ran. His easy gait made Adaka exert to his limit, huffing, puffing and panting. Try as he could he would not shake off the ornery urchin. It would also be setting a bad example to stop him physically. He tried a friendly chat backed by a smile. The smile which preceded the 'good' turned into a wince as the crack of the staff against his skull cut off the 'morning'. He dodged to the left into the midst of joggers but the urchin ferreted in behind him. Adaka hardened his fist for a quick karate chop to drop the urchin. As he edged close to the urchin he cried out and fell like a log. From the corner of his right eye Adaka watched Idigo waltz past appearing oblivious of Adaka and the dropped urchin. The mist made his over six feet six inches height spectral. His weirdly easy crawl slowed and Adaka caught up with him.

"Thanks" Adaka intoned.

"You are welcome." Idigo whined. "He was almost killing me."

"He did not mean any harm." "Why do you think so?"

"He recognized your squat sturdy frame as belonging to a well fed officer and decided to punish you for the inequitable distribution of rations. One recognized me from the school of infantry and tried to punish me for fast promotions. I dropped him a little more harshly than your urchin."

"Thanks anyway."

They ran a brisk six kilometers traversing the Ogwe hill, the Ure stream and attaining the plateau they sprinted round the makeshift parade ground. They slowed to a leisurely jog which soon degenerated to a brisk walk.

"When do I get your answers to my questions?" asked Adaka. "Whenever you want" replied Idigo with a smile.

"If I say now can you comply?"

"Yes sir but I will have the added trouble of reproducing the questions as well" Idigo said resignedly.

"Then do so now. I do not doubt you but I wish to satisfy my curiosity about something."

"Your questions will precede my answers and in the order in which you asked them. When we get to the quarters I will hand over the sheet of paper on which I recorded the questions. The answers were written immediately after each question. There is the possibility of slight changes in answers when I put my mind to it but especially in further expatiation. Their walk slowed further to long legged athlete's strides and Adaka headed off in opposite direction from where the instructors were mustering the joggers who had completed the morning runs.

1. What do you do in a jungle situation?
2. Blend into the jungle environment.
3. What do you do when action matures into a maelstrom?
4. Every man for himself and God for us all.

5. What do you do when you come under effective enemy fire?
6. Hit the ground, crawl to cover, observe, maneuver to advantage, and return fire.
7. What do you do when you come under ineffective enemy fire?
8. Pretend devastation and confusion. Dig in to lure them in.
9. What do you do when you are outmatched by enemy fire power?
10. Tactically disengage and seek advantageous options. Dissuade enemy advance by effective, selective firing at will. Attempt flanks to establish a cross fire.
11. When located by the enemy what do you do?
12. Relocate.
13. What do you do when fatally wounded?
14. Slide, slither, roll, crawl, scramble, be dragged or carried to cover. Assemble your arsenal of guns, riffles, pistols, grenades, rocket launchers, magazines, bayonets, knives and whatever else constitutes weapons. Even stones that are within your reach and then prepare for the worthy exit.
15. When in doubt what do you do?
16. Nothing.
17. What do you do when outmatched?
18. Exercise patience. Remain cool and composed and then think.
19. What do you do when you are finished?
20. Die.
21. What do you do when confused?
22. Stall and think.
23. What do you do when you are cut off?
24. Seek enemy weak link and cut yourself out.
25. When caught in an ambush what do you do?
26. Recognize the head or tail of the ambush and vigorously attack it.
27. When you run out of ammunition what do you do?
28. Create new weapons and change style.

29. What do you do when caught in a cross fire?
30. Form a triangle and fight on.
31. What do you do when you can't locate the enemy?
32. Keep searching and do Reece patrols.
33. What do you do when faced with female soldiers?
34. Stop taking prisoners.
35. What do you do when lost?
36. Disband into smaller units. Resort to jungle language and turn guerilla.
37. What do you do when taken prisoner?
38. Pray and feign conciliation and cooperation. Tell your captors the truth about all easily verifiable facts. Be carefully talkative. Naivety and a subtle friendly disposition will help. A hearty smile and the ability to make them laugh will prove invaluable.
39. When you are out of your depth what do you do?
40. Think, watch and pray. Be patient.
41. When wounded in action what do you do?
42. Assess the degree of your injury and your capabilities then act accordingly.
43. What is the difference between a withdrawal and a retreat?
44. Withdrawal is a tactical back stepping. It is orderly and often accompanied by a counter-offensive especially in the form of a flanking move. A retreat is a disorderly fall out of an untenable position. It precedes a rout.
45. What do you do when a situation is too good?
46. Exercise caution. Do the unusual.
47. How do you become combat effective?
48. By knowing a lot about fighting and its operation thus putting same to practice.
49. What is mature jungle language?
50. Kill or be killed.
51. How do you retain relevance in your environment?
52. Dominate it.
53. What is jungle motion?
54. Stealth.

55. How do you react to things you can't do anything about?
56. Disregard them.
57. What do you do in enemy territory?
58. Become like the enemy.
59. What do you do in a no-win situation?
60. Wreck as much damage as possible. Loose gallantly.

They became aware of the bellow of a slim, dark instructor clad in extraordinarily spick fatigues and a fat unlit cigar.

"You two Colonels over here on the double! You are in my domain so be amenable to discipline. I cannot get you to eighty percent fitness within forty days if you keep breaking off to yap."

They ran to him and he stiffened to attention while still talking. "Hilary Muofu, Commandant War College Training arm of no specific rank, formerly Colonel and Commander First Artillery Regiment, Nigeria Army Kaduna. Lost wife and two children to pogrom but retaliated at the market square with one fully loaded Bren gun. Got one hundred and sixty men including twelve soldiers and nine policemen? Mark it no women or children. When I ran out of ammunition I headed back to the armoury for more but was overpowered because I could not kill my comrades. I then spent six months in a solitary cell at the Kaduna prison. I was treated like scum without food, cigarettes or medicines. I was given only bread and water with enough space for exercises. I broke jail leaving sixteen people dead. I did not discriminate between guards and prisoners. All who tried to stop me died. It took a month of fat countryside feeding to reach Biafra. I lived off the land, raiding stores, stealing cars, bicycles and motorcycles. I would have arrived Biafra much earlier but I had time to think and saw the foolishness of revenge. At Kaduna, after a lot of medical examinations, I guessed from the patronizing and conciliatory looks of the medical experts that they thought I was mad. I tried to explain that I was not mad to no avail. During the court martial all the officers showed understanding except Colonel Hassan Katsina. I served with him under General Ironsi in the Congo. We became enemies because when the Moitse Tshombe group that kept brutally picking up and murdering peace keepers under him he kept mute. I waded in and bloodied their noses and we no longer lost anybody until we left. On our return he would neither talk to me nor drink with me. He even would not sit in the same mess with me. At the trial therefore he said nothing but just before the sentence was passed he walked up to me and scowling with deep hatred said:

"Moff, Moff, you will rot in prison and like rubbish your decomposed body will be swept out of the solitary cell."

He then smiled and turned away. The Chairman, Brigadier Jallo asked what that was all about? Hassan answered: "Sir we were comrades in the Congo and I just wanted to encourage him."

Jallo sharply upbraided him and order was restored. The sentence read thus: "The accused made no attempt to deny any of the charges brought against him. He pleaded guilty to all and also asked for the death sentence. He only asks for one favour: 'to be allowed into the city for one hour with any gun.' The experts have testified and we agree that it is a case of mental imbalance due to the macabre sight of his slain household. He is therefore reduced to the rank of Regimental Sergeant Major and to be kept in prison custody for adequate medical attention. The court rose and I was manhandled into Kaduna prisons with bruises. I never saw a doctor until I left without permission. I was hilariously welcomed into Biafra and my rank restored. Within weeks I was posted to the war college and further ordered to form a re-training section. Things moved well until I criticized most of the C-in-C's operational plans and strategies. Without much ado, he reversed his former amiable stance to me and stopped seeing me. I reacted by not attending three war cabinet meetings. When I went for the fourth, I was barred from the meeting. I made bones of it and the meeting rose in protest. The next morning I got an order demoting me to 'No Rank' status but keeping me in charge of re-training."

He looked cool and composed although his green vest was soaked and stuck to his flat stomach.

"Now that you know my plight, help me. I will do my re-training job but I need a favour. Please allow me to join your Reece and patrols or deep penetration strikes. I need some action to feel like a soldier again. Will you do this for me?" Muofu asked, supplicating and looking at Adaka. "You are a regular and should understand my need. I am suffocating with this training rubbish."

"That is alright" replied Adaka "We were in a few maneuvers together and I know about you. I have the authority to pick and choose good soldiers wherever I find them. Luckily you were not discharged but reduced to unspecific status. I will call on you when I need you." Adaka smiled.

"Thanks" said Muofu.

"I will race you back to the instructor's bay for a cigar. The winner gets two cigars."

They took off with Idigo slightly behind. Half way through he increased his pace and tore past them in his odd effortless crawl. He stopped long enough to watch the two struggle to breast the imaginary tape.

"A draw" Idigo whined in his odd breathless voice.

It was a morning for speeches and verbal instructions. Each instructor ended with a demonstration that awed the soldiers. Even the gun experts who instructed on marksmanship did trick shootings that made everyone stand on their toes in wonderment. The explosives experts talked on various explosives, their characters and characteristics. With steady hands they made some demonstrations that raised the hair on the napes of the neck. The sun was weak so none of the trainees bothered. It even drizzled a few times but that went unheeded. At midday Muofu rose from beside Adaka and Idigo moving casually through the seated men towards the middle. When he got there the three instructors that had just rounded up their expositions on mine laying hoisted their trick boxes and melted away. His voice cut through the air like a sharp whip: "My men will teach you styles, methods, ways and means, tactics, strategies and a few tricks. They will also get you physically fit. Your commandant with his assistants will hone you on the job to increase your efficiency and capability. I will teach you a few magic that will make the difference in any hard situation. I will give you three now and one everyday for the next one week. First will be the 'dead-leaf drop'. It is also called the 'Apache vanishing act'. Close your eyes immediately I drop, count up to ten slowly but not too slowly, and then open them. Without searching point to where you guess that I will be."

All eyes were on him and it seemed as if the ground opened and he dropped into a hole. When their eyes opened, all but a few hands were pointing downhill to his former position. Just some hands that included those of Colonels Adaka and Idigo were pointing uphill. When the murmuring died down he rose from close to the top of the hill. He appeared to be unaffected by the success of his first trick.

"Next will be the bullet dance. I have arranged for some soldiers with submachine guns, carbines and weapons that use nothing heavier than .45mm ammunition to gun me down."

He moved to the middle of the plateau and with his booted leg drew a long line. His men brought logs and sticks from the edge of the field and laid them along the line. He then took fifty long strides away from the line and the trainees and stopped. Twelve men armed with pistols, revolvers, submachine guns, and other small caliber weapons lined up and took aim.

"They will open fire on me and only stop when they run out of ammunition. This is the bullet proof magic that disheartens opponents. Colonel Adaka please give the command."

Adaka gave the command and Muofu started dancing. While dancing he watched the men. Frustrated one of them bellowed and charged over the line towards him. Muofu dropped and rolled away then flung a stone which hit the advancing man on the forehead and he fell like a sack. The others had ceased firing and the miscreant was carried away to the guard room.

"It was bound to happen. Out of every twelve there must be a Judas. He can't take defeat and that is why you must be on the alert when playing bullet proof. I prepared for it with three stones but one stopped him. The explanation of the magic is that I was not within range of the small caliber bullets. The dancing is to help me move fast if I hear the deeper sound of a high caliber gun. The bullets will strike the ground if aimed low or soar if aimed high. The third demonstration is the grenade magic. I will remove the firing pins of two grenades and play with them for fifteen minutes before making one safe again and playfully lob it among you. The one I will throw away from you will explode to prove that I was not playing with dummies."

A Warrant officer with the Ordnance section stepped to him and handed over two grenades. Muofu inhaled deeply and exhaled slowly. With his teeth he drew out the pins of the grenades, flung both hands up, down and around his body for some time and went into fluid calisthenics. He hummed all the while. When he tired of this he sprinted in different directions, ending each sprint with an athletic somersault. From the far end of the plateau he slithered, crawled and rolled towards the awed men. Ten feet from them, without the aid of his hands, he came to his feet and standing wide legged threw both grenades slightly above his head. Most of the men jumped up and ran away for safety. He caught both grenades at once and kept grinning until the men were seated again. Slowly he re-fixed the pin of one of the grenades. In a swift motion he flung both grenades. One sailed among the men and the other far away from them. Again the men ran in terror down the lee side of the plateau. Just as Muofu hit the ground, the angry crack of the primed grenade filled the air. He rose and mopped his brow. When the milling around and excited talking ended he spoke in his far reaching voice:

"First lesson in confidence over!"

He turned and left. The men were dismissed. Dennis and Oboyo joined Idigo and Adaka as they retraced their steps to their billet.

"I am impressed almost to death by this magic. The others were all right but the grenade stunt almost gave me a heart attack" Dennis mused aloud.

"Nothing to worry about for they were all normal stunts that can be mastered easily if you put your mind to it" Idigo answered.

"All but the flipping and catching of the grenades before the last move, which was really dangerous" countered Adaka. Oboyo made no comment for he had taught his vandals these tricks and much more before he was withdrawn from the ROB. While traversing cassava and yam mounds to their billet, he mused on the probability of leading men nearly as good as or even better than his vandals into the mid-west. He thought with anger of the lazy, lost, over armed men that commanded the parade ground soldiers. He thought of their land rovers, supply trucks, and well stocked stores. He cursed them and looked forward to the day he would march against them in full military offensive and not guerilla raids.

"I will make them look dirty. I will attack by day and attack by night. They will not have any respite. My vandals will raid them non-stop and I will sweep them back with relentless waves of attacks. I will punish them. I will make them feel small and untrained, I will"

Lost in thought he was shocked when Idigo interrupted what he thought were just quiet thoughts saying:

"No you won't. Whatever is the problem just forgive so that your judgment won't be impaired."

Oboyo apologized wondering when and why he started slipping into soliloquy. This was considered as one of the early signs of madness so he shuddered.

It was now the month of November and the rains had receded. The air was warm and slightly humid. The unarmed combat specialist Mr. Mba sat under a mango tree sipping water from a mud jug. He watched the over zealous karate instructor pick his way among the men sprawled in relaxation around the section of the field. As he came closer he looked up and asked: "He still refuses to spar with you?"

"Yes sir" replied Fidelis. "Today he just said 'I don't spar, I kill' and said nothing more despite my pleadings. The scarecrow Colonel friend of his called 'long juju' volunteered to fight or spar with me but Colonel Adaka waved him to silence."

He sat beside Mr. Mba the specialist and continued:

"I have watched him during training. He is very good and I think that he has achieved that rare cohesion and control of mind and body. I can't see fear or anger in him. Why does he not want to spar with me?"

"If I were you I would keep away from that man. He may be telling you the truth. My head coach in Korea, though over seventy years old, never spars. If troubled, he would allow one to come against him and then effortlessly maim the one with a permanent injury. This was to serve as a lesson in self preservation. Ask him if he trained under Kaochi? Stay away from him."

Mba dismissed Lieutenant Fidelis with a final wave of his left hand and Fidelis left. For almost two weeks he had tried unsuccessfully to get a sparring session with Colonel Adaka. After instructing on karate he always joined the others for judo, savate, kung fu and dombe training. He heard of Adaka's unparalleled mastery of these arts. He remembered punishing him that first day of training and wondered if that prompted the reason for his not wanting to have anything to do with him. He decided to seek Colonel Idigo's help in the matter.

A week later he was at the Iyi stream scrubbing the dirt out of his body when he felt being watched. He hurried out of the water to the Araba shrub under which he stowed his riffle, pistol and dagger. He stopped with his mouth hung open when he saw Idigo inspecting his supposedly well hidden weapons with an amused grin on his face. Anger did not cloud his reason for he paid the Colonel his due compliments.

"But sir, what are you doing with my weapons?" Fidelis asked. "I am a soldier and weapons are my business" replied Idigo.

"But sir those are my personal weapons. I hid them from view before going to wash my body" said Fidelis.

"You hid them amateurishly so they were easy to be located by skilled eyes. You are eager and will with time and training become a good soldier if well trained."

"That I know and that is why I have been trying to get the attention of Colonel Adaka reputed to be one of the best, and a near perfect all rounder. However it appears that he hates me and will have nothing to do with me. How else can I get him to take me on as a trainee to understudy him? I have done everything possible but still failed."

Fidelis looked as if he would burst into tears. Idigo's grin widened and he shook his head in disagreement.

"You have used all tricks, schemes and sly gimmicks but you have not asked him truthfully and straightforwardly. Try that."

"Where do I see him sir, and when?" Fidelis asked eagerly. "Here and now" replied Idigo.

"How do I do it seeing that he is not here?"

"He is here and you see him by keeping your eyes open and looking behind you instead of staring at me."

Fidelis swung around and swallowed hard when he saw Adaka buckling his belt and picking up his helmet and riffle.

"Speak now" urged Idigo.

"Well sir . . . . I mean . . . . sir I beg you"

He was much disoriented at seeing Adaka already bathed, scrubbed and standing quite close to him. His sturdy frame notwithstanding, he could move with feline stealth.

"I heard you and I know what you want. I have as from now accepted you and made you my ADC. You will meet my batman who will take you in tow for four days teaching you to box and helping you unlearn the low street tricks you call karate. You require the discipline of adhering to rules and regulations that only boxing will give you. Wrestling will come in later to build hard muscles. You will become party to our night patrols and must stop showing off. Showmanship is as bad as carelessness and just short of recklessness. These are all aspects of indiscipline that are the bane of a good military career. Go downstream and meet my batman."

A week later Fidelis had lost nine kilogram's in body weight. He had participated in six Reece patrols. He had killed his first human. Footwork and fleet handedness of boxing became points of fixation that drove his mind and body to the limit. His whole body was an aching, pain filled lump of sore flesh. Adaka's batman Ike spared no effort to teach him well. Dragging and pulling himself through the days like a very old man did not exempt him from the nightly patrols or the midday boxing sessions. Calisthenics, acrobatics, muscle control and lectures liberally laced with subtle pep talks accounted for three hours of his day. By the end of the second week, a quieter, less exuberant, more experienced, stronger and much better soldier had emerged. He became a shadow of his boss Adaka. Except for training sessions with Ike he was never more than a few yards away from Adaka. It was during this period that he discovered that Idigo was also learning from Adaka. Although they were aware of his presence during their many discussions and demonstrations, they never acknowledged it.

During the early days of his apprenticeship, he witnessed Adaka and Idigo grapple and tumble from a high branch of a tree. Idigo's fall was heavy but Adaka bounced off in a light roll ending on both feet in a crouch with knives in both hands. The heavy fall jarred the breath out of Idigo and he lay lifeless. Fidelis rushed to him and bending over him attempted to lift him up. He found himself sailing through the air into the middle of an algae filled pond. As he waded out of the pool Idigo commiserated with him:

"I thought you had learnt enough to keep out of the way. I mistook you for the Colonel and applied the force needed for his bulk to your slight frame. I am sorry."

He learnt his lesson and stopped asking questions, contributing to discussions, making exclamations or other noise indicative of his presence. These however never drew any response from either of them. Exactly three weeks after he went under the tutelage of Adaka, the Colonel gave him the first verbal instructions. He lay under a leafy araba brush for shade and was eating oranges when Fidelis yawned while squatting a few yards away and cradling his new Thompson machine gun. Adaka eyed him sleepily and said:

"Rather than break your jaw showing boredom, think up six words that mean togetherness. You have fifteen minutes."

"The fifteen minutes won't be necessary. I heard you expound on togetherness when you discussed with Colonel Idigo just before your practice session on the first day that I joined you."

Adaka held up his hand, palm forward to indicate 'stop'. Fidelis shut up looking perplexed.

"You talk too much. Do what I ordered you to do."

Adaka slit the peeled orange into four parts and threw one into his mouth.

"Togetherness also means agreement, concert, synchrony, unism and oneness."

He squatted on the alert waiting for the next instruction. While he waited he thought that Adaka was asleep and opened his mouth to talk.

"Shut up" commanded Adaka.

"Learn to wait. All things come to him who waits. The waiting training is the most difficult of military trainings."

Adaka sheathed his knife and spat the orange seeds out. He turned on his side and presumably went to sleep. Thirty minutes later he sat up stretching and yawning contentedly. Fidelis opened his mouth and hurriedly shut it. Adaka spoke softly but clearly:

All six words mean the same thing, unism. It talks of a number of different things or actions or persons or thoughts that are channeled to flow together. By that I mean in accord. For this flow to be good it must be smooth, unbroken, fluid and speedy. When this is achieved the effect of the move is in multiples of what it ought to be when taken alone. This phenomenon is called synergy. Combined effects rather than produce arithmetic balances shoot off to produce inexplicable multiples. Example will be one plus three amounting to eight instead of four. I have watched you learn judo, kung fu, savate, dombe, boxing and wrestling. In the last two you were poor. I put you through boxing and wrestling again to inculcate discipline in you. Now that you appear ready we will endeavour to mix the acts for you with enough physical control to reduce the energy you burn in their individual executions. With this training you will also practice reservation of energy. Who knows when the need will arise? This synchrony and energy economization will start tomorrow and last as time and convenience dictates. Go and be useful in the billet."

Lieutenant Fidelis Ude left and Adaka crawled to another cover where he instantly fell asleep. Two hours later he walked up from the stream, clean and fresh. He joined Idigo, Oboyo and Dennis as they planned the night's patrols.

Action synchrony and motion economy training proved destructive to Lieutenant Fidelis Ude. The flashes of smiles and laughs left in him evaporated. He became cynical and withdrawn with bland features. All through his unarmed combat training he never experienced the kind of devastating falls he received during this period. His whole body became one pulsating throb of fiery pain doing its best to drive him mad. He held his mind with the only religious recitation he knew which was Psalm 23. Practice sessions with Ike or Idigo were painful but with Adaka they became excruciating. At the end of the week he had learnt quietness, stealth and speed. He became better at control and economy of movement.

Adaka graduated him with a two hour fight session of mild blows, kicks and throws for diligence, endurance and patience. He was made free two weeks after Adaka graduated Idigo.

"Remember this always, only fools or mad people do not feel fear. Courage is not the absence of fear but doing the necessary despite the fear. Pictorially imagine what you want and determinedly go for it. More often than not you will succeed. The human mind thinks in pictures and not words or figures. Express no inhibitions just go for what you want and I assure you that success will attend most of your moves. You are now good so don't kill for the sake of killing. When the urge comes on, fight it with the knowledge that you cannot create a life. Maintain the human spirit in you and do not become a zombie. You will now improve with practice. Go."

Adaka turned and left as Fidelis remained rigid in salute grinning winsomely.

CHAPTER TEN

PATROLS

For two weeks Adaka led patrols into and behind enemy lines. Every night he led his core group of five with other twelve men and they infiltrated the enemy locations around the Port Harcourt sector. They covered from Afam through to Degema and back to Owerrinta and Ohaji areas. They became so good at it that there was no need to fight or kill anybody during the patrols. Dressed up in Nigeria Army uniforms, infiltrating their camps and lines proved easy for the lull in fighting and unofficial peaceful interaction made them lax. The relieved commanders were more often than not included in the patrol teams. When Adaka started sending out more teams the new and old commanders were scattered among the various teams. When Adaka had commanded a team twice, he would then pick men from those teams and spread them to other teams. In a month he had built up over thirty such teams that penetrated the enemy locations every night without a single shot being fired. No accidental discharges or disruption of the scanty mine fields was recorded. Any unfortunate soldier who stumbled upon a patrol team had to die silently and the body carried back to the Biafran lines. The scope of the mapping and intelligence gathering widened such that the baffling success intoxicated the Div. Commander and the relieved brigade commanders. By the end of the eight weeks retraining period when their commands were restored, they requested to continue as subordinates to Colonel Adaka in the

Lightning Strike Force. Even the Division Commander protested when he was informed that Colonel Oboyo will proceed with Adaka to 54th Brigade headquarters from where they would launch deep behind-the-line strikes. Brigadier Eze who for the first time in his army career saw the impact of infiltration, participated extensively in the patrols. He executed a few knife killings on the job. He therefore felt betrayed when it became obvious that the Strike Force would move on without him. This impression was hastily corrected by a signal introducing Brigadier Achebe to whom he should hand over. He was directed to assume command of the Strike Force from his present base while Adaka would be mustering, retraining and honing the men. Brigadier Eze's main job as commander would be target selection, assessment, planning and coordination. Adaka, Oboyo and Idigo would execute strikes while Dennis handled logistics issues such as ordnance, supply, transport, reinforcement and signals, thus he became the assistant to the commander of the Strike Force. Unlike Eze he moved with the others to the 54th brigade base to liaise between them and the commander. Brigadier Eze heaved a sigh of partial relief for he would do this desk and paper work but he was sure to get into action soon enough. The plot will thicken and needs mount. His experience would come into play and he would be on the move again. He remembered the first few days of jungle movement training under Adaka. Bent forward like baboons in quest of nuts they were made to pad on the balls of their feet through leafy, rocky, dry stick covered forest beds for many hours. Days of practice reduced the bush gear noise to a negligible level. Soon their duck-like single file quirky motion was mastered along with the neck swiveling motion to obtain at least three hundred and twenty degrees eye-view. He thought of the weeks of patrols and the one unauthorized strike at Eleme that he had accompanied Adaka on. He felt prepared for war, under Adaka his junior he had learnt patience and its virtues. The sniper courses organized by Oboyo almost maimed him. After eighteen hours on the tree and while adjusting to urinate for the second time, he miss-stepped and fell headlong. Thanks to the agility and acrobatic trainings, he had curled enough to hit lightly. He rolled to his knee as the enemy troops ran to investigate. He crawled away believing that a number of his ribs had been broken. Later he found out that except for aches and pains, he was intact. He did not need much work to best his Colonels and the weapons instructors at sharp shooting and marksmanship. He felt very ready and willing to await his time before hitting back at the enemy. He selected and discarded over ten targets every day. He pored over intelligence reports seeking targets he would initiate and occasionally lead patrols for assessment and evaluation. His hopes were high.

Two weeks after his assistants had left for 54th Brigade, he did a self evaluation and discovered why he was still seated at 12th Division headquarters. He noticed the unnecessary haste in all his earlier moves. He cursed Idigo whom he was sure was reporting on him for not pointing this out to him. He resolved to further learn patience, stealth and speed.

Three weeks to the pulling out of the Lightning Strike Force, reinforcements in men and equipment started arriving. Colonel Dennis had a list of over three hundred men specially picked as having met the standard required. In small batches, Idigo spirited them out of 12th Division to 54rth Brigade of the 11th Division while Adaka deployed the new arrivals among the better trained troops of the 12th Division. Training continued even after Adaka had left for the 54th Brigade. The beating received by 'Big' Major Nwadike hastened Adaka's departure. After a lot of consultations only six soldiers were penciled down as prospective 'Lethal Weapons'. They were all light in stature except Captain Nwosu who looked like a perfect replica of Colonel Adaka. Nwosu lay under an Araba shrub sipping gin from his flask. He appeared to be finding it difficult remaining awake. Instinctively he felt footsteps strolling down the beaten path to the officer's billets veer towards him. He made his lashes droop over his eyeballs and the 'Big' Major that appeared looked him over contemptuously. Mistaking him for a malingering private was understandable because he hadn't any rank insignia. His camouflage dress was fresh and new so it did not speak of combat experience. No weapon was seen on him so he appeared ordinary. 'Big' Major Nwadike, true to his reputation as a disciplinarian, a bully and a wicked man, swung his booted foot striking Nwosu on the ribs. Nwosu's roll saved some of his ribs from breaking for the kick was not gentle. The ribs were however slightly bruised. Nwosu was on the balls of his feet instantly facing Nwadike. Nwadike's palm fell on the revolver on his waist as he said:

"Idle civilian, what are you doing here?"

"Sir you could have asked this question without kicking me. I was resting and I am a soldier" replied Nwosu meekly.

"Idiot, Private, you dare not tell me how to ask questions. You will be exempted from action because I will shoot your leg and carry you to the Casualty Collecting Post myself."

He pulled out the revolver and as he made to cock it, Nwosu snatched it from his hand and flung it away. He noticed that the Major was drunk. Major Nwadike reacted instantly. He kicked out with his boot to catch Nwosu in the crotch but Nwosu was a mere inch from the trajectory of the swing. Nwadike threw ponderous swings at Nwosu's head but none of them connected. He shouted with rage and rushed in to grapple with Nwosu who obliged him by walking into his arms and encircling his massive chest with his hands.

Nwadike, who towered over Nwosu and was almost twice as big and heavy, had his hands free so decided to beat Nwosu savagely. His angry shouts, grunts, huffs, and puffs seemed to give speed to his hands that swung like a wind-mill. This noise attracted Officers returning to their quarters from the mess.

Seeing 'Big' Major Nwadike ostensibly pounding a private to stupor, they could not intervene. He was known as the 'Mad Major' at Afikpo sector and nobody toyed with him. He was known to have beaten three soldiers to death with his bare hands. He shot people at the slightest provocation, which included not paying him compliments. They stood and watched as his huffs, puffs and grunts turned to groans and wheezes. His swinging hands weakened and he stopped struggling. Nwosu lowered him to the ground and retrieved his helmet, flask and riffle. Donning them he stooped, lifted Major Nwadike onto his shoulder and passed the Officers gazing in perplexity at him. He deposited him at the C.C.P explaining that the Major was drunk and slightly asphyxiated.

Three days later, at the Officer's Group meeting designed to integrate the old and new Officers as they arrived, Nwadike saw Nwosu as Adaka ended his lecture dismissing them. He immediately sought out Nwosu and said: "Boy, so you are an Officer? That is all well and good. The other day I was drunk and you must have used chloroform or something like that. I could not breathe. Now I will like you to repeat what you did and at the same venue. I was able to retrieve my revolver yesterday and took the trouble of cleaning and oiling it. You have caused me a lot of trouble so you see that I must punish you."

He ended with both palms open in the sign that said he could do nothing less.

"What time sir?" asked Nwosu.

"I will arrange it and fix the time. I will inform you so where are you staying?"

"Around sir, I stay around. I will find you before the sun goes down." He saluted, turned and sauntered away. Nwadike looked after him with surprise. The way he had taken the revolver from him still troubled him. He had never seen such speed. The dead-fish eyes were ghostly. The civility and economy of movement was uncanny. After beating him to pulp he would find out more about him. For now he had to arrange an audience, especially men from his former unit. The lie had somehow slipped out that somebody bested him in a fist fight. Such rumors could not be tolerated. They must be corrected at once. He stayed off alcohol and did not go near the mess. He slept more to preserve his strength and be in top physical form for the fight. There was this nagging fear behind his mind reminding him of a beating he once took during his secondary school days, while building up his image as a bully. He shook the bad memory off. Spectators were already milling around waiting for him to give them a good time. It was a few minutes past five when Nwosu arrived. He respectfully knocked at the door and entered. He saluted saying:

"I will be available from now on at the venue."

Once more he saluted and then left. Major Nwadike got up, took a glass of water and stepped out of his door. Bent over, he sipped the water, swirling it around his mouth. He blew his nose clearing both nostrils, spitting out the water, he drank lustily. He washed his face and looked around at the officers waiting to get the time and ordered:

"Go along the path toward the Bofor Bunker. Stop at the guava tree and wait. He will be around the brush waiting. You will have to carry him to the CCP after I am through with him".

He turned into his room. They left immediately feeling sad and very sorry for the object of his maniacal attention. Five minutes later, he arrived. Standing close to the shrub he urinated while looking around and saying:

"It looks as if my friend has chickened out. Wherever he may be seek him out and inform me immediately. Running will not help him today."

Before they could answer, Nwosu dropped from the thick foliage of the guava tree and behind the men.

"That will not be necessary sir, I am ready and waiting. You may wish to give me the fight plan." Nwadike was looking curiously at him.

"What are you talking about?"

"I want to known how you intend to execute the fight so that I will respond commensurately" Nwosu replied. "I can see that you are mad. I will beat you slowly and not with overly heavy blows so that it will not end quickly. I will make you feel the pain. I will humiliate you and dehumanize you I will ensure that you do not leave the sick bay for at least six weeks. I will teach you a lesson that will remind you of your lowly officer rank most definitely bought by your corrupt mentors. What is your rank?"

"Captain Sir. I will do all that you wish, but in view of the Biafran need for fighting men, I will not incapacitate you permanently. The other day I only squeezed your chest. Today I will beat you. I am ready when you are."

Nwosu moved lightly towards Nwadike exhibiting a light-hearted jaunt. Nwadike threw a straight punch aiming for the nose. A slight shift in position by Nwosu caused Nwadike's force to carry him past Nwosu who drove stiff knuckles into Nwadike's midriff.

Nwadike wheeled around and rushed in to grapple, but Nwosu was not where he was a split second earlier. He drove stiff knuckles into Nwadike's jaw and two teeth flew off. Before Nwadike could turn a kidney punch drove him to his knees. He gritted his teeth to drive away the pain that flamed through his whole body. Shaking his head to clear the wooziness he slowly got to his feet looking around for Captain Nwosu who stood silently by waiting for him to recover. Nwadike got up and turned heavily towards Nwosu executing a boxer-like guard and cautiously moved in on him. His hands began flicking out in jabs that never landed. When he got the distance right for his jabs to connect Nwosu's head always snaked out of the way. Hard digs in the jaw, head, chest and ribs answered to all his enthusiastic attempts to rush in and make a rowdy brawl of the fight. Being punished and out jabbed, he adopted the one-two punching approach and fell twice to sucker punches. He began a windmill kind of swinging cum punching drive with the hope of at least one connecting. However, none connected because the eerie wriggles, timed twisting and turnings of Nwosu made him a mirage. Nwadike weakened. His legs became unable to meet up with the sleek footwork of Nwosu, who had meanwhile stopped punching Nwadike's face and body. He concentrated on Nwadike's hands and hip bones, further wearying Nwadike. When it became obvious that Nwadike could barely move or keep up his guard Nwosu stood unmoving before him and spoke out:

"Major Nwadike, they call you the 'Mad Major' of Afikpo Sector. It is on record that you have maimed and killed several innocent people on this false pretence. This has also been keeping you exempt from your erstwhile military chores and duties. Your commanding officer could not put you to any effective use because he believed you were genuinely a case of madness. When you were posted to Adaka's command then you realized that the game was up and that it would no longer be business as usual. You therefore conveniently fell into a ditch purporting to have dislocated your shoulder and elbow. Your relative at the base hospital hastily put you in traction and followed this up with plenty of cosmetic Plaster-of-Paris. Two days after Adaka pulled out you were healed. You have since resumed your drinking bouts and further acts of terrorism. The yellow streak in you makes you panic in battle situation so you want to act like the famous Achuzia and play some of his pranks and stunts. You now honestly wish that I should kill you and though I can do that easily I however will not. You must learn to be a real soldier not a fake. I will now punish you but l will not maim you. I will oblige you on that request."

A back-hand slap followed flashing across Nwadike's face and blood and gummy spittle dribbled from his mouth as a broken tooth sailed onto the ground. More slaps and kicks to the shin followed in slow measured succession. These were followed and punctuated by occasional knocks to the forehead. Bending over to avoid the slaps and knocks he quickly changed the tactics with open-handed slaps, raking his back and light punches tortured his hip bones. When he was forced to straighten up, open-handed chops cracked his sides without sparing the ribs. The spectators surged forward to stop what they thought had become a satanic beating.

"Keep away or come in fighting" said Nwosu stiffening in readiness while not relenting in the light but measured beating he was delivering to Nwadike. His words slowed them but their hasty retreat was more as a result of seeing five similarly clad, mean looking soldiers who had surfaced as if from holes in the ground around the venue of the fight. One of them, certainly a teenager, handed his assault riffle to another one and stepping out shouted:

"If anyone or more of you would like to participate in the fight they are welcome."

He waited and quietly looked over all of them gathered there. The same type of calm demeanor earlier exhibited by Nwosu was in the poise of the lad with the quiet conveyance, economy of movement and speech as well as the interpretation. They fell back further and with dread in their eyes watched the systematic and scientific degradation of the hard hunk of giant flesh formerly thought of as indestructible. To cap it all, the person doing this was not up to half of his size and shorter by at least nine inches. The spectacle had to be seen to be believed. The knocks had opened up both eyebrows which were now bleeding. The lips were bleeding from many points. The nose bled along side the mouth and the pool was increasing. While continuing to minister the beating Nwosu spoke quietly:

"Don't fall or I will be forced to kick you and then I will not guarantee that you will not be seriously injured. Stop pretending, and try being a soldier. You will discover that people do not die with every bullet fired in combat. A few battles will inoculate you and the terror will disappear"

"Yes sir" replied Nwadike.

"You are panicking again. Do not be ridiculous. You are a Major and I am a Captain, you should not be answering sir to me"

Nwosu administered a flurry of slaps to the belly and Nwadike's sniffs, grunts and groans went into loud cow-like bawling. He was neither fighting back nor defending himself. He put all of his remaining strength to holding his crumbling body up. This feat was short-lived because the next flurry of slaps to the chest and belly crumpled him and he fell like a half-filled sack of white cassava. Nwosu looked him over expressionlessly and stepped back wiping sweat and blood from his hands, face and dress.

"You are bleeding too much, so I cannot carry you to the C.C.P as you desired. I do not want to further stain my dress. You will frog-jump to the C.C.P holding your ears or I will kick you there. The choice is yours. You have only five minutes to make your choice."

Nwosu brought his wristwatch out of his back pocket and wore it on his left wrist. He stood back surveying the wreck disdainfully. Nwadike struggled up to his knees and managed to squat. He held his ears and attempted to frog-jump. He passed out. Nwosu turned to the spectators.

"Help him" he said and left.

The other five had quietly melted into the environment as the beating slowed to the end.

"God, he looks like the wreck of Hesperus." said an Officer with a limp.

"What is Hesperus?" asked another.

"I do not know" replied the first. "My father says it often about any thing that does not look good." said the officer nicknamed Limpie.

A fair-complexioned Captain fondly called Oyibo lit a cigarette and when satisfied that it was burning well said: "He is not so tough, yet l had always gone the extra mile to avoid contact with him."

"Be that as it may you cannot avoid this contact forever. You will help in carrying him to the C.C.P before he bleeds to death. The vandal that beat him said he wanted him alive not dead. If he should die the vandal is bound to know and come after us. We had better hurry." The fat squat second lieutenant bent and stretched out Nwadike while Oyibo looked around apprehensively.

"Did you call him vandal? Well I beg not to be involved in any way. He may still be around and considering what he did to the mad Major, let us get this body to the C.C.P at once, whether he is dead or alive. I will advise you to watch your tongue and not call people names."

Using the fisherman's haul they carried him in such a way as not to obstruct his breathing. Second Lieutenant Dimgba explained that he was not calling anybody names.

"If you have heard the story of the rebel Major Oboyo you will know what I am talking about. He disobeyed all the orders from his Brigade commander, Division Commander, Chief of Army Staff and the Commander-in-Chief. He also defied all the guns of the Nigerians, and the antagonism of the locals that wanted to patronize the conquering Federal Troops. He stayed back in the Mid West known as Republic of Benin. He retrained his men in dire situation survival strategies, guerilla warfare, and jungle effectiveness. His men had no consideration for others and acted only to survive. They pulled off considerable and unparalleled feats of bravery and courage and were reputed to be both brutal and totally heartless. They were also known to be hard as stones, and tougher than leather, endowed with the instincts of animals and with serpentine cunning. Oboyo was the one known as the Chameleon. They were nicknamed 'Vandals'. Rather than die of hunger they even ate human flesh. Their greatest strength however lay in their being entirely unpredictable."

He broke from the story when they entered the C.C.P and medical personnel relived them of their burden. They sat on the pavement, beside the ward, and shared tales of satanic fighters being bred all around Biafra while waiting to be informed of Nwadike's condition.

A guerilla-like sergeant walked out of the ward with the officer that had challenged them to the duel "if they so desired." The officer stopped, and the sergeant turned facing him saying:

"Go and tell him that he is alive and will live. They are patching him up right now. He should report to the Colonel and explain the circumstances that led to this development."

The officer returned to the ward. The sergeant saluted wheeling smartly to march away. Captain Harry Mgbemena stood and blocked his path. The sergeant stopped and saluted looking respectfully at the Captain.

"We arrived here only on Monday. We have not been fully integrated. Could you please tell me who this officer that spoke to you is. He looks strange."

"He is Lieutenant Fidelis Ude. He is one of Colonel Adaka's Lethal Six."

Kingsley moved to continue but the Captain still blocked his path. "Where do they live?" Harry asked

"I have never seen any of them in the Officers quarters."

"They live around. No specific place. Just under the sky in the environment, but not under any roof. They are different. Stay away from them." Kingsley advised.

"What is your name and what unit do you belong to Sergeant?"

As he asked these questions the Captain moved away from the path. "Kingsley sir, Heavy weapons support, reserve. Lightning Strike Force, under Colonel Adaka"

Captain Mgbemena made a sign of the cross, turned and looked after the sergeant who to some degree had the same eyes and ominous air as the now called 'Lethal' persons.

"Dimgba, you can see that they are not vandals. These appear worse than the vandals. This Biafra is no longer safe. One does not know whom to be afraid of, so wisdom dictates that one must be afraid of every body, comrade or not. It is already dark, so let us go for dinner and later meet at the mess. Rank or no rank do not cross anybody, for this kind of beating we witnessed today is worse than death. Any one of you who so desires, may come back and find out the condition of our Major."

With this he moved away, and the others followed. Their procession was funereal with everybody's thoughts keeping him company. After dinner, they furtively retired to the mess looking over their shoulders. Although the mess was full it had the silence of a graveyard. Low murmuring, throaty mumbles, assisted by hisses and sign language accounted for most of the discussions and conversations of the evening. Sign Language played a major role most especially for placing orders. The mess soon emptied fast when it was observed that the boys from Intelligence had arrived with their many questions. Adaka and Nwosu moved silently through the night flitting from cover to cover in a macabre dance.

"Sir after the kick I saw trouble in his eyes and knew that if I tried walking away he would attack. I had no option. I had to put him to sleep. Thereafter I made inquires through the Intel boys and got his dossier. I knew that a fight was unavoidable. When he came calling I had to oblige him. I pulled punches and generally handled him with kid gloves. I am sorry for not finding a less noisy way sir."

He walked on beside the Colonel, both mute, but ruminating.

"Be at the Division Commander's office, by 0200hrs We pull out tomorrow in order not to draw any more attention and compromise our force, that is supposed to be phantom, non-situational, but highly mobile and effective. Inform others. I will summon all of you to meet at the palm plantation beside the quarry. The signal will be three air bursts at five minute intervals, and yours for confirmation will be three claps. Good night."

He waltzed his way to his billet while Nwosu melted into the thin night air. Fifteen minutes later a shadow exited his room from the rear window crawling into the bush, its meteor-like passage going unnoticed.

Ekene farted, smacked his lips wetly and turned to continue his sleep. Training restrained him from the luxury. He stiffened, unmoving, surveying his surroundings. Slithering away he cancelled his position, re-establishing it in a leafy grove. He watched out for signs of any reptile but seeing only three snails and a turtle he chose a small strip. Cuddling his riffle while easing and drifting into sleep again he heard his commanders' voice quietly lancing into him:

"Be at the Div commander's office in thirty minutes."

The quiet voice faded away. Warrant officer grade two Ekene Oranwa applied all his senses to locate his commander but found he was making about four guesses as to the exact position. He hastily relocated to the cover of a large avocado pear tree. He knew that his unconscious fart had woken the Colonel who had then cancelled both his position and sleep. He consulted his wrist watch and it was just twenty-five minutes short of two O' clock.

"Why does he want me there before the air burst signal?"

He retreated deeper into the bush, selected a point, dug a shallow hole and excreted. Afterwards he flitted down to an arm of the Iyi stream, water of which was always clean and clear. Making sure he was alone and unseen, he washed his head, face, hands, feet and legs. He drank happily after scrubbing out his tongue with a sharp-edged stick. Putting on his uniform he filled his flask with water and left. Two minutes before two o'clock that morning he was reconnoitering the Division Commander's office surroundings. He and Captain Nwosu became aware of their presence at about the same time. Both eyes shot to the office as Adaka tapped lightly on the Commander's door and stepped in. He saluted smartly: "He is here sir."

"But my men on the observation post duties and those on sentry duties have not reported any presence including yours. It was only when you knocked that the double spit of the sentry warned of presence. That means that he heard your knock and looked to see you. How do you accomplish such a feat? I have been practicing but I appear unable to improve, please tell me how to do it."

He dropped the pencil with which he was working, and leaned back in the high-backed arm chair.

"Practice Sir Practice. Practice causes the improvement. Moreover you are doing too many things at the same time. You are still running a Division, in the process of handing over, running the Lightning Strike Force, which is yet to be fully established. Selecting and assessing targets—which should not be your job—and finally sir, you are still in a haste to have the opportunity to strike at the enemy before this war ends. All these are in conflict and reduce your jungle-craft. Accord of thought and action makes for the serenity that produces jungle effectiveness and competence. Just relax. It will all come with time. Captain Nwosu is out there waiting."

Brigadier Eze looked at him and nodded in understanding.

"Yes. The beating-man. Call him in. My Intel report says he is about half the size of the so-called Mad Major. Call him in."

Colonel Adaka clapped three times loudly. A pair of boots landed on the terrace indicating that the balustrade was scaled for entry. The knock had not really sounded before the door opened, and Captain Nwosu entered. He saluted, stiff at attention with his eyes flashing around the room like a trapped animal.

"Stand at ease Captain. Tell the Commander what happened" ordered Adaka.

"Yes Sir" replied the Captain. With characteristic economy he explained what had happened, clearly and precisely up to the point of depositing Mad Major at the C.C.P.

"I sent Lieutenant Fidelis to ensure that the medics gave him prompt and adequate attention. Although a little delirious, he is resting well and has no bones broken. He only lost three teeth, and the medics removed a loose one making it four. All things considered, sir he is hale albeit not hearty."

Brigadier Eze stood up and after studying Nwosu for some time said: "I have seen the report, and you are not to blame. If you had so wanted you could have avoided the second confrontation. Why did you not?" "Biafra needs fighting men and there he was pretending mad and maiming solders. Reports say he has killed several. He needed to be stopped, his mad bluff called and his self-worth increased by destroying his dread of military action. This can be done by breaking him down and rebuilding him. The first part has been achieved. The second part by retraining will restore his pride as a man and make him useful" Nwosu stopped.

"Adaka will you take him over or do l keep him with Achebe?" Brigadier Eze asked.

"My hands are full as it is but l will take him over, when he has recovered. If he were left here, he would want to disprove what happened as a fluke and thereby cause more trouble, and end up being court martialled and shot. His record can now be easily misread as treason. I will, reluctantly though take him on." Adaka looked at Nwosu.

"His physical conditions are poor. He needs a lot of physical training before you start talk of combat craft." opined Nwosu.

"Captain Nwosu" said Eze in a stern voice

"You handled the easiest part of the whole exercise. Now after the Colonel has finished retraining him, I give you the assignment of cultivating, retaining and maintaining his friendship. This is if he survives the training and honing. That more than anything else will restore his self-respect. That is all for now."

He leaned back in his chair. Captain Nwosu came to attention, saluted, spun around and marched out of the office. Looking seriously at the commander Adaka requested permission to pull out at dawn.

"Our continued stay will definitely compromise our security and our work here is done. I only picked five prospects from the last batch of Afikpo grown reinforcements, adding the beaten Major makes six with my remaining seven men. We will leave quietly and not be missed."

He stood up slinging his riffle in preparation to his leave.

"Find time for sleep sir, it will help in the total development we crave."

He saluted, spun around and left, but not before the Brigadier had countered:

"At least I steal naps in the office while you prowl the bushes, hills, valleys and ravines without a nap not to talk of sleep."

By this time Adaka had closed the door.

"Offering transportation would have been graciously refused. I know they will not trek to Oba but they prefer anonymity in travel. For them there are too many weak links in troop movements which is why they capitalize on enemy troop movement for strikes. It is best Adaka and his group leave. This will afford me the opportunity to effectively utilize the men I have selected for recommendation to the Chief of General staff. I may even carry out a few deep penetration strikes of my own. This will be for my friend and Commander Nzogwu."

He was still soliloquizing and pacing the office when the cock crew and moles intensified their chirping. He stretched out on the tattered sofa and willing himself to give thought to his next moves fell into a deep, dreamless sleep. No sleep for three nights in a row ensured the six whole hours of deep sleep. He woke up to a bright sunny day. Gritting knocks and efforts to force the door of the office open at that point made him to remember the twelve o'clock appointment he had scheduled for Brigadier Achebe. He had obviously come. Checking his wrist watch he noticed that it was forty-minutes behind the scheduled time. His cocked pistol dove behind the towel he held to his face as he opened the door. It was the Brigadier who looked puzzled and relieved at the same time.

"Good morning Eze, what happened that made you fall asleep? I thought you people had mastered sleep and don't need it any more." Said Achebe as he gently closed the door behind him and moved to a chair.

Eze produced a bottle of Gordon's Dry Gin and two glasses. He filled both took one up and raising it said: "Good morning."

He emptied it at the same time as Achebe, and he refilled Achebe's glass. Adaka would not approve of their tiny tot of body warmer. "Give me fifteen minutes to answer to the call of nature and do some ablution. The bottle is there and there are more in my drawer." He went behind into the bathroom.

Adaka sneered at Ekene when he rose from the thick grass to meet him as he came out of the Commander's Office.

"Your watch betrayed you. The moonlight glittered against it. Wrist watches do better under shirt sleeves. Leave now for Mbawsi Post office. We will rendezvous with you there between six and nine p.m. today. If you can peacefully arrange transportation do it. Do not commandeer anything. If this does not work out reconnoiter and spot bicycles to be stolen. We will require about fourteen bicycles. Spirit past the communities and avoid any incidents. The signal will be three tongue clicks to two."

Adaka left. Warrant Officer Ekene consulted his wristwatch and finding that it was seven minutes short of three o'clock, he pulled down the sleeve of his shirt to cover the watch and headed for the stream. For the first time since his arrival to the 12th Division head quarters, Adaka chose a lush spot beneath his favorite orange tree, stretched out and slept. At exactly a quarter to five he slowly opened his eyes and surveyed his surroundings without moving. Feeling satisfied he got up and plucked ten oranges which he put in his haversack to join the dry pack and first aid kit. Two smoke grenades and four anti-personnel grenades formed the base of the sack. He made for the stream. Approaching the Bailey bridge he loaded his riffle with three airburst rounds and fired the first. The other two followed at five minute intervals. From his pouch he extracted a fresh magazine and replaced the partly used one. He filled the partly used magazine with live rounds. He lightly ran across the bridge, taking cover in the sugar cane bush bordering the end-side of the bridge. This stretched into the shore of the river. Sergeant Kingsley had beaten them to the bridge. Loaded down like a mule, his ungainly sight struggled up the steep climb accessing the bridge from the shore of the river. Although weighted down by the many packs he was not slow in accessing the bridge or in crossing it. At the south end he instinctively turned to the cover of the sugar cane bush. Jungle craft advised him that the cover was too obvious and he veered off down the road. Adaka bleated from the cover of the sugar cane bush and relieved Kingsley turned once again into the bush. He was still unpacking when Lieutenant Fidelis and Captain Nwosu covering each other flitted across the bridge. Kingsley's jaws fell open when he saw a very old man in agbada holding a wooden walking stick and helping his wife up the hill come to the Bridge. The lady appeared older because the man's head showed no dark hair while the woman's were grayer and she looked frailer. They slowly hobbled across the bridge. Kingsley turned and nodded welcome to Fidelis and Nwosu then looked back to the bridge. His face furrowed in surprise for the two old crows had vanished. Before anyone could stop him he picked up his riffle and bounded toward the shoreline. Just before getting to the rim, he dropped on all fours and crept around looking for the aged couple. At about the same time, the couple had apparently rolled down the abutment to the shore. Picking themselves up they stared into the faces of Adaka and Fidelis. Fidelis with rock steady hands cradled the assault riffle, the snout of which was pointed at the exact middle distance between the chests of the old couple.

"Put down the gun Fidelis, welcome John Chukwuma and Isaac Iweka." Said Adaka.

A smile fleetingly crossed Adaka's face. The couple forded the little inlet, separating them from Adaka and Fidelis climbing up to where they both stood. Fidelis' smile broadened when he noticed Nwosu creeping out of cover and making his riffle safe.

"I was not the only one taken in by the disguises of Staff Sergeant John and Sergeant Isaac."

When private Ike came marching across the bridge, herding five soldiers with their hands held above their heads in surrender Fidelis' thin body rocked in silent laughter.

"What is so funny?" questioned Nwosu. Fidelis answered:

"They are prisoners yet they have their riffles slung behind them. Any fool can see that Ike has goofed." His contented smile called for comment but none came. The soldiers continued their march down the road, and around the bend. Five minutes later Ike burst into the clearing with one of the men. He left without a word and returned later with two men. Two minutes later he came back with the remaining two. Adaka looked them over and affected introductions all round. Kingsley shared out his erstwhile burden to them all.

"We leave now. John and Isaac will scout while you others take the new men in tow and teach them on the job. Our R.V is the Post Office Mbawsi, and the time between six and nine pm. The move will be clean and without incidents. Avoid these as much as possible. Go".

John and Isaac led and the others followed. Soon only Ike and Adaka were left. They sat down to a breakfast of dry yam and plantain chips. They topped these with oranges and water. Hiking up their packs they trotted out. Dodging in and out of the bushes to avoid road blocks, or overzealous military and regimental police, they had covered a reasonable distance before the sun announced midday. Scouting the outskirts of Aba Town to determine how best to traverse it Adaka observed two guava trees, the branches of which were weighed down with lush fruits. Ike followed his gaze and veered to the adjoining compound saying:

"I will fetch some bags.

He returned in less than no time with two bed sheets which he hurriedly tied into the shape of bags. Adaka had started plucking and the pile of fruits soon disappeared into the makeshift bags. They continued and two hours later were headed for the Umuikaa junction. To beat the road block and inquisitive stragglers who more often than not turned marauders, they took to the bush observing three hundred and sixty degrees watch. This procedure slowed their pace. The reason for this precaution was not far fetched. Marauding stragglers and predatory civil defenders who populated this junction did not discriminate between soldiers and civilians or even nationalities. Preys were not given the opportunity to report their plight. They almost always ended up dead. A measure of cannibalism was known to occasionally occur. At exactly 05.40pm the farmer who was abducted at Umuehi farmland pointed out Post Office Mbawsi to them. He was promptly released with a threat to keep his mouth shut or risk their re-visit. They had identified his homestead before making him guide them through a short cut to Mbawsi town.

10pm Fidelis and Claudius Johnson began maintaining tongue clicks. Adaka and Ike did not respond but kept surveillance of the area from the top of a bitter kola tree and a burly Indian almond tree. Believing that they were unobserved John and Isaac concluded a healthy meal of yam porridge made sweet with a cock trapped by Isaac. They knew that Adaka would disapprove of the fire but reasoned that they had made up for any lapses by assembling all fourteen bicycles ready for immediate departure. The owners would not miss these for a long time because they had taken their time to locate and avoid an outcry. After some naps, they decided to eat the remnant of the porridge and bury the pot and other evidence of the cooking. When John went to the base of the tree where the half-filled pot of delicious meal was hidden, the pot was nowhere to be found.

The ladle had been plugged into the ground showing some sticky mess on the base of the handle.

Returning, John informed Isaac that some body, presumably one of their own group, had beaten them to the meal. Isaac looked toward the base of the tree where the pot had been very well hidden and shook his head in dismay.

"It is the Colonel. He knows everything. It means that they have arrived.

Let us work at surprising them also."

They then made enough noise to attract attention and in full view walked down the sandy pathway leading to the stream. Ike watching them smiled while locating Fidelis whose eyes followed them.

Just before the bend in the pathway captain Nwosu and Henry Opara rose facing them. Henry's inexperienced gun was pointed straight at Isaac's chest.

"Watch that gun!" Isaac said in a tremulous voice. Henry lowered it. "What anger blinded you into this carelessness?" Nwosu asked.

"They ate our food hidden close by and I suspect it was done by the Colonel so we want to surprise him too by coming up behind him without his being aware of it." Isaac said.

"Pipe dream" replied Nwosu.

"Forget your suspicions. It is the Colonel and Ike his shadow. The Nigerians call Fidelis the shadow but actually the real shadow is Ike. I am sure they are watching us even now. It is almost eight o'clock and none of them has answered to the clicks so let us make ourselves comfortable while we wait for the rest. Fidelis and his pupil are also here."

Nwosu's clicks were replied to by Fidelis and they emerged from cover. Kingsley and three men he had in tow chose a ditch for cover; they had crawled into the ditch and waited. They were still waiting, watching and receiving snippets of instruction on jungle craft when three loud clicks sounded behind them. They spun around in surprise with riffles raised then they heard the two answering dicks from Kingsley. They then lowered their guns and stared at Ekene.

Looking them over dispassionately Ekene pointed: "Behind that plantain groove."

He fell into the lush grass and slithered away. Kingsley followed his example leading his men to the Colonel. Warrant Officer Ekene Oranwa had arrived Mbawsi Town at about mid-day reconnoitering and entering the town. This took up one and half-hours. He could not locate any roadworthy vehicle capable of conveying more than four men and five in a car will prove too constricting. If four then they will require four cars and getting fuel for four cars will not be easy. To compound matters the disappearance of four cars will be noticed. The anonymous movement expected would then be lost.

"The only buses I saw were of the Ford and Taunnus brand. They looked worn out and abandoned. I then decided to revisit the lonely homesteads in search of bicycles. That was when I saw the old couple with farm baskets hobbling down the road from Isi Ala Ngwa junction. I hid in the bush until they passed. Curiously I watched them and noticed some unusual things about them. The first was that they looked too casual and uncaring for wartime. They neither looked back nor threw furtive glances around. Secondly the woman who appeared older was using a restless left hand to stress points and emphasize. I remembered that our man Isaac had similar traits. Their animated discussion would appear noisy to a distant observer but when they passed me it was silent. This clinched it and I knew it was a disguise. I caught up with them and from the cover of a collapsed mud house sent clicks. Instinctively they vanished into the gutters on both sides of the road. We united and discussed my problem and they volunteered to steal the bicycles. Later I smelt cooking and traced it to see John busy stirring the contents of a big pot. When I retreated Isaac came in with the last of the bicycles about three hours before your arrival. They must have eaten and are resting."

Ekene finished his report not knowing what to expect.

"Good work" commended Adaka and extracted four lush green guavas and gave them to Ekene.

"Eat those and go with Ike to collect what is left in their pot. You said that the pot is big? There must be something left. Ike will distract them while you steal the food."

All had gone well and on the dot of nine three loud clicks sounded, the men responded and emerged.

"What kind of scouting got you so fast to the rendezvous?" Adaka queried John and Isaac.

"Before the Umuile by pass we saw a lorry approaching the hill. We did not look in its direction but the lorry stopped after passing us. The elderly RSM who climbed down said that I looked like his mother and asked us our destination. I told him that we were going to Umuahia so they let down the tail board and helped us in. we had no option. At the bumpy stretch before Isi Ala Ngwa junction the lorry slowed and we disembarked. We checked to see if they noticed but passing the stretch the lorry accelerated. Our disembarkation went unnoticed. We saw people at work in the farms and stole the basket and hoe. We were almost inside the town when the Warrant Officer accosted us. Even while in the lorry we kept our eyes open for anything unusual. We did not notice any cause for concern sir."

Isaac stopped and looked at John for confirmation and John nodded.

Adaka considered for some minutes and then spoke:
"You will scout to Oba while Ekene will lead. Watch him and learn Isaac that expressive left hand of yours is tell-tale. It will blow your disguise to an experienced eye. Secondly I remember Idigo saying that confidence is very necessary but overconfidence kills. Ekene while you navigate keep your eyes extra open because the Nigerian troops from Okigwe are pushing for Umuahia. We leave in thirty minutes, five minute spacing between pairs. Kingsley you and your men will take the rear."

They were feasting on the guava and cherry provided by Ike. Some went to the brook beside the rail line to refresh and fill their canteens. Most were back when a cripple with a big supportive staff under the left shoulder hopped down the road with a lantern, no one including John who was already dressed as a Pastor gave him a thought. Adaka's undivided attention was on him and the others followed suit.

"Get that man back here." ordered Adaka. Kingsley returned with him and to show respect the bald headed youth with a game left leg tried to salute military fashion.

"Good night sir" he croaked in a hoarse fear laden voice. He fell and picked himself up wobbling around to pick up his staff.

"What happened to your leg?" asked Adaka.

"Machine gun at Omoh sir and I was discharged non-combatant from military hospital Uli.

Adaka lost interest.

"You can go but lower that lantern."

He hopped off after an awkward salute and realizing that he had no cap on Adaka who was buckling his belt jerked his head up and asked after the disappearing back of the wounded soldier:

"What is your name boy?"

"Sergeant Adaka Iweka sir reporting for duty."

He rolled into the bush and surfaced beside them to see them all grinning foolishly. Even the Colonel could not immediately control the grin.

"That is excellent, I knew that something was not right but Idigo would have spotted it right away. It has to do with the confidence thing I mentioned earlier."

It was twenty minutes short of midnight when Ekene moved out and two minutes later Pastor John and cripple Isaac mounted and rode after him. In that prescribed order and timing the others followed. Kingsley waited for Adaka and Ike to move but they stayed relaxed.

"What happens now sir?" Kingsley asked.

"You are falling behind schedule. You ought to have moved five minutes ago. What is keeping you?"

Kingsley and his men mounted and left. Ike reported that the car had enough petrol for the whole journey to Oba. He had parked it at the Primary school.

"I drained four cars to fill the tank, engine oil, water and brake fluids are all checked. I loaded our kits and I will also load the bicycles in case the unforeseen occurs. With the exception of your pistol, the guns are all cleaned and oiled. I stripped the Thompson because the firing pin was doubtful. The canteens are full and we have enough fruits and yams to last a week. I am ready sir."

Adaka listening showed signs of irritation saying:

"You talk too much." and moved to the brook to return fifteen minutes later.

"Let us go." he commanded and Ike led the way to the car. In full military dress uniform, both of them contrary to practice displaying their rank insignia settled in the car and drove off. At Ibeku junction they passed Kingsley and his men. They were well spaced out and pedaling purposefully. Kingsley like the mother hen led the way dutifully looking his wards over by criss crossing the road and pretending to enjoy the scenery.

"Kingsley's ankle knife is showing." Adaka said and lapsed into a nap. The dark night became darker and the weather from being cool became cold. Flashes of lightning at intervals illuminated the pitch darkness. The strong headlight of the Vauxhall car gallantly penetrated the darkness and assisted Ike in navigating. There were holes, bumps and ditches that pock marked the roads around Umuahia. This was evidence of Nigeria's unsuccessful attempt to take the city. There was no drizzle before the heavens opened and rain poured down like water cascading down the Niagara Falls. The valiant attempt by the wipers to improve visibility failed. The fleets of water flooding the windscreen were torrential. Ike selected a shade under some leafy shrub and parked. He put off all the lights, unrolled his McIntosh and went under the car. Adaka exited the car, bent over and vanished into the bush. Twenty minutes later he approached the car from the opposite direction in what could be described as leisurely strides. He opened the boot of the car and climbed in.

Kingsley and his men had hooked up with Fidelis and Nwosu. Covered by their thick rain coats they trudged on through the dark stumbling spiritedly. The deep throaty growl of the thunder masked the swishing of their boots and rain coats through pools on the road. The headlights of their bicycles criss crossed the road like will-o-the-wisps. Three clicks came as they crested the hill to Olokoro by pass. Nwosu replied with two sharp clicks and Ike stepped into their path saying:

"The Colonel orders you to seek dry cover around until the rain lets up."

Without another word he stepped into the bush and vanished.

"I did not see the Colonel's and his aides' bicycle lights after They....."

"Shut up" hissed Kingsley "survey the area and seek cover."

Laying down his bicycle he unsheathed his ankle knife and entered the bush. Rather than let up the fury of the rain increased. Kingsley after ensuring the safety and comfort of his men debated whether to hibernate like the others or investigate the presence of the dark car he believed he saw earlier after they passed Isi Ala Ngwa junction. Overpowered by curiosity he crawled toward the car. Circling the car twice he believed that he had located the driver. Knife in hand he hugged the dry partly burnt stump nearby and straightened to view the surroundings better. The point of a bayonet painfully probed between his clavicles. He stiffened and dropped the knife in his hand.

"Pick up the knife and go to rest as I ordered. Your ankle knife was showing when you rode out of Mbawsi town. Exercise more care."

Kingsley turned to apologize and acknowledge his mistakes but stared into empty space. He shrugged and returned to his cover.

'This on-the-job training although more effective is much more tasking' he mused. Stretching out he slept. When he opened his eyes the breaking dawn was bright portending a hot day although the morning was still cold. He also saw the smiling face of Ike who said:

"Up and rouse your men. You failed to obey orders as given and ran into the Colonel last night. At Olokoro by pass veer left and head for Afor Ugiri. The Nigerians are nearer than the news is reporting. Leave at once."

Ike smiled and left as unobtrusively as he came.

Ike found Fidelis by hunting fortune. He heard the desperate thrashing about of something heavy and noiseless. He took his bearing and zeroed in on the sight. Fidelis was squatting and watching the death throes of a beautifully coated antelope lost in thought. Ike straightened up and said:

"Is it not sadistic to ogle the death throes of such a beautiful antelope?"

Fidelis casually looked up and replied:

"That animal is more like a deer than an antelope. It is bigger and more brightly coated than an antelope. Whether deer or antelope is not important, what matters is that it is meat for the boys. I was waiting for it to die."

"No need to wait" said Ike flicking his hand and a long blade buried itself behind the left foreleg of the animal accessing its heart. It slumped and Ike retrieved his knife wiping the blade on the fur of the animal.

"With this attack on the heart, any animal, man inclusive dies without pain or struggle. Take it to the blue car parked up the road and drop it in the boot." said Ike.

Fidelis faked a cough and bow-legged Claudius Johnson bashed through the bush like a tired wart hog saying:

"Did you hear my noiseless approach?"

"Not really" answered Fidelis "although at exactly the time you executed your noiseless approach an angry bull thrashed through the bushes to this very point and vanished as you arrived."

Claudius' face fell and he lifted the stag hauling it behind Fidelis as he sought the car. Ike delivered the order about veering to Afor Ugiri and the reason for the detour. He turned to go in search of Nwosu and stopped abruptly as Nwosu called from the top of an avocado pear tree:

"I have heard the order. We leave in ten minutes."

Two long ropes lowered his bicycle and from the tangerine tree another bicycle was lowered about twenty-five yards away. Henry Opara dropped from the tree clutching his riffle at the ready. He straightened when he saw only Ike standing relaxed and Nwosu swinging down the tall tree, Ike left without another word although he was curious as to what the bicycles were doing on trees.

CHAPTER ELEVEN

NIGERIAN PATROL

Just before the Afor market square at Ubakala, Ekene spotted a Nigerian patrol. He made a rough estimate of sixteen persons and backtracked to Isaac and John. A swift conference activated the disguise specialist. Within thirty minutes Major John Ede from Kogi state and Sergeant Momodu Okunola entered the market square. The 'lightning' emblem of the 12th battalion Nigerian Army, tagged 'military power' reclined smugly on the top of each arm. The freshly ironed khaki uniforms and shining booted feet told the patrol team that these were more of tradesmen than infantry fighting men. Clean shaven, spick and span effeminate looking as all men of the artillery corps.

"They would do better behind their pencils, rulers and slide rules. They would also do better ciphering and deciphering trajectories and demolishing from a distance" mused Lieutenant Lekke. "Reconnaissance patrol does not fit them. See how they are clutching their riffles like magic wands. Challenge them sergeant Ibrahim."

"Halt who goes there!" shouted sergeant Ibrahim on guard position, his finger resting on the trigger. The two soldiers stopped moving and thrust both hands up above their heads, holding their riffles like firewood. Lieutenant Lekke laughed quietly and beckoned all three to him saying:

"Major you should not be here. We have not secured the area and are on path finding patrol to plan our move. This place is still dangerous until we can open, establish and maintain a corridor between Umuahia and Okigwe. Flushing the rebels out of Umuahia will be easy then. Please go back."

The 'Major' and 'sergeant' had lowered their hands before approaching the patrol and one of them said:

"We are getting ready for the whole operation. For the past five days we have been mapping out the area to soften it for you boys to enter easily.

There is an airfield around this area and we wish to locate it. Intelligence reports that there are about thirty French made jet fighters and over ten short range bombers there. Brigadier Adikunle of the marines and Jallo are agreed that we must locate the field and camouflaged runways for their destruction before the offensive begins. It is my duty to do this and I have followed the trail and know that it is fifteen kilometers south east of the market square. I was on my way to the road leading there when your man challenged us. We will leave at once. I am sure that we will establish the location and be back in two hours. Adikunle's offensive has opened up more fronts so we may only meet deserting soldiers and refugees seeking charity organization camps. There is no danger."

He turned and moving away heard Lekke volunteer to assist him by providing security for the important task. The 'Major' considered for a moment and agreed.

"I have told you that I am now sure of the road and there is no danger but then why not? Teaming up we shall do a better job and return earlier. I will personally report your part to the Brigadier who briefed me personally for this assignment. You will give me your particulars on our return."

He moved off and was followed by Lieutenant Lekke and his men who became enthralled by their catlike movements as the journey progressed. Thirty minutes of brisk and heady movement brought them to what looked like a formidable erosion site. Lekke was now very much impressed with the bush savvy and physical attributes of the soldiers he had thought of as dumb and effeminate. The Major hopped onto some rocks and peered down the erosion site. He beckoned to Lekke pointing out the shallow stream flowing at the bottom of the gully. He said:

"I will traverse these rocks while you lead the boys down the gully. According to the intelligence reports uphill beyond this gully is the plateau on which the airfield lies. I will drop ropes to assist your climb up the hill from the 'gorge' as the intelligence reports describe the place. You Momodu, hunt for some creeping ropes. We should be through here in the next fifteen minutes."

His Kogi accent and the authority of rank ensured unquestioned compliance. The soldiers so addressed moved off immediately to comply. From behind another rock, Ekene who was attired like a Nigerian Artillery Warrant Officer clicked and winked as John caught his eye. He climbed down to Ekene who gave a mock salute.

"Where is the Colonel?" he asked.

"He, Ike and Fidelis will receive them. They have mounted a guard of honour down there." Ekene replied. Lekke thought to impress the Major by arriving the bottom of the gully and utilizing his obstacle crossing expertise to attain the top of the hill without rope assistance. He considered the Majors task of climbing the high rocks more arduous than his. He rushed his men down the gorge. The rivulet formed by the water exiting the belly of the rock was so pure, clean and cold that when they got there all sixteen of them unlaced their boots, pulled off their stockings. They put off their helmets, leaned their riffles against the convenient rocks and went into the water. Some drank with cupped palms while others knelt beside the water, lapping it up with relish. Having drank to his fill and still intent on impressing the Major, Lekke surveyed the sharp incline of the hill face. He wondered how to climb it without a rope. He became aware of unusual clinks behind them where they left their riffles and other things. The ravine became very quiet and all his men were enjoying the coolness of the water and surroundings. Nobody was left on observation post because he felt they were totally alone in this cave-like world of the cold rock water. Without turning he knew that somebody was behind them. As abruptly as the feeling emerged it subsided. Reason told him that the fellow behind them was sergeant Momodu accompanying the Major. He knew they were nimble, he thought, and possess ghost-like qualities. He continued surveying the hill face choosing a path with more foot and hand holds. He then noticed that something appeared more ominous. The swishing and gurgling noises from the waterbed had ceased. He looked to the right and saw all his men intact and in good health. This did not please him much because they all had their hands held high in the air above their heads. He turned to see a kid dressed in faded army uniform which appeared to have been stolen from an army camp. He may be a camp follower, he thought, those always running around the mess room doing errands. He may also be a member of what the rebels call 'Boys Company' but whichever it was he must die. His hand dropped to his waist holster and his big pistol surfaced. Before the hammer clicked to signify that the pistol was cocked, and ready for firing, a long blade flashed through the air and buried itself in his biceps. The pistol fell and slid into the water. The kid walked back to the large rock on which he sat. Lieutenant Lekke's size deceived him and he flung himself at the boy intending to smother him and throttle the life out of him. His intention was good, the execution perfect for he landed on the back of the boy but like a camel the boy humped his back and jerked upward. Lekke flew over his shoulder and hard landed on the rock with his shoulder, arm and side of his head. He passed out. His men did not make any move to go to his assistance because Ike's riffle pointed unwaveringly at them.

"Undress!" ordered the boy. All but staff sergeant Solomon Olokun complied, casting their shirts and trousers at the boy's feet.

"Listen boy, I cannot for if I remove my hand from the wound, I will bleed to death. Have pity on me because my mother is Ibo like you and told me that you people do not kill your daughter's children."

He bent his head to indicate that he was pleading.

"Don't bother, I will help you." the boy walked up to him, slit open the trouser and pulled it off him saying:

"You have lost blood and need warmth. Go and seat beside the Lieutenant. Ike go and dress their wounds." He unslung his riffle, sat down and covered the men.

"Please kneel in the water to dissuade you from making sudden moves.

I do not want to kill any of you for this is a war among brothers." They all knelt down and one of them asked:

"Are you the one they call Shadow in the Ukwa area of Port Harcourt sector?"

"Nobody has called me that to my face." Fidelis smiled as he replied. Ike treated the wounded prisoners and tied the hands of the other eleven behind them. After unloading their riffles, he removed the magazines dropping them into two bags made from the discarded trousers. Their riffles were slung on their shoulders before their hands were tied. Their helmets were put on and the only free one carried the bags containing the magazines. The climb was difficult for the encumbered prisoners. At the top of the gorge Ike bleated and an answering bleat came from behind them. They all turned in surprise to see Colonel Adaka following behind them. He had a big roll of rope in his right hand. When he crested the mouth of the gorge he handed the rope over to Ike saying:

"Join them by the waist giving walking space."

This was speedily done and it also embraced the magazine carrier with the two wounded men.

"This way they will not think treacherous thoughts." Fidelis murmured. Ekene and John joined them when they reached the main road. Lekke looked unwaveringly at John the 'Major' who still had on his disguises and the hatred was obvious. Adaka saw the look and smiled saying:

"John I know that you don't want to be shot by a jittery Biafran soldier who will prefer questioning a dead Nigerian Major. Put off that uniform."

John entered the bush and emerged the Pastor he was before the patrol was sighted. Almost an hour elapsed before Isaac hobbled in with a military policeman and six other ranks from the nearby brigade. Isaac executed his wounded soldier salute and reported that both the brigade commander and brigade Major refused him audience.

"They both showed interest when I mentioned your name but looking me over waved me away. They did not believe me. I was dragged to the guardroom when I angrily told the Captain here to give me five minutes or I will end all our lives in two minutes. They all laughed but he listened to me and taking me outside I showed him my suicide belt. I also exposed my disguise which convinced him and so here we are."

Adaka looked at the military policeman. He beckoned the Captain over and said:

"Take these men to your brigade and report the situation to the commander. These are Prisoners of war and should be so treated. Treat the wounded and feed them all. I want to meet them alive on my return. My complements to your commander, I am Colonel Adaka Ekwo."

He looked at Fidelis and Ike saying:

"See them down to the road and return, we are already behind schedule and the Okigwe-Umuahia channel is getting hotter this morning. We may take a brief hand before continuing. Captain Nwosu and Kingsley are heading for Eziama. We will as soon as possible meet up with them. We have salted dry meat in the car so open the boot and take enough to carry you to Oba. We rendezvous at 14th Brigade Eziama. Take a hand by doing a few patrols and leave tomorrow for Oba through Anara, Orlu, Awo-Idemilli, Uli, Okija, Ozubulu, Orifite and Akwukwu, avoid Nnewi I do not want to explain to curious Brigadier Amadi. There will be no pack movement so break off and travel at will. Use your discretion but preserve your bicycles and weapons. I hate loosing any person so move out with your back ups."

In no time the clearing was without a sign of life. Colonel Adaka withdrew into the cover of the weeping willows with Claudius Johnson. Ike chirped and Adaka responding came into the open with Claudius. Fidelis and Claudius checked their packs, hefted them and left. Ike backed the car into the open and Adaka climbed in. He spent thirty minutes on the radio gathering information and charting a course.

CHAPTER TWELVE

RUMINATIONS

They drove off twisting and turning through dirt roads and bush paths. The fear laden stares of the locals in the hamlets and villages followed them. Immediately the car drove out of sight, relief showed on the staring faces. The civilians had one thing in common and that was their fear of soldiers be they Nigerian or Biafran. Soldiers meant rudeness, intimidation, taunts, commandeering of valuables, rape of wives and daughters, beatings, shooting and killing. This was for anybody bold enough to claim God or Constitution given rights. To the subjugated civilians soldiers meant death. At the hands of the Nigerians death was brutal and immediate. At the hands of the Biafrans, it was slow and tantalizing but certain. Their prayer was not for any side to win but for a quick resolution of the conflict. The hunger from economic blockade and vandalization of farmlands by soldiers aggravated the situation. Ever present was the danger of Nigerian long range artillery guns, menacing jet fighters and bombers. This frayed all nerves. Rumours of Nigerian offensives, sabotage, coups, unconditional surrenders and others did not leave grounds for hope. The poor, sick, weak, frightened and emaciated people had their hope, trust, and faith in God. Kwashiorkor was killing more people than enemy bullets. The stares that followed Adaka's passage though not emotion filled, spoke clearly of hatred and not love. He continued through not oblivious of this fact. He deeply longed to hold them and tell them that he identified with them and shared their views without reservations. He wanted to be their brother and friend. He longed to sit with them sharing kola nuts, roasted yam, palm wine and raffia palm gin with them. He wanted to do this in an atmosphere of peace, swapping stories and hoping for a future filled with joy. That was why he had to train more people to fight better and ensure that this lethal weapon he has been commissioned to create, prime and hone is potent enough to bring the commanders of the federal troops to the negotiating table. Seeing the helpless looks of the civilians always triggered his mind back to the Kano military evil.

There were killings in Jos, Kaduna, Minna, Jaji and other military bases. These killings were devastating but nothing to compare with that of Kano. Killing in anger is a whole lot different from premeditated killings where comradeship bound people. Deceit and hurt where truth, love and trust were in abundance or spirit-de-corps in lay language. This spirit meant that it was always teamwork so the corps will take care of its own. A soldier will not only defend another with all of his might but will defend his spouse or that of his comrade with his life. They trained, lived and exercised together in order to defend their Nation's territorial integrity but also the well being of their civilian brothers. There were no murky recesses in their minds and their thoughts were not hate-filled. This was until the smooth, devious, slimy, scheming frauds called politicians decided to prey on them. Lies, deceitful surmises, fraudulent suppositions and devious schemes easily took in the good, straight forward and simple-minded military corp. Evil spawned hatred, hatred spawned misunderstanding, misunderstanding spawned coups and coups gave birth to counter coups. Fear and dishonesty took over and destruction arrived. Destruction of lives, property, valuables, codes, ethics, hopes, aspirations and beliefs followed.

Sectionalism, ethnicity, tribalism and other discriminatory vices followed in the wake. A pogrom ensued enveloping the tribe dominating in commerce and with a population that was more widely spread than others throughout the country. The Ibo tribe was the victim and Lieutenant Adaka, Iloma and Awoni were of the Ibo tribe. They went through the School of Infantry and were commissioned together. They attended courses in India, England,

Australia and Philippines together. By the same long whim of fate they went on peace keeping assignment to the Congo at the same time. They served in the same unit so naturally, a relationship deeper than the usual comradeship developed. They did all things together within the confines of rules and regulations, never antagonizing authority. Together they planned getting married after consecutive bouts of veneral disease. The windy homilies of Major Mojekwu, the matron of the regimental medical station at the Kano cantonment went a short way to dissuading them from seeking the doubtful pleasures of prostitutes. The job of turning them off was done by the matrons' insistence on administering the injections personally. Each drug was administered separately and the needles plunged deep into the muscles to prevent abscess. Treading the path of caution and wisdom meant getting married. They planned for it and put their savings together. When they felt that they had enough for one of them to get married they sat in conference to choose who does it first. Because they were all about the same age, the traditional custom of eldest making the first choice did not apply. The fear of the unknown hazards of marriage often hinted at by elders dissuaded any from volunteering to pioneer the move. That none of them had a fiancée or heart throb indicated that marriage was the least of their worries. They all wanted to be great soldiers. Adaka wanted to be like General Patton. Awoni wanted to be like Field Marshall Montgomery and Iloma wanted to be like Hitler. He knew all the great Hitler speeches by heart and spouted them as occasion arose. He was the cynic of the three, never excited or over enthusiastic about anything. With the opinion that women were the cause of all problems on earth he declined taking the lead in the marriage experiment. They cast lot to choose who takes the lead and Adaka was picked. The support was overwhelming. Even the Officers wives did not stop at the customary cash contributions and gifts presentation. They traveled the long distance to the east and fully participated in the customary rites. At the wedding Iloma and Awoni led the guard of honour. They were ramrod stiff with the tips of their swords clenched in a symbol of tight unity. All went very well and Awoni who was next according to the cast lot started looking forward to the event.

Adaka appeared healthier and happier, exuding satisfaction and contentment. When Awoni sent word home for a wife to be sought for him, there was great joy in his Ogbu village. His father had wept profusely when his son after taking a delightful degree in Geography rather than take his pick of all the many government and company jobs available, opted for the army. The traditional belief that military service meant a short life span still held sway. His father sought solace in drinks and married another wife to replace the lost son. Awoni's protestations that he was not lost fell on deaf ears. They both rarely exchanged words except for austere greetings. Awoni continued to send monetary presents to thaw his father's wrath. Mbegbu thus went around the whole town and surrounding villages seeking a worthy spouse. His son's many courses abroad and healthy salary were his boast but most parents' mouth drooped in disdain when they were made aware that the groom was a soldier. The task was hard but the diligent and fortuitous search paid off and a beautiful girl who was a trained nurse and midwife was picked. Before the customary rites took place, the first coup-de'etat took place in Nigeria. The traditional marriage was postponed indefinitely.

The hustle and bustle in the military heightened the fear and suspicion. Distorted truths coupled with misrepresented facts brewed hatred. The Politicians were at work. The result was a bloodier counter-coup and a pogrom followed by loud calls for secession. Troops were confined to barracks and the latent storm was seething while the ill-equipped and short handed police corps battled ineffectively to quell the pogrom. The politicians stepped up their play and the volcano erupted in the military. Comrades were marched out, made to dig ditches and shot inside the ditches that became graves.

Suspecting the unusual happenings of marching men out peacefully and not returning with them, others resisted, insisting to be armed before such trips. This of course was not possible and orders were disobeyed. The officers that were out of unit on duty or leave could not contact their household or colleagues. There was a silence that portended evil. The pogrom had flowed into the barracks although most military formations stuck to the old comradeship and shunned pogrom. Even those that accepted it were not proud of it and only had to execute the shameful act under cover of darkness or unobtrusively. Soldiers of other tribes would identify with the victims and a real bust up will occur. Soon after the lull of reason, arrangements were made and soldiers from the eastern part were shipped to units in the east. This was the situation that befell Adaka, who was engaged in Military exercises and maneuvers at Ibadan when the trouble erupted. Believing that his six months' pregnant wife and friends, Awoni and Iloma had been shipped east to safety, he boarded the military truck that conveyed him to 82nd Division Enugu. At Enugu he saw his colleagues from Kano and other detachments and their wives, but his friends and wife were nowhere in sight. Blank stares met his questions until Captain Nsofor of the signals' saw him and waved him over. He gave him the keys to his quarters and told him to go and freshen up so that they could sit up at the mess to await news of his wife and friends. He complied and left. They spent half the night at the mess and Nsofor got so drunk that Adaka could not question him at all. He had to hold him up and half carry him to their room. After parade the next morning, where Colonel Ojukwu explained the happenings across the country, his fear heightened and bile rose in him. His mind raced in overdrive yet he had no solution. By the third day, sitting in the signals' office beside Captain Nsofor did not seem to be paying off. Feeling useless and not given to drinks but not being a teetotaler, he headed in blind haste to the mess. Rather than order his usual rice or garri and egusi soup, he ordered a small shot of whisky. Three hours later, after many small shots of whisky, gin, brandy, rum and beer to clear his head, Nsofor reciprocated the good gesture of the first day at the mess by carrying him to their room. Laboring with Adaka's bulk, R.S.M Jude who as other rank had seen action in almost every part of the world walked up to him saluting carelessly:

"I don't know what you boys are up to but the other day I saw this very officer carrying you home dead drunk. Today you are doing the same for him. I have never seen you drink even beer! What are you boys playing at?" Nsofor moved away from Adaka to the R.S.M saying:

"I was putting up an act for him such that he would not be able to question me closely about his wife. The situation is bad and his course mates returned to Kano cantonment for a rescue mission, which to my mind is suicidal. I am trying to help him maintain his sanity. When he sees others and the gruesome effect of the pogrom he may calm down."

He went back to his task and the old RSM helped him. By the fifth day, Adaka was no longer talking or responding to talks or questions. He also stopped eating. The RSM tried taking him under his wings and explaining the commonness of death and he withdrew further into his shell. Captain Nsofor had become evasive to his queries about the signals so he quit bothering him. After the Division Commander's lecture, he cornered Second Lieutenant Clifford Ozor of the Reece unit Kano and asked after his wife and friends.

"Your wife was sheltered by RSM Dauda's wife. When the evacuation transport came for the women she and two women were not seen. After we searched everywhere Corporal Idahosa of the signals promised to keep us informed but urged us to leave at once. According to him an unmilitary signal was received and that night would be bloody. We left without your wife. At Kafanchan we saw Lieutenant Iloma. He told me that Awoni had continued down east that morning believing that the ladies had passed Kafanchan. When I told him what happened he went into the barracks and soon passed us on his way up north in a Zephyr 4 car. We fed the ladies and they freshened up and we continued down home without incident. We arrived early in the morning so the officers and men came to collect their wives. Other women from the town that sought refuge in the barracks were provided with transport to their destinations. I was busy with this when I saw my friend and school mate Awoni, frantically peering shortsightedly into the faces of the ladies. I knew that he was searching for your wife. I avoided him until I sat to eat in a buka. He entered and sat beside me and when he asked me I told him the truth. The truth was that your wife was safe with the Dauda family. He jumped up shouting: "That mad drunkard, that devil" and ran from the mammy market. The last I heard was that he commandeered a signals' land rover, some arms and ammunition from the armory and drove off. Signal was received that afternoon that he threatened the border guards and headed north. I have heard nothing ever since."

He finished lamely dabbing tears from his very red eyes.

"If he had made his intention known to me I would have gone with him. I am sorry sir."

Without a word Adaka left. The time was 12.35pm and he began loading a land rover with sacks and boxes when RSM Jude led six tough looking men to arrest him. Forming a half moon around him the six men held their riffles pointed at Adaka. He became aware of their presence before they showed themselves. Like a big cat he crouched beside the land rover with its side providing cover from some of the riffles. His right hand rested on the skeleton butt of his FN riffle and his left hand had his big pistol cocked and pointing at one of the men when RSM Jude barked:

"Lower those guns and wait for me near the kiosk."

He walked to Adaka ignoring the pistol, stopped and brought a large kola nut out of his pocket then he intoned benedictions:

"It shall be well with us. We shall not know sudden or untimely death. We shall live to see our grand children and our wives and children shall live to see their great grand children. The Lord that instructs us to catch the skunk will give us water to wash our hands. Faith that makes us eat pepper will provide the drinking water to salve the tang. Your wife shall return. A war is looming but we shall survive it. As we chew this kola nut we chew life, health, wealth, joy, peace, love, promotion, and all good things in Jesus name."

He broke the kola nut, counted the lobes and smiled widely:

"Five lobes, good omen." He threw one lobe into his mouth and dropping the other into his pocket he opened his palm holding the lobes and Adaka who had straightened from his crouch, uncorking and holstering his pistol, moved forward and took two of the remaining three lobes. RSM Jude threw the last lobe into his mouth chewing and clearing his throat:

"Do you need alligator pepper?" he asked and Adaka answered in the affirmative. Jude produced a dry alligator fruit and taking some seeds from it, threw them into his mouth while chewing the nut. He gave the fruit to Adaka:

"That will ensure that you won't sleep while doing the long drive to Kano. It would be better if you had somebody to relieve you when sleep comes knocking. I would have volunteered to go with you but I am neither used to prospecting holes without cricket or using the gourd with holes to fetch drinking water from distant streams. I" he made to continue but Adaka interrupted:

"What do you mean?"

"I mean that many roads lead from Kano to the east. Lieutenants Iloma and Awoni left about five days ago for Kano. They have either succeeded or failed. The likelihood of success is more. If so they are on their way back and you may miss them and via another road go barging blindly into an angry barracks already bested by these resourceful young men. I know you will take a lot of them with you but you are sure to die. How will that help your rescued wife and very loyal and valiant friends? I was once youthful like you are now and understand the exuberance. You are however better trained than I was then. Like you, I was in the Congo and witnessed the bloodbath but this is a different thing and calls for reasoning more than brawn. Like you, but long before you, I was in the Philippines and trained in jungle craft and warfare, there is a difference though. War situation has arisen but war has not been declared so by your training you will discover that you will not be able to perform at top capacity. You will be restrained by many conditions that are not yet defined in your mind. Call this off while we prepare better and gather more information. I will accompany you if you will just give three more days." He lit a cigarette and ate the last lobe. Meekly Adaka unloaded the land rover. The men were ordered to carry everything to the RSM's house. There they were well stowed and Adaka returned to his room angry, bewildered, yet convinced of the reasoning of RSM Jude. He started that morning to go on long leisurely walks within which period he hoped and planned for the blissful reunion. He was away by the third day when a gaunt looking, tired Lieutenant Awoni drove into the Division at about 10.00am. The guards allowed the dirty Zephyr 4 through the checkpoint and the quarter guard zeroed in on the car as it zigzagged drunkenly into the roadside gutter. The beautiful girl with flat tummy tied hands and feet in the back seat had wild eyes. She raved noisily but wordlessly like a dumb person. Lt. Awoni passed out and a pool of dry blood on the front foot mat indicated he had serious injury. They ended up at the Medical base and the dedicated doctors went to work. Infusions of blood and dextrose-saline were set up immediately while the Psychiatrist and Psychologist were ferried in. The beehive of medical activities rather than revive Awoni pushed him deeper into unconsciousness. The doctors were confident that he would pull out of it but they all had reservations about the girl who appeared to have lost her sanity. Further investigations revealed that she had also lost a near mature pregnancy. A D&C was done and the Psychiatrist administered some injections that put her to sleep. When Adaka strolled in at about 4.00pm, 2nd Lt. Clifford met him and gave him the news. He raced to the Medical Unit, looked the two of them over and asked of Iloma. The doctors and nurses did not know what or whom he was inquiring after. Their blank faces made him angry, and by the first burst of rage, 2nd Lt. Ozo rushed in with RSM Jude:

"Relax man, first of all let us ensure that these two are revived then we can get information on Iloma before we act. The thing is now narrowing down."

Jude walked over to Awoni's bed and picked up the chart saying: "This is the fourth pint of blood and sixth unit of dextrose-saline, he was really far-gone. The miracle is that gangrene had not set in and the real miracle is how he managed the far drive from Kano in this condition."

Adaka snatched the chart and reading it said:

"We are both B positive blood group, I will donate as many pints as he needs."

The severe doctor Mike Ogboto sternly ushered them out. They sat at the verandah sharing kola nuts, alligator pepper and the occasional star beer that was forced out of Adaka's pocket to celebrate the rescue of his wife and the safe return of one of his friends. RSM Jude arranged a two weeks leave for Adaka and a week's leave for Ozo to enable them attend to Awoni and Mrs. Ekwo.

Taciturn Adaka attracted many visitors including Major Chukwuma Kaduna Nzogwu. Captain Nsofor of the signals had received firsthand information from signals Corporal Idahosa in Kano. He knew that Iloma had been fatally wounded while rescuing Adaka's wife from RSM Dauda and the drunken soldiers raping her. He shot them all at close range in the head but shot Dauda in the crotch and the belly. Dauda begged him to take him to the Base Medical Center. He agreed to do so if Dauda told him where the other two women were. He explained that they died by jumping two stories' down the non-commissioned officer's quarters when they wanted to start raping them on the third day. Iloma gave him a head-shot and lifted Adaka's wife to his shoulders. He had crossed the parade ground and was heading for the tennis grounds when a shot rang out and he stumbled and fell. He tried to get up but could not and was still struggling to move himself and Adaka's wife to the car when Awoni arrived on the scene. He was reconnoitering the barracks when he saw Iloma with his burden traversing the parade ground.

He took up position to be able to offer him cover in the event of pursuit. That was when the shot rang out and stopped him. In a flash Awoni was beside them and he checked and saw that Iloma hadn't much time to live. He could not contemplate leaving him there but there was no sense taking a corpse over a thousand kilometers to bury. He had difficulty restraining Adaka's wife who was totally irrational in talk and action. He knocked her out dragging her over to the land rover then he returned for Iloma.

"No don't bother about me for I will go soon. I am already feeling cold.

Just set me up for the worthy exit."

Blood leaked from his mouth as he spoke:

"Tell Adaka that I killed all those who raped his wife. Dauda's wife named them all and I killed them all." He stopped talking for a while.

"Set me up fast and leave. They will come after me soon."

Awoni moved him carefully and with much difficulty behind the wrecked table tennis boards. A shot rang out and the bullet plunged into the ground. Awoni set him up activating the exit grenade belt mined with twelve British Mark 7 grenades. He exchanged his rapid-fire assault riffle for Iloma's telescopic Swan Six sniper riffle. Crawling to a nearby cover he positioned himself to start picking off those sure to come hunting Iloma.

"No." mumbled Iloma "Go. Help Adaka. Use the Zephyr 4 its tank is full. They destroyed his wife. Go."

Awoni hesitated and Iloma shrieked with blood spraying the air: "Go"

Awoni peered through the telescope and saw somebody pointing to their location with many soldiers surrounding him. Awoni took aim, drew in his breath and squeezed the trigger. The man crumpled and before others could take cover Awoni nailed another with the second round. He then cut across the yard to the Zephyr 4 car and loaded in the unconscious body of Adaka's wife. He fought through three checkpoints. After Ukpilla he had no more trouble for the soldiers at the checkpoints were not happy with the killing of comrades-in-arms. The signals corporal knew no more and cut off transmission. At Agbor, Awoni stopped to refuel. He had noticed that Adaka's wife had revived and was making a strange noise. Not long after, the smell of faeces wafted forward and urine trickled down the seat. He filled the car tank and drove off and not knowing what to do, he increased speed to reach his destination earlier. At Okpanam he drove through the town and stopped to urinate.

"Dauda look" He heard the girl say, and was turning before the sixth sense made him throw himself sideways. A stream of five bullets rushed out of the berretta pistol she held all but one missing him. Hit in the left thigh he hobbled back to the car retrieving the pistol. Awoni then tied her hands and legs, and dressing his wounds as best he could he headed for Enugu. He arrived at Enugu hours later drained of blood and strength but filled with determination.

This last part of the story came from Awoni when he recovered. His tearful convalescence period made every ear that heard the pathetic story tingle and saddened every heart that opened to it. What minds that dared think on it always cringed and blanked out.

Mrs. Olivia Adaka Ekwosimba never recovered sanity before the war finally erupted from the tentative "Police Action".

Corporal Idahosa was accused of giving information to the rebels. His court martial was summary and he was dismissed. Although the allegation was weak and not proved, his denial was vehement and soulful. No facts were available to convict him but somebody from the Kano cantonment signals' unit sent a very detailed report of Iloma's death. According to the anonymous signals man, the execution of the rapists agreed with Iloma's version to Awoni and Olivia's version during her few lucid moments. Iloma's exit started with a white handkerchief tied to his riffle and waveringly raised above his head. The troops moving in on him and the lady stopped to confer. Few minutes passed and they continued towards the white handkerchief less cautiously. When thy got near him they heard the whinnying, whimpering groans of a dying man. When they saw the blood soaked wreckage they abandoned all caution and rushed to him some slinging their guns.

"Hospital, hospital" he kept crying.

They felt that calling for a stretcher or ambulance will waste precious time so shirts were pulled off and rifles used as rods to form a stretcher. As they bent to haul him onto the makeshift stretcher he smiled and said:

"Goodbye for Adaka and Awoni"

The explosion was so thorough that there was no way to separate the shattered flesh and clothes, sixteen souls perished with Lieutenant Iloma.

Ike pulled into the shade of a cashew tree. He had seen the signs before they took off after handing over the prisoners. Adaka looked lost and had to be helped into the car. Before long tears were coursing down his cheeks while he recited the Kano horror and rescue as if he was reporting the matter to someone. Ike drove slowly twisting and turning through dusty villages and hamlets. At the 14th Brigade headquarters' entrance the guards at the checkpoint dutifully looked into the car at the Colonel's dead fish eyes and withdrew, waving them on. Adaka refused to move until Ike began asking him questions about the rescue. In a subdued voice he answered until he slept. Usually the longer the trance lasted, the deeper and longer the sleep.

His men had all arrived and in place of the Colonel, Captain Nwosu and Lieutenant Fidelis had gone to see the Brigade Commander who complained:

"We have a big problem. The federal troops captured Oraobodo village and took over the Nkume shrine at the top of the hill. They took their time to fortify the hill, building a warren of bunkers and machine gun nests. Veins of trenches now crisscross the body of the hill and the cliff side that adjoins the stream at the base has been made steep by ingenious engineering. No hand or footholds are available. From the top of this hill they can see troop movements all around, covering a distance of not less than fifteen kilometers. They thus cover the road from Okigwe to Umuahia. You can see why all our moves are checkmated and even when we, at great cost in men and ammunitions, breach the channel it does not take them time to flush us out. I don't know what to do any more, after eight well planned concerted efforts to destroy the fortifications of the hill."

He looked at them to see the expected bewilderment but they were nodding as if they understood and would soon come up with the solution. This angered him and loosing patience he asked them to leave if they had nothing better to contribute than nodding like red head lizards.

"Sorry sir" answered Fidelis "Have you thought of artillery attacks?" "Yes boy, our 106 and 105 guns did a valiant job and were blown to smithereens within thirty minutes. We sneaked closer almost to the base of the hill and deployed twelve howitzer guns. We breathed a sigh of relief, believing that our travails were over. They were taken by surprise when our guns opened up. Our joy and hopes were short lived for the fury of their response made everything we had seen before insignificant in comparison. We lost all the guns, and ninety percent of the crew. The infantry escort lost about thirty percent. The rest returned with burns and shrapnel lodged in different parts of their bodies. About six men returned intact. So you now see that there is no way."

He uncorked a bottle of brandy and drank straight from the bottle without offering to them.

"Two more questions sir, what of our air force?"

"That option was exploited to our enduring pain. My pressure reached the limit that they assigned a Cessna plane as bomber, and two helicopters equipped with cannons and heavy machine guns. In ordinary battleground this worked like magic but at Nkume hill it fizzled out like soap bubbles, without a fight. The bofor guns we never suspected were there opened up and before our crafts could get in place they were burning balls of fire plummeting to the earth. No survivors."

Nwosu spoke for the first time:

"Can you give us explosives and men to guide us?"

"That is no problem. How many of you?" asked the Commander?

"We are thirteen sir" Fidelis answered.

"Odd and unlucky number, does that mean that you are going for a Reece patrol?" Colonel Onugha asked.

"No sir. We are going to take out the hill and the guns there. Some of the soldiers will die but others will retreat hastily. Just get your men to move in and take it." Fidelis looked at Nwosu.

"We will leave now sir" said Nwosu saluting.

"Which of you is Colonel Adaka? I have heard of you but never met you. I got your signal and confirmation from Brigadier Eze. Which of you is Adaka?"

Before they could answer the door opened and Adaka walked in. "None of them, I am Adaka. I heard you all and my men spoke my mind.

We will attack the hill this night. You have to in addition to explosives and guides provide armor bearers. We have to destroy all the guns there unless you are ready to move in and hold what grounds we take. By hold, I mean hold and defend, not loose to a counter attack. My men and I leave before midday tomorrow. Fidelis meet Ike outside and take a guide. I want you back from the patrol before six pm. Leave."

Fidelis left and Adaka turned again to Colonel Onugha:

"You must pick out five good machine gun crews to keep the enemy busy if you intend to hold what we take."

"Yes sir" Colonel Onugha answered. "Get Kingsley" Adaka ordered Nwosu.

Kingsley stepped in as Nwosu opened the door.

"The Colonel will assign five machine gun crews to you for this night's operation. Take them, pick the best guns they have and train the men on their use before we leave."

Kingsley left and stood outside the door waiting.

"My man Captain Nwosu will contact you for anything we need. Thanks for your time."

He made to leave but Colonel Onugha would not have it. He urged him to stay for dinner but Adaka declined.

"If you wont eat then drink. I have very good quality alcohols." "I don't drink." Adaka answered.

"We can discuss the army" Onugha said.

"That leads to coup plots and attempts." Adaka answered turned and left.

Nwosu stayed back a short minute to apologize for his boss's curtness.

He did this by putting both palms together in supplication. He pointed to his head and dodged out the door. Onugha nodded in understanding. He was still sitting and wondering what manner of people these men were, who thought they could do what had for so long defied solution, when a gentle knock sounded and the Captain Nwosu came in. He saluted and presented a list of what was needed for the operation. Colonel Onugha summoned the Brigade Major, and the Adjutant. They arrived within minutes of summons and Onugha addressed them:

"We have guests who will do some work for us. They need the following within an hour. Ten long ropes, six walkie-talkies tuned to each other's frequencies, and to mine, seven strong torchlight's, twenty strong and sharp wooden spikes, seven padded hammers, six strong tarpaulin sacks, and thirteen two edged, very sharp pointed bayonets. Six flasks of dry gunpowder, and fifty Molotov bottles. Supply these within one hour to this office."

"Yes sir" they chorused and left.

The supplies were delivered as Adaka and his men were preparing for the operation in total silence and darkness. Kingsley and his men needed light and words to recognize themselves and communicate orders and instructions. Within the hour he had convinced the machine gun crew that they knew next to nothing about machine guns. He instructed them on emergency nesting and setting up unmanned but active machine gun nests. He spoke with the armor bearers and ended with these words:

"We don't abandon our men, wounded, whole or captured. At the end of this operation we will all return to base, wounded whole or dead if possible."

He padded over with them to Adaka. At 2100hrs they were on the move with the guides who now only tagged along. Ike's report showed that they did not know the terrain. Fidelis had to escort them back to camp and keep them with Isaac and John. He returned and they thoroughly reconnoitered the area reporting back to Adaka.

"There are six weaknesses we observed:

1. Too many communications gadgets chattering and making the place noisy thus easily penetrable.
2. The trees they left for cover will also provide the cover for infiltration.
3. The steep east end that shows no foot or handholds for climbing from the stream is less watched. They think it is formidable and unassailable. That is not true, the soil is soft and muddy and shielded from open view by the many leafy shrubs at the top.
4. The troops there are from different units and movement appears freer than it should be.
5. The northern end with direct access to the guns at the top is too heavily guarded, that communication problem is inevitable, in an emergency situation when close combat is being fought.
6. Their power supply depends on two twenty-four KVA generators buried at the base of the hill, in the west side.

7. All the roads and paths are heavily guarded, but the bush is free for anyone who dares.

They seem to dread the bush and darkness. We can infiltrate and be in position to strike in an hour."

Adaka called up Colonel Onugha on the radio:

"When the explosions start, move in but don't engage until you hear from me."

They filed out led by Ike. Fidelis followed him, often disappearing into the bush and reappearing. An hour later they were at the base of the hill, split into four light groups. The large machine gun group began deploying under Kingsley's command. He went to confer with Adaka and was still at it when he noticed that Fidelis, Ike, Nwosu, and Isaac were almost at the top of the hill. He returned to await developments. Fifteen minutes later, he saw Ike and Nwosu flit past his men towards the lip of the open trenches. Isaac and Claudius followed with more stealth than Ike and Nwosu. When he went to survey the surroundings again, there was nobody left around the stream. He looked up to see if they were still climbing but there were no persons or ropes to be seen. The wooden spikes dotted the hillside. A few bodies rolled down the sides of the hill. It was a full hour after deployment that all hell broke loose. Grenades were exploding and two mortar guns at the top of the hill opened upon the federal troops deployed at the shielded side of the base of the hill. A massive eruption occurred, and bedlam was let loose. Except for the mortar guns and bofors that were now being used as anti-personnel weapons, all the guns on the hill were silent. The occasional grenade explosions only helped to increase the tearful screams of the fleeing men. Their flight was so intent on putting a lot of distance between them and the hill.

The spectral demon mask produced by Isaac and John had well trimmed moustaches, and bushy gray beards, the large tongues sticking out were red and broad. The eyes were red and blazing with fury. John, clad in Nigeria army camouflage uniform, with the artillery insignia, ran out of a bunker now devoid of life screaming in Igalla language:

"Ghost, ghost, ghost."

He ran with bloodied hands and lobbed grenades into bunkers.

Ike, Nwosu, Isaac and Claudius, were emptying trenches of lives. When Fidelis tired of the bofor and mortar play, he unsheathed his blade and posting Asuquo and Tim to the guns, joined Colonel Adaka in the close combat furores. By 2330hrs the hill was devoid of federal troops. The explosions ceased as the mortars, grenades and bofor guns eased off. Kingsley and his men redeployed to beyond the hill. Onugha arrived with his troops and occupied all federal bunkers and trenches. Majority of them were deployed far beyond the hill.

"Colonel" called Adaka "we are done here. Hold, keep and maintain. With this hill you can easily keep the corridor closed, that way Okigwe and Umuahia will not join. Most of the known guns were saved, so our people will use them."

He left ignoring Onugha's salute. When the hill and recaptured grounds were secured, Onugha and his aides returned to base. He slept until seven in the morning. He woke up to the smell of a delicious breakfast and sent for Colonel Adaka to join him. Neither Adaka nor his men were located. Only the guides, armor bearers and machine gun crews were seen sleeping at the quarters, allocated to Adaka and his men. Their bicycles, a motorcycle and car were all intact. Some of their packs were resting undisturbed. At about 2300hrs, they trickled back into base and prepared to leave. Onugha jumped into his land rover and drove over. He saluted and Adaka responded.

"We leave now." said Adaka "thanks for giving us the opportunity to serve with you."

Ike opened the car and as Adaka entered they left. Looking around Onugha saw the others were cycling out of the base in twos.

CHAPTER THIRTEEN

MILITARY POLICE POSER

Adaka ordered Ike to head back to Afor Oru Mbaise, headquarters of fifth Division. At Afor Oru he met Colonel Njoku and discussed at length with him. Njoku, a graduate engineer before joining the Nigerian army was in command of the Nigerian Army Engineering Corps before the war. He was very good at his job and could impart knowledge to others with ease. Any army engineer that went through him became an explosives expert. They were exceptionally good at demolition, mining and de-mining. To train under Njoku meant to be a good infantry soldier because he saw both departments as complementary to each other. His principle was that a good soldier should be able to shoot well, demolish properly, secure an area adequately, read maps correctly, and assess situations speedily. This person is the good soldier. Adaka and Njoku had met in Ibadan during maneuvers and struck up a friendship based on mutual respect. Njoku had tried commiserating with him for his friend's demise and his wife's illness but Adaka would not acknowledge the gesture. They had discussed intelligently about military matters while they served together at Adani, Ogbede, Igbo-etiti, Okuku, and Enugu but as soon as conversation went personal he shrunk, blanked out and left.

Promotion to Colonel brought him face to face with Awoni. Every body knew about them and expectations were varied as to what would happen on that day that the Commander-in-Chief will decorate them. Five of them stood at attention when the Commander-in-Chief entered. The ceremony was short, citations short and powerful without being flowery. The decorations took place and the ceremonial toast was drunk. Colonels Njoku, Nebo, and Armah drank theirs but Awoni and Adaka touched glasses and poured out the red rum on the rugged floor. Brows were raised but they seemed unperturbed. The Commander-in-Chief and the attending Generals left and the party commenced with the arrival of all kinds of dishes, and exotic drinks.

These, were served by skimpily dressed, army entertainment girls. Hykkers 70 was the performing band Adaka turned to the door and Awoni followed. Adaka climbed into his land rover and before Awoni's driver could move Adaka's vehicle was beside his. Their eyes locked:

"How is she?" asked Awoni. "No change" answered Adaka

"Have you seen her?" asked Awoni "No" said Adaka

"Why?" Awoni intervened

"I have been busy. Iloma died because of her."

They bowed their heads in thought and were not aware of their drivers' taking off or the ranking participants at the party starring at them, and after them when they had driven out of sight. Conjuring up the past Njoku thought about everything and in sympathy, parted with his five best engineers. He could train others up to their standards.

"Christopher, Felix, Jonathan, Obi, and Okon, you are now my men. You will work for me by teaching my men all you know about engineering. You will then work better for me by practicalising your knowledge. You will be taught to fight. Now you will start working for me by reporting at 54th Brigade headquarters by 0800hrs tomorrow."

Adaka looked them over as if memorizing their names and faces and shaking hands with Njoku he left.

Njoku looked at the big bowl loaded with rice, stew and meat that Adaka had devoured without tasting the food. He discussed the important business that brought him as he wolfed down the food. He did not touch the beer or palm wine served but gulped down two mugs of water. He also discussed the incendiary and explosive nature of the Molotov bottles, wondering why they don't detonate sympathetically.

"Please work on this. If the bottles are made smaller for ease of conveyance and can detonate sympathetically then the only thing left to make it the most devastatingly effective conventional explosive is achieved."

Njoku just ate about a quarter of the meal served for him, Adaka and his aide. He was surprised to see the empty bowl that the aide returned with the empty water mug, empty beer bottle and empty palm wine bottle

"Does the A.D.C smoke?" he asked the steward.

"I don't think so sir. I offered him and he shook his head. They don't talk much."

Njoku stubbed out his cigarette and shut his mouth when he wanted to talk more as thoughts flew about his head:

"Yes he is a great soldier. An all rounder but he is insane. He can never be normal again. He wants to die and takes risks that he calls calculated. I am sorry that he has been through two severe traumas. I am truly sorry. I wish I could help. He was a good fellow before this mess erupted."

Njoku allocated transport for their conveyance to 54th Brigade.

Oguta sector was brimming with activities. Troop movements for both sides were crablike. Gain territory today loose even more tomorrow. Try flanking move in the morning hurry back in the evening to contain enemy counter. The dead and the wounded increased, as reinforcements arrived. All the medical units in and around the sector worked round the clock. Many were dying and being buried. The fury of the fighting rather than abate heightened with time. Both sides were determined. Monday Debekeme was making waves with the ridiculous navy, Volkswagen engines motorized his canoes in which were mounted light machine guns, bazookas, anti-tank grenades fired by SL rifles and anti-personnel grenades. During ceremonial parades that took place for propaganda purposes, the Biafran navy was beautifully attired in their immaculate whites, and blue arm bands and lanyards. Even their fleet of shinning gunboats with mounted guns and canoes exuded life as if raring to engage in battle. The beehive of activities on the quays was all part of the ploy. But for the machine gun bunkers and shore batteries the quays were normally empty of life. The gunboats were Nigerian navy boats knocked out and captured in battle. Some were sunk and later salvaged to decorate the quays. Attempts were made to repair service and re-commission them into active service but spare parts were not available. The research and production centers came up with spare parts that did not match and those that matched did not work. Further attempts were abandoned and they started doing the valiant window dressing jobs to deceive the enemy and jerk up the Biafran propaganda machinery. Foreign nations would think that a long drawn out war, costly in life and materials, could only be stopped by either recognizing Biafra or like Emperor Haile Salesie of Ethiopia suggested, press for speedy and peaceful resolution.

The boats did not work, and the guns on them were mainly painted scrap metals. Foreign journalists came, saw and left deceived. The real Biafran Navy were a few motorboats and canoes motored by Volkswagen engines, as designed and armed by army Colonel Idigo. He added specially made long and broad bladed machetes, with red scabbards, worn by the rag tag men of the navy to cut the picture of daredevil pirates. This worked very well against the over equipped, pampered and inexperienced Nigerian Navy. Their heads were loaded with theories of great sea battles, employing great guns, broadside barrages, depth charges, torpedoes and various types and calibers of deck guns. Surrenders, taking of prisoners and observing Geneva Convention agreements and treatment of war prisoners and battle codes brimmed around their skulls. They dreamt of merry ceremonies that attend exchange of war prisoners. They did not know that the fight was against a frightened, hungry, angry, sad, and desperate people that had not much to live for. The very successful propaganda machinery, headed by Okoko Ndem, ably assisted by Armand Odogwu and Chukwumerije did not leave the people with much hope. Pictures of slave like domination, iron fisted rule, torture, rape, scorn, and despise of people in areas that had fallen to the federal troops, made the free populace pray for death rather than fall into federal hands. Gruesome tales of dire combats and great offensives, with attacks and counter attacks always ended in valiant victories for the gallant Biafran army. These always sounded good, but disheartened the wizened Biafrans.

After such victories the guns always sounded closer, and situations in Biafra got more frantic, with refugees streaming helplessly in all directions. Every rout of the federal troops portended tighter conditions for Biafrans. Biafrans prayed for cessation of hostilities not either Biafran or Nigerian victories. The international communities were also taken in by the federal propaganda of love for the misguided easterners that cannot free themselves from the rascally, brutal, hard drinking and very wicked rebel soldiers. On the flip side they were deceived by the Biafran propaganda that depicted a balanced and equal military might, always hinting at special weapons, strategies, and connections that will shift the balance in her favour. The chaos was brewing.

The brutal Biafran pirate navy always sucked in the open-minded Nigerian boats, wiping out the naval crew and hauling the damaged boats ashore. The Nigerians who dreamt of Geneva war codes and exchange of prisoners never had a chance to see such niceties. The battle for Oguta was getting different from other battles where after days of heavy fighting a side capitulates and the victorious side digs in for a deserved rest after taking the territory. No side would give up. Deserters on the ill equipped Biafran side increased and companies of military police men sprouted everywhere well armed. They were deployed as the third defensive line along all routes leading into and out of Oguta. After the severe flogging that went with the punitive doubling of deserters they returned them re-armed to locations needing reinforcement. The ingenuity of deserters did not work this time because the bushes, hamlets, towns and villages, were well manned by the military policemen. Even officers were not allowed out of the sector. The wounded were treated and returned to unit or if the injury was a bit more serious, they were turned into couriers or amour bearers. Rank not withstanding except for the dying, or conceived very seriously wounded but saveable, nobody was allowed to leave the sector. A summons from army headquarters or state house was ignored and the holder returned to unit. This was the situation when Adaka's men crested the Awo-Idemili hill. Ekene who was scouting signaled the others following and they went for cover. Ekene dismounted and took his time urinating. At the checkpoint an officer with bushy beards but immaculately uniformed beckoned to him. He waved in response but still took his time. The officer sent a lanky NCO to bring Ekene to him. The NCO with gun at the ready walked jauntily to Ekene:

"Idiot what are you doing here with this fine bicycle and that new skeleton butt Madison 70 that is meant for senior officers?"

Ekene feeling and acting unperturbed spread both palms upward smiling widely.

"See" he said pointing to his right where Isaac and John were locked in mortal battle, a bag from which some mint quality Biafran currency notes poured lay beside them. Ekene peeped and saw the officer busy searching a ten-ton lorry.

"I will kill you if you don't show me where you buried the Nigerian notes!" John panted.

The military policeman ran to them smelling money and forgetting himself, his attempt to separate them ended in his hands being bound with strong ropes, and his mouth stuffed with a handkerchief and taped. He was hurried into the bush and Ekene also had time to mount and disappear the way he came.

Three clicks sounded and dismounting he entered a dark cocoa plantation on the left side of the road. All the other members of their group, including Kingsley and his men were seated there and smiling, within minutes John and Isaac dragged in the resisting sergeant.

"If he struggles again kill him." Nwosu ordered.

The sergeant stiffened and managed to show penitence and pleadings from the look in his frightened eyes.

"Tie his legs giving walking space and untie his hands. Remove the gag so that he does not choke. If he is right handed bind that hand to his belt."

"He was seen to be left handed for most of his often needed valuables like lighter, handkerchief, kola nuts and alligator pepper, were in his left pocket. His pen size sneak pistol was hidden in the left side of his waist."

His left hand was therefore tied to his belt on the left side. "Sit down" commanded Nwosu.

"We are Biafran soldiers and have an important assignment. We cannot afford to waste precious time with you military policemen. We want to use you to save your men. We will do that by making you guide us through to Ozubulu avoiding all the checkpoints. Is that clear to you?" Nwosu touched his ankle knife.

"Yes sir" answered the sergeant.

"But it must be at night because our men are scattered around all the villages in this Oguta sector to stop deserters, guard against infiltrators, and keep saboteurs in check. Infact sir, the instruction today is to shoot deserters and my boss is doing just that. At night they will relax and you can safely travel Sir."

He looked expectantly at Nwosu.

"Time is of the essence sir, so we will touch base before the Colonel" Fidelis said.

"In that case we have to take out the checkpoints. If they resist strongly apply whatever force you deem fit. Fidelis pick three men and take out this point. You have thirty minutes. The cackling butcher, Asuquo should not go with you."

Nwosu turned to Claudius saying: "Pick his brain; find out all he knows about the area and checkpoints so that with or without him our passage will be smooth and speedy. The Colonel will frown if we leave so many bodies behind. Go to work."

Fidelis looked at John, Isaac and Ekene, turned and vanished into the bush followed by the three. An hour and fifteen minutes later, Fidelis returned with a mortally shaken Captain Udechukwu, of the military police. He had called for an extra hour to do a better job. They dumped four large sacks of military police wears inclusive of face caps, arm bands, lanyards, belts, hip holsters, and pistols. The bearded Captain, who served under Adaka at Ehamufu, nearly had his windpipe slit before he understood Fidelis' seriousness. Having complied with the demands, and learning that Adaka was in command, he volunteered to guide them through. He provided three land rovers that would arrive before sundown. The others were arranging papers and fuel for the vehicles. Captain Udechukwu tried to make conversation with his mate but found him rather uncommunicative, but with a listening ear.

"I breached one of Adaka's laws. I talked out of turn and that boy nearly severed my gullet. I served under Adaka as a Corporal and continued with him to Ezamgbo, Okposi, Afikpo, and Uburu. We were doing assignments for shackled regiments. It was on one such assignment at Uburu that I was blown into a ditch by a mortar bomb. I learnt that they had successfully concluded the operation and returned to base when Adaka discovered that I was missing. Nobody confirmed me dead so picking up a platoon he came in search and saw me still bleeding in the ditch. He got me out and took me to a hospital. Adaka who saw to my field commission as second lieutenant also recommended my promotion to lieutenant, after my discharge from the hospital to the convalescent camp. I tried joining up with him but he turned me down declaring me non-combatant. His name got me into the military police and his discipline and adherence to orders got me promoted to Captain. I don't shave again because of the web of ugly cuts, scars, and keloid decorating my jaws, chin, neck and face. I am very pleased to be of any assistance I can."

When he paused, Nwosu quietly asked:

"Who told you about Adaka?"

Fidelis got up and moved toward Captain Nwosu. He made to talk but Nwosu's eyes stopped him.

"This boy sir" said Udechukwu "after he spared my life I commented that he moved like Adaka and but for his slight physique, carries the same air that I see you also carry. He answered that he is of Adaka's regiment. That is all he said and I started co-operating, and quit looking for a way out."

True to his promise some vehicles stopped nearby, just before six pm. Second Lieutenant Tim Anowi on observation point duty with corporal Eme showed his head and raised his right thumb to indicate that all was well. Almost at the same time three clicks sounded from the main road, which was answered by two clicks.

While Isaac was guarding the vehicle John glided in from the road and Ekene came in from the bush, beyond the rendezvous spot. Rather than take them all by surprise he saw Nwosu's gun barrel pointing up the left side of his chest. The new arrivals were clad in military police uniforms.

"Sergeant" Nwosu addressed the lanky military policeman:

"You will return to your checkpoint and release your colleagues who were bound and gagged for their own good." The sergeant nodded.

They pulled the MP uniforms over their own, and discarding their steel helmets they put on peaked caps and white berets. With everything in place, without an order passing to or from anybody, they ghosted out to the land rovers. Captains Nwosu and Udechukwu sat in the lead land rover and they pulled out. The journey to Akwukwu was smooth and uneventful in spite of the many checkpoints. They disembarked with their bicycles returning all the MP uniforms and equipments. John and Isaac asked for permission to retain four of the uniforms and were granted. Udechukwu dutifully saluted not knowing if Nwosu was a Captain or a Major. Nwosu raising an open palm and shaking same briefly, in a farewell bid, acknowledged this compliment. The land rovers left. Through the foot paths the men cycled into Oba with Ekene scouting. They rendezvoused at a clearing beside the Idemili stream south of the Brigade. Tim and Ekene set out to reconnoiter the area, and reported back to Nwosu after the brigade's tattoo roll call at 2000hrs. They made themselves comfortable on the trees and bushes around the brigade awaiting the Colonel's arrival.

Anara junction was as always a beehive of activities. The research and production, RAP, moved their headquarters to Anara when Okigwe got threatened. The Biafran Army Engineering Research Unit was stationed at Okwelle about five kilometers from the junction. The Air Force Helicopter base at Amaigbo junction was not far from the place. From Ikeduru down to Anara, army camps dotted the fifteen-kilometer stretch. Checkpoints were everywhere, but existed just for the purposes of extortion, and collection of tolls from weak-kneed soldiers on AWOL. It was chiefly a clearing point for stolen goods. Commodities were bartered, but monetary sales and purchases were also made. There were only two accepted currencies, the Nigerian currency and the Biafran currency. Business was transacted without questions being asked. The crowd heightened because refugees were then pouring in from the suburbs of Okigwe. Ike carefully drove through the crowd leaning on the sharp horn of the Vauxhall. He thought in his mind that the car had two very good aspects. The first was the powerful headlamps which would make any train turn green in envy and the second was the piercing horn, suggestive of a ship's bullhorn at work. He maneuvered the car into the RAP headquarters, where Colonel Adaka went in for a time consuming meeting with Engineer Roy Umenyi the explosives genius, who with Engr. Tim Ch Efobi manufactured the Ogbunigwe. This wonder weapon was supposed to bring the war to an end. When launched it had truly put the federal troops to flight in many sectors, until they discovered it was more bark than bite.

The noise and smoke that reverberated sounded and looked like an erupting volcano but was practically all there was to it. It was once known to have landed on a small cottage housing the federal troops. It broke through the zinc and roof and exploded on the dining table injuring some of the diners. The former fear of the Nigerians that it was a nuclear weapon was thus doused but the fame of the great RAP grew in leaps and bounds, in hopeful Biafra and apprehensive Nigeria. Roy welcomed Adaka and went into a windy monologue about new weapons capable of sinking Nigeria.

"If you remember sir that Nigeria a few years ago included Biafra and Republic of Benin you will not be in a hurry to sink Nigeria. I have come to make enquiries concerning one of your earlier products, the Molotov bottle. In a nutshell I would prefer if it could be made to detonate sympathetically, and if it can come in smaller bottles. We will engage in about six weeks from now and the offensive will be continuous not sporadic. Often we infiltrate an area or location, at great risk and have to take greater risk, dawdling to launch every bottle separately. The incendiary and explosive qualities meet expectations but the conveyance and separate detonation are a drawback. I think this can be remedied. Can I return in three weeks?" Adaka asked rising to evade another round of lectures on explosives and wonder weapons.

"No. Come back in five weeks. We need to source materials and test the product. I must however warn you that the model you require will carry less punch and be less stable. We will be ready when you come. I am rather busy and can't spare you any more time."

He turned to his flasks, test tubes, pipettes and jars. Adaka turned away smiling to his car. It was already getting late so he told Ike to head for 54th Brigade. They had no problems at the checkpoints, until he came to Ibiasoegbe. The military policemen were adamant to his rank and name. His ominous presence rather than coax assent, triggered challenge. The Lieutenant in charge of the checkpoint made a speech.

"Listen Officer, I don't know your rank but we are in the war front not AHQ and other rear bases. Your names, or rank that you are not wearing, mean nothing here. The instruction is to arrest anybody passing out of this sector and return such a person to the nearest forward location. You and your driver will join the reinforcement to Oguta this night. I will keep the car for you until you return."

He drank gleefully from a beer bottle half full with raffia palm gin. His men had their guns at the ready and appeared eager to use them.

Ike saw some bodies lying beside the road. He made a mental note of the first two to die by knife, before he would have space for the Thompson machine gun to speak. He quietly eased his door open, took out both ankle knives and under cover of a raucous cough he cocked the Thompson. He blew his nose into a brown handkerchief that covered the short blade in his left hand. Adaka climbed out of the car, brought out a signal and pushing it at the Lieutenant said harshly;

"This is from the Commander-in-Chief. Read it. It empowers me to kill any known or perceived enemy of Biafra."

The inebriated Lieutenant had never seen an order or signal from the Commander-in-Chief. In curiosity, he stretched out his hand to take and read the signal. Iron fists clasped his wrists, flung him about using him as a shield and the right hand fluidly produced a long barreled black pistol. His men on turning to them both to ascertain the true situation looked into a deadly weapon held in a rock steady hand. Meanwhile a thin blade pierced through the broad signal sheet, painfully touching his Adam's apple. The little distraction was enough for Ike to dash out of the car and slash the throat of the most eager of the two MP's covering him. The left hand knife was almost at the throat of the second person who in fright tried to fall back when Adaka said: "No"

Ike restrained and curved his thrust and the knife slid into the shoulder of the man. The man shrieked falling to his knees, his fallen gun abandoned. Ike, Thompson in hand, kicked him unconscious. The other six had their hands raised over their heads. Adaka backed against a mango tree having the officer in tow.

"Those bodies, who were they?" he asked, "Deserters sir" the Lieutenant answered.

"So they were Biafran soldiers, and you killed them?" Adaka asked. "Sir, the Provost Marshall gave the order" he answered.

"How many are they?" Adaka asked. "Twelve sir" answered the oldest of them all.

"Since this morning sir, some of them were wounded, and some of them sick."

"Shut up" ordered the lieutenant remembering his authority. "Who shot them?" Adaka pursued.

The old MP with crooked kola stained teeth answered:

"The lieutenant and that dead Theodore, I told them that anybody who kills like that will die in the war but they laughed at me."

"Ike kill him."

Adaka withdrew the knife and the lieutenant ran. Ike slowly looked at him and flicked his right hand. A long blade outran the lieutenant embedding itself under his left armpit. Like the stag he slipped onto the ground and into eternal darkness.

"You others, return to unit, and tell your unit Commander that Adaka sends his compliments. He should ensure that the deceased families are informed, and the bodies buried adequately."

Ike drove down the road and Adaka vanishing into the bush, soon appeared beside the now stationary but steaming car. He entered and they drove off. The circuitous route and bad roads slowed them down such that they arrived in Oba at about midnight. Ike stopped at the Girls Secondary School and Adaka alighted with some of his gear and said:

"0645hrs at the Commander's Office remember a clap for a cough or vice versa."

He stepped into the bush while Ike continued into the brigade. There the dutiful brigade guards insisted on searching everything and everywhere. Although Ike did not mind the bother at the gate he was relaxed, knowing that he had reached his destination.

Ekene who was ensconced on a tree close to the gate however, did mind the embarrassment. When by the growl of the car before the engine idled in neutral he scanned the car, he saw that the Colonel was not in the car and that Ike looked fatigued. He slithered down the tree and crawled further into the bush. He began cackling like a king cobra. The guards at once lost interest in the car. They stoked the fire giving them warmth and light. Every one of the guards put on his boot and cocked his riffle. The deadly king cobra's bite had no cure. Ike drove off smiling. 'The boys are already here' he thought. When the cackling stopped the guards felt the snake had moved on and away from them. They tried to relax although still casting furtive glances at the bushes. Ekene happily sought another bed. The morning dew forced him to unwrap the McIntosh spread and use it to cover himself. Two hours later the grating sound of an aged pickup van disturbed his sleep. He crawled closer when voices started rising, and learnt that the new arrivals were engineers requisitioned from 5th Brigade by Colonel Adaka.

"Colonel Adaka asked us to report to him by 0800hrs at 54th Brigade headquarters Oba. If this is 54th Brigade headquarters Oba, then we are at the right place. You can look over the vehicle but not open boxes, jars or cans. These are volatile materials for our work." Sergeant Christopher that did not look a day older than sixteen explained.

"Rubbish" said the guard commander.

"We search everything, even if it is Colonel Enwe or Nkita that you are reporting to. Infact you are under arrest. There is only one

Colonel here and you come insulting my intelligence. I was in the University when the war broke out."

The riffles were leveled at the engineers, and they wisely acquiesced to the guard commander's instruction. They marched to the guardroom. The driver was disarmed and kept at the gatehouse. When the guard commander returned he summoned him and ordered him to open the boxes in the vehicle.

"No sir. I won't touch anything there. I want to survive the war."
"Shut up and do as I say or . . ." shrieked the commander.

"Or what sir? I will face anything but an explosive death. I witnessed a ten-ton Mercedes 911 lorry blown to rubbles, taking out three buildings near it. There was a lot of blood and charred flesh around for days."

"Alright don't touch anything. Drive the car under that Iroko tree and park there until we sort out this minor problem."

The guard commander gratuitously gave quarters.

"I can't do that sir. The engineers are not here to control their chemicals, so I will not even step near the vehicle."

The guards nearest the vehicle hurriedly created space, between them and the van. Nwosu and Fidelis who had been summoned by Ekene strained not to laugh. Beaming smiles covered by their forearms as they enjoyed the mischievous drivers' play.

The guard commander got confused.

"What then do we do? We can't leave the van blocking the entrance" his brow furrowed.

"You are right sir. We can't leave it here. As an Officer, sir, and having been in the University before the war, I humbly suggest that you use your authority and knowledge to drive it and park it anywhere you want. It may not explode at once."

His humility and genuine attempt at finding a solution to the problem at hand, showed in his face.

"You idiot, I was only commissioned last month, and I was studying History, not Engineering or Nuclear and atomic Physics. Do you want me to die? If your stupidity will not allow you to contribute sensibly then shut up" the guard commander fumed.

"Yes sir. I am sorry sir. The Commander Colonel Adaka will be here any moment from now. He was right behind us when we passed Ozubulu. He will be able to defuse the explosives in the van and drive it off the way. He is not a very wicked man and does not shoot or put people in guardrooms. His only punishment as I saw was to send those that fall short of his standard to join the vandals in the Republic of Benin. He calls it going to learn sense at the best school of infantry. Although severely wounded and declared non-combatant people have been known to return alive" the driver continued.

The guard officer who bent his head in thought looked with blistering hate at him.

"Idiot can't you shut up? OK, you corporal take him to the guardroom and tell them to lock him up. Tell them to release those engineers at once. He looked at the ranking NCO on guard and added:

"That fool was driving me mad with his foolish talk." He brought out a cigarette, his lighter appeared and he was in the process of lighting the cigarette, when the NCO dove into the gutter for cover. Herd mentality prevailed and they were all in the gutter when somebody asked what the matter was? Another asked if the Adaka had come? A third asked if the Adaka was a person or a real baboon.

The NCO pointed at the van and said:

"Sir that is highly inflammable and like the driver said I want to survive the war."

The officer threw away the cigarette and lighter and started shaking. They refused to leave the gutter. Nwosu waved Fidelis away and rising walked to the post with Ekene, he said:

"Come here all of you. Where are the engineers and the driver?"

"I am very sorry Colonel, they said they had a long drive and would like to freshen up, and refresh with, I mean refreshments. I will bring them now sir."

The guard officer turned and ran into the camp. He met the engineers coming back and told them to hurry for the Colonel was waiting, and continued. At the guardroom he released the driver and advised him to run to the gate for the baboon was there. He plunged further into the compound and hid.

The engineers and driver hurried to the gatepost hoping to see Colonel Adaka. They saw Nwosu dressed exactly like Adaka in jungle combat dress. In size and physique they were alike but this looked like a less potent replica of the real Adaka.

"Get into your van and drive in. Camp around your van after all it is almost morning. Turning to the humourist he asked: Driver, what is your name, rank and unit?"

Nwosu looked appreciatively at him while Ekene squirmed in suppressed laughter.

"I am Corporal Nathaniel Egwuenu of the supply and transport department, temporarily attached to the fifth brigade Biafran army" he stiffened in respect.

"See me before returning to your unit. I will be there when you keep your appointment with the Colonel." He turned and slid quietly into the cassava farm and Ekene still shaking in mirth walked down the beaten path to the Idemili River.

Six am saw Adaka's men positioned discreetly around the Brigade Commander's Office. The Intelligence Officer, Lieutenant Muturu, walking with a limp and favoring a right hand still in cast, knocked frantically on the commanders' door. The door opened and the commanders' aide surveyed him from over a green towel. Muturu knew that a cocked pistol was peering at his heart from behind the towel.

"I wish to see the commander immediately" he appeared jittery and on edge.

"The commander can hear you. Talk, he is listening."

"This is Intelligence matters, and for his ears only" Muturu insisted. "If it has to do with the lady ghost, he is not interested. If it is of military importance, speak and don't waste my time." The aide spoke harshly. "My men reported strange military types around this camp. During the night two strange vehicles came into this camp. There was much problem at the gate. They can be spotted around the camp trying to look like they belong."

"Lieutenant you can go. Relax and do nothing. They are part of the troop mobilization here." Awoni spoke from the toilet.

Muturu shrugged and left. At 0640hrs Awoni stepped out briskly and walked to his office. At the entrance he met Adaka. Their eyes locked. About five minutes elapsed before they both started and acknowledged the compliments of aides and provosts. They nodded and entered the office. The aides stayed out. Even the clerk who was cleaning the office suspended the job.

"You smell badly." Awoni said.

"I have not had a bath since the day before yesterday. I brought in more men and will see five engineers by eight this morning."

He went near the window and clapped. A cough sounded and Ike came in.

"Get Nwosu" he ordered.

Nwosu padded in coming to attention to honour the other Colonel.

"Interview the engineers that will report here this morning and find them accommodation. We will use them. Tell Idigo that I am here. Keep the men on leash. No incidents."

He turned away dismissing Nwosu. Nwosu still stood unmoving which surprised Adaka. He faced Nwosu questioningly.

"I will suggest we retain the driver that brought the engineers. He is a man of parts and has guts. With just words he turned the officer and men on guard to jelly. I will give details later." Nwosu finished.

"That is fine. I will see him later. Keep him in sight so that he doesn't go back to familiar territory."

"Thank you sir" Nwosu said and left.

"We will go to my apartment to remove the smell and feed you. We can talk or think after that."

Awoni opened a drawer in his table and withdrew a bottle of Irish Cream. As they left, Colonels Idigo, Oboyo, and Dennis ascended the steps up to the porch. They halted a respectful distance away and executed a parade ground salute. Awoni responded although he knew it was more for Adaka than for him. Adaka looked at them without expression. He felt like embracing them in joy but restrained himself. Anything he touched got spoilt, and in the same vein anybody he loved died either physically, mentally or psychologically. He was tired of destroying people with his odd love. He saw brilliant, cynical, strong, and knowledgeable Iloma, beautiful, lithe, happy, joyful, fun loving Olivia, and energetic, inventive, experimenting and hilarious Awoni.

His mind went back to his first love Christie Gbalite, who died during houseman ship, immediately they decided to get married. This forced him to seek a military career. He remembered his father who was cycling home to join his family in the celebration of his University admission, and full government scholarship, he never got home. The bursar of the government college at Ughelli mistook him for a grass cutter and swung to the roadside to kill him. He died instantaneously.

When the drinks cleared from the head of the bursar, he cried ceaselessly. The pain was more because Ekwosimba was his classmate, drinking partner, town's man and bosom friend. In the boot of the car he had a goat that he was taking to Ekwosimba's house as his own contribution to the celebration of the admission, and scholarship of his best friend's son. After all he was his guardian through school at Government College, so he was his son also. Weeping through the wake keeping service and funeral, he lapsed into a mournful frown. After the burial he handed one hundred pounds to Ekwosimba's wife urging her to use it to look after her family, and to remain friends with his family. He drove off. Cutting through town slowly taking in the views ruminatively, he headed for the Ikor River, a tributary of the river Ethiope. He parked beside the road, and sat in his car for hours. To onlookers and passersby he appeared to be enjoying a quiet drink and appreciating the serene beauty of the setting sun which painted the environment a rusty brown. Like cold water down the spine the cool evening breeze turned cold. He emptied the last bottle of Gordon's Dry Gin, closed his car door and walked down the river bank. The Ijaw beach dwellers saw him and felt he was visiting a medicine man or scouting for cheap fresh fish, just caught and brought in by canoes. He did not respond to the greetings of those he passed by. His slow walk was purposeful, until he turned out of sight behind the mangrove trees bounding the wider and deeper side of the river. Brabra the net maker, and bone mender, widely sought after by accident victims in the whole of Ughelli, looked after him. It irked him that his teacher, who he was sure, was not as rich as himself, would disregard him and neglect his salutation. He was deeply grieved because he had mended the leg of the man's son, broken in a testy football match between Government College Ughelli and Emevor Grammar School. He had charged him a very small fee because he shared a drink with him every time he called to reassess and treat the wounded leg. He thought they had become drinking partners as they indiscriminately swapped stories of deep drinking and frolicking with the girls. Now when he thought the friendship was getting tighter, he snubbed him, before his folks and low life friends as if he did not exist. He remembered boasting to his low life friends, who saw him as their hero that he had moved higher in life and that though he would not forget them, he would from then on spend more time with the Senior Service section of the society. He was still thinking and planning how to retaliate for the insult when it occurred to him that the man was staying too long. He went to the groove which led to nowhere, and it was empty. He ran back asking the others there if the man had come back, but they said they did not see him, moreover that his car, which was well known in the town, was still there. A cry was raised by Brabra, who led men in canoes, to search, the waters near the bank.

They dived, and used bamboos to rake the river bed until late that night. Brabra wailing like a child, ran to the Police station to lodge a complaint, and there he met the wife and son of Celestine Nwankwo Iloma. The desk sergeant was telling them that it was too early to file a missing persons report. He advised them to come in towards the evening of the next day, if he still had not returned. His tear filled eyes, and sorrowing mind were shut to his surroundings that he did not see them, even though they sat a few yards away from him.

"My friend, teacher Iloma has fallen into the Ikor River. We have searched since seven o'clock this evening, and my people are still searching. He has not been found. Come at once."

He sniffed, coughed, blew his nose, and putting both hands on his head, he began wailing again.

Iloma's wife and son ran to him and held him. "Where?" they both asked.

The desk sergeant did not wait to follow procedure:

"How did you know that he fell into the river? Let us go now. Which part of the river? Corporal, take over. Writer please come with me."

The answers to the questions were not in the order the questions were asked, but the howling Brabra supplied the answers in between sobs and howls and mumbles. The desk sergeant, a tribesman of Iloma who had many times benefited from Iloma's hunting prowess, mounted his bicycle and rode out to the bridge. He stood his bicycle beside Iloma's car and ran down the bank to the shores. Fires were lit and burning to give warmth to the men that dove in search of the bursar. Oil lamps, kerosene lanterns, and torches lighted the beach such that there was no darkness. A group of men were standing in front of the illicit gin sellers' shack, some were kneeling and massaging a pot-bellied man, lying face up on the ground. Two men were kneading his feet, legs and thighs. One was gently pressing the stomach while another was pressing the chest with vigor. A small fire smoking and smelling of the leaves of chosen medicinal plants used to revive unconscious people was burning near his head. The desk sergeant stepped into the crowd, identified Iloma and shoved the man who was working on the chest aside, and applied all the first aid knowledge from the Southern Police College Ikeja. He was tiring when Brabra led others there and relieved him. He also did everything he knew including forcing illicit gin down his throat and nostrils.

Nothing worked. It was past midnight when the station officer arrived in the station's land rover. He did not waste time asking questions. The body was taken to the hospital and the police driver took home Iloma's wife and son. The Resident Medical Officer was waiting when they arrived. He did not need a second look to confirm that death had occurred. He certified Iloma dead and they conveyed him to the mortuary. A week later, the local St Paul's Church, brimming with personalities from Warri, Sapele, Burutu, Forcados, was the venue of the funeral service, which progressed solemnly.

Mournful dirges filled the air. The ordinarily soulful performance of the organist got so mournful that many of the choristers of the church choir chocked tearfully. The Reverend Agoriwe from St Andrews Church Warri mounted the pulpit purposefully. Looking sternly at the congregation he spoke as if they had made him very angry.

"The question now is who are we burying today? Iloma or Ekwosimba. Last week my friend Ekwosimba was laid to rest, and I was battling with malaria in hospital. Discharged, I billed to be here this Sunday to console the family. I am here this Friday, instead of consoling the family, to lay his best friend to rest, at the same church and the same cemetery. My mind has milled out many sermons for today. I can't remember any of them. I have officiated in many funeral services but today I am tongue tied. I knew these two very well. As a young priest I wedded both of them. I baptized all their children.

I have eaten many meals with them, and have preached many sermons to them about the vice of drinking and the demon of alcohol. I confess that I have shared some drinks with them. I also confess that I have been jealous of their friendship.

I wanted to be a part of them, to make them look up to me for spiritual guidance, and as close to me as they were to each other. I failed for I found them as inseparable as the biblical David and Jonathan.

I thought that no friendship will surpass that but now I know better. Death separated David and Jonathan. It could not separate Iloma and Ekwosimba. In my mind I know that this is stronger. I have thought of Saul and Jonathan not separated in death, but it is not the same thing. They were in life, not such great friends. I thought of Romeo and Juliet, and my mind says fiction is fiction, not fact. Take this as the funeral sermon. Love one another and be close. There will be faults, arguments and misunderstandings, but love, the God-like kind, by which he gave his only begotten son, covers all. Love, don't hate. Love, love, love   " and the tears were cascading down his eyes and cassock, from red eyes.

"Whatever anybody says, hints at suicide notwithstanding, as a servant of God I tell you this. Iloma and Ekwosimba flew on the wings of love to heaven, where I am sure that they are filled to the brim with love, and ministering to God with the twenty-four elders. Today's texts are:—1 Samuel 18:1-4, John 3:16. God bless us all with love as we send off our friends Iloma and Ekwo in this solemn ceremony."

He executed the sign of the cross and descended from the pulpit.

There was no dry eye in the church, and all the cars, motorcycles and bicycles remained parked in the church premises as the whole congregation followed the hearse to the cemetery.

"The Lord gives and the Lord takes away. These have sourjourned on this earth as pilgrims and left their mark. They left a large footprint on the sands of time. The footprint of love enduring and inseparable love, they have fought a good fight and have left the stage for other performers to endeavor to do better. We will now conclude the funeral rites by laying the bodies to rest."

Reverend Agoriwe removed his spectacles and wiped his balding head and face with a white handkerchief. He cleaned and polished the glasses meticulously, while the choir led the congregation in an even more mournful "Peace perfect peace"

"Sand to sand, dust to dust, ashes to ashes, the Lord gives and the Lord takes away, the body returning to the dust from which it was made, and the spirit to the Creator and owner of the world" he droned on and on until the choir discreetly took over. An attempt at hilary by the choir's rendition of "Stand up stand up for Jesus...' 'Onward Christian Soldiers...' 'When the saints go marching in..." did not affect the heavy air. They switched to "Be thou my guardian and my guide..', 'Thy will be done Oh Lord..', Thy will not mine Oh Lord.." stuttered to a mumbling close. The choir tired and the even more mournful wail of the siren of the hearse, replaced the quietness of the march back to the church. There were not much of greetings, salutations, embraces, or interaction as the congregation dispersed. There was food for thought and everyone, the children inclusive, all mulled on it. The Reverend gentleman had quoted Mathew chapter seven, verse one through five, wondering why instead of loving one would go against the Master's instruction by judging. The reverend had even admitted to drinking alcohol, and also said nothing about the empty bottles of gin found in Iloma's car or the suicide allegation.

The churchyard emptied fast. Even the mischievous children who will not allow an opportunity pass without attacking the church orchard's guava, mango, almonds, tangerine, and oranges forgot the fruits. The sexton normally turned a blind eye to the children's antics by forgetting to lock the church gate. This Friday he did not even push the gate close so the children did not need to push it open as on other days. The wheezing whistle of the weaver birds increased the eerie quietness that suggested ghosts were assembling for a meeting. The children looked longingly towards the orchard, but lacked the courage to approach it. They went home hoping for a day that ghosts will not meet, especially the ghosts of drowned people or accident victims. Love or no love, ghosts were ghosts and given to slapping and knocking people.

Awoni learnt of the double tragedy from both Adaka and Iloma. He heard the story and others from a disoriented and tearful Adaka, on his discharge from the military hospital as he carried him to the hilltop army convalescent camp, Enugu. He visited him a number of times and on the last visit explained that they would not see again.

"I have told you all about me. You now know the truth. We won't be friends anymore. If we continue, you will die and if you die I will have no excuse not to go like Iloma's father. I don't want that so we part today in spirit. We meet no more except military duty calls, and even then no personal interaction. I am sorry for destroying this good thing we had going."

He was weeping shamelessly as he left. All eyes were on them and shocked at the height of emotion expressed.

"Listen Adaka you are always right, your judgment is often sound and right but this time you are wrong. Christie Gbalite died of hepatitis when the medical world was still not sure of its treatment. Iloma died taking on a barrack of soldiers. Soldiers are trained to fight and he died fighting. What is odd or unusual about it? You married a good and normal girl and the pogrom put her in the path of that illiterate drunken psychopath, Dauda. The trauma of what she encountered blanked her out and it will pass with time. How is it your fault? That I went to rescue her and her confused mind mistook me for Dauda cannot be your fault. Why are you trying to destroy yourself? Relax my friend. Time will heal everything. Iloma will not want us separated. Why are you doing this?"

Adaka clamped his mouth shut and entered the taxi that took him there. The taxi drove off and Awoni stood looking after it weeping. As if from a deep sleep he started and rushed to the camp commandant's office. The commandant was leaving when he limped in and requested to use the telephone.

"Is it to call your homosexual lover? He has just left and it will take some time before he reaches the base. You can use the phone but stop crying."

The Captain turned away. Iron fists dug into the collar of his tunic and his one hundred and eighty pounds of flesh sailed over the balcony, onto the flower bed. Easily scaling the balcony, Awoni placed the heel of his right foot on the throat of the prone Captain.

"But for your wife and children, I will just crush your throat and spare human ears of the rot that comes out of your mouth. Next time you die." He withdrew his foot and the commandant got up slowly. He could not talk at once, so he waved Awoni into his office to use the phone. Awoni spent some ten minutes trying to convince RSM Jude that Adaka would attempt suicide. Jude was convinced and spoke with Lt. Col. Njoku snr. He in turn called in the Division Intelligence Officer. A short meeting rejected the suggestion of arrest, guardroom, house arrest or a rebuke. Medical attention was agreed to be the best option. The meeting was breaking up when Major Nzogwu walked in and was briefed by Colonel Njoku. "I beg to defer sir" said Nzogwu

"I agree with the twenty-four hour surveillance, but what he needs now is action to keep his mind and body busy. We are already planning the defense of our northern borders. The best thing is to co-opt him and draft him to anywhere it erupts first. He will not stop thinking of dying, which is the end result of suicide. He will think of taking others with him while dying. Leave him to me. He is a good soldier and will not take much to turn aright. If you accept, I will arrange for him to receive the signal this night."

Nzogwu's hands folded across his chest waiting. Colonel Njoku sighed in relief, the problem having been lifted off his shoulders.

"It's alright major, handle as you see fit."

He arose and responding to their salutes, left. Nzogwu's theory proved right and Adaka metamorphosed into a rare mix, a lethal soldier and a good commander and motivator of men.

"Oboyo, take over, I may not be in a position to do any work for some hours. Tell Ike to wake me when I should wake."

His eyes were glazed and pain filled. He walked with a slow heavy and shuffling gait, appropriate for someone three times his age. Awoni led him to his billet and pointed out the bathroom to Adaka. Without much ado, he ordered rice and stew with fried plantain.

"Use bush meat for the stew, and tell my batman to go to Ose and buy fresh raffia palm wine. It must be very sweet."

They were left alone, and the tears began to flow. "We failed Iloma" mumbled Adaka tearfully.

"We did not" said Awoni with tears coursing down his cheeks.

"We swore to defend and protect ourselves. We did it during the confusion at Katanga. Just the three of us stopped the Kasavubu and Moitshe Tsombe troops and their allies. We gave respite to the enveloped United Nations' peace-keeping troops across the Nkanga River. I was lost in the thorn bushes west of the Nkanga River, located by the Tshombe group, pinned down by the Kasavubu men and running out of ammunition and physical strength, in the one-man last stand that spanned fifteen hours. Against orders, you pulled out of your duty post in the U.N location, and crossed the rushing Nkanga River to cut me out of the closing crossfire established by the Kasavubu and Tsombe troops. You even carried my tired body through the thorns and over the Nkanga, to the secured U.N location. I survived because you acted fast and intuitively. If I had done the necessary I would have met you in Kano and made enough impact in the skirmish to keep Iloma alive. I would have covered his back, but I was sitting back lazily at the division, waiting for you to do my work for me. I failed the two of you."

Adaka railed on adamantly.

"You did not. It was already late for you to catch up with us, when you arrived at the division from Ibadan. Iloma took the heroic last stand and executed the worthy exit, taking more than a platoon of soldiers. What more can you want? He even took more soldiers than our mentor Kaduna Nzogwu. What else do you want? We have the opportunity to punish the genocidal madmen with our rank and command. We have thousands of men to mould and use to punish the Nigerian army, for allowing it to be used against itself. Who ever heard of soldiers killing unarmed comrades and burying many alive? Or soldiers raping their comrades' wives, and killing their kith and kin, instead of protecting their nation's territory? Well we have fought our way to the position to really hand out some telling blows, even if our efforts don't help the experiment called Biafra to survive. Please don't fall apart. If you do it will mean that Iloma left and you abandoned me. Pull yourself together. We have a job to do."

Awoni held onto Adaka's glazed eyes with his wet and sorrowful ones. Six hours later, after pouring out their hearts and minds, the two sat to a hearty meal of rice, stew and bush meat, with kegs of raffia palm wine that boasts of minimal alcoholic content. They talked far into the night, never again mentioning Iloma or Olivia. They shaved, bathed, with reminiscences and ruminations, on plans, targets and strategies. Five thirty saw Adaka dressed in full combat gear and eating from a bowl full of oranges. Awoni leaned up from the bed on his right elbow:

"Are you going anywhere today?" he asked.

"No" replied Adaka "I will address all my men mobilizing here and start preparing for our strikes. Over a hundred targets have been suggested, and about the most likely twenty-five reconnoitered. Peripheral patrols start today prior to deep behind the line patrols. The strikes start five weeks from today, give or take one week."

He drank cold water from a large jug. At 0600hrs he gave a shrill bird-like whistle and immediately an answering replica came from the door. Adaka stepped out to see Ike leaning against the balustrade.

"Good morning Colonel" Ike greeted without saluting.

"Good morning Ike. I would like to see Idigo, Oboyo and Dennis in an hour."

He moved into the open compound and walked the long legged athlete's walk around the brigade commander's office until Awoni arrived at the office. Oboyo, Idigo and Dennis arrived Awoni's office, thirty minutes later. Formalities were quickly dispensed with and a round table conference that included Awoni began. The agenda was:
"Strike targets"

Suggestions were made, thoroughly debated and either discarded or kept in view. At about 1650hrs, feeling fagged out they took a well-deserved rest. During the recess, Adaka forbade any military discourse. Dennis took the floor, spewing ribald and rib quaking jokes that forced genuine mirth and loud hilarious laughter, from even the most taciturn of them. The refreshment that cannot be described as light by any length of imagination, made them want to answer the call of nature. They freshened up and reconvened at 2000hrs. The targets were agreed. Colonel Dennis, coordinating, read out his notes.

"Target one is to clear the Onitsha, Anam, Ogbaru and Abala stretch of the river Niger of Nigerian presence. Their gunboats patrolling the area make sneak attacks impossible.

Target two is to take out Nigerian Navy base and army transit camp at Onoghono.

Target three is to clear the Ozeh hills' artillery guns that have pinned down all the Biafran regiments around Onitsha and its suburbs.

Target four is to blow the Agbor Bridge, to slow down Nigerian reinforcement.

Target five is to sporadically attack Nigerian army bases at Otuocha, Umueze, Anam, Oroma-Etiti, Mmiata Anam, Nzam, Igbokenyi, and Aboh camp, Ika, Ugeh, Aya and Ozugono.

Target six is to connect Omoh, from liberated Otuocha and make the Federal positions south west of Nsukka untenable.

Target seven to secure the Omamballa River and use it to open supply lines to the Biafran troops cut off by the Enugu-Awka stretch, heavily secured by the Federal troops.

Target eight is to break off and attend to Biafran distress calls and special duties.

Target nine is to unrelentingly continue the guerrilla attacks on Nigerian army bases at Ebor, Illa, and Agada.

Target ten is to re-establish links with the vandals and mobilize them for pre-emptive attacks to open grounds for deep and far-reaching strikes.

"We will give priority to these in order of need."

Dennis looked up from his notes and turned to Adaka expectantly.

"I have not had time to consider targets or plans. We will, I am sure be hearing from Idigo who has been around and conducted series of Reece patrols. Let us hear from you Colonel."

Adaka leaned back opening his note-book. Idigo leaned forward without looking at the thick file and note pads before him.

"I think it is best to adjourn at this point, and through the Chief of Defence Staff summon Colonel Ifenso, who hails from this riverine area. He was in command of the eighteenth, twenty-first and twenty-seventh battalions, which kept the Federal troops busy along these areas. He has also liased between us, and our troops behind enemy lines in these areas. He knows these target areas and the natives. He is the ace we will require for priority and planning. Clearing the river Niger of Federal presence need not be classed a target. I have assessed the situation and don't consider it difficult to achieve. I have conducted reconnaissance patrols through these areas to as far as Igbokenyi. Our men have infiltrated these targets and are doing a good job of familiarizing themselves with the troops there. I personally planted them all and gave them vague local identities. We can clear the river Niger in one week. We are well planted in their repair and maintenance workshops, so the barges, ships, and gun-boats can be taken out in one night. By that I mean any night we choose. The Agbor Bridge was mined last week, when we chose it as a target. Our men are in Nsugbe seeking ways of penetrating Ozeh. Tunneling is impossible. The area is too rocky. Infiltration and sabotage are the most obvious options. I have also dispatched patrols in these towns. Except for emergencies they will start reporting in by weekend. That is the extent of work already done by me."

Idigo leaned back and pouring cold water from the large jug into a glass drank it down.

They sieved Idigo's report, asking pertinent questions. Fully satisfied they agreed to commence operations the following week, after picking Colonel Ifenso's brain. The meeting broke up at 2220hrs. Dennis went in search of the signals officer on duty to seek authority for and dispatch the signals to summon Colonel Ifenso. Idigo was ordered to give details of his plans to clear the river Niger. The detailed plan should include ordnance requirements and logistic support. Total reinforcement expectation was from the 54th brigade. Colonel Awoni should therefore put his brigade on blue alert.

"Oboyo, I suggest you see these new engineers and their odd driver with me so that we can asses what use to put them to. Their knowledge of explosives should be put to work in our planned massive and extensive demolition jobs. We meet with them at0900hrs this morning."

He turned to leave and Awoni said quickly:

"I will like to be in on everything from now on. After the failure of Hiroshima and Zero Four operations, the Ozeh artillery guns have pinned us down. My men need the retraining that happened at 12th Division to improve. Collectively we can upgrade their fighting status to above average in a short while. After all I am supposed to supply the reinforcements in men. I will pick out twenty-five of my engineers, with heart and brains. I trained a special squad of twelve grenade lobbing and bazooka experts. They have accounted for over thirty ferret cars, Saladin cars and Salacin troop carriers. I fully support your operations and will participate fully, combat wise."

Awoni smiled as Adaka nodded agreement. They dispersed quietly their aides falling in behind them as they sought their billets. Adaka walked south of the camp with Ike slightly ahead of and to the right of him. Awoni looked after him and remembered their Filipino instructor boasting that since after his training on jungle warfare, when he was a second lieutenant, he had never slept in a house. He was then a Major, and had fought five different wars spanning twenty-five years. Adaka is trying to be like the gaunt, soulless wretch. He moved to his apartment, and pulling off his boots and beret, fell into a dreamless sleep.

That morning they met the engineers, and were thrilled with close to magical demonstrations of explosives. The engineers could produce gunpowder and use the powder to mould all types of explosives. Designing mines and projectiles seemed their strong point. They used even mud, chewing gum, garri paste, pounded yam or cassava to design potent explosives. They designed small and miniature mines capable of being hidden behind leaves, fruits branches and tree trunks as anti-personnel weapons. These they had effectively used to stop the determined march of the federal troops, to link all of Mbaise to Owerri and Okpalla junction without much fighting. The federal troops had been mined to a stand still. Most of their injuries were shattered knees, shins or ankles. The face, eyes, jaws, chin, cheeks and inevitably the mouth, had come close second in the region of more injury. The omen to the soldiers appeared weird and cooled their enthusiasm to fight. Colonel Njoku jr. had time to practice his first love, which remained explosives engineering. Even the gift of a handkerchief from him was always suspected. His men showed that he had put in much work to train them. Adaka and the others were very impressed. Dennis kept up a running commentary on the great potentials of the numerous designs tried and tested. His parrotty excitement made the onlookers except Adaka and Awoni, to laugh almost nonstop. Major Ozor the brigade major, Lieutenant Colonel Chiananti Nwalusi, the assistant brigade commander, and Captain Benji Ikeakor commanding the brigade's engineering unit, could barely stand straight for laughter. Dennis was at his best, but found a quieter side-kick in Corporal Nathaniel Egwu who enlarged the Colonel's humorous remarks with even more humorous wisecracks. The corporal caught Colonel Adaka's dead fish eyes a few times and tried to hold his tongue. This was not easy so he hit a compromise by lowering his voice. The engineers rounded up and were dismantling their equipment when Adaka spoke:

"You corporal, you drove the engineers here?" he asked.

Corporal Nathaniel Egwu stiffened to attention and saluted smartly "By the grace of God and authority of the licensing office, I am the driver sir."

Awoni winced, fury shadowing his face. Adaka remained expressionless for a short while. He shook his head as if casting off something unpleasant.

"You will return to your unit this afternoon with your van. Colonel Dennis will make out the orders."

Adaka pulled on his beret.

"On jet wings sir, my heart is not carved out for war. I suffer from systolic murmur when explosives explode around me and diastolic rumble when I touch a riffle. Thank you very much sir."

Every one burst out laughing. Adaka smiled but Awoni pinned him down with two red eyes bursting with anger:

"If I hear your voice again I will carve out that your cursed heart. Get out of here."

"Easy Colonel" said Oboyo

"If you remember the fools Isaac and John when we arrived at the twelfth division, you will see the potential before you. Post him to Colonel Idigo, like the other two he will turn him into what we need. He will be good."

"OK" said Adaka placing a restraining hand on Awoni. "Ensure that the van returns to 5th brigade tonight." They dispersed.

Training started with frenzy. Adaka's over three hundred and fifty troops were scattered amongst the 54th brigade troops deployed in the first and second defensive locations. The commanders, from squad leaders through to battalion commanders met daily with Oboyo and Adaka for one week of intensive training course on becoming good soldiers. Awoni never missed the sessions and only contributed when directly asked to. Training intensified, and Kingsley demonstrated his uncanny expertise with the machine guns whether heavy or light. He could dominate an area of more than one thousand feet radius with heavy machine gun fire. He could set up unmanned machine gun nests, and make them fire sporadically at his will and command. He could also create mobile machine gun nests. He demonstrated that one man could operate as many as ten machine guns covering an area of over a mile, effectively. Working with Colonel Idigo, they designed the mobile mortars, along the line of the mobile machine guns, but to be manned by a crew of one. Patrols intensified and a local war cabinet was inaugurated. Intelligence officers were inducted into patrol groups, especially for lucidity of intelligence reports on enemy situations, locations, attitudes and activities. Requisitions for machine guns and mortars were made and reluctantly supplied. When these requisitions persisted, the ordnance department gathered all the defective machine guns available and delivered them to the 54th brigade. The armorers who received these weapons shipment angrily reported to the brigade major that all the guns were defective. Sergeant Kingsley on return from a deep behind-the-lines patrol was informed of the arrival of the guns. The very next day he came to the brigade armory early and diving into the midst of the dirty, dust-laden guns began separating them into groups according to defects observed. He was still slaving on it all alone when Colonel Dennis arrived and berated the other armorers.

"In your ignorance and stupidity, you sit down here watching with scorn while an expert is battling with over a hundred machine guns. I bet you anything he will fix at least a half of these guns in the next few days. If you can't do an armorers job then convert to cleaner and clean the guns for the practical engineer to fix. All of you are only armorers by title. Clean the place and the guns and assist him by doing the odd jobs, while he does the expert jobs."

Dennis bristled in anger, cursing in his Nkwerre dialect. His knock knees showed through his baggy combat uniforms.

"If I find a moth of dust on this floor, or on any of the guns, I will ensure your transfer to the frontline where you will not be burdened with this job but face a soldiers' ordinary life of fighting with a riffle, bayonet and grenade. You lazy idle civilians, clumsily playing at being soldiers."

He stalked away.

Kingsley worked day and night. He did some welding and iron bending work, straightening of pins and barrels, and reshaping of breech-blocks. Triggers and trigger guards were fixed, and sight blades and knobs were repaired and welded back on. Broken bipods and tripods were fixed. The armourer's enthusiasm peaked when they saw the most impaired of the wrecked guns brought in, rapidly coughing out bullets after they had been serviced by Kingsley.

CHAPTER FOURTEEN

FIDELIS UDE

"Officer approaching Heiss!" bellowed Sergeant Kingsley straightening to attention.

The gamblers retorted with:

"Ha . . . . Ha . . . . Ha Baby Officer. The weight of that gun is pulling him down."

A smile appeared on Lieutenant Fidelis' face. "Ha" laughed Sergeant Ede the bully:

"Baby wants to cry."

All but Kingsley joined in deriding him, passing snide remarks and laughing raucously. Lieutenant Fidelis stopped beside them still smiling. Kingsley tried in vain to warn them but Corporal Johnson the gambler forgetting himself told him to shut up. Fidelis signaled Kingsley to oblige. "There are only baby gamblers here. Not one good gambler among you" he said condescendingly.

Johnson dropped his cards face down on the ground and looked up at Fidelis:

"Why do you think so?" he asked

"I don't think so I know for sure that you are baby gamblers. That means that you are immature gamblers and as such no gamblers. That translates that there is nobody here to gamble with me. I must leave you to your children's' moonlight play and seek out men who can gamble."

He slowly turned away dragging his riffle up to his shoulders. Sgt. Kingsley caught the bait and enhanced it by offering to join Lieutenant Fidelis to look up good gamblers. Enraged Johnson rushed up to Fidelis and hooking his fingers into his belt flung him bodily onto the gambling ring. Others gave way as Fidelis fell on the small of his back.

"Corporal you just flung down a commissioned officer of the Biafran Army" he said as he sat up cradling his gun. He wiped it of sand with his sleeve and only looked at Johnson who in great fury now knelt beside him, threatening his face with balled fists.

"If you mention rank again I will not only knock your baby milk teeth down your baby throat but also mash you like the yam with which I fed my baby brother. Now, whom do you consider as immature gamblers?"

Fidelis smiled ingratiatingly,

"Well, since you must know for it will quicken your maturity I will tell you. Card gambling is for girls, boys and bored housewives. It is no better than the ludo dice. Men who are learning to gamble start with these. Your stakes are also too mean. Imagine a gambler, gambling for shillings and the pound as the highest stake. Real gamblers will laugh at these."

Johnson stood up shaking his head. "This is a case of shell shock." "Not true" retorted Fidelis.

"I want to gamble so let me seek out real gamblers."

He stood up wiped his clothes, hefted his riffle looking at Johnson he challenged:

"If you are man enough, gamble with me." "What is the gamble?" Johnson asked.

"A fight, if you beat me then you will collect my salary for six months. If you loose I will collect yours anyway for you won't be able to do so. See how simple? No cards, not penny antes but real gamble producing real cash, real pains and real satisfaction."

Johnson accepted the bet by extending his open right palm and Fidelis struck it with his palm.

"The same gamble is open to all seven of you."

Fidelis intoned stretching out the open palm to them. All of them except Kingsley laughed and struck his palm with joy. Fidelis smirking gleefully blew on his palm to show that his palm was hurting from the enthusiastic striking.

"You Sergeant arrange the fighting venue, and prepare the documents to be signed before the fights. We will meet here after tattoo roll call for the execution of the documents and for the inspection of the venue. Also draw up the schedule. There is no way I can fight you all in one night. Please keep a closed mouth about this. We don't need a crowd. For good fights we can't afford distractions."

Although the men were truly disdainful of his petite stature subconsciously they had drawn up to attention while he spoke, following Kingsley's example. He stood rigid looking slightly above the Lieutenant's head. Fidelis turned away and casually walked off.

"Why are you afraid of him Kingsley? You may be a big for nothing cow dung as I see you." Corporal Johnson spat at Kingsley.

"If you think so why not find out and be sure. The men will form a ring and we will step in for five minutes." Kingsley's voice that was subordinate while Fidelis was around had turned hard and commanding without increasing in volume. Corporal Johnson noticed that and sought a way out.

"You are my superior and I don't want any strain before I flog that shit with his purchased Officer's pips. I heard that his father is a clergyman of some sort. They say he has spiritual powers and is very rich. That won't stop me flogging his son though."

Kingsley refused to be appeased.

"What of the flogging of me? The big cow shit? The fight won't go beyond here and now." He pursued belligerently.

Johnson's voice fell to a pleading whine.

"I am sorry sir." He stiffened to attention submissively and respectfully.

"Alright" answered Kingsley coolly pretending to thaw out slowly, "Now we must choose the fight venue. What do you say about the back of the toilet? It is secluded, not frequently visited at night, and well shielded by plantain and banana trees. There will not be any disturbance. Are there any objections to the venue?"

"No" chorused the others

"About the time, I would suggest an hour after tattoo roll call. Do you consider that suitable?"

"Yes sir." They responded.

"Schedule will be a fight a night. Is it OK?" "Yes sir."

"The order will be as you line up behind Corporal Johnson who will fight first."

They lined up behind Johnson, and pulling out his note book, Kingsley put down their names.

1. Corporal Johnson.
2. Sergeant Ede
3. Lance Corporal Ibur.
4. Private Kalu.
5. Private Ikpo
6. Sergeant Nelson.

"I will draw up the papers and meet you here after tattoo. I hope all is very clear."

"Yes Sir." They agreed. They dispersed. Lance Corporal Ibur followed him and catching up with him asked curiously:

"I know you are of the same division with that boy. I also know that you are a good person. Why do you want that boy dead?"

"I knew you would follow me and that was why I slowed my steps. I like your preaching, and I know you can do a lot of good. Your work with the Chaplain impresses me more than the destructive work we others do. I don't want you incapacitated. He will do it with ease. Stop the others from taking on this suicidal gamble. The fact that you see no threat in him is one of his very useful weapons. He is a sadist. If the others will not listen, you must find a way out."

"Sergeant, do you mean this little runt is all you are saying about him? I am curious and will really want to tangle with him. You may not know it but I was on my way to becoming a professional wrestler when the war broke out. I then joined the World Council of Churches personnel for the distribution of relief materials. I was the most promising star in Huck Fions' stable. I had training tours of Poland where there are phenomenally strong wrestlers, France, with wily wrestlers, and every part of Britain, meeting experienced English fighters, rugged Irish wrestlers, brawny Scottish wrestlers and the magical gypsies. My involvement was to spare him one real beating, because I know the others are bent on killing him. Now I am curious and may apply a little force, but I will exercise restraint." He smiled.

Kingsley looked him over with pity and smiled.

"I have tried at least for the sake of our Anglican denomination. See you later."

He walked off shaking his head sorrowfully. He changed direction from his quarters to the officers' section of the Shine Mess. Through the window he saw Lieutenant Fidelis savoring a mug of hot chocolate obviously either stolen from a Caritas relief center, or bartered by Lieutenant Dinah from the hornier of the priests or relief workers. He attracted his attention by waving his beret, indicating that he would like to have a word with him. A few large gulps emptied the mug and Fidelis walked out of the mess to him. Kingsley saluted and tried to talk Fidelis out of the fight.

"What is wrong with you? Are you afraid for my life?"

"Not at all sir, but I am afraid for our mission. We are to investigate and locate positions that will be fatal to the enemy. We are to seek out good soldiers that will be honed to lethal qualities. We are not here to antagonize the soldiers or the brigade as a whole. This is bound to happen when you are through with them, and their intelligence section starts suspecting a plan to systematically maim, and incapacitate the soldiers, stationed at the headquarters. This is bound to happen as more challenges come your way, and a death or two may occur. Please sir let us make our move to locate targets this night."

He stopped to catch his breadth having stood at attention all along. "Stand at ease. I understand your feelings, fears and sentiments, but you seem to be loosing sight of a fact, that the fights and ensuing fights will help us fish out good and sturdy soldiers for our division. Discipline must be maintained or else we will have a mob of unruly, armed louts, glorifying under the title of soldiers. Thirdly, consider my person. They spurned me, mocked me and physically assaulted me. Am I not within my rights to seek redress physically? Go and meet me at the venue after tattoo. By the way where is the venue and the exact time? I don't want to keep them waiting."

"Venue is behind the rank and file toilet. Time is an hour after tattoo, but sir can't any thing be done?"

Kingsley rolled his eyes heavenward in supplication.

"Something can be done to make the fight more equal. If they elect to fight with weapons, by which I mean knives or cudgels, I am game."

He smiled and Kingsley saluted, turned and walked away.

"Devil" he mumbled under his breadth "Someday you will meet your match."

Fidelis turned at the door to the mess and shouted to Kingsley; "I know, Adaka told us as much."

He entered the mess and Kingsley resignedly walked away, startled at the discovery. "This boy like the legendary Colonel Idigo, aptly nicknamed Oracle, and Long juju, can read minds."

He retired to await an eventful night.

The gamblers led by Corporal Johnson arrived in their fatigues. Smoking and swigging hot drinks from a Schnapps' bottle, they went into bickering about who would take the first pleasure of flogging the "baby officer". Kingsley sharply called for silence, looking them over as if inspecting men on parade.

"In the afternoon we made a schedule. Why do you want it changed?" he asked.

Sergeant Nelson spoke angrily;

"Because aside from you, I am the most senior in rank and including you, I am the most senior in age. There should be respect for rank and also respect for age. Traditionally I should choose before anybody here. I was the one totally snubbed by that spoilt brat. He just looked me over once and twitched his nose as if something smelled. He does not know that some of the wild oats I sowed in the north, as a trader, are older than him. I am sure that he thinks in his heart that I am an albino. I must flog him first. I claim the pleasure of being the first to flog the insolent fool. I challenge anyone who questions this right, to a fight to settle the matter. As a matter of fact,

I challenge Corporal Johnson to a fight to the finish for insolently forgetting his lowly rank and claiming first shot in this new gamble."

He stepped into the middle of the men, looking at Johnson. Johnson declined.

"You being a Sergeant outrank me. You can have first shot." Nelsons puzzlement showed in his creased brows.

Emm . . . . Emmm he stuttered, then collecting his wits smiled:

"I thank you snake I mean Corporal Johnson for conceding but I still want to fight you before I flog the boy.

Lance corporal Ibur stepped towards Nelson, just as Sergeant Ede, the bully, spat at Nelsons feet moving catlike towards Nelson. With equal agility, Nelson rose on the tips of his toes spreading his palms open. Before Kinsley barked to halt their moves, Nelsons' feet spread eagled in the air, the right thwacking noisily into Ede's face while the left toe forcefully stuck Ede's carotid artery. Kingsley's bark stopped Nelson who had whirled facing Ibur. Smiling indulgently, Ibur flung him bodily over fifteen feet through the air into a newly dug lavatory pit. With feline grace Nelson landed feet first but all attempts to climb out failed because the pit was deep and had no foot holds. His anger intensified, and he threatened to kill 'that fat cassava bag of a lance corporal' for taking him by surprise. In the interim Ibur was being revived by Johnson from the strange touch to his Adam's apple by Kingsley. Kingsley fearing he had hit too hard, asked Johnson to step away. He then urinated on Ibur who was startled back to life by the urine pouring on him. He licked some off his face and cupped his hand to catch more mumbling 'water, water.'

All but Nelson who was still cursing and threatening Ibur, Johnson and Ede, while unhappily prancing around the base of the pit, were laughing roarously as lieutenant Fidelis spoke:

"Gentlemen"

They all turned to see him seated on the trunk of an uprooted palm tree

"You were all late for this rendezvous. Lesson number one is never be late. Lesson number two is always being early to reconnoiter the venue. I was here twenty minutes before the time. I heard the red oil albino tell the one he kicked unconscious that I have run away. For that reason I will fight him first."

Ibur who had sat up spitting out the urine from his mouth interjected;

"No sir, he will kill you. You must permit me to soften him up, by breaking a few of his bones, before you fight him."

"Shut up" barked Kingsley.

"For interrupting me you will be number two. Thanks for thinking up this good ring into which you flung number one contestant. You all have a lot to learn but that will come after. If any of you wants to, he can choose any weapon he is good at and I will fight him with that weapon."

"No weapons" said Kingsley and the others agreed. Fidelis stood up and moved towards the pit. They saw that he was dressed in a pajamas gown and looked like an underfed, flat chested girl approaching puberty.

"Are the papers signed?" he queried.

"They will be signed now" answered Kingsley.

The papers were signed and Fidelis threw Nelson's down to him in the pit.

Nelson signed it and wrapping it round the pen threw it out. "Are you ready for the fight this night?" Fidelis asked.

"Yes idiot baby officer. Come down here so that I will kill you. You are as bad as that cheating snake Johnson. Come on." He was still speaking, looking up at the men who now assembled at the brink of the pit when Fidelis, now clad in tugs tapped him lightly on the shoulder.

"Bloody sneak" he cursed, whirling in the dombe fighting stance only to run into a well placed temple punch, half way through his whirl. He sat down heavily and hit his head against the muddy side of the pit. This time his fall was nothing like his earlier feline landing when lance corporal Ibur threw him into the pit. His head was woozy and his knees and legs were too wobbly to carry his weight. He leaned back, shaking his head, to clear it of the wooziness. Fidelis backed to the other end of the pit. His body no longer appeared petite. His shoulders were reasonably broad and his tawny muscles looked round and hard. His belly was flat and hard but his legs were the unusual features of his body. They were curiously muscular and thin. The feet were ape-long, his ankle bony, and his calves thick and hard. All these differed to his thighs, which were thick, hard, and sleekly lengthy and rippled as he gyrated on the balls of his feet.

"You breeched four rules of fighting. They are;

1. Don't rush into a fight.
2. Don't be angry when fighting.
3. Don't be noisy in a fight.
4. Don't talk in a fight unless it is absolutely necessary."

As he spoke, he counted it off on his fingers.

"When you feel better, sober and rested, you can indicate by rising to your feet and raising your guard. By this I mean your favorite fighting poise. If you will need over thirty minutes to recuperate, I will go up and handle another person before returning to continue with you."

Sergeant Nelson slowly stood up looking dazed. "What did you do to me?" he asked.

"You were in too much of a hurry to fight, so I had to cool you off with a moderate knock to your temple. It is not painful but remains one of the six most effective ways to halt an angry charge. Are you better?"

Cunning light shone in Nelson's eyes.

"I am better sir. Do you know that we share the same complexion yet you call me albino? No problem there sir, I can see that you know the art of judo. I will like to learn it." As he spoke he inched forward.

"It is very effective and my commander at the 4th Commando Brigade Major Steiner taught us a little bit of it, but I did not pay much attention. I will now . . . ." His left foot shot a spray of sand and mud straight to where Fidelis' face was a split second before. Not waiting to confirm if it hit target, Nelson, vaulted into the air, his scissored legs closing together in what ought to be two hammer blows to the temple. The heels of his feet connected to themselves because Fidelis slid forward in between the wide spread thighs, cupped Nelson's testicles and squeezed forcefully. Nelsons' attack was accompanied by a lingering smile, an energy exerting war cry of: 'Bura ubanka'

And a momentum gathering grinding of the teeth, in theory and in accordance with the generally realistic suppositions of the adept practitioners of the dombe fighting arts, the foregoing was guaranteed to incapacitate, if not kill the opponent, no matter his strength. Unfortunately this did not work out as expected.

The sand and mud sailed over the shoulders of Fidelis, by reason of his slight shift of the neck to right carrying the targeted head, face and eyes out of the trajectory of the earthy missile. If the sand and mud had hit target, the victim would have back stepped with both palms going to alleviate the discomfort of the eyes, and exposing the temple to the crushing dombe heel blows. The target was disobedient to Nelsons will and rather than back step, Fidelis slid forward in a counter attack. Instead of lying dead or wriggling on the ground, pulverized, disoriented, suffering excruciating pain, moaning, groaning and whining sorrowfully, Fidelis stood looking down on Nelson who was replicating all that was expected of Fidelis. Prior to these agonizing theatrics, his smile had turned into a grimace depicting great pain, his war cry into the screeching scream of a bull ape caught by a sharp pronged iron trap, his rigid body turned jelly and he lost every pride, hope, integrity and interest in the surroundings. Tears flowed shamelessly down his cheeks. He made no attempt at sitting up or composing himself. Fidelis looked him over and called for the rope. He carefully strapped his chest under his arms, threw the rope up to Kingsley and bending hoisted Nelson onto his shoulder. Kingsley and Ibur hauled him up onto the ground where they started reviving him. Fidelis surveyed the pit and backing to one end, ran against the other, bounding monkey-like out of the pit. Without turning he donned his pajamas and walked away wishing them goodnight, and the hope of meeting the next night. Nelson was revived and wanted more of the hot drinks to salve his sorrow and humiliation. He was obliged. When he emptied the bottle, he stood up wobbled a bit, sat on a dead tree trunk and lit a cigarette.

"He did not give me a chance to fight. He is difficult to touch. He is not so strong but I will not wish to fight him again. He can collect my salary for the next one year, if I live that long. My advice is to fight him from close quarters. How did you get us out of that hell hole?"

Ibur answered kindly;

"He secured you with that rope, hoisted you on his shoulder and we hauled you out. He ran up the sides of the hole like a monkey."

"I have lost the gamble. I don't want to be part of this mad game any more. If somebody will lend me a hand I will like to leave immediately. Others can have a meeting to determine their fight schedules and strategies."

He waddled wide legged toward the dormitory blocks, and the silent Ikpo took his hand to assist him. He turned to Kalu, asking him to pick the lot for him and inform him when his turn will be. Sergeant Kingsley spoke solemnly;

"I don't see what good this gamble will do. He will mark you all and best you no matter how strong you are. If he wants he can kill all of you."

"Rubbish." Ibur interrupted. "Like us he is flesh and blood. He feels pain and will work real hard to defeat me. If it be a kill or be killed situation, he will have to put in his best, and even at that I will place my bet on my walking out alive. You have not seen me in a desperate fight. I am Ibur that trained alongside the polish dumb kid Igor. I never bested him in our training sessions but he sweated to win. I will fight my turn in accordance with the fight schedule you drew up in the afternoon."

"You brainless bag of cassava, you must abandon this fight. He will strain more to just defeat and not injure you. To kill or incapacitate you permanently, he will just let himself go. Not pulling punches he will spend little time dispatching you. Please believe me." Kingsley pleaded.

"He is not like you or I. He was already good before Adaka honed him. He is a killer and is very good at it. If any of you crosses him, such a one will not fight again in life."

They stared at him passively as if wondering what got into him.

"I will make one last try after which I will just do my job and collect ten percent of the bet. You have all signed and Sergeant Nelson has lost. Corporal Johnson is next. The venue remains here and time is twelve thirty a.m. To show that you have no chance against that person I will tell you this, I can handle any three of you in a fair fight and best you but he can handle four like me without much exertion. He is the one the Nigerians call Shadow and our Reece people call 'Spectre'. Others call him ghost. I don't call him devil to his face. Not that he will make bones about it, but like what I know he is, he has a long memory. I will see you tomorrow night."

Sergeant Kingsley left quietly.

Corporal Johnson could not sleep all through the night. He located Ibur and discussed tactics with him till the early hours of the morning. He contracted Ibur to train him for the night's fight with Fidelis, and also act as sparring partner. They talked, trained, shadowed, and feinted far into the day, missing meals and muster parades. By four pm. Ibur stopped him eating dry packs and drinking water.

"The time is rather short but you will dry out until twelve fifteen am. You will neither eat nor drink until after the fight. You will only wet your lips and throat with a little water before the fight. Remember to stay close to him. That is your only chance. If you get the opportunity, head butt him with all your vigor. Don't take a chance with him, so fight to kill and not to win. If you catch a hold of him don't let go. Hang on with your life. Most importantly start praying now and don't stop till after the fight. Sleep now if you can. You will fare better than Sergeant Nelson. Remember no more discussions, exercise or fretting. Relax."

Ibur went back to his corner, fell on the bunk and slept at once. Johnson's unsuspected strength and skill had tasked him to the limit. Tattoo roll call was uneventful. The officers in charge were lax and nobody was missed. Soldiers kept canceling their positions to ensure the presence of absent comrades. Lieutenant Fidelis headed back to the shine mess where he was discussing explosives with Idigo, Oboyo, and the engineering wizard Ifudu. Multiple air explosion charges, depth charges and mine laying were the topics of the week.

The idea was demolition of enemy vehicular weapons. Real British spawned gunboats were decimating the make shift Biafran Navy. The Scandinavian ferrets were bloodily dissuading gallant Biafran attempts at regaining lost grounds. This resulted in the amputation of more Biafran soldiers whose shins were shattered by the low flying bullets from the ferrets.

"Adaka's urchin is back" said Oboyo laughing.

"He won't be much use to us this night. He has some devilry to effect.'" Idigo countered. Fidelis was taken aback. His mouth fell open in surprise. He thought his new gambling escapades would remain secret until he had punished the insubordinate soldiers.

"Sir . . . I mean Sir . . ." he stuttered but Idigo waved a silencing hand at him:

"Go and rest, you need it, and I will want to watch you unobserved. Sergeant Nelson mumbled in his sleep at the 'MRS' this morning and the INTEL boys dug in and discovered your new game. You will need the exercise soon."

Fidelis left immediately. Later he arrived at the venue and saw Kingsley and Ibur quietly sitting on a felled log, chatting dispiritedly about the foolish risks of the strange gamble. They became aware of his presence as he glided through the light drizzle that had made the venue soggy and cold.

"Good morning" he said amiably.

"Corporal Johnson is sleeping under the squat cashew tree to your left, and the others are noisily sneaking up on the venue. Tell them to make less noise, and look out for Colonel Idigo who may come to observe proceedings. Don't cross him, it took me two weeks to recover from my brush with him at our first meeting."

They both jumped to attention and chorused "Good morning sir". Ibur moved to the cashew tree and hesitated as he saw the smile on Corporal Johnson's face. Reluctantly he shook him awake asking why he was smiling.

"I got the solution to this weird fight in a dream now. It will end in a bloodless draw." He stretched and slowly walked to the open space. Soon Kingsley shepherded the others into the venue.

"Good morning gentlemen" purred Fidelis.

"Morning baby officer" growled Ede before the others could respond. "They are afraid of you but I am not. I know that your father is a native doctor, juju priest, spiritualist, influential and rich. Yet I am not afraid of you. I would have waited for my turn but I have a reece that may take me out for a long time. I have already served my time with the second commando brigade, DMI, BSS, and divisional reece, before they raided your rich father's cradle to make you an officer. Your fancy fighting style does not impress me. I will show you bone, grit, sweat and blood. Come and fight." Sergeant Ede rolled up his shirt-sleeves. He stood with balled fists and hands akimbo expectantly watching Fidelis.

"It is not within my right to change the fight schedule" said Fidelis but if the gentlemen don't mind and Corporal Johnson agrees, I have no quarrel with the new arrangement. Infact I will take both fights today."

A cunning smile graced Johnson's face.

"I defer to the Sergeant; he is my superior and has choice advantage." He bowed theatrically, and looking around sat on a felled log.

"Come and fight" challenged Ede. Fidelis put up his guard and shuffled towards him. He sent a tentative jab to which Ede did not react. The second and third jabs were not so tentative. They hit Ede's forehead but rather than draw a grimace of pain or confusion, Ede smiled and shuffled forward to meet Fidelis. Fidelis threw jabs and punches in quicker succession, which Ede blocked without sweat. Ede's booted right foot shot out in a mule kick towards Fidelis' chest. Despite the lightning speed of the kick, it did not land on the targeted chest. Fidelis' "peek-a-boo" guard blocked it. The force of the kick did not break the hand bones that blocked it, but it uprooted and flung Fidelis across the space on his back. Ede bellowed in triumph and ran in to boot Fidelis' supine body into unconsciousness. As the same right leg shot out again, the sole of the lieutenants' foot cushioned it, more than half way to its target. Sergeant Ede had no time to think, grimace or groan, for the lieutenants' open fist slashed in a fierce cutting motion across his neck. His light went out. Fidelis rushed to the prone body, pressed the Adam's apple to open the airway and held the mouth open. He turned to Kingsley:

"Hold the mouth open and don't give him anything to drink until he can croak, otherwise he will choke and die."

He turned to Corporal Johnson; "Come on, we don't have all night."

"We will fight sir but I want all formalities observed. We are not enemies. This is a friendly gamble there shouldn't be any hard feelings. When Ede is declared all right we can commence formalities." Johnson sat swinging his legs and looking worriedly towards the huge almost lifeless body of Ede being revived. Ede was sitting up and sipping raffia palm gin. He stared shortsightedly at the lieutenant, blinking rapidly and shaking his head in disbelief. He looked pointedly at Kingsley and pleadingly enquired;

"I easily blocked his blows. He appeared slow and had no real punch to talk of. I nailed him with that kick and rushed in to put the boot. Thereafter I can't remember anything. What happened? Does he use juju?" he paused expectantly. Kingsley cleared his throat addressing everybody there not just Ede:

"I told you before. I will tell you again. You have no chance against him. You are like helpless babies in his deadly hands. He just sucked you in with what you thought were jabs and punches. He tricked you into your foolish move to quickly stop you without disabling you. Thank God you mentioned a pending operation. You others are you still fighting?" he looked at Johnson.

"Yes" replied Johnson "just a friendly gamble. No anger, no bitterness, no hard feelings, no animus. Yes no animus" the word animus pleased him no end and laughing with supposed candor, he approached Fidelis with hands stretched out for a boxing tournament-like shake. His head revolved as he beamed his smile on the others, mumbling 'no animus' to show that he had no care on earth. He did not see the disgust on the face of the lieutenant, neither was he aware of the disapproving clicks of Colonel Idigo, who was well ensconced on the bushy avocado pear tree bordering the clearing. As they touched hands he seized the lieutenant's hands, he pulled him to himself and locked him in a powerful bear hug, pinning down both hands. The former amiable smile on his face was replaced by anger and hatred.

"That was not so difficult fancy fighter, now to crush the shit out of you."

As he crushed harder, Fidelis started making choking noises and buckling his weakened feet no longer supporting his weight. Johnson had to hold him up to increase the effect of his bear hug. Exultantly he shouted "Ibur! I told you that none can stand the Russian bear. I will break his ribs and this mess of fancy fighting shit will go to the grave. The Russian bear has again dispatched another." As he spoke, Fidelis who had stopped resisting was slumping down head against Johnson's chest. Straining with what he thought was Herculean might, Johnson gloated with more cruel words;

"Now hear the bones cr . . . . aa aaahhh" he did not finish.

Fidelis firmly placed his feet on the ground, dropped his head at a good angle to Johnson's jaw and shot upward like a dolphin surfacing out of the water. His hard skull made contact with Johnson's jaw as Johnson was still talking. The teeth closed on part of the tongue and severed it. Two of the front teeth fell out and many more were loose. Johnson fell down choking and mumbling obscenities on his knees as blood and spittle escaped from his mouth. Hot tears flowed from his eyes. Turning to Kingsley, Fidelis said;

"Take him to the casualty collecting post. He fell down and cut his tongue."

Others helped Kingsley to carry Johnson away, while Ede followed with bowed head. As Fidelis slid silently away through the path from which he arrived, Idigo dropped from the pear tree into his path.

"Another lesson, don't use the same path twice, unless it is unavoidable. Oboyo and Adaka will confirm that. You could have incapacitated him without these permanent injuries. Your hands were close to his scrotum."

Idigo led the way into and through a leafy plantain and banana patch. "I had used that before, and I wanted to practice another move. Sorry sir. When did you arrive here sir?

"I was just behind you. I trailed you." "I had no hint." Fidelis said.

"If you had it wouldn't be a trail. Good morning." He vanished as into thin air, and try as he could, he was unable to locate him. It was about midday when Ibur, Ikpo and Kalu caught up with Kingsley at the brigade ordnance depot. He was instructing armorers on the similarities, differences and peculiarities of the heavy machine guns, like the British water-cooled Burr, the Browning and the German M 42 vis-à-vis their lighter counterparts. He eyed his visitors without enthusiasm waving them to the umbrella shade of the Indian almond tree. Nearly an hour later he rose from the clamp bench he was using for the stripling and assembling of the machine guns. He lit a cigarette and walked to them.

"I have no business with you now and certainly not before midnight.

What do you want?"

Ibur was still trying to find the right words when Ikpo spoke:

"We don't want the gamble. I personally will not fight him. Not even with the added advantage of an assault riffle against his bare hands. My aged mother is ailing. My father is already past ninety. Must they go to their graves mourning the foolish death of an only son who walked into suicide with his eyes wide open?"

Kingsley looked at Kalu and Ibur as they enthusiastically nodded their agreement with Ikpo's emotional speech.

"I warned you but you would not listen. I tried to make you know the devil but you turned a deaf ear. Now you have only seen the tip of the iceberg and confirmed the old saying that 'seeing is believing' that is for fools. Why don't you wait and go by the other saying that "experience is the best teacher"? He made to continue berating them but Ikpo rushed in again;

"I don't want to experience anything. I may not be as lucky as Nelson, Ede or Johnson. Nelson is now castrated. Ask him. Ede's voice box is broken. His former authoritative drawl is now a froggy croak, Johnson lost a quarter of his tongue, which the doctors could not attach. He will never speak again." He fell on his knees, head bowed and fists clasped in supplication.

"Please help us out. Kalu is also an only child."

"It is too late" began Kingsley "he has smelt blood."

They began thinking of how to get out of the suicidal gamble. They were still at it when Colonel Idigo who had glided into the ordnance depot observed them after his instructions were given. They were so engrossed in the noisy plans that were jettisoned as soon as they were formulated that they only became aware of Idigo's presence when he was less than ten feet from them. Kingsley who knew him led others to salute. Without the pips and with forever rumpled and faded khaki dress uniform, his clumsy nature not helping matters, no one ever suspected he was an officer.

"I want to help you out. The gamble must go through but it could be changed to arm wrestling. To catch his interest, increase the stake. Don't be deceived by his small stature. You will most probably all loose against him. I suggest that you ask for all to take place this night to end the shit."

He turned and left."

Kingsley's furrowed brows creased into a wide grin.

"That man that just left is the Colonel Idigo, the Oracle. The Long juju, or Brain box. He is more dangerous than them all including the fighting Colonel Adaka that trained lieutenant Fidelis. See how he easily solved a problem that kept us jawing for over an hour. Leave the rest to me. We will meet at the venue at the same time. Just show normal respect to him. Don't whine or suck up to him. Be manly but respectful. See you later."

He left them going back into the ordnance section. Joyfully they went back to the other ranks mess to celebrate their success. They celebrated so much that when they were missed at tattoo, Kingsley went searching and expended some cups of cold water to wake them from their drunken stupor. They were herded to the venue walking gingerly to show that they were sober. Forgetting the plan on how to broach the change of plan of the gamble, Ikpo's fear laden brain set his tongue loose:

"Good morning sir, lieutenant. I hate to change the plan but beating me in a fight won't prove anything. I may be big and strong but I don't know how to fight. My size has always attracted challenges. The many cut lumps and bruises marking my head, face and body will prove it. I learnt my lesson when I got carried away by a fellow student's beauty and became too enthusiastic in chasing her. Her hands argued for her. The first slap, which was backhanded, showed so much disdain that I forgot her gender and beauty, and rushed in to beat her to submission. Somehow she was not where I thought she would be. More than a dozen hands beat me relentlessly until I found myself doing unpracticed levitation. Surely such a petite, dainty girl cannot turn octopus with more than a dozen hard hitting hands, easily lifting me far above her head. I did not feel or hear the noise of any fall. Fellow students who witnessed the spectacle assure me that she delivered the beating single handedly and that she was sorry for me after the beating. She arranged the cab that took me to the chemist where I was revived and treated. They quietly informed me that although on hitting the ground I urinated and farted, I did not defecate. It did not help my ego much. A week later I found a boxing gym. After a month of punishment and wicked beating called sparring with thin but muscular heartless people, I called it quits. I tried wrestling and broke my hip bone. When I quit after telling my wrestling coach my story, he taught me arm wrestling. At this I am unequalled. I therefore challenge the lieutenant to arm wrestling. If I win I won't touch your salary. The satisfaction of defeating a master of the fighting arts will wipe away the shame of my Igbeli affair. Let us do arm wrestling."

He stopped. Kalu, Ibur, and Kingsley all nodded their heads in agreement.

Lieutenant Fidelis burst into a raucous laughter.

"You already met my sister. She is in this brigade and is the Captain in charge of the entertainment. I agree to the arm wrestling and for no stakes. I am ready when you are.'

The night wore on as they laughed and arm-wrestled, the looser buying drinks and cigarettes. Even Kingsley participated and came out second best after Ibur. Fidelis, Ikpo and Kalu placed third, fourth and fifth respectively. They all parted at dawn and Fidelis tore all the allotment sheets signed by the earlier losers A week later, as Idigo led Fidelis and others out of the ordnance depot, where they were preparing for a week long, deep, enemy territory operation, Kingsley looked curiously at Fidelis and asked:

"Do you play tricks in everything including arm wrestling?" Fidelis looked at him blankly, but Idigo rushed in:

"Yes, to mend battered egos."

CHAPTER FIFTEEN

DIOKPA OLISA

Diokpa Olisa was said to be over sixty years old, but still could out swim young men in the Ogbaru area. He was not one to boast about any thing because he rarely talked. Many did not feel comfortable around him for they did not know whether he was an old man or a young man. He was among the first thousand men shipped out of Africa under the banner of the West African Frontier forces. He returned to Nigeria in 1956, neat, clean ramrod straight, clear headed, bright eyed, displaying strong healthy limbs with his sprightly soldierly walk, and hairy sinewy hands. On his right hand rode a chunky hunk of milky-skinned, bow-legged, five feet three inches, laughing white woman. Her curly auburn hair, deep blue eyes, small mouth that seemed to continually mock and the small snub nose appeared non-European. There was a catlike oriental slant to the eyes and brows that enhanced the beauty of the face. They both descended the steps that were rolled against the side door of the large British Overseas Airways Corporation DC3 aircraft that left London Gatwick Airport the night before the morning of seventh July 1956 when Captain Celestine Olisa [Diokpa] saw Nigeria again. His immaculate white beret and many decorating ribbons did not demean the glistening dress uniform of Her Royal Majesty's Army. The ribbons and Captain rank insignia raised every eyebrow in surprise and deference. This was a dark skinned Captain in the British Army and taking liberties with a beautiful white woman, swinging a black bag that reminded one of a doctor. The looks and furtive glances did not last long because four soldiers led by a white lieutenant marched towards him, halted, and saluted. His amiable features hardened when he saw them and he responded curtly. They fell in behind him while he passed through Immigration and Customs. The Policemen on guard duty chested out in salute and looked after him in bewilderment. A black Captain in the British army was not an everyday occurrence. Their luggages were stacked in the boot of a black Opel Rekord. The white lieutenant climbed into the front seat beside the driver after Diokpa and his wife had climbed into the rear seat. The lead land rover engine coughed to life and was about to pull out when dancers emerged from the wing of the arrival hall. They danced with grace and litheness to the melodious singing of a mermaid-like, beautifully decorated maiden, leading equally beautiful maidens in an odd duck-like, quaking motion. The backing drums, flutes and gongs so blended that it was difficult to tell the instruments apart. It became obvious that the troupe was there to welcome their illustrious son Celestine Olisa. A musician dressed in leathers and feathers like an Apache Indian held a guitar strung across his chest and shoulders. His enthusiasm was infectious. The dancers and acrobats demonstrated in accordance with the tempo of his strings. The frenzy soon drew sweat from them all. Even onlookers that included passengers from the British aircraft and others started to sweat when they joined in the alien wriggles. The sun was only just peeking out of the horizon and the atmosphere was still humid, but everybody present was sweating. A lull was called when the voice of the lead dancer assailed the atmosphere: "Cele left for the Great War and like everyone we lost hope. Diokpa Olisa mentally waved goodbye to his only son. The war ravaged the World and when there was not much left to consume it simmered to a halt. Very few participants returned because the death tolls were beyond anything the world had experienced before. Those that came back, returned short of limbs, eyes, ears or intellect. They were all marked, and came home angry. Not so our Cele! When others were hurrying home, like the great warrior he is, and the successor to the Diokpa Olisa Chief Priest of the ever flowing Oshimili, god of the waters, he stayed back and confounded the white people."

She paused to demonstrate beautiful callisthenic movements that had everyone on their toes, while the Ibos present interpreted to the non-Ibos who gyrated alongside them. The exotically clad guitarist pulled his strings along in musical salutation.

"He showed them how to fight, and when it was time for peace he showed them how to love. The King could not let him go. He took him away from the black man's army and gave him a big rank in the white man's army. They are said to be great healers as they demonstrated when they came into our land but our own Cele showed them what healing was by the power of our flowing god the Oshimili. They quickly made him the chief of their healers, but kept him still as head of their army, in case war broke out again. The king, grateful for his many services, gave him his beautiful daughter for a wife. Our Cele took the wife but despite her great beauty insisted on coming home."

She gyrated like a snake on a spot, bumping and grinding her waist. The white lady led the clapping which drowned out the twanging of the guitar, and called for a tattoo to be played on the wooden gong. She set her eyes on the white woman, and with a gliding watery crawl edged closer to her with arms wide open and an enticing smile on her face. The white lady rushed forward into the waiting embrace.

"Thank you, daughter of the sea. Your beauty says you are a daughter of the great lady of the big waters. Thank you for gracing our land with your person. We welcome you and acknowledge you the head wife of our own Cele. We will serve both of you in all things."

She slid on her knees to their feet, flattening on her belly before them in subjection. Five equally beautiful dancers, although not quite as tall, graceful and regal as the lead dancer, slid behind her, flattening on their bellies in total subjection to Cele and his white woman. Before the clapping died down, Captain Celestine Olisa was firing questions at the guitarist.

"Osita, how is your father, town crier Osadebe? He must be too old now to spread the community news. Is your elder brother the new town crier? Is my father alive? Who tends Oshimili shrine now? Do the Oshimili maidens still appear? These dancers are they of

Okumili breed? How did you know I was returning today? Take your time and tell me everything. I am so thrilled to be home."

Guitarist Osadebe answered happily with enthusiasm:

"We are all fine. My father is still the town crier. My brothers and I have spread out to the towns to make money and become important instead of rotting away in the village. Your father insisted that all the young men should leave the village and go hunting for the white man's money and also gather his teachings. Your father who is very much alive and with all his faculties sharpening instead of dulling said our gods are dying. When asked if Oshimili was dying, He laughed and said that Oshimili was dying faster than the other gods. Well, we know that he is never wrong so all the healthy young men and maidens are in the towns schooling, working, trading or following the white man's ways, to imbibe their culture and become rich like them. My brothers and I are playing music and I must tell you the truth we are making more money than we ever thought was possible. Only the deformed, stupid and careless are still in the village. Our brethren along the riversides are more into farming and fishing. Welcome home. Only the lead dancer is an Okumili maid. The others are from our village. Your father told me that you were alive and would return to relieve him. He told us that you will return this morning, with a white woman caught from far away lands over many big rivers. The town union arranged for some of us to come to this entry point from over the seas. Our Austin lorry transport left home two days ago and we arrived here very early this morning, just before your flying ship floated in. Welcome. You will go with us to see your father and our people. You are to be the Diokpa when your father joins his ancestors. Welcome."

He made to continue but Captain Olisa of the British Army stopped him with a wave of the hand. Moving among them he placed a penny on each forehead, and ten shillings to take care of their feeding and accommodation, until they leave the next day.

"Tell my father Diokpa Olisa that he saw correctly and that I will be back in two market weeks from today."

He then got into the car beside the white woman who was his wife and they drove off. Ogbaru community, joined by other Ibo speaking riverine people, hosted the troupe, and they thereafter, left Lagos, the following morning. The troupe so thrilled the crowd that the cash takings astonished them. This made guitarist Osita Osadebe think of moving from commercial Onitsha to obviously richer cosmopolitan Lagos.

Retired Captain Celestine Olisa was driven to Mahon Barracks at Obalende where his wife and himself were feted for days at the mess. Some musicians like Kokoro, I.K.Dairo, and Victor Olaiya were invited to perform in his honor. Almost bursting with joy, satisfaction and contentment, Captain Olisa pleaded with Lieutenant Colonel Ogundipe to allow him go to his aged father. Ogundipe agreed on the condition that he would consider taking up a contract with the Nigerian army medical corps as well as his wife Doctor Sheryl Olisa [nee Bones] of Middlesex England. Both were offered honorary ranks of Major, with full benefits, allowances and pay. Captains Donaldson and McIverson of Sussex and Major Gerald of Manchester were suborned to persuade the couple to engage in a few years of post military service with added financial benefit.

They consumed bottles of scotch doing their bidding, but were not successful and by the seventh day Captain. C. Olisa [rtd] handed his wife into the shining land rover jeep. His luggages had been neatly stacked into the rear to allow for seating space for the batman attached to him. He was to escort him home and remain with him for one whole month before returning to Lagos. Even the land rover and driver were assigned to him for non-specified number of months. They were to return to base after he had purchased his own car and secured a driver. Full of thanks he left the barracks bursting with excitement at the happy prospect of seeing his folks again and going swimming and fishing. They left Lagos that morning and arrived at Asaba late the next day because they rested and freshened up at the Eku Hospital where Sheryl's course mate was the Chief Medical Director. Excited that Sheryl married a Nigerian, he had sent mail and telegrams to her to 'come home to beautiful, warm, grassy Nigeria from the cold and wet England.' He remembered working with handsome second lieutenant Olisa at a military hospital in London after Germany capitulated. He conveniently forgot that he competed for Sheryl's favor, but lost to Olisa. Overjoyed when he learnt that they were coming home, he sent letters and telegrams offering to host them even for a few hours. They could not but accept. So they spent two delicious hours eating, chatting and planning exchange visits. The other two hours they spent sleeping to regain strength before continuing. Doctor Bennett Doe saw them off with beaming smiles playing on his wide mouth. His fingers were happily laced through his ebony black Nigerian wife's jutting backside. After all, his Norwegian ancestors traversed fjords and wide turbulent seas and oceans before settling in Cork County, England. What could be wrong in him, Sheryl and others putting down roots here in Nigeria? That was how the Dutch pioneered the move into the veldts of South Africa over four hundred years ago. Already there was a sprinkling of English nationalities like the Hathaway's and McKinley's in the south eastern part of Nigeria.

Dreaming of wonderful holiday visits he watched the dusty road as the land rover's rear lights disappeared. The Olisas' slept awhile at the marine dock before exploring the surroundings bare footed. They ran gleefully from one point of interest to another, basking in the early morning sun. By five thirty, the pontoon's bull horn blasted, and the vehicles rolled down the quay into the ship to be ferried down to Onitsha. The land rover was sixth in line, and was already studded down before Celestine and Sheryl toddled onto the dock. The horn sounded three more times, and the ship, lifting anchor sailed off the shore into the deep waters of the river. The crossing was made in fifty-five minutes. By seven forty, the land rover drove off through the shores of the great river Niger toward the mud covered untarred road to Ogbaru. Just before ten am they drove past Atani. Villagers were beaming with smiles and waving happily to welcome their hero. He drove into his father's compound at the dot of eleven. The atmosphere of expectation was high. Within a short time the very large compound was filled with visitors. The elders, the priests, and chiefs felicitated somberly, while the more energetic youths ate, drank, and went into competitive acrobatic displays. One whole market week was taken up by the most colorful celebration ever seen along the whole riverside area, from Osamara to Otuocha. It took Celestine Olisa one week to choose a mud brown Peugeot 403 saloon car and hire a driver. He immediately released the driver of the land rover as well as the batsman and they returned to Lagos with a bounteous load of dry fish, yams and cocoyam, gifts for themselves and some Nigerian Army officers. Sheryl soon got occupied with professional visits to some government and mission hospitals. Her surgical skills were very welcome as the dearth of qualified personnel was the bane of medical management. She became more popular as her fame and humane nature traveled far, with the speed of lightning. She was immediately faced with a host of corrective surgeries where over enthusiastic general practitioners veered into unknown fields, thereby over reaching their capability. Everybody loved her smiling visor and her phenomenal healing touch gave her the name 'Angel'. Everybody, including institutions, wanted her to grace their parties or other occasions and she was buffeted by many invitations every time. She always had a mind to accept and honor but some very sick persons, rank, status or position not withstanding, always needed her urgent attention. So she rarely attended or when she did would be whisked off soon after arrival at such parties. Sheryl was the toast of the whole area. She even delivered the Okumili maiden of twin boys that were identical and looked like miniature replicas of Celestine Olisa. For weeks after, cloudy turbulent features indicative of worry replaced her radiant smiling face. One day, as she returned from answering over ten emergencies, her husband Celestine presented her with dry eel fish, to be pushed down the throat with a tumbler full of coconut water. This was her favorite snack as Cele knew and therefore used it to assuage her anger. She pushed the tray away but Cele pushed it back.

"Why?" she asked.

"Country behaviour to present my apology." answered Cele. "Why the apology?" she asked.

"What you think of is the truth. I have wronged you." replied Celestine.

"I may have concluded that it was your father's doing not yours. He is still virile." said Sheryl

"Then you would have concluded wrongly." said Celestine.

"What if I deliberately concluded wrongly in order to ease my mind?" she countered.

"Then that ease of mind would only be temporary and will create ground for enthroning falsehood, which will foster hate and its virulent kin discord. We don't need that, so you must know the truth. My father will leave by the harvest season. I have trained under him for almost two years. I will replace him and so have a need for replacement myself. You know the custom. I have explained it to you in detail. I thought the priesthood would shift to another family, but I now know better. The powers are inborn not learnt. You just get to know what you ought to know, and do what you ought to do. Your will is not involved. The dreams directing you come on their own impulse. It is not forced on you as in hypnosis. I am beginning to see that the spirit world is stronger than our physical world. Forgive me." He lapsed into expectant silence, picking up a piece of coconut and fish. He took a bite of each and fed Sheryl with the same. She ate and they drank. Soon they were eating and drinking and laughing again. He looked anxiously at the piece of dry fish in his hand, de-boning it he said:

"I now give these children to you. Do with them what you will. Hate, love, kill or enslave, it is your decision that counts and has my full support. Just know that I have never been and will never go near any of those maidens betrothed to me by custom except this one time that my consent was not sought."

They shared the de-boned fish, and Sheryl spoke;

"I accept. The need for qualified medical practitioners is much in this our land. They must be guided into the medical field, and away from your water deity that your father said is dying. This is resolved so mention it no more. If the deity calls on you along the same line, do your duty. Undeveloped uterus barred me from the joys of childbirth, but fate has given me a set of identical twins. God be praised."

The very old Diokpa Olisa Sr. died in the hamattan season that preceded the Christmas. He was not sick, ill or weak, but stretched out on his vono bed, died on the 23rd of December 1958. The Saint Andrew's church members Odoakpu participated fully in the funeral but were excluded at the interment. Certain rites were not for the uninitiated into the spirit world. Celestine replaced his father, and his fame spiraled. He healed in the white man's fashion, administering medicines and injections, but rarely cutting people open to heal them like his wife did. His native touch appeared nearly as efficacious as his white ministrations. All along the banks of the Niger, Oyi, Idemili, Edo and Omambala beaches, the deities, their shrines and priests, sought him and his Oshimili shrine deity for help, direction and spiritual sustenance. Amongst the heathens he was very popular.

He was said to have returned from a spiritual sojourn in India, before retiring from the British army to come home to his beckoning Oshimili shrine. This combination of forces placed him far above other priests and native doctors, and the fame of his shrine advanced with his. His clientele was not limited to civilians. Soldiers and policemen consulted him for bulletproof charms, charms for promotion and others. Transport drivers seeking charms for disappearance in the event of a motor accident, trooped to his shrine. All claimed satisfaction by him. He knew the waters of the river Niger so much that he could tell from where to wade through, in the rainy season, or in the dry season. He was unequalled as a fisherman and never missed target, when he went game hunting, with his Arizaga double barrel gun. He did not need to look up to aim at birds; instead he looked down and dropped them with a shot. What gave spice to his life was the fact that he was a diligent churchgoer and participated in all the church programmes. Because of his deep knowledge of the bible, the pastor of his church gave him the liberty to preach at church meetings. He even wanted him to preach at church services but the parochial committee's petition to the Bishop, restrained him.

Idigo had not only heard of retired Captain Celestine Olisa, now Diokpa Olisa, but had seen and talked with him. Idigo's maternal uncle, police sergeant major Nze, known as man-mountain, had taken Idigo to the retired Captain for bulletproof charm before he went into the school of infantry. Diokpa Olisa welcomed them in his living room that looked like something out of a foreign magazine, and offered them a jug full of sweet palm wine. They sipped with trepidation, eyeing his gamming guns. He discussed the strengths of the Nigerian police force with Nze, probing subtly for vital information as regards the personalities therein. The white kola nut and alligator pepper that preceded the wine had been gulped down before sergeant major Nze narrated their mission. Diokpa Olisa listened and nodding understandingly, accepted the cash gift they brought him. It was known that he did not charge for services, but accepted gifts in whatever forms it came.

The food items went to orphanages and the destitute around his community. The cash took care of about forty secondary school scholarships. He had only three University scholarships going when hostilities started threatening in 1967. He got up and entered his room. Returning he told Nze to feel at home in his living room. He led Idigo to his shrine, a smile laden with mockery played on his face.

"Tell me about yourself." He commanded. When Idigo finished Diokpa said:

"You are patriotic, very idealistic but not very realistic. Most of these myths are based on ridiculous folklores, held up and transferred down ages by mischievous tricksters, preying on over-believing weak minds. I was part of a conflict fought with great fury. I saw people killed in their thousands, but I did not see a single case where charms saved somebody from bullets or explosives. I am well over sixty but have not ever witnessed any such event, either in this country or in the countries that war took me to. After the war, at the officer cadet school, being born an African with my fair share of superstitions, I asked my instructors about charms, and I became the laughing stock of my course mates. If there is any such thing, I have not yet found or been exposed to it. Your mind is your charm. With your mind you think, and whatever you think about with intensity must surely happen. Your mind is your brain not your heart. If you think well you will always position yourself to advantage. Don't rush into any situation blindly. Study situations and don't forget circumstances. Train well to master your act. Put yourself in the other man's position and then guess what his reaction will be, then you can counter it. Try to excel in your doings. Don't over indulge in food or drinks. Handle medicines cautiously. Viciously fight mental and physical docility. Exercise and keep fit. Don't shirk duties, don't abdicate duties but don't volunteer for anything. Don't kill for killing sake. Don't loot or rape. Don't hurt anyone for nothing. Most importantly, don't dare anyone by asking what he can do, by this I mean insinuating impotence or ineffectiveness. If you avoid these, and do the necessary you will survive this looming war. This is the charm. Come."

He led him further into the shrine he scooped water and washed Idigo's head, letting the water run down his clothes.

"Think correctly and even the bullets will avoid you. Whatever god it is you worship, pray to him for help to always think well. To learn to think is to learn to live. God help you."

Diokpa led him out of the shrine. Nze was overjoyed and suggested that the charm be tested with the gamming guns on display at Diokpa's home.

"No need for that." Said Idigo "doubt weakens charms" "It is already working" said Diokpa smiling:

"I see you at the end of the war. I see you writing on a black board with pupils studying around you. You are a teacher not a soldier."

His voice this time came out differently. He shook his head as if trying to shake off a disturbing foreign thought. They left.

INTEL COLLATION AND STRIKES

Idigo knew that his responsibilities were demanding because any error in intelligence work could ruin everything. He had only one week to collate the intelligence fodder gathered, sieve them of chaff, assess them and formulate plans for the war cabinet to consider and choose from. He remembered his mentor Diokpa Olisa, who knew every inlet, tributary, island, beach, and clan of the river Niger, from up Ndoni down through Otuocha to Ozugono. His mind fluttered with joy and anticipation. Diokpa with his cultured voice and queen's diction had not seen him since that great juju day when his uncle "man-mountain" Nze secured a bullet proof charm for him. Events were to show him that he had one mentor in the military, and that in the retired Captain Celestine Olisa, the Diokpa of Oshimili shrine deity of the flowing waters. He headed for the Diokpa's compound.

Ekene and Tim, explored captain Nwosu's terrain, which was Osamara through Akili-Ozuzu, Akiri-Ogidi, Atani and the entire Ogbaru area, to the Niger bridge. Six hours of fishing and interacting with villagers, hunters, and fishermen gave the required intelligence. When they met Nwosu and Asuquo at the Ozugu ponds, they turned blind eyes on them. Idigo's four hours with Diokpa Olisa were usefully spent. They mapped the river, indicating useful beaches, islands and shallow waters. They had Intel on patrol boats operations patterns, and the sandy beaches where they go to carouse with the local ladies and drink sellers. He was asked to return that evening for a fishing expedition to see things for himself. That night they went as far as to Onoghono, and on their return at about two am, were challenged by a patrol boat, full of very drunk soldiers. First, they demanded for their total catch of fish, which was not small. After they complied, the officer in charge of the patrol boat said that he was a good man and so would not just gun them down. He said that he needed a canoe for his in-law who was an Ibo man, and a fisherman. He would therefore seize their boat and give it to the man. For allowing him to take the boat, he will save their lives by allowing them jump overboard and swim to shore. He started counting and Diokpa slid into the dark waters with the word: "Think".

He immediately changed position and swam below the motorboat. Idigo pulled off his suicide vest, and pulling the cord flung it into the motorboat as he dived into the water. His dive got him close to Diokpa who was pulling out a knife from his belt. Idigo kicked out, back-shooting his body forward to Diokpa. He pulled, indicating movement away from the boat.

Their combined efforts got them a few yards away from the boat when it exploded. Five minutes later, Idigo and Diokpa rose from both sides of the boat holding on to the side and surveying the carnage. Nothing was left alive. The engine had stalled and water was entering the boat from its sides. Diokpa climbed aboard ordering Idigo to reclaim their canoe.

Diokpa went to work, throwing the dead bodies overboard. He patched the leaks and tried unsuccessfully to revive the engine. He scooped water out of the boat. Stabilizing the boat, tied it to the canoe and climbed into the canoe with the riffles that were not destroyed

"What do we do now?" asked Idigo.

"We head for the shoals where their ship won't dare for fear of running aground. We hide the boat there and then paddle home from Osamala end. Pulling the heavy patrol boat along made them paddle with all their might. They secured the boat and were able to paddle home before the sun rose.

On their way to Diokpa's compound, he asked Idigo:

"You had twelve grenades in the vest all wired for action. The explosion was rather light considering the number of grenades involved. Why did the boat not sink?"

Diokpa walked into a side road when a motorcycle crested the hill.

Idigo followed him.

"The lower part of the vest contained only anti-personnel grenades. As they bore down on us, I sensed that a fight was imminent, in which case we will take the boat. I hurriedly separated the anti-personnel grenades from the others, scooping the others under our nets. The vest had only three anti-personnel grenades with high shrapnel propulsion capability. That is what I used because we shall surely need the boat in the coming weeks."

He cut a small branch from a shrub and began chewing it to sanitize his mouth. Diokpa nodded in satisfaction.

"You think very well and fast. Your reaction time was fast." He congratulated Idigo.

"You taught me to think and Adaka taught me to fight. I am grateful to both of you."

Idigo slept until midday, when Ekene and Tim woke him up. They fed thanked Diokpa and left. Diokpa had not only given them detailed geographical description of the whole area, and the behavioral patterns of the Federal troops stationed around, but also had offered to join them in the furore. Idigo was overjoyed, and decided to hurry away to have enough time to collate other Intel, in order to expedite action on the clearing of the Niger and Omambala rivers of federal presence.

They left and met Nwosu who was rendezvousing with Fidelis and his men at Nsugbe. Ike had opted out of the rendezvous to hurry back through the Oyi area, and report the interesting developments he had espied at the Ozeh big guns fort. He was excused. He lent them Isaac for the familiarization patrol along the target area. At Nsugbe they met with Colonel Ifenso and discussed far into the night, examining possibilities, options and alternatives. They made preparations for infiltration, hours before the zero hour. They returned to base by the weekend. The camp was simmering with excitement, without knowing exactly what was brewing. It was Tuesday and all the camp activities were as usual well observed. Muster parades, tattoo roll calls, maneuvers and battle simulations were strictly performed to the rather active new schedule, jointly prepared by Awoni, Dennis and Adaka.

Oboyo sneaked into camp with wild looking men that could only be described as brigands, and the feminine looking fair-complexioned Captain Henry. Except for Henry and the sad, frightened lady with them, others including Oboyo needed a bath. The lady left and a few minutes later sergeant John joined them, beaming with smiles. It was not possible to accuse them of stinking because the skunk's smell that wafted from a distance from their presence did not invite interaction, or familiarity. They did not look human. Their furtive, restless, shifty eyes did not present them as epitome of love or friendship. They were like animals. They slunk around the commander's office like leashed hounds, until Oboyo came out with Adaka and Awoni. Behind Oboyo who did not deign to look at them, they slunk away. Captain Henry and the lady broke out of their ranks and moved to Adaka. He looked them over.

"Meet Ike for further briefing. Nwosu will discuss plans and make you familiar with the target area. Brief Ike on R.O.B as you saw it."

He walked into the office and they left. News soon circulated that real Biafran vandals had come to join Adaka's men to clear Onitsha and Enugu. Rumors and speculations flew around as on the job training and refresher courses continued in the front lines.

The federal troops got more restive and the Ozeh guns became more active. To keep everybody busy, Colonel Awoni ordered trenches to be turned into bunkers. The now numerous bunkers served as machine gun nests, and Kingsley shifted to the forward locations with his heavy weapons support trainees. His trainees grew in knowledge and confidence and he allowed them to gather experience by keeping the front busy, with long-range machine gun harassment of the federal troops. Their losses in men to the new MG assaults got alarming and they pulled out of range to newly and better-constructed trenches. Sergeant Kingsley had with the assistance of Idigo, a welder and an engineer, using three heavy machine guns and three light machine guns, formed the Biafran version of a gattling gun. It was so effective that it could cover a radius of over three hundred yards, remotely controlled, and a radius of five hundred yards, manned. 54th brigade had shaped up to peak standard of combat readiness.

Brigadier Eze and Colonel Ifenso arrived at the 54th brigade and went into marathon meetings with the Colonels. They X-rayed the riverine areas, put up plans, dissected them, sieved out suspect aspects and studied the out come for performance. After four days of these meetings, Colonel Dennis who was coordinating as secretary read out the decisions reached.

1. Colonel Oboyo will return to Republic of Benin [ROB] with one hundred men and two engineers. His act will be guerilla hit-and-run. Take no prisoners. Demolish and destroy. Maintain no territory. Keep in touch with Biafra and call for the Lethal Squad when necessary.
2. Colonel Idigo will clear the Niger stretch from Osamala through Onono and Otuocha to Ogwurugwu and eventually Ozugono.
3. At Onono Colonels Awoni and Adaka will join him as they roll through the slated targets. Clearing the Ozeh hills gun fort will be done simultaneously with clearing the Niger.
4. Oboyo and his vandals, sorry, his men, will strike important targets in the Republic of Benin, acting simultaneously with the strikes from Otuocha to Ozugono. This is to give

the impression of a looming massive offensive, targeting the former Mid-west region, part of the west, and Lagos.

5. As we start rolling down these riverine targets, we will establish guerilla nests in the surrounding villages.
6. I will coordinate and liaise between us, and our commander, Brigadier Eze. Also between our commander and both army and defense headquarters, especially for ordnance reviews and supplies. My job appears to be the most tasking so I will require a platoon of disguise and infiltration artists, for security and communication. I need at least a week of training in disguise techniques from Colonel Idigo. What are left are our weapons requirements.

Dennis filled a glass cup with what looked like brandy, but smelled like raffia palm gin. He sipped it ruminatively, expecting questions, and points of correction. None came.

"About weapons, we have a number of urgent needs for amendments on existing weapons. I don't particularly care for RAP's new but untested wonder weapons. I want to rely on known weapons with few amendments and adjustments. The Kingsley gattling gun and unmanned machine gun nests are not for our kind of fighting. They will give the impression of a fortified 54th brigade location with much heavier firepower. Its one major setback is that the mindless firing spends much ammunition. I am happy to announce though that information from the sectors show that this Kingsley's brain wave, re-engineered by Idigo and Njoku's engineers, has balanced the firepower on both sides. The adjustment belts that make the machineguns fire almost all caliber of ammunition are a compensating factor. Sergeant Kingsley who has officially been posted to 54th brigade by AHQ will receive a field commission to the rank of lieutenant. Colonel Awoni will perform the ceremony. The order has arrived at this brigade and I have a copy as his former commander. By this I mean the officer who leads him in operations."

He did not look at Brigadier Eze, who merely laughed thinking in his heart "you are the real commander"

Adaka continued:

"I have spoken with engineer Roy Umenyi and Colonel Njoku about reducing the size of the Molotov bottles and making them more incendiary, and also to detonate sympathetically for maximum effect. Those will obviate the need for individual and selective detonation. Secondly we need thicker and longer lasting smoke screen, to shield our advance when the enemy is expecting us. By this I mean a slightly discomforting smoke screen, not the asphyxiating gas that was used at Agulu lake area, which petrified and suffocated indiscriminately, among all the soldiers in that sector. Anthrax was suspected until investigations were carried out to show that it was a large load of diethyl-chloro-tri-nitro-toluene, and other chemicals that blackened into thick clods of black smoke. Thirdly we will require small and light, green coloured, almond-shaped anti-personnel mines, bunker blasting grenades, multi-load grenade nests for anti-personnel use. Most of these will be delivered by this time next week. Tentatively we will place OP date as next week, and zero hour will be communicated when established, just before commencement. Meanwhile this "O" group meets from 1600 hours to 2000 hours everyday. And Dennis, do not mistakenly refer to vandals, even though they have matured to monsters. Oboyo, we await your schedule and targets. Every act should be stepped up. Time is of the essence. There is need for marine transports. Idigo see what you can do in this regard. I expect contributions to improve on the plans as they stand and to pad up the bone."

He eased back his chair preparatory to getting up. "So far so good" said the Brigadier,

"Dennis, I want a detailed report of the entire goings on. I have to show the need to both the CDS and CGS in order to get allocation of supplies. If we do not say 'we are' nobody will say 'they are'. They need to know all that we are doing and the impact we have made. Meanwhile we shall adjourn. Ifenso is still convalescing so he is excused from the 'O' group to return to his treatment. Sixteen hundred hours is the time. 'O' group adjourned."

He stood up and the others followed.

Refining and fine-tuning of the plans and strategies continued until their supplies and ordnance requirements were delivered. The last meeting took place on the 5th of December '69. The meeting convened with all the participants carrying large file jackets. They also carried note pads on which the terrain, approved plan, options and alternatives were fully documented. Weapons and equipments were distributed according to individual requirements. Last minute briefings took place and all present had time to talk about their specific objectives, while others silently acquiesced or corrected a mistake here or there.

"This Operation is code named Niger Furore" declared Brigadier Eze. "Oboyo, you will leave this night. Adaka, take over as I return to my base. I will join you shortly after I have briefed the CGS, good luck." He rose and they shook hands all round and dispersed.

"I will see Roy Umenyi for additional supplies." Said Eze

"What did he call that chemical weapon you spoke about? I thought it was all a bundle of rubbish. I did not know it was as effective as that. Why was it not controlled to kill only the enemy?"

"The lay man's term for it, is the 'Stand still' solution. He mentioned however that it was only 2-ethyl-4-chloro-flouro-Tri-nitro-toluene. He mentioned that he could not control the wind, so the weapon went haywire. He feels justified in his intention to only kill the enemy. He heaps the blame on the unsteady wind direction."

"The fact remains that I think he is mad, and only useful to the extent he can be controlled. He requires close supervision. He actually does not know the side to which he belongs. He is just interested in manufacturing weapons of mass destruction, to give him fame, wealth and power not Nigeria or Biafra. However he is a genius as his dynamites show. He has delivered five hundred sticks to us."

CHAPTER SIXTEEN

10TH DECEMBER. OKOKO NDEM

The dawn of 10th December '69 broke with a very excited and sing-song voice of the ever present Okoko Ndem, hailing:

"Brave and courageous Biafrans"

Followed by news of the demolition of the Agbor Bridge and the successful attacks on three Nigerian locations at Okpanam, Ubulu and Ogwashi. Although he did not mention the ongoing confusion on the Niger, he hinted at a concerted effort that will in a short while clear the Republic of Benin of according to him: "the rag tag army of vandals. The Republic of Benin will be used to launch great offensives that will clear these vandals from our beloved fatherland. We will then be at liberty to use our new lethal weapons once tested at Agulu, which drew international outcry. Now in a matter of weeks these weapons already rolled out of the manufacturing lines at our great Research and Production Laboratories, will engage the vandals. We will not relent. We will remember our churches, schools, children and women who have suffered from the wicked indiscriminate bombings, strafing and shelling of these animals in uniform. We will turn our new marshal sufficiency against them. We shall flow through their lands and they will see, feel, and taste of the dark potentialities of our new marshal sufficiency.

Long live the Republic of Biafra. Long live the Republic of Benin."

Brigadier Eze was in conference with the Chief of Defence Staff, and the Chief of General Staff, when Okoko Ndem's tirade hit the airwaves. The conference paused as Okoko Ndem verbally tore the Nigerians. He loudly proclaimed the might of Biafra, threatening the terror that will soon be unleashed against Nigeria, and not so subtle hints at a massive offensive that will end the war.

"Where does he get the little facts that he balloons with his wishful thinking?" General Effiong asked. Brigadier Madiebo answered soberly:

"He gets most of his information from our research and production people, and from hospitals where men wounded in action, in their delirium conjure up great battle scenes and their heroic performances. If his wishes were horses we would have won this war." He chuckled.

"I think sir that this time he has glimpsed some solid facts. Colonel Oboyo has started operations in the Republic of Benin. He has been very effective and as I earlier reported, operation Niger Furore commenced this morning. Colonel Idigo has trained four of our entertainment girls, in disguise arts. They have infiltrated the Ozeh forts and are presently cooking delicacies for the enemy officers and senior NCOs. Captain Dinah Igbeli leads them. I have no doubt that these officers and most of their senior NCO's will be near comatose from exhaustion—thanks to the ministrations from these girls—before Adaka will lead his men into the gun fort. There is no way we can capture the guns and move them into Biafra. They will be demolished. By midday Adaka will be withdrawing from the fort. Our engineers will mine the area to prevent the federal troops from attempting to re-fortify the hills again. We have delivered new generation anti-personnel mines that are difficult to detect. They will decorate the leaves, branches, trunks and rocks for a radius of about three miles around the fort. Any Nigerian soldier curious to re-access the fort to evaluate the degree of the loss, or retrieve the dead, will mark up the statistics of lives lost, and these will be more in the end than in the actual attack and fighting.

Eight pm is zero hour for swamping Onono Island. With the seizure of Onono, all the other small islands will become untenable for the federal troops. Our noisy and equally smoky shore batteries, that create the impression of volcanic eruption when fired, will do more to ridding the Niger of the federal troops than the actual fighting. They will be frightened off. Adaka and his men will join Idigo in the battle for Onono that is if the wily Idigo has not taken the island by then."

Eze cleared his throat, and took a drink of water. He made to continue but stuttered to silence as Okoko Ndem's piercing voice came again on the airwaves:

"Fellow Biafrans, a couple of hours ago I told you of the devastating strikes of the gallant Biafran soldiers that have made broad inroads into the Republic of Benin. The vandals are cowering like poltroons in their ever-weakening locations as they become more untenable. As interesting as that is for us from a military standpoint, the general position has improved beyond imagination. A Joint Task Force of the Biafra army and navy cleared the river Niger from Osamala to Onono of Nigeria army presence. Over one hundred soldiers of the Nigerian army were taken prisoners and other not-so-lucky thousands were fed to the hungry fishes of the river Niger.

The carnage was so devastating that our gallant boys refrained from pruning them down into oblivion. Some were allowed to escape to relate the horror to their evil oligarchy. As I am reading this news to you, information has just reached the studios that the much-feared guns of Ozeh, forted up like the Second World War guns of Navarone, have been taken out by the Lightning Strike Force, of Biafra, under the command of Colonel Adaka Ekwo. The explosions are still going on, and like rats out of their warrens the Nigerian troops are being flushed out of the hills. The lucky ones will be herded into prisoner-of war camps. I put my mouth to prophecy and declare that it is the beginning of the end.

Brave and courageous Biafrans, we are now on the offensive. The next few weeks will record more fighting than was done on the Normandy beaches during the Second World War. The tide has turned. It will be remembered that only a month ago, the same Lightning Strike Force took out the Okigwe sector dreaded guns at Oraobodo hills, and closed the channel hitherto established by the vandal army between Okigwe and Umuahia. The die is cast."

Brigadier Eze opened his hands wide with palms facing up.

"Sir you can see that he actually has means of gathering information. He also exaggerates so much that nobody on either side will be daft enough to believe him. But for the opportunity it affords him to rain abuses on the enemy and their high rank officers, his newsreels are embedded in so much half truths that the true situation becomes difficult to unravel. More confusion follows his ever-hopeful reports. From what he has said now, you can deduce that Adaka and Idigo have achieved their targets, and will join forces to sweep the river Niger as planned."

"That is alright Eze said the CGS. You should brief the CDS at least twice a day. This meeting shall rise."

He rose buckling his belt and putting on his cap. Eze also rose, requesting permission to join the Lightning Strike Force immediately, and direct operations. This was curtly refused and he sadly withdrew from the office, heading for the Signals Unit.

'King to Lord K legs

> Calling to raise Sitrep
> OB vandals strike. Confirm.
> ID river-rats, How much pie
> eaten? Ogun Fort rep.
> Confirm refortification?
> P. Coop
> Eagle
> Flying top birds. Essay.
> Supply ordnance Oliver
> twist Eagle to eagle.
> ^X not K legs
> Confirm all. Complete
> essay. Six-penny man
> Furore.
> Onono too Otuocha.
> Pressing inexorably. Roost
> Otuocha. Cheerio King. Bravo
> Top Bird.
>
> Dennis who was not yet conversant with the "Diarrhea code" preferred the long hand transcript.

DECODE.

Date: 10-12-69.
Subject: SITREP. LIGHTNING STRIKE FORCE.
Brigadier Eze to Colonel Dennis:
"I demand situation report on the activities of Oboyo's men in the Republic of Benin. Also require report on Colonel Idigo's activities on the rivers Niger and Omambala. What is happening at the Ozeh artillery fort? Confirm post-action fortification. Co-operate swiftly. A good and detailed report to the High Command will assure the release of the desired weapons. Hurry. Stop."

ENCODE.

Date: 10-12-69.
Subject: SITREP. LIGHTNING STRIKE FORCE.
Colonel Dennis to Brigadier Eze:
"I confirm that all objectives are being addressed. I will send detailed comprehensive report by 1800hours. Fighting is raging from Onono to Otuocha. Our men will rendezvous at Otuocha. Stop."

Eze shrugged resignedly. No degree of pressure would get more out of Dennis. A perfectionist, he would like to personally confirm events, and obtain all possible facts and figures before going into his lengthy narrations. Eze sighed in relief. He had dreaded the results of the first encounters.

Training had been hard. Conditioning under Adaka had been a gruesome experience. It was a living torture, but they had all graduated. Expectations were high, and Dennis had elevated organization and administration to a new height such that efficiency was to be seen in every sphere of the Lightning Strike Force activities. The Idigo invention—the diarrhea code—made it easy to get the flesh of the message, but entrenched the bone of the message in the unimportant flesh. He knew he was condemned to wait until Dennis had established the facts before sending in the usually lengthy report in long hand.

It was at half past one in the night that Dennis' dispatch rider Sergeant Egwuenu Nathaniel stopped his BSA motorcycle in front of the AHQ Signals office. He entered the office and enquired about the whereabouts of Brigadier Eze. He learnt that the CGS was hosting the Brigadier for the night, but that the brigadier had hung around the signals office hoping to get information from the now boiling Onitsha sector, and the formerly dormant Republic of Benin. He had left when he became sleepy, but asked to be woken up if any messages came in. the Signals Officer then called up the brigadier's aide on the walkie-talkie. Brigadier Eze instructed that the dispatch rider come across to the CGS' billet immediately. Before he drew up to the gate, Brigadier Eze was already standing there expectantly. Sergeant Egwuenu saluted and handed over two sealed and waxed envelopes. Each bore a title. The first was "Ozeh hills" and the second "River Niger/ROB."

Eze tore open the second, which was less bulky and started reading as he retraced his steps to the living room. He called for a mug of coffee and drinking absent-mindedly, he read and re-read the first memo titled "ROB". He learnt nothing more than he had gathered from Okoko Ndem's news report and newsreel. Putting aside the report he ordered the steward to feed the dispatch rider, and provide him with a bed for a short rest before he returned with further orders. He opened the second memo and a wide grin made his face resemble a half moon sitting precariously on a deep heavy ladle.

"Thank you God." He said under his breadth and read on, tense with expectations.

OZEH.

Colonel Dennis to Brigadier Eze. Stop.
"The situation is shaping up right. Ozeh hills were cleared and all the guns destroyed. The guns were seized and secured at about 0815 hours this morning, but fighting spread through the surrounding hills to deter the federal troops from hurriedly re-grouping and forcefully taking the fort. When the fire power of our mobile machine gun nests, assisted by the six rapid firing Oerlikon guns captured that morning overwhelmed the confused resistance, they withdrew into no-man's land, between them and our hitherto beleaguered front lines. Our defensive lines, unaware of Operation Furore, instinctively reacted to enemy rush into the no-man's land by forcefully attempting to drive them back. Our men entrenched in bunkers established deterrent rain of bullets. The seized guns of the fort started belching smoke and raining shrapnel on the now very confused Nigerians. Nwosu, Asuquo, and eight artillerymen borrowed from Oba manned the seized guns, and with superb directions from the captured Nigerian artillery officers, put in place a very furious and devastating fire all around the fort, decimating the Nigerian lines. In some areas the Biafran defensive lines suffered the same fate. Broken men, dead and dying, littered the hillside, while those still able to move sought whom to surrender to. Not knowing how effective the attack had been, Adaka's men mined the hills and the gun nests in the fort, and demolished the guns that would otherwise have improved our firepower. Captain Nwosu, Ike, and newly promoted lieutenant Kingsley fought their way through Nkpor junction through Obosi to Oba. The breeches were established and fortified before Nwosu, Ike and Kingsley hurried back to Nsugbe to join up with their men. Adaka lost thirteen men but none of his lethal troops. Running to the

Nkisi stream they connected the prison yard, Akpaka forest and the Marine police quay. They saw no troops or boats but looked out and saw Onono boiling. With the dusk darkness settled on Onono and its surroundings but angry guns of small, medium and big calibers, spat furious flames for hours. No side could give ground because there was just the small island to fight on. Giving ground would mean taking to the waters and the swim to the mainland or the other neighbouring islands. This feat was not possible considering the rain of bullets slamming into the waters and could only really be accomplished by an athletic fish. There were no boats in sight. They were either already sunk or captured otherwise sequestered for safety. Idigo's river rats' actions will follow in the next report. The Ozeh hills have been taken and well fortified such that the enemy cannot easily come near, as a matter of fact, the whole area is now an uncharted mine field. Stop.'

Brigadier Eze tore open the big envelope and took out the first report which consisted of three foolscap sheets stapled together. It read thus:

"Colonel Dennis to Brigadier Eze stop.

SITREP IN RE-OPS NIGER FURORE Stop. Too juicy for Diarrhea code, permission to report in long hand.

10 days to Zero hour Adaka released his troops led by his lethal men and commanded by Idigo into the River Niger. They disguised themselves as fishermen, traders and illicit gin brewers. They then infiltrated all the nooks and corners, getting acquainted with the Federal patrol boats and troops. Their generosity and respect for the Federal troops earned for them easy acceptance and they started to study the patrol patterns of the troops. They soon moved into the islands. As the occasion warranted, they attacked and seized the patrol boats or sunk them. They took no prisoners but always recovered the uniforms of those they killed. This enabled them to disguise as Nigerian soldiers at night and do their own patrols along the Niger with impudence, sailing the waters with Federal gunboats. The entertainment girls who infiltrated the island as fish sellers or gin and palm wine vendors, also doubled as free women. They discretely spread the lore of a river mermaid that frequently devours

men and their boats. This well orchestrated rumour reassured the Nigerian commanders at Onono who were getting worried by the disappearance of their men and boats. The boats in the harbour that were not in active use were mined easily by these agents. They usually hid Molotov bottles in the engine compartments of these boats that detonated when the boats were started up. Before 10th December 1969, Idigo had fourteen gun boats refurbished, well armed and deceptively manned. On the 9th he interviewed the few prisoners, all officers, taken within the period and obtained from them the codes and passwords in use for communications. He also extracted the names, ranks and description of the soldiers and naval men. He was so thorough that he collated information on every possible item including meals and meal times. On that same day he released the boats manned by Adaka's specially trained troops. They were directed and coordinated by men of the lethal squad. They hid in the numerous inlets and sand dunes in the river. By 10:20pm they had cleared from Ossamara to the blown away part of the River Niger Bridge. Six dunes used as observation posts were taken and the sentries taken alongside too as prisoners. The many dunes between the islands and Onono posed a bigger problem because they were better defended and equipped with communication gadgets. These were used to alert the command at Onono or the Nigerian Army bases at Asaba, Ibusa, Ogwashi, Okpanam and others. Operation Onono was to commence at 20000hrs. The following day and nothing would rouse the enemy to suspect. Idigo led a squad of six men from Adaka's lethal warriors. Some of Dinah's entertainment girls that were stationed there were released to compromise the army and naval sentries on the eleven harbours, dotted from Atani to the Niger Bridge Head at Onitsha.

These entertainment girls turned agents, descended on the hapless sentries who were weary from fighting. They were dazed by the sight of beautiful, fresh and sweet smelling damsels hawking needed refreshment commodities. The eyes and alluring wriggles of these girls and the giggles which promised more than the commodities being hawked entranced the sentries. They started carousing lustily and lustfully until they slipped into unconsciousness. Small doses of lagatyl had gone into their drinks and coupled with the hemp respectfully rolled and presented by the dotting sex kittens, the lengthy slumber of the sentries was ensured. When Idigo therefore landed at these harbours, he discovered that the stealth applied was not even necessary. He took away the trussed up sentries in his boat, returning with them to Ogbaru as prisoners of war. At harbour six he was shocked at the bloodied quay. The trussed up lifeless bodies of two naval ratings and a soldier stared sightlessly at the sky. They were stark naked, and in addition to their numerous stab wounds, each had their hands chopped off from the wrist and their severed penis stuffed into their mouths. A nymph like damsel clad in hospital white was busy stabbing a soldier in the chest. From her squat position a rumble rose out of her throat. Her long eye lashes were drooped, clouding her happy visor with confusion. She held the knife she was using defensively, climbing out of her earlier squat. Her shapely legs bowed into the knife fighter's poise, taught by Colonel Adaka and the knife artist. Idigo spoke sharply his riffle pointing at her head:

"Chinyere drop that knife and kneel down at once."

She stopped, looked up into Idigo's face with a smile as she recognized him. Fear had turned her visor weird, but reassured, she dropped the knife and glided towards Idigo with reddened hands thrown wide open for embrace with tears flowing down her cheeks.

"Daddy, daddy, daddy." She cried in a small relieved voice.

"They molested me and beat me. They asked me questions and called me a dumb idiot. A soldier brought the food and they asked me to warm it with the optimus stove. When I told them that I don't know how to light it they slapped me and after he lit the stove he did to me what the others did. While they were taking their bath I warmed the rice and put two lagatyl and soneryl inside the drinks. I doctored the food as you taught us. They drank my drink without paying and called me a mermaid. They said that they would continue to punish me as the male nurses did at the hospital. Eventually they ate and prepared to start again and had undressed when the medicine took effect and they slept. I had to tie them up as you instructed and wait for you but knowing how bad they are I decided to remove what they use to molest people. I also punished them a little with their own knife. Have I done well?"

Her smile was as radiant as the sunshine. Idigo held her at bay with his long hands but did not know when he drew her into his bosom stroking her head and back.

"Poor child, poor sick child, I remember warning Adaka that you should not come on this or any other mission."

His eyes were wet and he looked at Fidelis saying:

"Take her back and drug her at once. Don't tell anybody what happened here because she is very sick and must be transferred to a good hospital. Watch her very closely because she is used to the drug and I am sure you have seen how dangerous she is."

The dead bodies were pushed into the river and the quay washed clean. Idigo hurried to the other quays and discovered that the sane entertainment girls had done a marvelous job. Nobody could blame Chinyere because she had been a hopeless case at the Psychiatric Hospital. It was this same maniacal cunning that got her enlisted into the army after the slaughter of her BOFF instructor who molested her. She was being treated for sprained ankles when Doctor Izuorah at the military hospital saw and recognized her. It was his intervention that stopped her being commissioned into the medical corps. She had presented a nursing certificate which fooled the commandant and his men. In sympathy therefore, the commandant quietly transferred her to the entertainment unit where she was enlisted as a private. This meant nothing to her as she trained alongside the others, impressing her instructors with her sharp mind. News of her however spread and it became difficult to find her a unit until Captain Dinah Igbeli specifically requested that she be transferred to the 54th Brigade. She did well at her job but shied away from entertainment proper. Fidelis had overheard Idigo, Adaka and Oboyo discussing her. Adaka's opinion had been in line with that of Oboyo who wanted her eliminated painlessly with a head shot. Adaka wanted her eliminated but in the biblical David/Uriah fashion during a tight no escape battle situation, such as a suicide mission. Fidelis gave her a drink from his canteen and Idigo nodded approval thinking that she was fed a dose of lagatyl. A small canoe equipped with a two horse power engine was rowed into position and Fidelis guided Chinyere into the boat. Climbing in, he started the engine. The canoe slid fluidly away into the water as the engine purred gallantly in the direction of Ogbaru. Out of sight Fidelis immediately went to work on Chinyere. He unslung his spy glass and studied the sand dunes after the Niger Bridge. He angled into the open water and edged toward the shores of Asaba. He let the engine idle and began speaking to Chinyere:

"These men that like molesting you are hiding from you because they know how strong you are. You can out think them but don't forget what they have been doing to you every time. You have suffered so much but you may forgive them if you like."

Chinyere shook her head in disagreement.

"Well I am not forcing you to forgive them because there are other fine girls that they will molest beat and cal names if you don't stop them."

Fidelis bowed his head sadly.

"Lieutenant Sir, I will not forgive them. They must be stopped to save the girls." Chinyere's wrath transformed her face to a weird mound with indescribable contortions. Her eyes were flaming red and her otherwise luscious cupid lips were thinned out as a slash in the weird visage. Fidelis shook his head sadly:

"Dear child" he tried to mimic Idigo "it is already late. They have trapped the innocent girls in that small island that I was looking at with the spy glass."

He looked again and shook his head.

"I told you that they have hidden the girls so you will have to outthink them, outsmart them, outfight them, and destroy their radios and walkie-talkies then kill them and rescue the girls. If you do not find the girls there then know that they have been moved to the next island. If that is the case then remain calm until I come and take you to the next island where they are sure to be hiding and molesting the girls."

Chinyere hissed: "Take me there at once."

Her flaming eyes were now dark red and cloudy with hate, the long lashes were drooped and the left side of her cheek twitched.

"Not so fast, first of all you must study the island, and decide how to appear there like a spirit. I don't have to remind you that they will start to think that you are a mermaid and start molesting you. Do not be worried but endeavour to please them while you concentrate and do your duty. Make sure that none of the men is left to go unpunished. You will need more medicines and I have brought them for you so take these."

He handed over two packets of lagatyl and a packet of soneryl to her saying:

"Take this spray gun also and make sure that you do not inhale its fumes because if you do you will sleep. Use it on the wicked men that don't want to be drugged."

He handed over the spray gun. Chinyere laughed and her angelic face broke out as the sun from a cloud.

"I know that spray, it is chloroform and my daddy Colonel Idigo taught us how to use it, I can use it safely." said Chinyere happily.

"I hope that you will not need anything else, remember to outthink and outsmart them." Added Fidelis assuredly, he engaged gear and the canoe moved as the engine purred softly. Under the bridge Fidelis removed his Army shirt and disguised himself to look like a fisherman. Chinyere hid under the nets unbidden and Fidelis paddled tiredly. Thirty minutes later, right under the noses of the bored sentries Fidelis launched the human torpedo. She slid into the water and surfaced behind the sentries quickly climbing ashore to select a weedy area of the shore where she was shielded by the weeds. The setting sun did not trouble her but she needed privacy to encourage the sentries. Humming like a bee she made her cleavage show while slowly she parted her legs and hiked her short white gown to expose her laps. One of the sentries attracted by the humming went to investigate as Fidelis paddled away. Dusk was already casting dark shadows when Idigo, dressed as a Nigerian army officer beached his craft and jumped ashore.

"Sentry!" he called but there was no response. He cursed in halting Yoruba language and looking around in feigned anger drew in his breath. Littered around were dead men in grotesque shapes, hacked to different and varying shapes of dismemberment. Idigo and his men with the exception of Fidelis shuddered in cold sweat. As they moved towards the tail of the sand dune-like island they met shallow water which separated the dune from a bigger one, they heard a form of throaty growl.

Three wet thwacks sounded and then Chinyere strode out from a thatched shack. She adjusted her gown and headed back to the dune now occupied by Idigo's men. Wading through the shallow knee-length water separating the dunes she caught sight of Idigo. She hefted the meat axe in her hand above her head smiling: "I made sure of them with this. I could not find the girls but I made sure that they would never molest me or the girls again. I killed all twelve of them here."

She climbed ashore pressing the water from her gown.

"Seven bodies sir and I thought that she would be more effective than us and if you agree we should use her more often. This will be a better option than destroying her in line with Colonel Oboyo's recommendation of a shot to the head." reiterated Fidelis. He then looked at the apparition which was treading through the sand towards them.

"Daddy, daddy" she cried as she hurried towards Idigo with open hands.

"No head shot, I will put her to sleep myself." Said Idigo as his hands moved in a blur and he caught her in a tight embrace. Her smile remained on her face while Idigo held her up and wept:

"My daughter, oh my God! Oh my daughter oh! I have killed myself." He continued to wail as he let her down on the ground, and cried until no more tears flowed.

Fidelis at about 8:00pm went and carried away the body of Chinyere; he then gently pushed her body into the water. Idigo rose and boarding the boats they swamped the remaining three dunes emptying them of life. No prisoners were taken and they were just finishing when Onono erupted. Idigo cleared the Niger stretch without firing a shot and the Nigerians were oblivious to the momentous happenings. END OF SITREP EXPECT MORE SOON.'

Five sheets of foolscap paper stapled together fell out of the big envelope when the Brigadier opened and shook it out. He picked them up and read:

"Colonel Dennis to Brigadier Eze. STOP."

Onono Operation is over and continuing to other islands. Onono was swamped by our men whose infiltration was made possible by our friend retired Captain Olisa. The shore batteries opened up splitting water and not much else and our men on the island led by Tim, Ekene and Claudius attacked their command post, offices and armoury by stealth. It did not last long because the subterfuge was not as stealthy as it should be. They could not take the armoury so they blew it up and meanwhile fighting erupted in which grenades played a loud role. Each side was determined to repel and expel the other. This continued until Adaka and his team was ferried into Onono under cover of darkness. Drawn by the fighting Idigo attacked the patrol boats in the harbour blowing them to smithereens. The blazing woodwork and red hot shrapnel was doused in the waters. With the destruction of the gunboats retreat was no longer possible for the Nigerian troops. Idigo's boats then spread out facing all possible routes of reinforcement.

Adaka and his men from Ozeh stomped around impatiently as the fighting progressed. He was about to break his no-signal-during-offensive rule when ten boats drew up to the marine police beach. In command was Captain Dinah Igbeli of the army entertainment unit. Adaka stared at her as she nimbly jumped ashore and ran over to him. Saluting curtly she explained that she had come to ferry them to the island. Adaka nodded and his men boarded the boats.

"You will join me sir in the lead craft." Dinah said and Adaka followed her into the boat. Nwosu conferred with Adaka and moved alongside the other boats relaying instructions. An unaccustomed smile played on Adaka's face as he watched Dinah efficiently handle her command. Meandering to take advantage of every possible cover and the darkness, the boats purred speedily to the island. The well sandbagged command post was proving hard to take and the machine guns of the observation post angrily challenged the approaching boats. Dinah's lead boat veered off as she ordered the last five boats to withdraw out of sight of the island. She ordered them to await her signal of air bursts and tracer bullets to signify approach. The deluge from the machine gun bullets had claimed five lives and Adaka fumed silently for being hamstrung and unable to react. He wondered if Dinah would justify Idigo's trust and confidence, but at the back of his mind he had his doubts. The other four boats at this command appeared to turn tail and head down river.

"Get me toward the shore!" ordered Adaka

"That is exactly what we are doing but you will remain in the boat while we engage the rear battlements from the north quay."

Dinah pointed at six men and ordered them to remove their boots, helmets and grenades and swim with her in the company of two other girls to the shore.

"Vero take the boat around the darkness and approach with the Colonel and his men when I fire air bursts at you in one minute intervals" commanded Dinah. She then handed out Macintosh bags for the conveyance of grenades, arms and ammunition, and also distributed bayonets and cutlasses. Adaka watched as they slipped into the water and swam towards the island. Ten minutes later the north quay came alive with the angry crack of grenades punctuating the heavy and small arms fire. This did not last up to fifteen minutes when the tracers started coming. Adaka smiled with satisfaction as he tensed for action.

Thirty minutes of blazing fury saw the federal troops leaving the fortifications and retreating inland. The air bursts and tracer bullets heralded the arrival of the other boats. These joined the foray and shortened its duration. By midnight calm had returned to the embattled island. Over three hundred Nigerian soldiers were seated facing themselves with their booted feet tied together and their palms on their heads. Adaka spoke to them as he prepared to leave for some other island and sand dune on the Niger and Omambala rivers.

"Gentlemen I feel obliged to inform you that you are prisoners of war and will be treated as such. My men will secure you until we are able to move you. Please do not attempt to escape because I am leaving that lieutenant leaning against the wall in charge of you. Be very careful with him because he is a known neurotic which means that he is unstable. I know that he is very efficient and competent with every known weapon. I trained him personally and can therefore vouch that he is diligent and accomplishes every assignment. Some see him as a sadist while others talk of an unrestrained temper, but I know that he is cool, calculated and very cunning. His youth notwithstanding, note that he is more than ordinarily dangerous, he is lethal, do not cross him."

The scrawny looking Fidelis reclined unmoving against the wall like a lounging lizard. His thin neck seemed to strain against the weight of the steel helmet. The big pistol on his hips' holster gave the impression of trying to twist his waist. The long black self loading riffle [SLR.II] definitely pulled down the shoulder it hung on. Adaka looked steadily at him and said:

"Take over but remember that I want them alive when I return. Captain Dinah will assist you in this task."

Fidelis nodded imperceptibly, took out his canteen, uncorked it, and drank lustily while his eyes roamed owlishly over the seated men. Platoons of soldiers were strolling aimlessly about but to the trained eye there appeared to be a pattern to the lethargic stroll. Adaka was about to board the last boat with Diokpa Olisa when Dinah marched up to him and saluted and like a cobra his expressionless face turned on her.

"I do not want to stay back here and do warden job with my brother. If we stay together the forces will be too much and evil will occur."

She stood unmoving while Adaka spoke in a trance like voice:

"I do not want you to die, you lack fear and that makes you vulnerable. Is Fidelis your brother? You look alike but in any case stay here." He concluded with his hard features softening.

"Why sir?" asked Dinah

"You are hard and tough and like my commander Colonel Awoni you hate women. You hate me especially as your look shows. You refused to spar with me during the 'martial economy of motion' course we underwent under you. You hate me so why should you care if I die or live."

Her wet hair was now scattered all over her face. Shaking with tension her face glowed with her beauty, purity, and simplicity showing. Diokpa drew the back of his hand across his face and whispered:

"Okumili daughter of Oshimili, separate them."

His eyes brightened in excitement and Adaka nodded.

"Come with us" he commanded her and she climbed into the boat then taking the wheel pulled the five horse power Austin engine alive. She pointed the boat into the open water and asked for directions.

"North-East" said Diokpa Olisa as he huddled in conference with Adaka.

"I understand these matters. I saw you looking at her before the last attack at the central command post and knew that you would fall for her. I thought it was all right until I saw her clearly and knew that she belonged to Oshimili. They are spirit beings from the Okumili shrine that come and go as they please and the males from Okumili are better. They don't consume their mates and they don't marry but if they do they rarely make children. One truth must be told and that is that the brother is safe because they are normally warriors. The girl is not safe and if you stay around cuddling her, like the big spider that she is she drains and kills her mate." Diokpa drank hot coffee from his flask as he finished his advice.

"I cannot love again so there is no hope" replied Adaka.

"You may think so but that is not the truth. I do not know you or your story but I can sense your weird nature and a story is always behind such nature. You even fight like one possessed. I have watched you and seen you perform better in battle situations. You relish danger and get your best excitement from it. You will even survive this war that you hope will consume you. You will survive and I see you teaching children, but don't know what you are teaching. I can't see more but you are relaxed and like a human being and not a war spirit." As Diokpa finished speaking he drank from his flask and offered the flask to Adaka who refused with a shake of his big head.

"I don't love her but I confess that most things about her appeal to me. My friend Awoni who is a ladies man and loves none but only enjoys frolicking with them actually fell in love with her. He nearly killed her when he knew that she consorted with other men. I will not have anything to do with her because I have never cheated on my sick wife though they look alike" mumbled Adaka.

"You certainly will have something to do with her because like me you have been chosen by her. You have no choice in the matter" said Diokpa.

Adaka smiled with unbelief while the other boats were overhauled in the early hours of the morning and they studied maps to choose the locations for attack. From behind them Dinah said clearly:

"Do not bother with those maps because I know the islands and the best approach routes to them."

By 0540hrs on the morning of December 11th 1969 they had gone through six islands and four sand dunes finding them all empty. Evidence showed that the former occupants had beaten a hasty retreat. On reaching the last island they decided to rest. The abandoned huts were well stocked with food, drinks and beverages. Even military wares had been left behind. The food was tested for poison and found to be clean so they prepared meals which after they ate, most of the tired men slept. Adaka felt something rub against him and edged away. It happened again and his right hand shot out closing on the neck while the left hand held the long bladed okapi knife poised to stab.

"It is me" croaked Dinah through a compressed windpipe. She lay prone not moving and Adaka heaved a sigh of relief and sheathed the blade. His hand softened against the neck kneading it gently.

"What is it?" he asked on a tremulous voice.

"I searched the huts for you but could not find you so Diokpa told me that a lion can never be willingly caged and that I should look in the lion's habitat in the bushes not in huts or houses. I therefore came looking and found you" Dinah said laying a trembling hand uncertainly on Adaka's shoulder.

"Why?" asked Adaka.

"I had to see you and be sure" replied Dinah. "Be sure of what?" queried Adaka.

"Your hatred of me and why you hate me so much."

"But I don't hate you. Why do you think that I hate you?" Adaka mellowed further.

"You always look at me with a blank expression which tells me that you disapprove of me. You refused to train me physically during the economy of motion courses while you trained the other boys and girls. Each time I came into your line of vision you shook your head in disapproval. Whenever I stay around you it will not be long before you leave as if I carry around a disgusting body odour or I fart each time I am around you putrefying the air. I even see your nose twitch and your mouth curve up."

Her hot palm on his shoulder had tightened while tears coursed down her cheeks. No sob indicated that she was crying so Adaka was not aware. Adaka's hand instinctively traveled over every part of her body in what appeared to be a wild caress but infact was a frisk for hidden weapons. He edged away slightly raising his head to survey her unbuttoned shirt. His eyes lingered on her big navel, moved down her middle to flitter briefly over her flowery nylon underwear to her shapely straight legs. Adaka's eagle eyes saw a small sixth toe and shifting to the other toe saw the same thing. Seizing both hands he saw the stumps of sixth fingers. He shuddered and Dinah, who partially pulled up to sitting position when he wanted to see her fingers, fell back on his chest. Her tears were flowing unrestrained onto Adaka's chest.

"Why do you hate me?" she asked.

"I don't hate you, I love you. Why are you haunting me? I am sorry that I was away or else it would not have happened" he was sobbing.

"What are you talking about?" asked Dinah.

"My wife, you are my wife. I knew it when I saw you at the brigade. I was not deceived but why don't you just get well?"

From his breast pocket he brought out a picture of Dinah's look alike in a gown. Dinah did a double take.

"Colonel Idigo told me about you and warned me not to hurt you so now I hope you understand. I cannot hurt you and will even give my life for you. I have never loved in my life but now that I have met you I will shout to the whole world that I have loved after this day. My heart is on fire."

As she spoke her hand went to work and Adaka squirmed uncomfortably for a while. However the smell of Cocoa butter pomade and the lavender scent emanating from her hair melted his resolve. He buried his hair in her head and twisted and turned in an ecstatic wrestle worshipping at the altar of passion. Idigo playing watchdog had tailed Captain Dinah closely to the shrub where she located the sleeping Adaka and tiptoed towards him. Five yards from him she had unbuttoned her trouser and the top part of her shirt exposing two throbbing mounds of mammary flesh and enticing cleavage. Idigo then sheathed the knife he had held at the ready and his smile widened when he noticed Adaka tense into consciousness. The girl was in for a frightful surprise he thought. He listened to everything and as the events took an amorous turn he pulled himself away. He retraced his steps to the island's command post where he met Colonel Dennis and Ike trying to communicate with Colonel Awoni who was engaging the federal troops at Omoh, plugging the front line. He was reported to be thrashing his way through the federal troops at Otuocha like a lawn mower decimating grass. As commander of a mixture of his own men and a detachment of Adaka's men he brought out the best from them by keeping them apart and making them compete.

By the morning of the 12th Otuocha was cleared and secured with Aguleri, Umuleri, and Mmiata Anam freed of Nigerian troops. Awoni lost over five hundred men as against Adaka's one hundred and thirty four dead and seventy six wounded. Those not severely wounded joined the defensive lines thrown up against the federal troops at Omoh. While awaiting further orders Awoni planned and launched patrols into ROB as far as Ika, Igbokenyi and Ozugono. Because static made communication barely comprehensible, Idigo's men ferried Dennis to Otuocha. He was briefed by Awoni and then he returned to the 54th brigade and thence to army headquarters Orlu to report to Brigadier Eze.

Eze in excitement took him to the COAS, CDS and CGS where he gave first hand report of the battle situation. The Brigadier again sought permission to rejoin his command and it was granted. This was specifically for collating information at 'O' groups and clarifying plans and strategies. The CGS looked at him and said:

"You will be in the way so allow those war spirits to do their thing. Do the liaisons job for me, after all you are a general officer and not supposed to be totting around guns, grenades and bayonets. You have one week to report back to me, more things are happening than you suspect. The rapidity of the events is chaotic and I can't see my way through the confusion."

He closed his eyes shaking his head in despair. The Chief of Army Staff, Major General James Ogunewe, Chief of Defence Staff, Major General Madiebo and Chief of General Staff, Lieutenant General Effong all sat morosely avoiding each others eyes. The excited rendition of the Operation Niger Furore situation report appeared to fall on statues. Except for Eze's excited response to Denis' frenzied rendition the others bit their fingers to the quick and dawdled on their pads illegibly.

After the conditional permission was granted to Brigadier Eze he hung around to know what was amiss. Dennis sensed a good story and stood stock still pretending that he was waiting to be dismissed. They did not notice him as the Brigadier. Eze saluted and turned to leave but no response or comment followed his action so he turned again to face them.

"What is wrong sir?" he asked to no one in particular.

Nobody replied and he stubbornly stood unmoving with Dennis hiding behind him. Effong slowly looked up saying: "Why are you still hanging around? Go and return in one week. If we are still here then you will know everything then. This Lightning Strike Force move may turn the tide. Your men can do the magic so go now."

Eze's withdrawal was neither professional nor energetic. He turned slowly mumbling in protest:

"We are militarily stronger now than ever before. In less than one week we have regained vast areas of land that we lost in these months of war. Our martial insufficiency has been remedied by this Adaka, Idigo and Oboyo tonic. Why should we despair now?"

No response followed him so when he got to the door he turned to them saying:

"They have been cut off at Onitsha and we can clear Onitsha in two weeks so I will . . ."

"Go!" roared Effong his famed juju green eyes replacing his ordinarily brown eyes. Even his brows appeared to bristle catlike. He looked devilish. Eze left with Dennis tagging behind.

"To capitulate at this time of our new found ability then in the next six months they will be converging at the borders thinking of defence and not offensives anymore. To capitulate now that our military potentials are on the climb is sabotage. I must talk to Adaka, Idigo and Oboyo. Oboyo must have seen the weakness in our command and toed the path of honour by refusing to conform and setting up his own army in R.O.B. known as the Biafran Vandals. I was instrumental to convincing him and making him return to this enclave of spineless, uniform, rank, medals and laurels, chocolate cream soldiers. They can't arm, feed or manage the patriotically motivated army. They can't negotiate good armistice and they can't do anything well, even this God given turn of events they want to truncate. All they think about is oil empires to rule. I will not permit this because it is sabotage." His musing would have continued oblivious of Colonel Dennis hearing everything but Dennis stopped him.

"Sir, this is seditious and you know that in a war situation the trial is as farcical as it is summarily inept. You could be shot for these truths you are voicing. Mull on them but don't speak out. I would suggest that you first discuss with Oboyo before you involve Adaka, Idigo and Awoni."

Eze stopped and looking Dennis over said:

"I am sorry I spoke out of turn."

They continued to his office. He cleared his office then took out and after cleaning, oiled his personal arms. His aides were waiting when he exited his house with Colonel Dennis walking slightly behind him to his right side.

The loaded land rovers stood waiting the lead jeep on top of which was mounted a light machine gun. Eze remembered

Archdeacon Adewale Cole the then vicar of the Breadfruit Cathedral Church Lagos. At the same time he realized that he was humming 'Abide with me fast falls the even tide.' This was the Archdeacon's favourite hymn. The mood of despair fell on Dennis and he joined in the song. As they were heading to Ihiala the singing had changed to 'Thy will not mine Oh Lord.'

Dennis put off the radio as Okoko Ndem came on air, and thinking drowsily while Eze hummed on, he slept. The vehicles stopped at Oba and he woke up to see the guards presenting arms. Brigadier Eze screamed at them:

"Stop that nonsense! It is for cream-puff soldiers. There is a war on." Confused, they stood still and the vehicles drove past the raised bar.

Lieutenant Colonel Ozor who was acting Brigade Commander in the absence of Awoni made provision for the entourage's brief stay and further provision for their river journey to Otuocha. Driven to his wits end by Brigadier Eze, Dennis was able to organize an 'O' Group at Otuocha to include Oboyo, Diokpa Olisa and the non-combatant Ifenso. Although he was still recuperating, Colonel Ifenso demonstrated a ubiquity of presence by surfacing at the battle ground as soon as the fighting abated. Hindered by a game leg and a shattered humerus that was healing nicely he was forced to keep away from the fighting. He however still savoured the reek of the carnage as he hurried to the frontlines to confer with the commanders and advice on whatever uncertainties that arose. By the third day they left the 54th Brigade using canoes to cross from Ose Ngwo through the Idemili River and row into the Niger River. At the Niger two of the Idigo boats were waiting and transferring from the canoes they had a smooth journey to Otuocha.

They kept away from the Asaba shores where angry federal troops were spoiling for a showdown with the sneaky Biafrans. They kept to the middle of the river aware of the many pockets of stray federal troops on the Biafran side seeking marine transport to join their counterparts at Asaba. At Otuocha they were welcomed and made comfortable by Captain Nwosu and Captain Dinah. A hot meal and drinks were presented within minutes of their arrival. Eze only picked at the food, grumbling to protest the absence of Adaka, Idigo and Diokpa. Seeking new targets they were conferring with Oboyo when Dennis' courier arrived. They had to hastily conclude and embark on the tortuous return journey to Otuocha. They arrived late that night and went into conference two hours later. Awoni had commandeered the estate of Cornelius Chinwuba, the Okpocha-Ngene of Ngene shrine. The big neatly kept estate contained three buildings. One storeyed building was for his many wives married from many clans and their daughters. The other was for him and his sons from where he held court as a chief and consulted his Ngene oracle. A former U.A.C Manager, he did not like the dirty mud shrine so he retained it and appointed a dwarf from Nri to minister there. He did his consultation and divination from a room adjoining his living room. The third was for very important guests. Diokpa who gave refuge to the Chinwuba family when the federal troops overwhelmed Otuocha, advised Awoni to put a tight reign on his troops. They were to desist from looting the estate or desecrating the shrine.

"There is a measure of power to these things, by which I mean shrines and deities just as there is in Devils and demons. We as Christians know that their power is subject to God and that all power belongs to God. Let them keep away and not dabble into what they don't know." Awoni had heeded his advice and kept the estate in good shape. When the Senior Officers gathered for the 'O' Group, all were full of expectations as to target selection and reinforcement. The ordinarily talkative Dennis seemed withdrawn and thoughtful. He even forgot to make his playful remark about cannibals euphemistically called vandals when in truth they had matured to demons. The atmosphere was bleak when Brigadier Eze walked into the room in trunks only, carrying his riffle, pistol, knives and suicide belt like a heavy load. He laid them all on the table as his subordinates stood up to salute. He backed to the wall with hands above his head.

"I have come to confess and surrender to you. You are real soldiers not the powder puffs glorying in high sounding ranks and mismanaging a worthy rebellion. From my deep throat agents at army headquarters, defence headquarters and State house, I know that they have moved all the important documents from Biafra via night flights. I also know that orders have gone out for Biafran army to quit attacking or carrying out patrols pending the shameful act they wish to perpetrate. I know that whatever we do will have no effect on their decision to surrender."

He made to continue but the noisy intake of breaths stopped him. "Yes" he continued

"They plan to surrender and have been planning it for over a month. You can see the rapidity with which the federal troops are over running Biafra. No offense and no resistance, only the amicable entry of Nigerian soldiers with slung riffles like boy scouts going for a picnic. It is all well planned. I am not a part of it and will resist it. Our top men will all fly out of Biafra in the next two weeks. This is sabotage of a strange kind. The people sabotaging the Biafran cause are the very people who led it. They wish to give up now that we have found our military rhythm. We can now see that but for the initial pain and anger at the pogrom, there was never a genuine desire to secede. It was just a ploy to obtain better bargaining power in order to secure enclaves and oil blocks to administer. Where are the patriots who truly wanted fair play or secession? Where are the Nzeogwus, Chude Sokeis, Emmanuel Ifeajunas, Alades and Victor Banjo my course mate? Where are they? Outside in the trash can is my dress uniform with the useless rank insignia and the senseless paraphernalia of worthless medals. I have quit the Biafran army whatever it truly is. On my own I have turned rebel and will fight Nigeria to a standstill as our boisterous Okoko Ndem would say."

He stooped and looked at them. No one moved or spoke so he continued:

"Now you know the truth. I will provide evidence of all that I have told you including the evidence of our leaders' rejection of very important supplies of arms, advisers and mercenaries vital to our survival. China and France are just two of the many countries that wanted to come to our aid for specific oil concessions. They turned them down hoping to bluff the Nigerian government into a more favourable armistice. This appeared possible but was slow in coming.

They were prepared to wait under the guise of seeking military muscle especially in the form of wonder weapons. They brainstormed and came up with a wonder weapon which turned out to be truly lethal to their utter disappointment. This weapon, the Lightning Strike Force bettered everybody's wildest expectations. I was the cog in the wheel of operations they infused as commander to shackle lethal soldiers. Like you all here, I found out early and decided to cheat them. Rather than fight you with the rank and hierarchy clout which they banked on, I cooperated with you. The result is this deadly command that can turn the tide of the whole war within one month. They therefore decided to pull the carpet under our feet by surrendering. If we allow them to do that there will be no Biafra and no banner under which to fight. I have resigned my commission to be free to prosecute my rebellion against Nigeria. Now I am at your mercy. Arrest me and by tomorrow evening I will be shot. Let me go and I will start a guerilla war and become a bee in the Nigerian bonnet. Join me and we have two options the first of which is to swiftly carry out a coup-d'etat and set Biafra on an even keel. We will spend quality time thinking not drinking, doping or gambling like they are doing now. We will retrain our untrained men and a real army will emerge, then Nigeria will hurriedly talk peace and let us go. Even they know that things have fallen apart and the centre cannot hold, if I may quote the sage Chinua Achebe. The second option will be to go the Oboyo way, break all links with the tottering Biafra army, establish a new identity and harangue common sense into the Nigerians. I am done and now the choice is yours. Cursed be dishonest people. Long live honest people."

He turned and stepped aside for them to take a decision but was stopped by Oboyo.

"Don't go sir for I share your sentiments, I am with you."

Oboyo followed him dropping his beret on the floor. Dennis and Idigo got up; Dennis now tongue-tied just walked across to Eze and stood behind him.

"I am at your command sir" he said.

Idigo cleared his voice and began in his tiny voice:

"It is not exactly as you say sir, I have known for some time that they are seeking a way to call a truce but then the suffering was too much. We could not match them militarily and there did not seem to be any hope. Now we can reverse the situation. We have muscle and the savvy to hold them. Our present move if sustained will make them have a rethink and usher in a sane armistice. After all, we were one and are still linked by too many things for a clean break. In view of the foregone, I am with you and hereby submit to your command."

Idigo moved towards Eze, stopped before him and saluted. He took off his beret and flung it down. Donning his helmet he stood behind Eze. Adaka stood unmoving and expressionless. Diokpa Olisa stood up stretched and yawned widely, he said:

"The bane of African Countries is that they find it difficult to follow up with an idea. Coups and counter coups chase themselves and the resultant confusion buries all the initial good intended. I am a civilian and not involved in this thing with you. When there is need for me just get in touch."

He stepped onto the porch and sat on a padded bench.

Colonel Ifenso got up with some difficulty, he refused to meet any of the eyes staring at him.

"I will not be involved in any coup or coup plot. I here and now resign my commission with the Biafran army and apply to Colonel Oboyo for a place in his army, be they vandals, monsters, ogres or evil spirits. I will avenge my comrades that were buried alive. I will fight on for my wounds are healing."

He stepped out to the porch and sat beside Olisa. There was silence and as minutes succeeded seconds and hours succeeded minutes, nobody moved or talked except to go and urinate.

Ike, Nwosu, Asuquo and Tim kept peeping and wondering as to the nature of this 'O' Group where nobody was talking and the commander was sitting relaxed in boxers.

Idigo walked up to Diokpa Olisa and spoke quietly:

"We are in a fix so direct us. Today is the eleventh of December and it's barely twenty more days to the end of the year. We must be patient and see how Adaka and Awoni are thinking after which we will know how to progress. Either we self-destruct by ensuring that nobody leaves here alive or we start planning."

Diokpa had his jaw resting on the cupped palm of his hands and the elbows resting on the knees. Idigo moved and stood in front of Adaka and Awoni, before he could speak Adaka said:

"Theatrics is over and no coup. How do we move? We move into the mid-west with Oboyo and watch events which I am sure will determine our next line of action. I repeat that there will be no coup."

Awoni stood up straight and said:

"I am with you, coup or no coup we must fight on. I don't know any other trade and to get mercenary openings is not easy for blacks. Fighting is my trade so I am for any party that votes for the continuation of the hostilities. A number of us understand guerilla warfare and it is easier to operate, more effective and less dangerous. I follow Adaka's lead in operative option but disagree about us all going into the mid-west. The thick forests, bushes, woods and swamps that abound around the Niger will easily hide a million guerillas. I am of the opinion that we should have hideouts on both sided of the Niger so that we cannot be cut off by the opposition and we can control the river as pirates. The Niger will be ours and any attempt by the authorities at full scale military offensive will be easily frustrated. To cap it all, I am with you."

He sat down and Dennis stood up with his face resolute.

"With Awoni coming across positively we are all acting in concert. There is no need for a coup. We have by our agreement today severed all links with Biafran army. We are no more soldiers but technically 'rebels' that are prosecuting guerilla warfare against any opposition be it from Nigeria or Biafra. Words like thieves, robbers, renegades, vagabonds, or vandals do not count. If we continue in our lethal tradition, we will in no time be known as wizards, devils, demons and ghosts. Owing no allegiance except to our rebel selves we are free to choose targets without interference. No more big names and empty ranks milling around purposelessly at beurocracy clogged headquarters. We have crossed the Rubicon so there will be no going back. Meanwhile there are important things to be addressed immediately. Some of these are camp locations, strengths assessment. This will include arms and armour enumeration, the planting of deep throat agents in the two enemy administrations and establishment of hierarchy. We should start immediately."

He mopped his face with a towel and sitting down he drank from the coffee flask proffered by Diokpa Olisa. They had all returned to the room from the porch. The atmosphere was so charged with tension that the early morning breeze could not soothe the heat or dry the sweat. Idigo stretched and laughed nervously saying:

"A recess and some lavish entertainment will not be out of place. Momentous and far reaching decisions have been taken in the last few hours for which most of us, if not all were unprepared for. I suggest a two hour recess."

Oboyo lit a cigarette before adding:

"I suggest we remain within this estate until all have been sorted out." He drank gin from his canteen.

"I suggest that somebody outside this group be put in charge of the men while we address the necessary and come out with a complete blue print or a road map of goals or objectives, plans, strategies, and command organogram. A management that is objective and based on the underlying principles of democracy will guide our actions from now on. If we all agree then we will start by drawing up a memorandum of understanding to be signed by all of us before the recess. After the recess copies will be made for signing and retention as guiding keepsakes."

Diokpa Olisa finished licking his dry lips before drinking from his flask. He looked over their faces and relapsed into a waiting silence. Adaka spoke with an unaccustomed drawl:

"It is a time of suggestions so I make bold to humbly suggest that Nwosu assume command of our forces for the next three days. That should be ample time to collate our thoughts, formulate plans and devise strategies preparatory to execution."

"Agreed" said Awoni.

"Okay by I" chorused the others.

Dennis descended the staircase and two minutes later came upstairs with Captain Nwosu, Lieutenant Kingsley and Sergeant Ike.

"I brought these other two to assist him if it be alright with us all." The perplexed men stood unmoving starring at the mound of caps, berets, and rank insignia on the floor. Adaka threw his beret and pips onto the heap saying:

"I have today resigned my commission with the Biafra army as I did with the Nigeria army at secession. I hereby join former Brigadier Eze now Mr. Eze as a guerilla fighter."

He looked at the men and added:

"In three days you will all know everything. Now we want Mr. Nwosu to be in command of our forces temporarily assisted by two of you if you will sever all links with the Biafra army" he stopped.

Captain Nwosu threw his beret onto the heap saying: "I am Mr. Nwosu from this moment on."

Kingsley and Ike did likewise. Hearty handshakes and embraces sealed the thickening plot and they went on recess.

Steaming basins of rice, beans, and stew were carried in under the direction of Sergeant Nathaniel Egwuenu. Plates and spoons were provided and the famished soldiers set to voraciously. Large well spiced and fried lumps of meat made the meal more delicious. Bowls of steaming fresh fish pepper soup followed while sweet raffia palm wine arrived in foaming gourds to wash down the meal. None of them had eaten this well in years. Diokpa recommended small sips from the bottle of gin provided by the jester Egwuenu to mellow their tense temperaments.

Egwuenu soon returned with packets of assorted brands of cigarettes and two more bottles of Scotch whisky: "Courtesy of Captain Dinah Igbeli" Egwuenu explained: "She regrets her inability to join you since she has transcended the entertainment duties and ventured into the realm of fighting. She is presently on observation post duties."

"Go away with your stupid English" Adaka said as he waved him away.

"My pleasure sir to carry out your considered instruction but I would rather like to, however...."

"Get out and stay out jester, this is no time for foolery." Awoni spoke sternly.

Egwuenu withdrew hastily.

'No sense of humour' he complained smiling mischievously.

As the day progressed Diokpa cornered Adaka and Awoni and by gentle probes dragged out their whole stories from the sad duo.

"This wife of yours Olivia, did you court her before marriage?" asked Diokpa.

"No sir, I sent home for a wife and my people did everything. I only went home for the final traditional rites and collected her. We are from the same local government area. We had no time to get to know ourselves well because military duties intruded harshly into our honeymoon."

"Did she ever mention a twin sister or sisters? asked Diokpa.

"I have this vague recollection of an odd brother who hates going to church but loves bible stories especially the David and Moses stories. He knew the names of David's mighty men by heart as well as the details of their acts of prowess. He made allusions to special religious books where these narrations were found. He cited the existence of these books whenever simple bible stories turned fantastic with his narration and it was pointed out that he was exaggerating. She told me so much about the brother that I had no difficulty recognizing him the day he harangued me almost to death. Their great resemblance awed me such that I bore the harassment for longer than I ordinarily would have. Idigo actually came to my rescue. She did mention a sister on rare but moody occasions. There was always the air of not being disposed to discuss the sister. She was however free with information concerning their ageless grand father said to be over a hundred years old. According to her the man doubled as a Priest of Udoh and a catechist of the Anglican Communion. Being clairvoyant from his priestly office, which he rarely functioned as age wore on, he was sought after both by Christians and pagans. Versed and experienced in herbal treatment and nature cure for almost all ailments, including orthopedic needs, he was always in demand. Ministering to people's health needs always went with ministering to their spiritual needs. He did the latter with lucid bible stories and credible works of God in recent and contemporary times. Numerous little gifts made him a rich man and he thus spread out his freely got bounty to all and sundry. He did not discriminate. Religious persuasion was to him like choice of food. Rice, beans, garri, yam or cassava meant physical health just as Anglican, Catholic, Presbyterian, Lutheran or Methodist meant spiritual health. To him the road to success lay in doing well. I never met the father or the grand father. The father died of a broken heart before I married her." He stopped and looked at the Buler watch on his wrist to indicate that the recess was over.

"You can now see that your Olivia, Dinah and Fidelis were triplets and that is the Okumili tradition. You will also father triplets. They don't stay together. When they stay together they cause destruction but when they are separated they perform well and give joy to their environment. We will talk more during the recess." said Diokpa as they filed back into the living room.

CHAPTER SEVENTEEN

THE NEBUCHADNEZZAR

Eze now dressed in khaki trouser and grey vest sat looking tired and exhausted as the meeting reconvened. Dennis assumed chairmanship of the proceedings without saying as much. He began by saying:

"Idigo the Oracle should read the minutes of the last deliberations and expand on the decisions concerning our future. The minutes he took will I am sure be better than the one I took. I suggest that we all keep pen and paper handy to take notes and questions should be asked when clarification is needed on anything. Any brain wave resulting from reasonable and realistic contributions should be noted and discussed at the first opportunity. Mr. Nwosu has taken command and Oboyo has called in a reinforcement of one hundred men from the mid-west. Take your minds off everything else so that we can concentrate and iron out the issues as they arise. If we are all agreed then Idigo will take the stage" he concluded as he wrote on his pad and consulted his wrist watch.

All of them nodded in agreement and Idigo pulled back his chair requesting permission to stand while addressing them. He put his pen and pad on the table in front of him and spoke in a voice slightly stronger than usual.

"Before the recess we agreed that we would disengage from Biafra while seceded from Nigeria. This we did by burning our hats, berets, rank insignia and medals. We put a tried and tested fighter in charge of our forces. This is to enable us formulate policies, plans, strategies, command structure and address existing issues. We are well guarded by mainly our lethal fighters and other loyal hand picked good fighters. However I still made provisions for the unforeseen. I have converted the master bedroom of this house into a well stocked armoury. I have installed a scanner with a bird's eye view of two miles radius here to ensure that our security is intact. We are supposed to elect a leader and establish a chain of command as the meeting progress. However that should come after we have done all the necessary things. Issues should be addressed and decisions taken democratically. This is necessary to avoid deferring to rank and position instead of to better thoughts, arguments and suggestions. Our decisions will stand as unshakeable as the American Constitution. Anybody not sure of total commitment to this cause should indicate now so that he will be excluded from now on. He will however not be allowed to go for another one week. In one week our movement will be firmly established and our forces in place to answer adequately to any challenge. After a week such a one will be allowed to go. He will be well treated prior to his leaving and will be released without ill feelings. We have fifteen minutes to consider and take a decision so I will pause now." He consulted his time piece and sat down. Nobody moved and fifteen minutes later he entered the bedroom and emerged with a large pistol which he placed on the table saying:

"We are all in this together so we will take the oath of unity before commencement. It will be in the order of our sitting and as I am the nearest to the gun I will start."

He picked up the gun and said:

"I am part of this move and will either float or sink with it so help me God."

He replaced the pistol and sat down. All the others took the oath without much ado.

"Next will be the formation of the agenda for this meeting. It is as stated here: subject your inputs, corrections and rectifications for debate. These are not in any order of priority so should be re-ordered. I propose the following agenda:

1. Objectives.

2. Command Structure.
3. Commands.
4. Locations.
5. Logistics.
6. Ordnance.
7. Target selection.
8. Plans and strategies.

My ideas as regards these topics I will now read out to you for your consideration and adoption or rejection. Amendments are expected to solidify what is agreed.

OBJECTIVES: these will be split into two namely long term and short term objectives.

Long Term: seeing that the Biafran high command has been compromised thereby has jettisoned our ideals, thus tainting our cause, we shall toe a different line of action. We will even more effectively continue to agitate militarily and otherwise for the good of our dear people of the Eastern region of Nigeria. We will learn a lesson from the Biafra experience and put an organization in place that will not tolerate, accept or sustain dictatorship.

Short Term: establish camp sites on both sides of the Niger River. We will as at now require ten such camps on each side. We can use the present Oboyo camps in the mid-west which are located at Ogwu, Ikpelle, Abala oshimili, Abala agada, Elah, Ibusa, Ogwashi, Okpanam, Igbodo, Onicha olona and Onicha ugbo.

On the eastern side we will establish camps in the follwing areas;

Akpaka forest, Odume Mkpikpa, Ose Umuhu, Ugbo oshimili, Akiri ozuzu and Ude sands.

Camp sites should be chosen to have at least two obscure escape routes. Immediate arrangements for underground armouries at the camp sites will commence so that as each camp is established arms and ammunition will be delivered. The Camp Commandants will take delivery personally. I suggest that we lure the commands around here to release their cache of arms and ammunition to us since they will not need them after the surrender. We will explain our moves to our troops to cement their loyalty and commitment. We must establish a strong security network and I dare to suggest that we recruit that jester Sergeant Nathaniel to circulate and monitor developments." Idigo said in conclusion.

"Why?" asked Adaka.

"He was posted to me and I suspected him right away. He is overly curious and takes risks to unearth information. I put tabs on him to see who he was spying for but found out that he is just a curious cat by nature. Being a born jester or fool, whichever you prefer, helps him ferret information with which he formulates jokes. He is brave and courageous as the fighting at Ozeh and later Onono showed. He is very intelligent and possesses a memory that is near photographic. Like Asuquo he is very efficient with the knife and kills without compunction. If trained he will become lethal. With his native, flimsy and sharp mind, skill at killing, compunctious and curious nature, I know that he will excel in security work and can be used for deep penetration strikes. Even Asuquo that crows in action has the disappearing trick which I have not been able to unravel; in fact I think it is real. He can be used." commented Idigo.

"The Command structure from down up would comprise of Commandants in charge of Camps who will be assisted by two capable hands and one security personnel. The Camp Commandant will be responsible to the common council as constituted here now. It remains for us to choose the head of:

> Logistics
> Intelligence and Security
> Operations, Planning and
> Strategies Ordnance, Supplies
> and Transport

Decisions and Target selection will be the joint responsibility of this council. I will pause now while you make inputs before voting starts to fill in the vacancies in the Command structure."

He sat down and drank from the water jug before him. Eze sounding quiet and somber said:

"So far so good, we are making notes and mulling on your ideas. If you are exhausted then we will come in but if not then continue.

A break will not only waste time which we don't have but also may distort thought patterns. If it is all right with the others then please continue."

The others nodded and drinking again from the jug Idigo continued:

"We will require a head of Administration and Liaison because infiltration and subterfuge will be our main strength. Considering the superb job of infiltration executed by Diokpa Olisa I cannot but nominate him to head that department. Now we will start nominations and voting."

He shared out small pieces of paper for the nominations preceding the voting.

"I like democracy but I hate politicians. Let us not be like them, loquacious, lying and prevaricating."

Awoni described the ease and speed with which Diokpa Olisa got his over six hundred men into the Aguleri area enabling him to plug Omoh to take Otuocha and the surrounding villages.

"Diokpa is obviously the man for infiltration. All those that agree with me should indicate by raising up their right fore finger."

All hands shot up.

"Now I suggest that we handle the other positions this way."

He sat down and Idigo standing again wrote on a broad sheet of paper: Admin & Liaison.

"Dennis!" chorused the others with their fingers shooting up. In this way all the other positions were filled up.

Oboyo for speed, instinct, fluidity of movement and disguise got Security.

Idigo was assigned to Intelligence.

Ordnance and Logistics went to Eze as the one with the clout to convince the brigade and battalion commanders to part with some or all of their stock of arms and ammunition.

Supply and Transport went to Ifenso who understood maritime travels and the geography of the area more than the rest.

Adaka was assigned to Operations. Planning and Strategies went to Awoni.

Nwosu in absentia was seconded to Adaka while Ike was seconded to Awoni.

Kingsley was seconded to Eze while Oboyo already had Asuquo and Nathaniel Egwuenu. Idigo picked Dinah as assistant and lewd knowing chuckles lightened the otherwise serious mood of the council.

Dennis, Ifenso and Diokpa were asked to pick assistants of their choice. It took a further three hours to sift the ideas and ideals and come out with solid decisions. A thirty minute recess followed and on resumption they dotted the I's and crossed the t's.

Meetings followed meetings and members of the council rarely saw the sky except from the porch of the living room. By 2pm on the 18th of December 1969 the meeting broke up. Eze in his immaculate dress uniform displaying the rank of Brigadier hand picked ten assistants and returned to the 54th Brigade headquarters. He commenced work on his project sucking the commanders in the area into releasing the whole stock of the arms and ammunition in the armouries to him. With Lieutenant Colonel Ozor it was easy and armour bearers were picked from the Brigade's able bodied men and placed under two lethal fighters—Tim Anowi and Claudius Johnson. The second, third and fourth battalion armouries were accessed through forged orders from Army Headquarters. The big wigs of AHQ were too busy to notice the security breaches. Lieutenant Colonel Ozor sent a signal to his former boss Lieutenant colonel Nwalusi. Nwalusi had taken over the command of the 53rd Brigade when the erstwhile commander was killed in an air raid and when he received the signal he came to see Eze. Three other Brigade commanders were taken in by Eze's clout and fervour as he described the continuing fighting in the Republic of Benin. He showed them orders from both the State House and AHQ which befuddled them and elicited their willing compliance.

Meanwhile Adaka and Ifenso traversed the established camps and supervised the crafty construction of armouries and bunkers. These were chosen with care and the actual construction work was limited to a select few very trusted fighters for security. By the 30th of December all the armouries at the various camp sites were well stocked, the bunkers fortified with the camp site camouflaged and secured. Tattoo roll calls at the camps established the numerical strength of the guerillas at four thousand eight hundred men. To the council this was very satisfactory and Nwosu traversed the camps setting up training schedules. Ideological teachings and indoctrination followed the training. Ifenso went out of his way to lure Medical personnel from the surrounding regiments. The engineers of Njoku aided by Henry a fifth year architecture student at the University before the outbreak of hostilities, veered from armament construction and manipulation to construction engineering. They were so good that not even members of the group could locate the bunkers and armouries without a blueprint or road map. Only the camp sites were visible albeit camouflaged. Idigo and some of his aides kept busy with familiarization tours of the camps to meet with the inmates. Nothing was left to chance and camp operations soon became efficient like clockwork. Nothing seemed out of place. The New Year was being celebrated when news of strange happenings hit everywhere.

"Brave and courageous Biafrans I salute you. We have for thirty harrowing months endured a genocidal war prosecuted by our kith and kin across the Niger, egged on by the British neo-colonialists and their strange bed fellows the Godless Soviets. The Organization of African Unity (OAU) through some illustrious sons of Africa have tried to negotiate an equitable brotherly armistice. This has not been possible because of the subterfuge of the British and Soviet neo-colonialists. They would rather have a horse and rider armistice forced on us.

Our Nigerian brothers are becoming reticent in the prosecution of this genocidal war. Across the sectors there has been marked reluctance by the troops on either side to continue the senseless, wholesale destruction of life and property. The indefatigable Emperor Haile Selasie, General Afrifa, Leopold Senghor, Houphet Boigny and others have not relented in seeking peace to halt this carnage. However this will not augur well for the covetous British and Russian governments who have scented fossil oil in abundance. Our brothers' reluctance to continue with the prosecution of this genocidal war becomes and remains of no import. Willy-nilly they as lackeys must adhere to the wills of their overlords. They continue to fight without enthusiasm, sending unofficial delegations to discuss cessation of hostilities with our frontline commanders. Initially we had our doubts and planned towards decisive victory and its accompanying carnage. Time has shown their honest desire for peace. We have absorbed all their combined might, not discounting the military advisers from their overlords and mercenaries both African and European. We have soaked up all that they can throw at us until they came up with this infernal blockade. Malnutrition has ushered in disease and malaria, kwashiorkor, hepatitis, scurvy, hypertension and other ailments. These have torn our heroic people to shreds. What they could not achieve militarily they decided to achieve by emasculating our civil populace. In a fast response to this unconventional move which qualifies as spiritual wickedness in high places, the War Cabinet decided to employ our lethal military weapons to obtain quick victory and relieve our people. I personally voted for that but was overruled by the Military High Command and other civil advisers who felt that the weapons cannot qualify as conventional and would cull the wrath of the United Nations.

The World has looked on silently as we soaked up their wicked fury. To the white world it is nothing. Only blacks are dying and dissident blacks at that. We have the equalizer but are not allowed to use it. We persevered, and knowing the fighting qualities of our people we created a lethal weapon beyond ordnance sphere. We activated them and started operation to hold the enemy and show them how vulnerable they are if only we should go all out. They felt the heat and as we wanted to release our full lethal potentials the saboteurs arrived. The overlords had infiltrated our political icons and military high command promising them pies and pastries in their gullible horizons. Three coup attempts have been exposed and quashed, all financed by these overlords. The crass propaganda now is that our lethal personnel weapon, the Lightning Strike Force is being bad mouthed. It is variously and wrongly called vandals, terrorists, demons, cannibals, deranged persons, wizards, juju men and a host of other such negative appellations. Collateral propaganda is that the War Cabinet and I are fighting to carve out oil empires to rule as Arabian Sheiks. Far be it from me. These lethal fighters so evilly badmouthed have been activated and we are unable to defuse them. I leave their defusing to the educated, disciplined and trained minds of their commanders. They are capable of destabilizing any nation they are released against. The hope remains that their fine minds, civilized nature, discipline and Christian virtues will curb their military potentialities. My ambition is not for oil or other mineral empire to rule or any great military career. My ambition is to see my people safe, sound, happy and not under bondage. To prove this I have conferred extensively with members of the War Cabinet and decided to give peace a chance. The ball is now in the court of the Nigerian High Command. As they make their bed so shall they lie on it? The Lightning Strike Force can only be defused by their actions. Our intention is not to achieve victory at all costs. Technically some victories can be so called but in reality their pyrrhic nature leaves equally abrasive taste on the palates of winner and looser alike. I advise everybody involved in this chaotic situation and the ensuing circumstances to tread with restraint and caution. With high hopes I repeat my decision to seek peace by leaving the country now. God bless you all."

Tapes of the short surrender broadcast of the Biafran government and the Commander-in-Chief's departure broadcast were played and replayed until the last packet of 'Berec' batteries were used up. The bewildered conferees sat speechless. It was 9th January 1970 and at Base Camp 4 Okpanam in the Mid-West of Nigeria. Adaka, Eze, Oboyo, Idigo, Awoni, Nwosu, Diokpa Olisa, Ifenso, Nebo, and Dennis all sat quietly in the bunker listening to Nathaniel Egwuenu narrate the happenings at the AHQ and the State House in the past seventy-two hours. Dressed as a Lieutenant Colonel in the Medical Corps, Egwuenu who posed as a Medical Doctor was able to access the Commander-in-Chief's drawer. He retrieved the original surrender tape recording by Major General Effong as directed by the C-in-C and also the C-in-C's departure broadcast.

"They were putting things in place after the first coup struck and was quashed with minimal loss of lives. The second coup to terminate the rebellion was carried out mostly by NCOs. This was bloodier and was angrily repressed. When the third attempt to unseat the Biafran High Command came as moral persuasion, the C-in-C, CGS, CDS, CNS, COAS, and the Inspector General of Police took only two hours to reach the decision to give up."

According to Major General Effong:

"We appear to be fighting for ourselves so let us quit. We have lost the people's mandate."

Nathaniel Egwuenu in his military and medical disguise blended and made himself useful. Working with Henry and Tim, they duplicated the taped messages and sent back the originals.

As the Navajo Chieftain hugged the air for the C-in-C's departure all three took off for Base Camp 3 at Akpaka forest but hurriedly returned to Amichi Nnewi. Bedlam unfolded as a high-handed Effong with his hand picked aides maintained order with iron hands until he drove down to Amichi to read the re-drafted surrender broadcast. As he handed over the Biafra flag he broke down and wept. He informed the Commander to whom he surrendered—General Obusonjo—that the symbolic pistol was fully loaded and that he should use it to put him out of his misery. General Obusonjo contemplated him, turned and walked away with the corners of his mouth turned up in disdain.

After Egwuenu's graphic report, the tapes were played and a somber atmosphere descended on the bunker. They all sat unmoving playing and replaying the tapes. Dinner arrived and remained untouched. The palm wine unattended to kept overflowing from the gourds onto the earthen floor, fermentation taking place.

"What do we do now?" was the question on every lip. Through couriers questionnaires were sent to every cell and the responses received and collated.

Sixty percent which represented the majority wanted immediate resumption of hostilities. This was not surprising for they hadn't the full complement of necessary facts to reach knowledgeable decision. Thirty-five percent felt that hostilities should resume at the appropriate time. This should be when preparations have been made thus the Nigerians will not have the advantage of weapons or equipment. In such situation real military battles would be fought and real earth-shaking victories won. Five percent which included the top hierarchy felt that the Nigerians' actions would determine the next moves.

The 15th of January was billed as the decision day. Spies were sent into the towns and surrounding villages to collect information on the unfolding events. The information collated was heartening. Both sides shared great joy at the cessation of hostilities. Military units became magnanimous to the Biafran populace with the beer and cigarettes trucked in from nearby Nigerian towns. Friendships were struck up by former foes and love flowed freely. Drunkenness produced a few frays but these were quite easily settled. Love, friendship, camaraderie and understanding reigned and peace set in. This information was received with mixed feelings for the broadcasts kept whirring around their skulls. The downing of the Biafra flag and the surrender speech proved a much more severe trauma than the Commander-in-Chief's departure broadcast. Who could imagine thirty months of a gurgling bloodbath, anger, fury, pain, hunger, disease, and sickness? Or thirty months of frustration and dehumanization and then the flag of the would-be Utopian enclave is downed. Her military muscles are frayed into inability. The rising sun as depicted by the flag sets with a suddenness and finality that speaks of oblivion. This gives birth to a midnight of harrowing thoughts of slavery, forced labour, stockades, garrisons, cells, rape, torture, firing squads and hangings. In this tense situation the Lightning Force Cabinet wavered nonetheless tilting towards resumption of hostilities, albeit the guerilla version that is not guided by the Geneva Convention. According to Eze:

"That way we will make them suffer as much as our people suffered. We owe our people the obligation to fight for those that cannot fight. We know how and thus cannot in conscience abdicate this duty."

Idigo would always counter with:

"That will be if the conditions that led to this rebellion still exist."

Dennis and Ifenso did a lot of paper work, always consulting Idigo. Diokpa Olisa debriefed the agents that went in search of information and reported to the council. Adaka, Oboyo and Awoni remained ominously silent, never missing any sitting. They always listened to the broadcasts that now included the surrender broadcast and the secession broadcast.

Nwosu assisted by Ike laboured at the very arduous task of running the cells and the onerous task of establishing control over the well trained fighters. Nwosu was unobtrusively assisted by Fidelis who had released all his prisoners in batches without loosing a soul, or striking up friendship with any of them. The prisoners had feared him more and traded long tales of his fiendish nature. He reported to Adaka after dispersing the men and was deployed to Nwosu. Nwosu immediately put him and Ike to good use cutting law breakers and dissidents down to size. It took two deaths and a fortnight of salvaging supposed hard unbeatable fighters to instill a discipline more rigid than routine army discipline. Nwosu pulled punches as he cut down trouble makers, especially those dubbed vandals. Ike and Fidelis went out of their way to display their youthful unarmed combat skills but Adaka's silent rebuke called them to order. Dinah and her girls were in their elements. Flitting through army camps and collecting information they relayed these to the council. At meetings held in the cells, Diokpa made members of the council listen to the broadcasts repeatedly. They also heard, assessed and sieved information gathered by the field agents. Opinions remained varied but still tilted toward resumption of hostilities when the unexpected happened.

The Nigerian Head of State made an epoch making broadcast that pulled the carpet from under the war mongers. The council met on the 15th of January and Nathaniel Egwuenu submitted the tape-recording of the Nigerian Head-of-State's broadcast to Diokpa Olisa. Fresh tapes and recorders were activated and the blurred recorded message grated through metallically.

"It is not unusual for brothers to strike discordant tones in our African traditional setting. The only regret is that this went beyond all imaginable limits before peaceful resolution began. This has cost the nation millions of irreplaceable lives and property. It is based on the foregoing that I declare a no victor no vanquished situation.

I declare the biblical joyful open handed loving embrace of welcome that was accorded the prodigal son. Our decisions, actions and domestic policies will be based on three R's namely: Reconciliation, Rehabilitation and Reconstruction. The re-integration of our previously estranged people into the Nigerian polity is a priority to be fostered by our unhindered display of love and equity in all spheres of life. In a nutshell there shall be no victory parades but a celebration of our people's return from an unpalatable sourjourn. There shall be no mention of treason, trials or dismissals. Members of the civil and military services should return to their former posts without delay and with no more than refresher courses to get re-integrated. Remember the words of our National Anthem: 'Though tribe and tongue may differ In brotherhood we stand'

This remains true and will be upheld by unity, love and peace not discord and war. Thank you God for keeping us together."
ANTHEM.

There was grave like quiet as the national anthem ground to a screeching halt. The faulty recorders' harsh grating did nothing to detract from the blissful message. Nobody spoke or moved for upwards of fifteen minutes. Their cloudy faces showed brows furrowed in puzzlement. Eze started shaking his head in disbelief.

"It is a trick. It cannot be true" he said repeatedly like a cracked gramophone record.

"What if it is true?" asked Diokpa.

"What if it is not a trick?" questioned Idigo at the same time.

"They wish to buy time to assess our situation and bidding their time strike when we are fully disorganized and disintegrated. I will not be deceived. Then we will only know oppression and repression and their genocidal pogrom will mature to tribal cleansing. German concentration camps will be as nothing compared to what I foresee." Eze's taut emotions drew tears from his eyes.

Adaka spoke for the first time:

"It is all right and there is a solution. We do not have enough weapons to match them now. We do not have enough information to correctly chart the path they wish to tread. Moreover we do not have the organization to respond stunningly and adequately to stop them if they choose to renege on this their beautiful hand of friendship proffered. We all need time to get ready. We must utilize the available time maximally. I therefore suggest that we use the next two months to intensify training to map out vital areas, select targets and infiltrate military formations. If need be we may kidnap the Research and Production egg heads if they will not come peacefully. We will need details of their poisonous gases and poisons. If we must fight it must be fierce and short. Ifenso will seek out more arms as the need arises and if the council approves Oboyo will assist him to plan our future campaigns with their usual thoroughness. Dennis and Idigo will plan our integration into the country that will be our pseudo-country without the conditions that led to secession. Within these two months we shall be meeting regularly to review the situation. Finally play back the surrender broadcast and let us match it with the General's clemency broadcast."

Every member of the council except Eze, who looked bewildered, agreed with Adaka. Eze was mute, looking at Adaka with more of confusion than suspicion.

Diokpa Olisa plugged the cassette into the recorder and the strong voice of Phillip Effiong flowed out in a long, grating, screechy audition:

"For unacceptable conditions that made our people of the Eastern part of Nigeria unaccepted in their own land, the erstwhile Military Council comprising mainly Senior Officers of Eastern Region origin and some of Western and Mid-Western origin decided to break all links with the Nigerian government.

On the 30th of May 1967 we seceded and responded to the Nigerian declaration of war dubbed Police action. For thirty long months of bloody grit, death and suffering we withstood the onslaught. The situation now is that we cannot continue this rebellion due to our martial incapability. The conditions that led to this aborted rebellion may or may not still exist but we have no choice but to give up."

His voice had dropped in tempo, a few decibels as he signaled the lowering of the Biafran flag. As the flag was folded and handed to him he continued in a stronger voice, handing over the folded flag and his service pistol to General Obusonjo:

"By these actions, I Major General Phillip Effiong of the Biafran Army, representing the Biafran High Command and the Biafran Nation do hereby surrender to the Nigerian banner."

He had stood sturdy and ramrod stiff, looking straight into the distance and expecting a shot to ring out ending his life. General Obasanjo could not take his eyes off him and returned the stare haughtily. He had clicked his heels and saluted, while responding to the salute Effiong broke down and wept, pleading for an honourable death from the hand of the enemy. He was denied that.

Nathaniel Egwuenu kept reeling out the details of the attendant happenings as the tape recording reeled to a stop. Sweating despite the harmattan cold, Diokpa Olisa ended the meeting.

"Gentlemen, it is time for work. We must have a well-oiled organization primed to full cock in the two months time available to us. All hands must be on deck so protect what we have with your lives. We shall meet weekly for reviews. All information accessed will be collated by Eze and me. Remain steadfast."

Without touching the food or drinks they all dispersed.

CHAPTER EIGHTEEN

IDES OF MARCH

A sense of calm, quiet, peace and serenity pervaded the atmosphere at midnight on March 20th 1970. The mufti but neatly clad members of council arrived and felicitating lightly descended into the hidden bunker of the Mkpikpa swamps dubbed Cell 7. Before descending Adaka stood and stared long and hard at Dinah who was looking uncharacteristically sickly and was vomiting. Idigo patted Adaka's back reassuringly and edged past him into the bunker. Awoni walked up to Dinah and offered her a cup of water. Dinah thanked him executing some dry heaves.

"How long?" asked Awoni "Two months" replied Dinah

"Him?" asked Awoni pointing to Adaka.

"Yes" mumbled Dinah while spitting out the water with which she rinsed her mouth.

"He is married" said Awoni

"Yes, to my sister I know. Her mind has traveled and will never return. I represent her and Adaka had done his duty. He owes no further obligation. When he returns home his wife would have traveled bodily. I ought to go with this war but I will now remain."

Dinah straightened from her crouch flicking water onto her hair and face. She looked straight at Awoni and turned to leave.

"There is something I wish to ask you. You need not answer if you do not wish to. I knew of your radio and the nocturnal weekly Morse code messages. The I.O knew but would not report to Military

Intelligence because he thought that you were a ghost and would seek him out and kill him if he dared reveal your secret. I had you under surveillance but could not act because to me I saw Olivia. Why were you spying for Nigeria?"

"I never spied for Nigeria. I was also of the Military Intelligence and reported to Idigo since he was responsible for my transfer to Army Entertainment as cover." Dinah smiled as she replied.

One more question and this is personal. Dinah nodded in understanding.

"Are you really a nympho?" Awoni asked seriously. "Keep guessing" replied Dinah laughing.

"One question for you sir" said Dinah.

Awoni who was moving toward the bunker stopped. "What?" he asked.

"Are you really a homosexual or impotent?" asked Dinah. "Why do you think I am either of these?" responded Awoni. "Your total hatred of women is not hidden" replied Dinah.

"I am not homosexual and I am not impotent. I don't hate women but I came close to killing you that day because you looked so much like Adaka's wife and I felt you were committing adultery. Secondly your presenting yourself as a sex kitten, your lewd and wickedly graphic description of your junketing added to your pornographic motions and squirms turned me on and I found myself craving for what I had sworn never to do again. Are you now satisfied?"

"Yes sir and I advise that you resume life for living is loving and without love one is dead" so saying she ran towards the kitchen.

Idigo welcomed Awoni into the bunker and the initial foreboding atmosphere of uncertainty lifted. Everybody was eating bread and sardines—Nigerian Army ration—and drinking real Star beer. Packets of cigarettes were scattered about with lighters but nobody smoked.

"I thought that you will quiz Dinah till dawn. Now that you know the truth, you can come in and not hold up the meeting any longer" Idigo rebuked him gently. Awoni smiled apologetically while Diokpa called for a short prayer to declare the meeting open. Jokingly all fingers pointed at him.

"You are the Priest, both of God and juju so pray for us." Ifenso said laughing. Diokpa performed the sign of the cross and prayed:

"God our creator, we thank you for getting us through the war. We ask you to guide us into the right decision this day. We make this prayer through Christ our Lord."

"Amen" they chorused.

Nwosu took an hour to explain the massive improvement in the arms cache situation and the millions of pounds obtained from three bloodless bank raids. Also he reported the successful infiltration of all the army formations and a detailed work on target selection. Training had peaked as Adaka had neither spared himself nor his lethal troops trying to put his skills and spirit into the trainees. He ended his report jokingly:

"Our state of readiness is above ninety percent and the boys are raring to go. They are calling for just one month of action before we reciprocate General Gowon's amnesty by granting them our own amnesty. Rest assured we can do so much damage and double the number of casualties in just two weeks than that of the thirty months of fighting. We will"

"Stop!" screamed Diokpa.

"You are supposed to report on our strength and capabilities not fan up embers of war."

He mopped his creased brow. Awoni stood relaxed and smiling with a big chunk of bread stuffed with corned beef in his hand. He put the glucky mound in his mouth and swallowed while nobody spoke. Everybody waited for him to speak and he drank from a beer bottle and then spoke:

"We are here today to know if the Gowon people are doing what they promised or are reneging and if so we strike within the week."

He sat down while smiles and laughter oozed forth. Eze drinking from a bottle of schnapps straightened up. He looked mellow and beamed happily at everyone present.

"I am sorry I got neurotic with fear and looked the gift horse too closely in the mouth. Please forgive me for I lost both of my parents and a kid brother to the pogrom. I believe that if we go straight to the point it will be the best approach we can use as this is no speech making occasion. The Nigerian people and the Nigerian government seem to be determined to do everything promised by the Head of State and more too. They have welcomed us with open hands and it is no trick. God bless a good leader and good followers."

He sat down and Idigo stood up saying:

"The information is positive so we should now plan reintegration and disbanding. The safe keeping of our arms caches should be a priority. Dennis is already far gone in the plan to establish at least one thousand of our men into commerce all over Nigeria. We have over seven hundred artisans and we have the money to set them up in towns of their choice. They will then apprentice another one thousand of our boys. We plan to make scholarships available to the academic oriented ones. This will be done through the men we will establish in major towns as contact points. Those of us in the services will return to their former duty posts. From our total strength of three thousand we should pick out one hundred who will devote a hundred percent of their time to preserving this legacy and coordinating our activities. These activities will not subvert our host government in any way. Our force will remain a sentinel on the lookout for evidence of oppression or repression to nip such in the bud. As I said Dennis had done a detailed work with regard to these tactical reintegration activities. I will answer questions as they come."

He sat down and Diokpa lit a fat cigar. He filled a glass and lifted it in a toast while the others did likewise.

"To Nigeria. To the Biafra spirit. To this our thing."

They all drank the toast and suspending the meeting went celebrating until the break of dawn. Nwosu and Dinah kept the security at peak when the meeting reconvened functions were delegated. It took two weeks to disband the men but by the 20th of April, Adaka's lethal fighters were still hanging around.

Oboyo, Nebo, Ifenso and Eze elected to return to the Nigerian Army. Adaka and Awoni had more on their minds than reintegration. Oboyo's men dubbed vandals were easier to turn lethal because they thought like animals and once mastered became wholly amenable to discipline. More lethal fighters were thus created with the now unrealized hope of fatally releasing them against any government. It was unheard of for fifty-two lethal fighters, counting Adaka, Awoni and Idigo to be poking around the fast emptying control camps 7 and 11 like sore thumbs. Any five of them could easily sack a town. If left undirected by a greater authourity they would ease into crime. For them to be trained they had been chosen as much for their brains as their brawn. What security agency could match them if they were to turn robbers, pirates, kidnappers or terrorists?

Adaka and Awoni opted out of a return to the army. Eze tried to talk them out of this resolve but failed.

"I have killed enough but have not been able to make even one child. Much as I agree that the politicians were at the root of the problem, I cannot see one Nigerian soldier as my comrade anymore. I want to get productive so I will go back to the University and pursue a teaching career" said Adaka and continued:

"my friend Awoni wants to get married and become a merchant. He went through secondary and University education with a scholarship award from A.G Leventis, so he wants to be like his Greek mentor. It was the Greek who pointed him to the army instead of towards merchandizing."

Eze laughed and nodded in understanding.

"All well and good but what happens to Nwosu, Ike, Fidelis and Dennis?" he asked.

"Ike and Fidelis have refused to leave me. I have tried everything to no avail. I explained to them that as a poor post-graduate student or even a graduate assistant I would not be needing aides. However they remained adamant. Idigo and Nwosu want to retain the lethal fighters and seek ways and means of keeping them under control until they are needed. My prayer is that they will never be needed again. I read Idigo loud and clear for he wants to do the only thing feasible with them which is to hire them out as mercenaries. Many places in the world today are heating up into a boil. I suspect that this is the only solution and I warned the authourities and the men involved of the impasse that occurs with these lethal persons. They have learnt to kill and it has become a way of life with them. It comes so easy with them that they can think of nothing else. I am in this trouble because I created them. I primed and fused them but now I cannot defuse them. If I allow Nwosu and Idigo to have their way in this mercenary issue, how can I then say that I have stopped killing when the weapons I created are performing efficiently."

Adaka would have continued but Eze interrupted:

"With time they will obey you and their restive nature will come to a boiling point and they will self-destruct. Order them to hibernate for a further six months before you can decide on your joint fates."

Adaka shook his head saying:

"You have forgotten that Idigo is the Oracle and can read us all like a book. I know that he is clairvoyant so I will not try deceiving him. He has sworn not to kill again except in self defense but he cannot pull himself from these men. Diokpa Olisa whom we all know of his mystical powers has predicted that Idigo will become a teacher but that does not palliate my worry. A teacher of what is the question? If as I suspect he wants to start teaching violence and like I did create more lethal fighters and lease them out for their kind of work then we will be in for trouble."

Adaka mopped his wet brow while Awoni spoke as if in a dream: "You cannot kill him because you cannot kill kin which he is. This is a real dilemma."

Sitting and standing around for a long time Eze said:

"I have the solution! Diokpa Olisa has paid off almost everybody and is still discussing with the Nebuchadnezzar and Dennis who is still opting for a banking career."

Awoni interrupted:

"Who was made Nebuchadnezzar? I thought that Idigo was unanimously elected."

"He was" explained Eze "but he opted out saying that he was tired of spying on people. Dinah the runner up is the Nebuchadnezzar. Dennis is helping her to tag everybody for call up when the need arises. Idigo is teaching them both the diarrhea code and making up the code book for them. If I may continue then know that Diokpa can change the course of his mind. I am sorry to say this Adaka but he worships you. He only sees Diokpa as an oracle the way other people see him as one. Get Diokpa to work on him and he will thaw out. I leave now and will be at the monthly meetings. The newspapers and our men and women to be installed into the Radio stations will broadcast the situations, dates and venues of meetings. Like I said try Diokpa."

He embraced them and left but at the entrance he turned to them saying:

"Awoni, fix the wedding date and inform us meanwhile monitor Nebuchadnezzar. There is something strange about her and I wish that you will not fall for her charms. You two, your eyes are always on her but I don't understand what I see so bye for now."

He ducked out of the bunker.

All through the next two days Diokpa continued with Idigo, Dennis and Dinah. On the third they pulled down to the Idemili River where Awoni and Adaka were supposedly cooling off with a quick swim but the thwacking sound coming from one side set them into jungle motion. Circumventing the path they planned to come up behind the perpetrators of the sound. When they got to the point they saw no one but a wet clay pot filled with clay on which twitched short wooden arrows. Four more thwacks came from behind them and turning they beheld Adaka and Awoni dressed in tugs fitting fresh arrows into their wooden bows. Close to them was a heap of more than a hundred freshly made arrows?

"I thought that you both have given up fighting so what are you doing here?" Idigo asked.

Diokpa laughed and said:

"They cannot but that does not mean that they cannot try, which is what I have been trying to tell you and Nwosu." He lit one of his big cigars.

"We are only exercising and keeping fit for we will leave as soon as this lethal fighter issue is settled" said Awoni.

Idigo spoke choosing his words carefully:

"I was beside Adaka when he created the lethal fighters including myself. In time I discovered the joy of killing but thanks to my mentor Adaka, I became able to suppress it. Religion has helped temper me down so I am now a better person than I was. However

I must confess that I am now a better fighter than I ever hoped to become. The better person in me is stronger than the better fighter that I am. I know the struggle that is in the mind of my boss. I wish to request for six months within which to plan out a strategy to defuse the men. Like drug addicts they will have to be gently and systematically weaned from killing and the fighting propensity in order to be rehabilitated into better careers. If we do this correctly then we can retrieve about fifty-four percent of them within three years irrespective of the toll accidents, death and other professional hazards may take. The remaining sixteen percent we shall leave to fate and the professional hazard. I believe that only fourteen percent would be left to be used as mercenaries so as to keep them busy and out of domestic troubles. However as I see both of you now I know that it is easier said than done to defuse lethal persons. I will leave for different camps with the men today and will ensure that they do not get into domestic mischief. This I promise. We shall be at Nebuchadnezzar's beck and call as and at when needed. We will make payments to Diokpa and still maintain large bank balances in case of need. We will ensure that the cells are guarded and endeavour to stop any leaks or attempts at investigation. If any of our other men become miscreants we shall leave their being taken out to the security agencies of the nations. If that fails, the boss, Awoni, Ike and Fidelis will take care of those for we shall certainly operate outside Nigeria, thank you sir."

He finished and looked at all of them except Dinah and Nwosu. Adaka nodded and they embraced. Nwosu furrowed his brows and Awoni buried six arrows with blurring speed into the clay pot. Idigo picked up ten stones and with equal speed pocked the clay pot in ten places around the arrows. Adaka nodded again.

"Guns are too noisy and less effective."

He walked to Dinah and putting his hands on her shoulder said: "Awoni will wed in seven months time when Dinah will put to bed, so Dennis endeavour to fix the next meeting for then."

GLOSSARY

1. Amansea—a town in Eastern Nigeria.
2. Agu-Awka—vast grassland between Awka town and Oji-River.
3. Abagana—a town in Eastern Nigeria.
4. Afor-Igwe—a popular market in Eastern Nigeria.
5. Afor-Oru—a market town in eastern Nigeria.
6. A name common among South-Easterners.
7. Adikunle—a name borne mainly by the Yorubas of Western Nigeria.
8. Awomamma—a town in Eastern Nigeria.
9. Amadi—an Ibo name.
10. Akwukwu—A waterside town in Eastern Nigeria.
11. Awoni—a rare Ibo name.
12. Ahukanna—an Ibo name.
13. Abudu—a town after Benin City in Mid-Western Nigeria.
14. Abala-Oshimili—name of a riverine town.
15. Afrifa—name of a former African Head of State.
16. Alakuku—a giant that hailed from Eastern Nigeria.
17. Abala-agada—name of a riverside town.
18. Azunna—an Ibo name borne by both males and females.
19. Atani—a waterside town in Eastern Nigeria.
20. Adakamma—full form of the name Adaka.
21. Achebe—an Ibo name.

22. Araba—a small shrub that is widespread and easily ignites.
23. Afikpo—a town in Eastern Nigeria.
24. Achuzia—a mid-western Ibo name.
25. Asuquo—a name from the soth east of Nigeria.
26. Agbo—an Ibo name.
27. Adewale Cole—Yoruba names.
28. Agorigwe—a delta provincial name.
29. Arizaga—Spanish shot gun.
30. Alade—a Yoruba name.
31. Akpaka forest—a forest reserve in Eastern Nigeria.
32. Aguleri—name of a town.
33. Anyamene—an Ibo name.
34. Aniogu—an Ibo name.
35. Aba—a town in Eastern Nigeria.
36. Mbebo—an Ibo name.
37. Amuma—name of an Ibo village.
38. Abakaliki—a town in Eastern Nigeria.
39. Agbor—name of a town in Mid-Western Nigeria.
40. Afam—name of a riverside town.
41. Awo-Idemili—name of a town.
42. Adani—name of a town.
43. Armah—an Ibo name.
44. Anam—a town in Eastern Nigeria.
45. Anowi—an Ibo name.
46. Amaigbo—a town in Eastern Nigeria.
47. Banjo—a Yoruba name.
48. Biafrana—name of triplets coined fron the Bight of Biafra.
49. Chukwuma Nzogwu—Ibo names.
50. CCP—casualty collection post.
51. Cele—short form of the name Celestine.
52. Chude Sokei—Ibo names.
53. Bofor—anti-aircraft gun.
54. Buka—a roadside cafeteria.
55. Burutu—a riverine town.
56. Chukwumerije—an Ibo name.
57. DMI—Directorate of Military Intelligence.

58. DHQ—Defense Headquarters.
59. Diokpa Olisa—Ibo names.
60. Dimgba—an Ibo name.
61. Dauda—an Hausa name.
62. Degema—a town in the riverine area.
63. Enugu—the capital of Eastern Nigeria.
64. Ede—an Ibo name.
65. Ekene—an ibo name.
66. EZe—an Ibo name.
67. Egbue—an Ibo name.
68. Ehamufu—a border town.
69. Eme—an Ibo name.
70. Efobi—an Ibo name.
71. Enwe—Ibo name for monkey.
72. Egwuenu—an Ibo name.
73. Ekwosimba—an Ibo name.
74. Egwu—short for Egwuenu.
75. Elah—name of a town.
76. Ifeajuna—an Ibo name.
77. Eziama—name of a town.
78. Fidelis—a name.
79. Fions—A polish name.
80. Debekeme—an Ibo name.
81. Effong—name from the Cross River area.
82. Eleme—name of a riverine town.
83. Egusi—a type of soup.
84. Ezzamgbo—name of a town.
85. Ethiope—name of a river in the mid west.
86. Emewor—name of a person.
87. Furore—name of a military operation.
88. Forcados—name of a town.
89. Gowon—a name borne by people from the middle belt of Nigeria.
90. Gbalite—an Ibo name.
91. Haile Sellasie—the name of a former Ethiopian Head of State.
92. Ibrahim—a Muslim name.

93. Idigo—an Ibo name.
94. Idemili—a river in Eastern Nigeria.
95. Uloma—an Ibo name.
96. Ilo—an Ibo name.
97. Iweka—an Ibo name.
98. Ike—an Ibo name.
99. Idahosa—a mid-western Ibo name.
100. Igbokenyi—a town in mid western Nigeria.
101. I.K. Dairo—name of a musician.
102. Ikpo—name of a river.
103. Ikeakor—an Ibo name.
104. Ibur—a name of non specific location.
105. Jallo—an Hausa name.
106. Juju—voodoo.
107. Jaji—a military location in Northern Nigeria.
108. Jos—a town in Northern Nigeria.
109. Garri—food made from cassava flour.
110. Hassan Katsina—Hausa names.
111. Hykkers '70—name of a musical outfit.
112. Igbeli—an Ibo name.
113. Ironsi—an Ibo name.
114. Ibeku—a district in Iboland.
115. Ibadan—a towm in Western Nigeria.
116. Ikeja—name of a town.
117. Ika—name of a town
118. Kogi—a town in Northern Nigeria.
119. Kano—a town in Northern Nigeria.
120. King-Kong—a fictional giant gorilla.
121. Kafanchan—a town in Northern Nigeria.
122. Kokoro—a renowned Yoruba blind musician.
123. Lekke—a northern name.
124. Lagos—the former capital of Nigeria.
125. Lagatyl—brand name of a sedative.
126. Leopold Senghor—a former African Head of State.
127. Muritala—an Hausa name.
128. Minna—a town in Northern Nigeria.

129. Mojekwu—an Ibo name.
130. Mbegbu—an Ibo name.
131. Mbawsi—a town in Eastern Nigeria.
132. Momodu—a Yoruba name.
133. Madiebo—an Ibo name.
134. Mgbemea—an Ibo name.
135. Mkpikpa—a swampy area in the east.
136. Ntoko—a town in Eastern Nigeria.
137. Ndikpa—a town in Eastern Nigeria.
138. Ndiora—a town in Eastern Nigeria.
139. Ndiowuu—a town in Eastern Nigeria.
140. Kwaku Arya—names of a Ghanaian.
141. Kaduna—a town in Northern Nigeria.
142. Kaochi—a Japanese name.
143. Kassavubu—a Congolese name.
144. Liston—name of a boxer.
145. Limpie—a nickname.
146. Morse—type of code.
147. Mbagwu—an Ibo name.
148. Maliki Odiakosa—Ibo names.
149. Muofu—an Ibo name.
150. Mba—an Ibo name.
151. Mgbemena—an Ibo name.
152. Okunola—Yoruba name.
153. Mmiata Anam—a riverine town.
154. Nwosu—an Ibo name.
155. Nnewi—a town in Eastern Nigeria.
156. Nwobosi—an Ibo name.
157. Nebo—an Ibo name.
158. Nwafor—an Ibo name.
159. Nwadike—an Ibo name.
160. Nkume—an Ibo name.
161. Nkita—Ibo name for dog.
162. Njoku—an Ibo name.
163. Nsugbe—a waterside town.
164. Onitsha—a town in Eastern Nigeria.

165. Okoko Ndem—names of a famous broadcaster.
166. Okigwe—a town in Eastern Nigeria.
167. Olokun—a Yoruba name.
168. Ozubulu—a town in Eastern Nigeria.
169. Okija—a town in eastern Nigeria.
170. Orifite—a town in Eastern Nigeria.
171. Orlu—a town in Eastern Nigeria.
172. Ozubulu—a town in Eastern Nigeria.
173. Opara—an Ibo name.
174. Oboyo—an Ibo name.
175. Ogbu—a town in Eastern Nigeria.
176. Okpatu—a border town.
177. Ogwe river—a river in the east.
178. Opi—a border town.
179. Okafor—an Ibo name.
180. Ojoto—a town in Eastern Nigeria.
181. Oba—a town in Eastern Nigeria.
182. Ozoadibe—an Ibo name.
183. Ozugono—name of a town.
184. Ojuru—name of a stream.
185. Obigbo—a town in the riverine area.
186. Osamarra—a riverine town.
187. Ojukwu—an Ibo name.
188. Obinze—name of a town.
189. Onyaa—an Ibo name.
190. Okwara—an Ibo name.
191. Obidi Amaka—Ibo names.
192. Okon—name of the Cross River people.
193. Oranwa—an Ibo name.
194. Ohaji—name of a town.
195. Owerrinta—name of a town.
196. Olona—name of a town.
197. Olokoro—a riverside town.
198. Oguta—a town in Eastern Nigeria.
199. Ogbede—a riverine town.
200. Onugha—an Ibo name.

201. Okposi—an Ibo name.
202. Okwelle—an Ibo name.
203. Oroma-etiti—a town in the riverine area.
204. Omamballa—a river.
205. Oyibo—a white man.
206. Ogbunigwe—a locally manufactured land mine.
207. Otuocha—name of a town.
208. Osadebe—an Ibo name.
209. Oshimili—a big river.
210. Oraobodo—name of a hill.
211. Ogunewe—name of a person.
212. Okpocha-Ngene—a diviner cum native doctor.
213. Ogwu Ikpelle—a trading beach.
214. Okpanam—a riverside town.
215. Onicha Olona—a town in the mid west.
216. Onicha Ugbo—a town in the mid west.
217. Odume—a valley farmed by the Ibos.
218. Ose—a waterside market.
219. Obusonjo—name of a person.
220. Ozeh—a hilly, fertile farmland in Eastern Nigeria.
221. ROB—Republic of Benin.
222. Ugwuoba—a town in Eastern Nigeria.
223. Umudioka—a town in Eastern Nigeria.
224. Ubakala—a town in Eastern Nigeria.
225. Umuahia—a town in Eastern Nigeria.
226. Ukwa—a town in Eastern Nigeria.
227. Ukehe—a border town. an Ibo name.
228. Umuehi—a clan in Iboland.
229. Ukwuo—a town in the mid west.
230. Uzuakoli—a town in Eastern Nigeria.
231. Umuoba-Anam—a riverine town.
232. Umuikaa—a riverine town.
233. Umuile—name of a town.
234. Ukpi—name of a town.
235. Udechukwu—an Ibo name.
236. Uburu—a town famous for its salt.

237. Ughelli—name of a town.
238. Umenyi—an Ibo name.
239. Umuhu—a riverside village.
240. Ude Sands—an island.
241. Umuleri—name of a town in Eastern Nigeria.
242. Victor Olaiya—a popular Nigerian musician.
243. Soneryl—brand name of a sedative.
244. Warri—a town in mid western Nigeria.
245. Uyo—name of a town.
246. Unhoned—not properly trained.
247. Uzochukwu—an Ibo name.
248. Ure—name of a stream.
249. Uli—name of a town.
250. Umueze—name of a clan.
251. Ugep—name of a town in Northern Nigeria.
252. Savate—a type of fight tactic.
253. Yakubu Gowon—name of a renowned Nigerian Head of State.

READ ON FOR EXCERPS OF ANOTHER SERIES BY THE SAME AUTHOR TITLED 'BIAFRANA'

AUTHORS NOTE

BIAFRANA SERIES

Ω

Out of the bight in the Atlantic Ocean called Biafra shot an illusory menace that turned real. This was to ravage the land for thirty long months before expiring like a meteor resembling Haley's Comet.

Its passage spawned ills spewing verminous fumes across the formerly blessed amalgam of British Sir James Robertson which straddled the Rivers Niger and Benue.

Simmering strife born of anger resulting from decades of segregation in the form of tribalism, sectionalism, nepotism ensued. This got further inflamed by religious intolerance creating disunity and mistrust in the giant territory. Unparalleled corruption and loss of integrity at all levels of the society followed.

Politicians commandeered choice positions in this odious melee while their cronies in the civil and public services who were favored with juicy crumbs, for ravaging the treasury, sang their praise, helping to hold down the oppressed masses.

It was into this cauldron that the identical Biafrana triplets were born. Their characters were worlds apart but excelling in their different fields they succeeded in combining good and bad into acceptable social alloys.

Their first line identification was by the numerals One, Two and Three. Followed by gender, two of them were female while one was male. Character traits come third but remain their main identification marks. Their uniform Christian beliefs diverged into individual moral, social and doctrinal interpretations.

They are unusual, outstanding and inexplicable so they make the difference. Get introduced to BIAFRANA ONE.

CHAPTER ONE

THE BEGINNING

IGBELI

Igbeliude the husband of Okpubili, supposed Priest of Udoh, only appeared at Udoh's shrine to cart away sacrifices. He would distractedly rain abuses on Udoh and the populace whose sacrifices were measly.

He knew every local folklore, sang wonderful dirges, and told stories of distant clans and nameless deities brighter than the morning sun. He reviled deities and their priests and threatened shrines and grooves with vile railings, challenging them to power contests.

He was known to defecate on the supposed sacred ground whenever the priest was away. About the Idemili shrine deity or river, he had nothing to say. He however did not show any sentiment or emotion toward Idemili.

The Idemili shores were his bed and amply supplied him with sacrificial chicken for meat. He did not touch the Idemili cow or he-goat for that is forbidden. Some suspected that he fished at night and ate his catch that same night, but no proof ever was found.

It is believed that eating the Idemili fish and python results in swollen belly and gruesome death. Igbeli's stature was slim, average height and comely with a flat tummy. There were no signs to suggest that he fed on the forbidden fish and python.

Wandering distractedly through the villages of Ebosi he sang dirges telling of sad past happenings that tore the Anigbo tribe into small hate-filled clans preying on each other. In Akwum where the main shrine of Udoh sat neglected by Igbeliude, a very well kept compound adjourned the shrine.

This was erected by communal effort for Igbeliude to make him stay at home and live up to his responsibility as priest of Udoh and husband of Okpubili. These serious responsibilities he scorned and continues to scorn until he was physically brought home to perform for some days before breaking free to continue roaming.

His songs were numerous and varied. They were always slow, sad, mournful and heart-rending. The soulful rendition that always varied irresistibly drew infants, youths, the middle-aged and old to Igbeliude. Hours of these renditions sapped him physically and mentally such that he invariably swooned into unconsciousness.

Not one member of the audience ever left with dry eyes. He often woke before daybreak to rush back to his bed, the shores of Idemili River. On the rare occasions that Okpubili attended his sing-song, she carried him home and kept him for a few days.

Okpubili understood him because she was also the prey of a roaming spirit. She must of necessity roam the villages to welcome the new moon and sing as well as dance the death dirge that foretold the demise of a renowned person or an impending doom, or catastrophe. Igbeliude and Okpubili were like souls.

※

www.ingramcontent.com/pod-product-compliance
Ingram Content Group UK Ltd.
Pitfield, Milton Keynes, MK11 3LW, UK
UKHW022214230426
12048UKWH00016BA/834